the Istanbul PUZZLE

LAURENCE O'BRYAN

AVON

AVON

A division of HarperCollins*Publishers*
77–85 Fulham Palace Road,
London W6 8JB

www.harpercollins.co.uk

A Paperback Original 2011
3

First published in Great Britain by
HarperCollins*Publishers* 2011

Copyright © Laurence O'Bryan 2011

Laurence O'Bryan asserts the moral right to
be identified as the author of this work

A catalogue record for this book is available from the British Library

ISBN: 978-1-84756-288-3

Set in Minion

Printed and bound in Great Britain by Clays Ltd, St. Ives plc.

'We may our ends, by our beginnings know.'
JOHN DENHAM, 1615–69

1

Icy sweat streamed from Alek's pores. He'd been optimistic. Way too optimistic. Kidnapping in the Islamic world was almost always a form of extortion – so he'd been told. But the appearance of the knife, big enough to gut a bear, had changed everything.

He shook his head in disbelief. Only an hour ago he'd been happy in his hotel room, a place that was now as unreachable as a childhood dream.

His heart banged against his ribs as if it wanted out. He looked around. Was there someone else in the pillared hall he could appeal to?

The bead like eye of the video camera blinked on. Alek's arms and legs jerked, straining at the orange nylon rope binding him to the smooth pillar. Musty air filled his nostrils. He was trembling, as if he had a fever.

When the two men had entered his room, he'd gone with them quietly. How stupid he'd been. Why hadn't he shouted, roared, jumped for the window? He'd seen the look in this bastard's eyes, as hard as stone. Now it was too late.

'Let me go,' he screamed.

His voice echoed. A hand held his shoulder. He threw his head from side to side, straining his neck. The rope around his ankles, knees and chest held him tight. His pulse thumped against it.

The knife glistened in the air like falling water. Only the prayer his mother had taught him could help him now.

Agios o Theos, agios ischyros, agios athanatos, eleison imas!

Holy God, Holy and Mighty, Holy and Immortal, have mercy on us!

He closed his eyes. Iciness hit his neck. Then a hot torrent fell on his chest. Warmth gushed down his legs, soaking him. A foul smell rose around him.

An eerie calm descended.

He looked around the ancient hall, taking in its forest like rows of pillars. The entrance he'd found must have been sealed up over five hundred years ago, before the ancient city of Constantinople above him fell to a Muslim army and its name was changed to Istanbul. There were treasures down here any museum director in the world would beg for. But he wished he'd never found the place.

He stared at the aluminium tables nearby. What he'd seen on those tables had terrified him.

A black mist rushed towards him. Would Sean find out what had happened?

Agios o Theos, agios . . .

A minute later the two fountains of blood, two foot high at their peak, from the left and right arteries emerging from Alek's chest, bubbled like cooling coffee percolators. The flesh around them shone with a silky gleam. But Alek's eyes were closed and his face was peaceful.

2

Glass fell into the street. The four-storey frontage of the new American electronics store was collapsing. An animal rumble passed under me. Alarms sprang to life in a chorus.

I'd been on my way home. It was a Friday night in August. London was hot, sticky. I'd been crossing Oxford Street when I stopped, mid step.

Coming towards me, that glass behind them, was a mass of fists, hooded faces, rage. Every muscle tightened inside me. Was the city going up in flames again?

I saw an entrance to a brick-lined alley, broke into a jog. A girl with a pink afro, white stilettos and a lime green tube top was standing in the middle of the street, her mouth open, her arms at her side. I veered towards her.

'Come on,' I shouted.

She looked at me as if I was a ghost, but came with me. I didn't have to turn my head to know the mob was almost on us. We barely made it. We turned together and watched them pass. For one frozen moment I thought they might turn on us, that I'd have to defend my new friend. But they moved on, chanting a drum-beat rhythm of slogans I could barely understand. That's a sound I'll never forget. Because this lot weren't just looting. These bastards had found a cause.

Some of them glared at us as they passed, but luckily we

weren't their target. They were after symbols of their oppression. And they were out of their heads on it. After they were all gone, my pink-haired friend shuddered, then ran off.

Screaming alarm bells and broken windows were the most obvious signs of the mob's passing, along with a whiff of danger. Was a police raid on a mosque worth all this?

I caught sight of a woman in a tiny leather jacket on the other side of the street. Her face was turned away from me. She was running. My vision tunnelled.

'Irene!' I said, softly. My legs started towards her. I stopped them.

Irene was gone.

But even though I knew that was true, my heart still wanted for the woman to turn, to smile, for my heart to pound like a rocket ship going into orbit again. No one had ever affected me like Irene. Before I met her I'd never believed that a woman could make your heart thump, just by walking into a room.

And a big part of me still didn't want to get over what had happened to her, didn't want to move on, not now, not ever, no matter what anyone said or did.

The woman was almost gone now, her black hair flying behind her as she disappeared into a glow of flickering lights. If I went after her, all it would mean was that I was crazier than I thought.

I let out my breath, slowly. I'd had what my grief counsellor had called a legal hallucination. People don't come back from the dead. No matter how much you want them to. No matter how unfair their death was.

When my mom and dad had died back in the States, within eighteen months of each other, I hadn't felt this way. They'd both had a good innings, but Irene had barely got to bat.

A helicopter flew low, its searchlight wandering. It was time to get away from this madness, to get back to normality, to my own frustrations. Alek hadn't responded to my last text message. He was due back on Monday when the image enhancement program I'd spent the last week fixing would finally get properly tested.

If we messed up this project, I wouldn't be able to hide from the rumour mill.

I could imagine what they'd say. How can you expect a project director not to make mistakes after what happened to him? Wasn't it obvious he wasn't over his wife's death, wasn't up to the job any more? Wasn't this why he'd been demoted?

I started walking, checked my phone again. Nothing. Why was someone with every communication option the world had devised been uncontactable for six freaking hours?

Photographing mosaics of angels, emperors and saints shouldn't have been this difficult. Even if he was doing it in what had once been the Islamic world's St Peter's. We'd worked in the Vatican for God's sake. And in the British Museum.

Then it was raining and I was running. It was lashing in Piccadilly Circus by the time I got to the entrance of the Underground. I was totally soaked. My shoes were squelching. I knew I'd be looking like a half-drowned marsh creature, tails of brown hair straggling across my way-too-pale forehead, my four AM shadow even more pronounced than usual.

The train was packed. It was not a good time to be wet. But we all stood shoulder to shoulder, trapped, swaying, dampness and tension filling the air.

I read the headlines on a girl's iPad. 'New London Riots' was the big story. Her finger hovered over it, pushed it away.

'England Awakens' read the next headline. Our train lurched, then stopped. The lights flickered. Someone groaned. It was ten minutes before the train started again.

3

In the basement of a villa belonging to the British Consulate, in the affluent Levent suburb of Istanbul, two men were staring at a laptop screen.

Loud moaning noises filled the room. On the screen, a big-breasted blonde was bouncing up and down on top of a scrawny dark-skinned older man. The bed they were on, in a hotel near Taksim Square, where the Iranian biological scientist had been staying, squeaked like a busted door on a moving train.

Surely a man that age should have stopped to consider *why* a woman so young and beautiful might be interested in him.

As the man let out a gasp the blonde pulled back. The view of his face was quite a sight. The man sitting in front of the laptop clicked his mouse. A still image appeared for a moment, then flew to the bottom corner of the screen. Peter Fitzgerald tapped his colleague's shoulder.

'That should be enough for you to open him up,' he said. 'His superiors in Iran won't be inclined to forgive him for this.'

Peter frowned as he went over to the printer. It hummed to life. This was going to be easier than he'd thought. But had they moved quickly enough? The Iranian had been in Istanbul for two weeks already.

4

The following night, Saturday night, I went to a barbecue near my house in West London. The Institute had an apartment in Oxford, but I rarely used it any more. My attic office was more than good enough for the days I didn't feel like battling up the M40.

It had been over thirty hours since I'd heard from Alek. If he didn't make contact until he came back on Monday I'd give him a chance to explain himself, then I'd tell him what I thought of his bullshit.

The barbecue was one of those gatherings where everyone dressed in similar, expensively-distressed clothes to demonstrate their individuality. I left before midnight. The host had been trying to hook me up with one of her friends, and while she was certainly attractive, my heart wasn't it. All everyone wanted to do was talk about the riots starting up again.

And all I wanted to do was get away from thinking about them. I walked home, crossed New King's Road, passed a bar with thumping music, people laughing outside. Everything looked normal. Maybe the riots weren't kicking off again. Good. I needed to get some sleep if I was going to go for a run in the morning.

My plan was to do the Kauai Marathon in September, which was only six weeks away. Ten days in Hawaii was a break I needed. I'd been looking forward to it for months. It would be the holiday that would mark a proper break with my past. That was what Alek had said, and I was hoping he was right.

I kicked off my shoes in the hall downstairs as soon as I got home. They skidded across the black and white tiles. Then I hung my jacket on the pile over the bottom of the banisters. I really needed to sort them all out. But where would I find the time? God only knew how Irene had kept the place tidy. The cleaner who came in now had enough work keeping the kitchen from turning into a health and safety disaster.

I checked my iPhone to see if I'd missed anything. There was still nothing from Alek. No texts. No emails. No missed calls. No tweets. Nothing! What was he playing at?

Was this all some stupid game? Was he trying to make a point about how important he was? I wouldn't put it past him.

A creak sounded from above my head. The pipes in the building had a habit of doing that. I reckon they were installed when Victoria was a princess.

The house had four floors and was at the end of one of those white stuccoed terraces West London is famous for. We'd grown used to its moods. Living there was our greatest luxury, Irene had said. Working seventy-hour weeks and being one of the founding directors of the Institute of Applied Research in Oxford had to have some advantages, I used to reply.

But I knew I'd been fortunate to end up owning the house. I'd been lucky to get a place on an exchange programme with University College London. And I'd been lucky to meet Irene while I was there. The work I did that year led to an article on patterns in human behaviour, which was published in the New York Times magazine to some acclaim. The success of that article helped us start the Institute.

15

I'd worked in a software company in Berkshire for three years after we got married. Then a few of us from college decided to set up the Institute. It had taken off way quicker than we'd expected, with serious projects in each of our specialisations.

We'd been lucky in many ways, but I'd give up every dime of our success, if that meant Irene could still be alive. We'd had plans and a house that was just waiting to be filled up with the sound of children's laughter.

And sometimes in my dreams I could still hear the echoes of what might have been.

I headed upstairs. I always kept a light on on the floor above, so it didn't feel like the house was brooding. That was the theory, anyway. Though it didn't seem to have the desired effect.

As I was undressing, the landline rang. It had that insistent tone only a telephone ringing late at night has.

Was it Alek? It had to be.

I found the phone on a foot-high stack of documents by the bed.

'Mr Ryan?'

The voice wasn't Alek's. It sounded like one of those city types who wear their sock suspenders to bed.

'Yes?' A needle-sharp sense of foreboding is difficult to ignore.

The sound of a car horn came over the phone line. A tinny noise, a radio station playing what sounded like Middle Eastern hip hop, echoed over the line.

'The name's Fitzgerald, sir. Peter Fitzgerald. I'm sorry to disturb you.' He spoke slowly, emphasizing each syllable, his manner exceedingly polite. 'I'm with the British Consulate, here in Istanbul.'

A shiver ran through me, as if I'd brushed against a wall of ice.

'Yes?' I didn't want to talk to him.

'I'm sorry, sir. It's bad news, I'm afraid.'

My mouth was as dry as sandpaper. Then my stomach did a backflip.

'It's about Mr Alek Zegliwski, sir. I've been told you're his manager on a project out here. Am I speaking with the right Sean Ryan?' The tinny Middle Eastern music played on in the background. What time was it there? 3:00 AM? Had he tried calling earlier, when I was out?

'Yes.' My voice sounded like it belonged to someone else.

Alek was more than a colleague. He'd been one of Irene's closest college friends. Then a drinking buddy of mine. We free-dived together. He was coming with me to Kauai.

Laughter echoed from the street below, from another world.

'Please sit down, Mr Ryan.' The voice seemed distant.

All the kinds of trouble Alek might have gotten himself into flickered through my mind, in a bizarre slide show. I stayed standing.

'I'm afraid it's my unfortunate duty to have to tell you that the authorities here have informed us that your colleague Mr Zegliwski is . . . ' He hesitated.

'. . . dead.'

A void opened beneath me. That was the one word he wasn't supposed to say.

'I am very sorry, sir. I'm sure it's an awful shock.'

I opened my mouth. No sound came out.

'We do need someone to identify his body fairly quickly. It's the Turkish authorities you see. They do things differently out here.'

17

Alek was coming back on Monday. We were meeting up in the evening. He was coming to my house. We were going for a run.

'Are you sure about this?' Please, let it be a mistake.

'I am sorry. They found his wallet, his ID. It's a bad time to ask, I know, but do you have contact details for Mr Zegliwski's relatives?'

I slumped onto the edge of the bed. Its scarlet Persian cover, half off already, slipped to the floor.

'I don't, I'm sorry. They're in Poland. I think.'

'He's not married?'

'No.'

'What about a girlfriend?'

'Not for a few months. And that was only for a week or two. He rarely talks about his family.' I wanted to be more helpful, but Alek was about as single and as independent as you could get. The only time he'd been asked about his next-of-kin in my presence, he'd pointed at me. That was his idea of a joke. He never went back to Poland either – not that I knew of anyway.

'No relatives in the United Kingdom at all? Are you sure?' He sounded sceptical.

'Not that I know about, no.'

Alek couldn't be dead. He couldn't be. More than anyone else I knew, he was able to look after himself. He was six foot tall, full of life, in his twenties for God's sake.

Something around me seemed to be changing, as if a hidden door had opened somewhere and a breeze had begun blowing.

'In that case, Mr Ryan, we'll have to ask you to come to Istanbul to identify Mr Zegliwski's body. I believe the authorities here have some questions about the project he was working on too.'

I didn't reply.

'Are you there, Mr Ryan?'

'Yes.'

'When can you come out? The earlier the better, really.' His tone wasn't soft any more.

The line between us hummed. I took my mobile out of my pocket, scrolled to Alek's number, tapped it. I had a phone to each ear now. Maybe, just maybe, this was all some stupid mistake. A joke even.

'This is too crazy,' I said, buying time. 'Do you know what happened to him?'

My mobile beeped. I looked at the screen. Alek's number was unavailable.

'We're not sure. The Turkish authorities are investigating. That's all I can say for now.' The line fizzed. 'Oh, and I spoke to your colleague, Dr Beresford-Ellis.'

The conversation had turned a surreal corner.

'I know you're aware of the current sensitivities with our Turkish friends. So you'll understand why we want to get all this done as quickly as possible.'

'I'll be on the first flight I can get a seat on.' My voice was firm. The truth was, he couldn't have stopped me going to Istanbul.

He coughed. 'Very good. Now finally, and I am sorry, but I must ask you this: Was Mr Zegliwski involved in anything political or religious, or anything like that?'

'No, not really. Nothing you wouldn't hear in any pub in England.'

I could hear the line between London and Istanbul hiss again as Fitzgerald waited for me to add to my answer. But I didn't want to say any more. I had nothing to hide. Alek had nothing to hide as far as I knew. But would there be consequences if I repeated every crazy opinion he'd ever expressed?

'What work does the Institute do, sir? I haven't heard about you.'

I could imagine my interrogator's eyebrows shooting up as he asked me that question.

'We apply advanced research to practical problems. Imaging technology is one area we've been working on, technology to find criminals in crowds for instance.' It was the standard description I'd been using for years whenever anyone asked me what the Institute did.

'Very good, sir.' He didn't sound interested. 'I'll tell our people you're on your way. You'll be met at Istanbul airport by someone from the Consulate. We'll know which flight you're on. The Turks will do the identification formalities on Monday, most likely. And please, do ring the Foreign Office emergency helpline to verify this conversation. The UK number is on our website. Goodbye, Mr Ryan. I'm very sorry for your loss.'

The line went dead.

I held the handset tight. My knuckles were porcelain white. A picture of Alek grinning outside Hagia Sophia, which he'd emailed me only the day before, came to me. He'd looked so happy. What the hell had happened? My hand trembled as I called his landline in Oxford. I was still hoping that somehow it was all a mistake.

His answering machine took the call. I hung up.

This couldn't have anything to do with our work at the Institute, could it? Alek had helped us win the project he was working on in Istanbul. It was a real opportunity to establish our credentials in that part of the world. But I'd allowed him to go out there on his own. My stomach turned.

'How complicated do you think taking photos is?' he'd argued at the time.

I stabbed my fist into the mattress.

What was going to happen?

Beresford-Ellis would lap all this up. His appointment as Director of the Institute last year had been a not-too-subtle attempt to sideline me totally. It wasn't enough that I was demoted for the stunt I'd pulled in Afghanistan. The other founders of the Institute had demanded I relinquish, temporarily, many of my responsibilities, for my own good.

And I'd agreed, reluctantly. So the last thing I needed now was for one of my new projects to end in disaster.

I shook my head. What happened to me didn't matter. All that mattered was what had happened to Alek.

He'd been the one I'd talked to when things had gotten too much, when the emptiness had won, when I'd decided I couldn't go on. I would have never survived without him.

I checked the Foreign Office website, rang their emergency number. As I waited for an answer I thought about how people would react to the news.

Beresford-Ellis had been disdainful about the project in Istanbul from the beginning. When I'd told him we'd won it, he'd said, with his trademark pessimism, 'I hope you know what you're doing, Ryan. Isn't any project like this in a Muslim country a bit too controversial these days? We don't want a bloody fatwa on our heads.'

'It's a small project,' I'd said. 'Who gives a damn about someone taking pictures in a museum?'

'Hagia Sophia may be a museum, Ryan,' he'd replied. 'But it was once the supreme mosque ruling the Sunni Islam world, and the seat of the Islamic Caliphate. And before that it was the Orthodox Vatican. There are a lot of toes to be stepped on out there.'

Having made his point, he left our office, sniffing as he passed Alek's empty desk.

But he was right. Hagia Sophia was important. It had been built when the Byzantine Empire was at its peak in the 7th century and had been dedicated to Holy Wisdom, Sophia, a concept that spanned both the Christian and pre-Christian worlds.

The Orthodox Greeks had lost their Vatican when the all-conquering Ottoman Turks had captured Constantinople and renamed it Istanbul in 1453. In doing so, they'd snuffed out the Byzantine Empire, the direct descendants of ancient Rome.

Sure, fundamentalists were angered when Atatürk had turned Hagia Sophia into a museum in 1934, but their argument was with the Turkish state, not us.

In any case, our project – comparing digital images of mosaics to prints and sketches produced by artists over the centuries – was just about the least invasive thing you could do in a world heritage site. And it was also exactly the type of project our Institute had been set up to do.

A friendly Indian lady finally came on the line. After receiving permission from her superior, she told me about a note on her system from the Istanbul consulate detailing how someone called Alek Zegliwski had indeed been involved in a serious incident in Istanbul. Their contact in relation to the matter was a Mr Fitzgerald. She didn't have any more information to give me. She couldn't even tell me Mr Fitzgerald's first name.

I fell asleep as the first rays of dawn were softening London's skyline. I'd spent all night thinking about what had happened. One memory had replayed itself over and over in my mind.

The day before he'd flown to Istanbul – only a week earlier – Alek had leaned towards me and whispered,

'You do know the Devil's caged under Hagia Sophia, boss? Let's hope I don't disturb him, eh?'

I'd laughed. Such superstitions had seemed ridiculous in our shiny glass-walled offices in Oxford.

When I woke, the first thing I did was look for Beresford-Ellis' number. It was 8:00 AM, but I didn't care.

Beresford-Ellis was the kind of guy who kept pictures of himself with prominent people on his wall. He had one with David Cameron, another with the chancellor of the university he'd worked in before he came to us, another with Nelson Mandela, and another with the head of the US Geological Service. He was so good at social climbing he could have run PhD-level courses on it. The cherry on top of all that was that he was about as trustworthy as an Afghan warlord with an empty war chest.

When the other founders had decided to take on a qualified manager to lead the Institute, because each of us was immersed in our own projects, I'd said nothing. Irene had died only a month before. Getting Beresford-Ellis in had seemed like a good idea.

I soon found out that his appetite for corporate-speak was prodigious. We didn't have projects any more, we had 'collaboration initiatives' or 'research value actualisations'. And he'd been subtly critical of every 'initiative' I'd worked on since he'd joined. The work we'd done in Bavaria identifying Bronze Age settlements from satellite images hadn't identified settlements from the target period, he'd said. And our trial security initiative in New York, for a big American bank, hadn't turned into anything lucrative. All he wanted, it seemed, were projects that got us major contracts quickly.

He was right in his own way, if you disregarded the fact that it took months for the impact of many of our projects to come to light.

These faults weren't compensated by his demeanour either. He seemed to be uninterested in everyone around him, not just me. Most of the time, it was almost as if his colleagues were invisible to him. What he preferred to do was talk about his own achievements.

'Bad publicity is the last thing we need right now,' he said, after I got through to him and told him I was planning to fly out to Istanbul that afternoon. He was good, as always, at finding the down side.

'If there's anything in the press about the Institute being involved in something it shouldn't have been, it'll be a disaster for our fundraising this year, Ryan. I know this is a bad time to say it, but there are some board members who think we've given you too much rope already.' He waited for a moment for his words to detonate.

What a bastard! Not a single word about Alek's death. He'd be happy with our scalps on his wall next to those photos.

'I won't dodge my responsibilities,' I said. 'But I think you should reserve judgement until we know the facts.' I cut the line.

A few hours later I headed for Heathrow feeling sick, totally unprepared, and unplugged from reality.

It knew it could easily have been me who'd been murdered out there. I could have gone to Istanbul instead of Alek, if I'd insisted on it. And there was more too. If what had happened to Alek had been because of our work in Hagia Sophia, how careful would I need to be?

What was going to happen in Istanbul?

5

Malach walked slowly. He turned his head often. The yellow bulbs were barely bright enough to light the sloping brick tunnel in front of him. The polished sheen of his bare head, almost touching the roof, was elongated as if he had been bound at birth.

From his huge hands dangled two canvas bags, the type you see in army surplus stores. Both were empty. When he reached his destination, he put them down beside the tables. He had work to do. The project had delivered what was needed. It was time to tidy up. What had happened in the last few days had pushed the cleanup operation forward, but not by much. Soon, if anyone found this place, they wouldn't have any idea what had been going on.

As he filled the canvas bags he thought about their unexpected visitor. The man had soiled himself in his last few minutes. Westerners were so weak. Their soft comforts made them that way. They knew nothing about how to face their end.

He took the hunting knife from its scabbard under his armpit, felt the tip. It was still sharp. Good. He would need it again, soon if he was lucky. He loved the feeling of power that ran through him when he used it. It was exhilarating. He held the knife in the air, admiring it. Then he put it away. He had a lot to do.

6

Heathrow Airport, Terminal 5, the largest free-standing building in the UK, looked as busy the following morning as it had
during the nightmare snow storm the previous winter.

There were queues at the check-in machines, lines at the
information desks, people sleeping, huddled together on its
gleaming floor. The continued closure of French air space, due
to an extended nationwide strike, was taking its toll. Flights
that weren't cancelled were being rerouted. The knock-on
effect delayed my departure by an hour. And I was among the
lucky ones.

To distract myself I read anything I could find.

The English Sunday newspapers were feasting on the riots
in London. They hadn't spread, but some journalists were
saying that police leave had already been cancelled. It was
astonishing, one article suggested, that a raid on a mosque had
produced such a reaction. Another paper, which devoted two
pages to what had happened, linked the rioting to other incidents around Europe in the past few weeks. The article claimed
that there was a fear in intelligence circles that such riots were
being coordinated.

Another paper had a map of St Paul's and the City of
London showing how far a crowd of half a million would reach,
if that many did turn up the following Friday for the mass

demonstration planned by a different Islamic group. The police presence at such events was likely to be much heavier now, even if the event had already been approved, said the article.

My eye fell on a side piece about a video being posted on the Internet showing a Westerner being beheaded. It made me uncomfortable. Could that Westerner be Alek? No. There was no need for total paranoia.

But what had happened to him? Was his death the result of a random incident? A robbery? A car accident? That was certainly the most likely explanation. Our Institute was a world leader in applying technology to intractable problems, but I couldn't imagine anything we'd been working on out there being a reason to murder him.

We did uncontroversial things, like identifying lost settlements under forests with L-band digital imaging, or devising high-speed spectrometry techniques to date carbon-based compounds without destroying the sample. I was proud of our work.

And everyone I knew thought we were doing something good. Even my dad, who had seen us open the Institute, had been proud. And that was something, coming from a US Air Force pilot who had flown 212 combat missions, had bailed out over Bosnia in 1995 and had then evaded Serb paramilitary units for three days.

It was time to board.

I was glad I'd picked a window seat. The thought of identifying Alek's body had put me off idle chitchat. And the idea that it might have been me lying cold in some morgue, and Alek flying out to identify my body, didn't help.

I'd had more than enough of the sympathetic noises people make when they find out something bad has happened to you.

28

It's not that I don't like to talk about Irene or to think about her. I probably think about her too much still. But I hate to talk about it to strangers. The words have got stuck in my throat once too often.

It had taken ten days, after they'd come to our house to tell me she was dead, before the tears came. Something inside me didn't want to face how much I was hurting, how much I needed her, loved her. That's what the grief counsellor had said. I stopped going to see her. I wasn't ready for all the stuff she wanted me to do. I don't know if I ever will be.

Irene had been the best part of my life for twelve years. My friends at MIT had thought me crazy for staying in England: I'd earn a lot more in the States, they'd said, but I couldn't have been happier. I'd grown to love London.

Slate-grey clouds were rolling below the plane now and the guy in the seat beside me was reading a book called *Turkey – The New Power*.

I picked up my iPad. I'd downloaded a guide to Istanbul on it. I read a few pages, then the meal came. I only ate half of it.

My unease about the prospect of viewing Alek's body only grew as we descended over the inky Sea of Marmara, towards a long curving shore marked by the glow of early evening street lights. Istanbul, a grey tapestry of roads and buildings, was coming into view.

An hour later, the marble floor of the arrivals hall echoed as I walked through it.

I'd felt the familiar breath-catching August Mediterranean heat as soon as the plane doors had opened, but in that metallic cavern of a hall everything was cool, slick, antiseptic.

I caught my reflection in a mirrored wall as I walked by. I looked like a typical tourist in my short-sleeved navy linen shirt and loose cream chinos. The leather haversack on my trolley looked about as travel-scarred and worn-out as I felt.

Already, I'd been detained at passport control for minutes while the immigration officer had checked his computer. I'd bought a tourist visa at the nearby counter, and others were going through quickly, so there was no reason for him to hold me.

Unless the authorities here were expecting me.

'Enjoy your visit to Turkey,' he finally mumbled, as he handed me back my passport.

I was relieved.

The frosted glass doors that led out of the arrivals hall opened with a sigh as I approached them. The shiny public area beyond had a long curve of people waiting for arriving passengers. The hall hummed with a click-clack of activity. Acres of glass gave the place an airy feeling.

And directly ahead, advancing toward me out of the crowd, was a tall pencil-thin man with an almond-brown face, black hair and a thin nose. His hair was slicked back. He looked like someone who wouldn't put up with too much crap. And he was looking straight at me.

Following the man, about a pace behind, were two other men dressed in pale-blue short-sleeved shirts and navy trousers flapping at the ankles.

The charcoal suit, which the leading man wore, looked expensive. He held out his hand as he closed the gap between us.

'*Merhaba*, Mr Ryan. I am Inspector Erdinc.' He shook my hand. His grip was tight, designed no doubt to make criminals uneasy. There was a smell of tobacco on his breath.

He stared into my eyes, as if I was his quarry.

'I was expecting someone from the British Consulate,' I said, looking around.

There were a few people nearby holding up pieces of cardboard with names on them. Unfortunately, none of them was mine.

'I am with the International Crime Section at the Ministry of the Interior, Mr Ryan.' He looked over my shoulder, as if checking to see if anyone was with me.

'I am here to meet you.' He raised his hands in an open gesture, and gave me a brief smile. 'You work for the Institute of Applied Research and are here to identify your colleague's body, yes?'

I nodded. One of his eyebrows shot up. I got the feeling he was assessing me. It wasn't going to be easy to get away from this guy.

'You will come with me,' he said, assuredly. Then, with his head down, like a boxer on his way to a match, he walked away motioning for me to follow him, as if he needed someone to carry his sweat towel. His heels clicked on the marble as he walked.

I looked around. His two assistants were nodding, indicating I should go after the inspector. I sighed, and followed him, with them bringing up the rear. It must have looked, to anyone watching, as if I'd been arrested.

7

The black S1100R BMW superbike came to a halt at the back entrance of the steel and glass apartment block, its tyres scattering gravel. Its rider, Malach, was, within seconds, heading up in the service elevator to the penthouse apartment with the breathtaking views over the Golden Horn. Its wrap-around balcony had once been used to host a party for a visiting Hollywood star. That evening the balcony was empty.

Arap Anach was in the main marble-floored bedroom. A cocoa-skinned girl was lying on a white rug in front of him, face down.

'You are a devil,' he whispered. She moved her hips invitingly, then groaned.

She'd been well trained, and understood English. He made a mental note to use the same contact in the red light district of Mumbai again. This girl was, without doubt, a 10,000 rupee girl, exactly as he'd been promised. He would send the man a bonus. From what he knew had happened to the man's family, he'd appreciate it.

He fingered one of the gauze-thin veils the girl had discarded. Then he examined her body. A creak sounded from outside the door. He didn't react. He'd seen what he was looking for.

'You think threads on your wrist will ward away evil spirits?' he said.

She moaned. She hadn't understood the turn this encounter was taking.

He looked at the scar on the back of his hand. Then, reflexively, he glanced around, even though he knew the room was secure, that no camera could be watching them, no microphone listening. He'd done the bug sweep himself.

It was time.

He placed the palm of his hand a hair's breadth from her back, and traced the contours of her body without touching her.

'I will be your last,' he whispered. Would she react? Anticipation and adrenaline coursed through him.

Somewhere inside her there was a shard of anxiety, there had to be, but it was well hidden. She assumed, most probably, that because she'd survived thus far in her career, and had met many men, that the future would be the same as the past.

A tentative knock sounded from the door.

'Do not move,' he said firmly. He padded across the room, cracked the door open.

'There is an envelope. It was sent to the Greek at his hotel,' a voice whispered. 'What should we do?'

'Get it, fool.' He clicked the door shut, walked back to the rug. As he passed the small table he passed his hand slowly through the flame of the candle burning on it, until he felt its sting.

'Are you ready?' he whispered. He kneeled down beside her, put one hand on her back.

She wriggled in anticipation. He reached to his left, slid a steel syringe from under the mattress of the emperor-sized bed. He held the tip near her back, dragging out the moment. Soon she would feel something. Very soon.

Then it would begin.

8

The heat was like an open-air oven, even though night had fallen. I could hear a plane's engine revving. The odour of jet fuel filled the air. The inspector was striding towards a gleaming black Renault Espace with darkened windows, which stood beside a 'No Parking' sign.

'Where are we going?' I asked loudly.

'You will see,' was his nonchalant reply. He held the Espace's door open for me. His colleagues were a few paces behind me. Did they think I was going to run? Did they think I'd done something?

Or had Alek done something outrageously stupid? Was I going to be implicated in something illegal that I knew nothing about?

'This is quite a welcoming committee,' I said.

'Hagia Sophia is one of our national treasures,' said the inspector, as he put his seat belt on.

'Anything to do with it involves our national security, especially these days. I'm sure you understand. All deaths there must be fully explained and accounted for.' He sounded firm, and suspicious. About what I had no idea, but he was not in the least bit ashamed of it.

I belted myself in.

'How is London?' he said. 'I saw you had another riot.'

'It was good when I left.'

'I like London. I have a cousin there. Such a great city.' He tapped the driver on his shoulder. The car moved off with a squeal.

'I thought you were going to be British, Mr Ryan,' said the inspector. 'But your accent is American, I think.' He looked puzzled.

'My father was American. My mother was English. We stayed in England until I was ten, then we lived in upstate New York. I'm back in England twelve years now.'

'An English mother and an American father.' He repeated what I'd said, as if he found it amusing. If he was trying to annoy me he was doing a good job.

'That's what I said. I like Macy's and Harrods. And I'm proud of it.' I'd used that line before. And I didn't mind giving him more from where that came from.

He looked me up and down, then changed the subject. 'Were you close to your colleague, Mr Ryan?'

'We were friends.' I stared back at him. I had nothing to hide.

He stared out the window. Letting me stew, most likely.

The motorway we joined a few minutes later had five lanes. The headlights streaming towards us were like strings of pearls.

The reservations I'd had about coming to Istanbul seemed justified now. What the hell had happened to the contact from the Consulate who was supposed to meet me? And where were we going?

'You were Mr Zegliwski's manager, weren't you?' asked the inspector a minute later. The question had an aggressive undertone to it, as if he was trying to find someone to take responsibility for something.

35

'Yes, I am. That's why I'm here, to find out what happened to him.' I'd worked hard on this project. I'd spent months on research. Alek had too. There was no way I was going to allow this guy to dump anything on me, or on the Institute.

'And you haven't been told what happened Alek?' His eyes gleamed in the semi-darkness.

'Just that he's dead. That I'm supposed to identify his body.' There was still a slim chance that it wasn't Alek they'd found, that he was in a coma in some hospital. I clung to it.

The inspector opened his window. Warm soggy air poured in. It was well after 9:00 PM, but still as hot as midday on the hottest summer day in London.

'It's a little hot,' I said.

'Not too much,' he replied. 'This is cool by Istanbul standards.'

'Are you going to tell me what happened?' I asked, louder than I expected to. I wiped off a rivulet of sweat running down my cheek.

I could smell musky aftershave.

'Your colleague's been murdered, *effendi*,' he whispered. Occasional beeps and the drone of cars speeding around us almost drowned his voice out.

I stared back at him. I felt empty, numb. I'd assumed Alek had died in an unfortunate accident.

'I'm sorry for the bad news.'

I looked at his face, waited for his nose to grow.

'Why are you treating me like a criminal, when my friend's been murdered?'

He didn't answer. He just kept staring at me. His eyes were bloodshot. He had a thin white scar on the side of his forehead.

'Did your colleague have enemies?'

I shook my head. 'Are you going to tell me how it happened?' I said.

For a split second, I saw disdain in his expression, then it became impassive again.

The traffic reverberations around us were like a muzzled growl. Warm air sliced menacingly through the car. Anger rose up inside me. I had to close my eyes to calm myself, start breathing deeply. I had to be careful. Letting off steam into this guy's face would probably only see me end up in a prison cell.

Memories of Alek flashed through my head. Why the hell had he been murdered?

'Is it a secret?' I said.

'Later, *effendi*, later.' His tone softened.

We passed a conga line of minibuses. There must have been fifty of them. Each had a blue circular logo on its side, the outline of the minarets and unmistakable dome of Hagia Sophia.

I'd been to Istanbul twice before. Alek had been even more times. The grey crust of buildings that flows to each horizon gives the city an anthill intensity. It's what you get, I suppose, for having a population of almost fourteen million. No city in Europe has ever been bigger.

I stared out the window, trying to take in what had happened. It was all so unreal. Anger rose up inside me again. I put my fist against the glass.

'We will find out who did this, Mr Ryan. And when we do...' I turned to look at him. He put his hands together, motioned as if he was crushing something.

The motorway we were on soared over a valley encrusted with buildings. The scene was lit by a spider web of yellow and white street lights. Then the motorway turned to the right and a whole vista of curved steel-and-glass office blocks appeared in front of us, all lit up. TV screens flickered in one of the blocks.

Electronic billboards flashed by. Yacht-sized, red Turkish flags were draped down the sides of some of the larger buildings. The skyscrapers we passed would not have been out of place in Manhattan or Shanghai.

Mixed with all this modernity, on every ridge, were spot-lit minarets and the illuminated domes of mosques, each a mini Hagia Sophia. Every district seemed to have one. Some were half dark and had fewer minarets; others were lit up like football stadiums. But none of them came anywhere near Hagia Sophia's beauty.

'Alek loved this city,' I said.

'He was right to. This is the city of the future,' the inspector replied. 'We are growing fast. And we're managing it well.' His finger jabbed the air.

'Our birth rates aren't low, like the rest of Europe.' He raised an eyebrow, gave me a toothy grin.

'People are still moving here?'

'More than ever. From Turkey and this whole region. Everyone deserves a future.'

Who could argue with that? I went back to staring at the cars streaming past. People were changing lanes as if they were on a racetrack.

'And you're not sweeping aside the past,' I said.

'No, not at all. You Westerners think you are the best at conserving things, but you forget we saved Hagia Sophia, the greatest building in the world. Tell me, which 1300-year-old building is still in use in England?' He looked smug.

'I think the Greeks were already a beaten empire by the time they lost this city,' I said.

'It is true, Mr Ryan. And it was foretold. That was the Greeks' fate. And they were fortunate too. Mehmed's tolerance, the freedom he allowed different races and religions, was something your European kings and inquisitors could have learned from.'

He pointed at a skyscraper the size of the Empire State Building. It was lit up in electric blue and had a giant Islamic crescent on top.

'Look, this is the future. Islam and capitalism married at last. Faith and money intertwined. What our people can do will surprise you all.'

'I just want to find out what happened to my colleague.'

The motorway became elevated again. We were bowling along high up over a muddle of buildings. Then the road swung to the left. The lights of the city were spread out in front of us, as if a sack of diamonds had spilled over dark velvet.

'Where are we going?' I asked, as we powered through the traffic, sounding our horn at anyone who strayed into our path.

'The morgue at the New International Hospital,' was the inspector's reply.

I thought about telling him to postpone the identification, that I was too tired. I'd have preferred to speak to Fitzgerald before I did it, find out what the process was in Turkey, if there was anything I had to make sure to do. But maybe it was better to get it over with.

We turned off the motorway onto a dual carriageway running between pencil-thin office buildings, fifteen, maybe twenty storeys high. There wasn't as much traffic now. Soon

I lost all sense of direction. We were driving through a warren of narrow streets with old buildings crowding in on each side.

'The Galata area,' said the inspector, motioning at the hodgepodge of old and new around us.

I'd seen pictures of the Galata Tower poking its head up above the tiled roofs of old Istanbul. Venetian traders had built the stone tower on the top of a hill to the north of the Golden Horn, Istanbul's natural horn-shaped harbour.

We pulled up with a squeal in front of what looked like an office block. I saw a green cross sign. I wasn't looking forward to what was going to happen next. But I held on to a paper-thin hope that the body wouldn't be Alek's.

I followed the inspector through an oddly empty reception area into a marble-floored lift. We'd left his colleagues in the car. They'd smiled at me like factory workers who'd been given a day off.

The hospital looked new. There wasn't a scuff mark on a wall or a scratch on any of the shiny floors.

For a second I wondered if we were too late to visit the morgue. Then I remembered who I was with.

A moon-faced attendant in a loose virgin-blue uniform was waiting for us, clutching a clipboard, when the doors to the basement slid open. He mumbled something in Turkish. We followed him. Our shoes squeaked on the floor. He led us to a low room encased in white tiles. The smell of powerful disinfectant filled the air. He pulled a shiny metal morgue tray from a wall. Every noise was amplified. All eyes were on me. Things were moving too fast.

There was a covered body on a tray in front of me. I'd expected a long wait, documents to be signed.

'Mr Ryan, are you ready?' The inspector sounded uninterested, as if he'd done this many times before.

I desperately wanted to leave. There was something pressing into my chest.

I nodded.

He said something to the attendant in Turkish, who motioned for me to adjust the white cotton face mask he'd given me, hold it tight to my mouth, as he was doing.

I'd been talking to Alek only a few days ago. How could the white-swathed figure on this tray be him? No, it was impossible. This shape didn't even look like him.

The attendant pulled back the stiff white sheet just far enough to expose the face. Bile rose inside me.

The face I was looking at was pale, plastic, like a mannequin's, a waxy effigy of Alek. A bloody bruise disfigured his forehead. His lips were dry, closed tight, as if they'd been glued together.

I stared, unblinking. I was watching what was happening, but from far away.

I'd learned in the past few years to disdain pity, to look ahead, to act strong, to not think too much. I needed every one of those lessons now.

Alek's skin had a blue tinge. There were wisps of vapour emanating from under the sheet.

And his body seemed strangely disconnected from his head, as if his neck had been elongated. A shudder ran through me. He looked different, so still. He'd always been so full of life.

I took a step forward, put my hand out. I wanted to touch him, to say goodbye.

The attendant waved me back briskly.

41

'Mr Ryan, can you confirm that this is your colleague, Mr Alek Zegliwski?' said the inspector.

'Yes.' I looked away. This was not how I wanted to remember him.

'As your colleague was Greek, Mr Ryan, our investigation of his death must follow certain procedures.' He paused.

'He was Polish,' I said, cutting in fast.

'His mother was Greek, Mr Ryan. He had emphasised that fact himself to a number of people here in Istanbul.' He spat out the word Greek.

I took a deep breath. All Alek had ever told me about his mother was that she was dead. Had she been Greek?

The attendant pulled the sheet over Alek's head. Then, with a resounding clunk, he slid the tray back into its drawer. Neighbouring trays rattled. Something caught my eye high up; a tiny security camera staring down at us.

'Come, we will talk,' said the inspector.

He led me to a smaller room up the hall. The type of room where grieving relatives could be comforted. I sat on a hard plastic chair. There was a line of five of them down the wall opposite the door. Everything was white. The inspector stood facing me. He was hunched over, as if he was thinking hard, and his arms were folded. Tiredness pulled at me. My body had finally decided to react to everything I'd been through.

'Aren't Turkey and Greece friends these days?' I said.

'Of course we are, but you must understand there are a lot of crazy Greeks who claim Hagia Sophia, and this whole city, for themselves. They say it all belongs to them.' He sounded affronted at the idea.

'What does any of that have to do with what happened to Alek?' I said.

In answer I got silence. All I could hear were the rumblings from the air conditioning. I waited, imagining Alek lying cold in that drawer. The inspector stared at me, as if he was expecting me to answer my own question.

'I came here to find out what happened to my friend. And I still don't know,' I said, as calmly as I could. 'And I've no idea why you think being Greek would have any impact on Alek's murder.'

The inspector held up his hands.

'I will explain why. The last Greek emperor of this city, Constantine the 11th, disappeared in Hagia Sophia the day the city was captured.' He paused. His tone was firm as he continued.

'Some Greeks say the last emperor made a pact with the devil that afternoon. That his body was taken below Hagia Sophia and that he will come back, and retake this city when the time is right. So you must understand, Mr Ryan, a Greek being murdered in Hagia Sophia is a big deal.'

'I don't believe in legends and I don't think Alek did either.' I gave him the kind of smile I reserved for younger children. 'Our Institute was commissioned by UNESCO to do a simple task here; to verify how the mosaics in Hagia Sophia are being preserved and altered over the years. That's what Alek was working on. It's not a big project.' The air in the room was getting stuffy, thick.

'There isn't even a UNESCO representative overseeing us. We're just recording things, monitoring changes. None of this stuff could have anything to do with what happened to Alek.'

The smell of hospital disinfectant was getting stronger too.

'UNESCO is monitoring Hagia Sophia?' he said.

'We're taking pictures, inspector.' Frustrated, I held up my hands. 'Thousands of tourists do it every day.' I had to move the conversation on. 'Can you at least tell me where Alek was found?'

He looked at me as if he was debating whether to say anything more or not. Then he continued. 'Your colleague was found outside Hagia Sophia early yesterday morning.' He studied my face. 'His head was near his body. For that we can be grateful.'

'He was beheaded?' I said it slowly.

'Yes.' He said, matter-of-factly.

My stomach flipped. I thought about what Alek must have gone through. I held my hand to my chest. The pressure had got stronger.

And the room seemed suddenly smaller, as if its walls had moved in.

He said something I didn't understand. The words were in English, but I couldn't make them out.

The fact that Alek had died was bad enough. That he'd been butchered like an animal was too much. This was why they hadn't pulled the sheet down. I'd been right about his body looking odd. This was sick.

I walked towards the wall, leaned my forehead against it. A wave of revulsion rolled through me. The white tiles were shiny, slick.

How could any human do such a thing?

'I don't believe this,' I whispered. Then I remembered something.

There'd been a story in one of the Sunday newspapers about a decapitation. No details. Just a one paragraph story. Had it been about Alek?

It had all seemed so distant when I'd been reading it. I must have read lots of stories like it. Of atrocities, horrible deaths. There were so many that few registered any more. I swallowed hard.

'Did what happened to Alek get into the newspapers?' I turned to face the inspector. He was standing by the table.

'The media here hunts for such stories these days.' His tone was hard. 'There may have been a small item in a Turkish newspaper yesterday. I promise you, we did not give out his name.'

I closed my eyes. Would the media in England find out what had happened to Alek? Would people be tweeting about it soon, speculating about the details? I could only guess what theories would come up, how it would all spin out.

'Does this sort of thing happen often in Turkey?'

'This is the first case of beheading in three years. We are not Iraq.'

'So why did this happen to Alek?'

He shrugged, looked me up and down. 'Are you planning to speak to the press?' he said.

'No.'

His face was a hard mask. 'Good. We'll be finished with your colleague's body in a week or so. There'll be an autopsy, of course.' I closed my eyes. 'You can make arrangements for his body after the results are in. We will hand over all his personal belongings then. ' His tone softened. He was playing the understanding official again.

Where will you be staying, Mr Ryan?'

'The Conrad-Ritz. Where Alek is… I mean was staying.' Alek had told me about the place. I'd called it from Heathrow.

'My driver will take you there.'

I nodded.

'Make no mistake,' he said. 'We value human life in Turkey,

Mr Ryan, unlike in some places. We take a crime like this seriously. As you will see.'

He took a shiny black leather notebook out of his pocket and began writing in it. I wanted to leave, to be on my own, to think.

'Are we finished?' I said.

'Just a few more questions.'

I didn't say anything.

'Can you tell me exactly what Mr Zegliwski was monitoring in Hagia Sophia, Mr Ryan?'

I wanted to snap at him. I was too tired for this.

'The tesserae, inspector. The tiny cubes that make up the mosaics. In Hagia Sophia a lot of them were preserved by the plaster Ottoman workmen covered them with, to conform to Islamic prescriptions against figurative art.' I spoke slowly. 'Gradually those mosaics have been exposed. Now we have a chance to record them digitally using the latest techniques, in case they're damaged in the future. It will help us understand how they've changed over time by comparing the images with drawings made over the centuries, which we are also digitizing.'

He made a note in his book.

'Do you think any of this could be a reason for someone to kill your colleague?' He stared at me, his hand poised to write.

'Inspector, the layers of gold that form the sandwich that make up many of the tesserae in Hagia Sophia are thicker and more valuable than those anywhere else in the world. Perhaps he disturbed someone robbing some gold tesserae.' It was a theory I'd come up with on the plane. Alek had joked about how valuable the larger mosaics were, even broken up.

He took another note. Then he said, 'Did Mr Zegliwski send anything to you or to your Institute after coming here?'

What was he implying? That we'd been stealing, illegally exporting artefacts, not just photographing them?

'No, he sent us nothing but digital images. There's no law against that.'

He closed his notebook. Then, as an afterthought, he said, 'Do you know about the Orthodox Christian archives, the ones that are missing, Mr Ryan?'

I wiped my forehead. A slick of cold sweat covered it. Alek lay dead a few feet away, beheaded for God's sake, and this man wanted to know about archives!

'I don't,' I replied. 'Are we finished?'

'You didn't know they were lost when Hagia Sophia was taken over?'

I shook my head. 'We're here to record mosaics inspector, nothing else.'

'Indeed, but any item discovered in the archives would have immense value. They included a letter from Mohammad, peace be upon him, so it is claimed. You can imagine the interest there would be in that. They say it was addressed to Emperor Heraclius, the Byzantine Emperor at the time. He visited Jerusalem when the Prophet was in Arabia awaiting his return to Mecca. Such a letter would have a major impact if it was found. It might even be considered important in England, no?'

'Our project has nothing to do with lost archives or lost letters.'

Why was he quizzing me about this stuff? Did the Turkish authorities really think our project was more than it seemed?

On the way up in the lift, the inspector smiled at me. It was the smile of a reptile as it sunned itself, while waiting for its prey to come within reach. He patted my shoulder as I climbed into the police car.

'Take care. We wouldn't want anything to happen to you in our beautiful city.'

I doubted very much that he gave a damn about what happened to me.

9

In Whitehall, in central London, not far from Downing Street, Sergeant Henry P Mowlam was looking out the window. The office he was in had a spectacular view over the London Eye. It was rotating, imperceptibly, against a backdrop of blue sky and the puffiest clouds he'd seen all year. His own office didn't have a view like this.

'Sergeant Mowlam,' said a voice.

He turned. The meeting had been organised by the Ministry of Defence. The conference room, with its dark panelled walls, held over twenty people. Just his luck to get called the second he'd got a proper look out the window.

'Yes, sir.'

The brigadier general who was leading the meeting from the top of the shiny oak conference table looked around the room, as if wondering who had replied.

Sergeant Mowlam coughed. 'How can I help?' he said.

'I was saying, Sergeant Mowlam, that we have some new chatter that's just come in. Can you give us the latest on it?'

'We've been picking up email and Twitter feeds this morning, sir. We discount most of this sort of stuff, but these messages are between the organisers of the demonstration planned for Friday. They are about supplies. Shall I read them out?'

The general nodded.

10

The driver sped through the still-busy streets. I was in the back again. Inspector Erdinc had stayed in the hospital. His other colleague had disappeared. My forehead was pounding as if I had a migraine.

A lot of things had been stirred up in me in the last few hours. There were so many links to the past in this city. So much was different here.

My fists were clenched as we sped onto a wide, low bridge. It had black chest-high iron railings on each side. Below, eel-black water slid past. On the far side of the bridge the shadow of a hill loomed, crowned with the spot-lit outlines of Topkapi Palace, the palace of the Ottoman Sultans, and the dome of Hagia Sophia. The dome was glowing with yellow light, and with its four minarets it looked like an oil painting come to life. Above, stars shone weakly through a haze. We were crossing the Golden Horn.

I asked the driver how soon we would get to the hotel. He didn't answer. I had only one word of Turkish – *Merhaba*, hello – so I decided to shut up.

He stared at me in his rear-view mirror. Then he touched one of those blue and white circular evil-eye charms they hang everywhere in Turkey. When we stopped at the traffic lights on the far side of the bridge he spoke.

'Your friend, he played a dangerous game, no?'

His eyes were fixed on the rear-view mirror.

I looked over my shoulder. There was a car with blacked-out windows behind us.

'It shouldn't have been dangerous,' I said.

He tutted, as if he didn't believe me. The lights changed. We sped on, cutting across two lanes in a way that would have spelled disaster in London.

He turned the radio on. A wild song filled the car, part Arab lament, part Latin dance beat. Then he turned the radio down, as if he'd remembered he shouldn't be playing music while on official business.

Then we were rumbling up a cobbled street and after another tight turn, with the minarets and dome of Hagia Sophia looming over us, we stopped in front of a parchment- yellow building. It was an Ottoman era, five-tier, wedding-cake of an edifice. It dominated one whole side of a narrow and steep side street.

Alek had picked the hotel, he'd said, because it was in the oldest part of Istanbul, near the summit of the hill Hagia Sophia was on. That was where the original Greek colony had been founded by someone called Byzas hundreds of years before Alexander the Great's family even owned a single olive tree.

The site had been chosen for reasons any child would under-stand. It was easily defendable. It had water on three sides; the Sea of Marmara, the Bosphorus, and the Golden Horn.

Not far from the hotel were the remnants of the old Roman Hippodrome, a stadium Ben Hur might have raced in.

The Roman imperial legacy here was only part of the his-tory of the place though. Within strolling distance of the hotel was the palace and harem of the Ottoman sultans, rulers of an empire which at one time stretched from Egypt almost to Vienna.

I stepped out of the car. Old stone walls and sun-bleached Ottoman-era buildings lined the street. The hotel brooded above me. It felt strange, unsettling, to be following in Alek's footsteps, seeing things he'd seen only a few days before.

I stood for a moment watching the police car pull away. I could smell jasmine on the warm air, hear laughter, voices. I touched the yellow plaster of the hotel wall as I climbed the stairs from the street.

As soon as I entered the building I was hit by a blast of air conditioning. The smiling lady behind the glass-topped ultra-modern reception desk had the blondest hair I'd seen in a long time. She was friendly, and very sympathetic, after I gave her my name and told her I was a colleague of Alek's.

'We are all so sorry about what happened. We heard from the police that Mr Zegliwski had an accident. It's terrible. He was so nice. What happened to him? Do you know?'

'Yes.' I didn't feel like telling her though, so I added. 'And thanks. I appreciate your concern.'

She smiled, then held a finger in the air, as if she was trying to remember something. After a moment, she said, 'There's something here for Mr Zegliwski.'

She turned, scanned the pigeon holes that filled the wall behind her until she found what she was looking for – a large brown envelope. She held it out in front of her triumphantly, to show me what was written on it. *Mr Zegliwski.*

I took the envelope. As I walked to the lift I squeezed it gently. It felt like there were a few sheets of paper in it, and something else at the bottom.

A man in a puffy black jacket stared at me from an oversized leather sofa at the far end of the reception area. He gave me the creeps. I imagined his corpulent boss entertaining some underage hooker or three upstairs.

As I waited for the lift to reach the fifth floor, I slid my finger under the flap of the envelope and looked inside. A silver key-ring, with one of those USB memory sticks attached, lay in the bottom of the envelope. I pulled it out, looked at it, then put it in my pocket. The only other thing in the envelope were some photos.

I almost dropped them on the white marble floor of the hallway as I juggled my room card and bag. It wasn't until I was inside that I got a chance to look at the photos properly.

One of them was of a woman with long black hair and a winning smile. Alek had clearly been busy. Something tightened in my chest. Did she know what had happened to him? My shoulders hunched, as the weight of his death bore down on me. There was one thing I was going to promise myself, and Alek. Whatever happened, I would find out who had done this.

I steadied myself, looked at the photos again.

Two didn't fit with the rest. One was of a crumbling floor mosaic. Debris lay scattered around it. The other was of the inside of a brick-lined tunnel. It had an arched ceiling, sloping downwards. A yellow marble plaque hung on the wall near the top of the tunnel. I could just about make out what was carved on it; scales with a sword lying across its pans.

I put the photos on the round table near the window. I couldn't make sense of them now. And I didn't want to think about them. I looked around. The room was a pastiche of late Ottoman style, decorated in reds and golds. Every piece of furniture was covered in a thick layer of varnish.

After a quick shower I turned off the bedside light and lay staring at the shadows, my mind drifting. A faint aroma came to me. The smell of roses. It reminded me of Irene. It would have been good to be able to call her now, to talk all this through with her.

When I met Irene she'd been studying medicine. She hadn't been interested in me initially, but I found out she used to drink in the university bar before getting her train home. A week later we had our first date. A walk in Hyde Park. She was a great listener.

We got married three months after I graduated. One of her friends used to tease us about how perfect our lives were, how lucky we'd both been to be doing so well so soon after graduating.

And then she'd volunteered to go to Afghanistan with the Territorial Army. They needed doctors. Three of them had volunteered from her hospital. That had been reassuring. I'd imagined stupidly, so stupidly, that that meant there would be safety in numbers. That the odds were against all three of them being killed. Their tour started two years and three months ago.

And she was the one who didn't make it back. A roadside bomb, an IED – an Improvised Explosive Device – killed her two weeks into the mission.

And for a long time I felt powerless and angry, all at the same time. Irene had been about all that was good about England. All she'd ever wanted to do was help people. It wasn't right that she'd died. Not for one second.

For months after it happened I fantasised about her walking through our front door. And I used to hope, despite everything logical, that I'd wake up one day to find her beside me again.

Tragedy warps everything.

I was slipping away, on the edge of consciousness, back in London, walking towards Buckingham Palace. A man in a long white shirt carrying a pitcher of water was coming towards me. I turned my head. Somebody was behind me, way in the distance. I knew who it was. But she was so far away. I turned, ran, stumbled.

I woke up, sickly unease rising through me. The floor-to-ceiling curtains were shadows in the darknes. I could make out the vague outlines of the gilt-edged prints of Ottoman Istanbul that hung in a row on the wall, like Janissaries, the Sultan's guards, standing to attention.

Then I felt something move. There was something in the bed with me.

Bloody hell! I swung my fist, slammed it into the mattress, bounced up out of the bed, scrambled for the light switch by the bathroom door.

The room flooded with jaundiced light.

There was nothing. Nothing in the bed. Nothing under it. Was I going mad?

Relief soaked through me. Had it been an animal, a spider, something like that? My skin crawled. I should never have left the window open.

The phone rang.

'Mr Ryan?' A woman's voice, anxious. It was the receptionist who'd given me that envelope. I sat on the bed, cradling the telephone against my bare shoulder. The gossamer breeze from the window felt like water running over my skin.

'Yes?'

'Two men are on the way up to see you, Mr Ryan.'

'What?'

The line went dead. I could hear a truck grinding its gears outside.

For a second I didn't understand why she'd called. Then it came to me. She was warning me.

A sharp knock – rat tat tat – sounded from the door. The do-not-disturb sign hanging on the doorknob vibrated.

That was quick. Then the knock came again. It was even more insistent this time.

I walked over to the door, put my eye to the viewer. Nothing. Just blackness. Was it broken?

'Come on, Mr Ryan,' an officious female voice called out. Someone English.

'Hold on,' I replied. I grabbed a fresh T-shirt from my bag and pulled it over my head. An even sharper knock sounded.

Rat-tat-tat-tat.

'Coming.' What the hell was the hurry? I pulled on my chinos, pushed my feet into suede moccasins.

Another knock.

RAT TAT-TAT TAT-TAT.

'Come on!' She sounded petulant, as if she hadn't heard my replies, or had heard, but didn't think I was moving fast enough.

I jerked the door open but held my foot against it, just in case I needed to close it in a hurry.

An attractive-looking woman was standing outside. She was in her late twenties, I guessed, and was wearing a tight high-necked black T-shirt. Her face was symmetrical, her eyes dark green, serious, her black hair pulled back tight. She had a thin gold chain around her neck. Despite her slim frame, she was clearly someone who could look after herself.

And she was holding an identity card in my face. I saw a severe-looking face and an official stamp, a triangle with a crown and the letters EIIR above it, and the words 'British Consulate' below. Then the card vanished before I had a chance to read any more. I stood up a little straighter. And then it came to me. This was the woman from one of Alek's photos.

'Come with me, Mr Ryan. Now.' She glanced towards the lifts.

'There are some people on the way up that you don't want to meet. They were demanding to know your room number down at reception. You have to come with me. I mean it.' She looked up and down the corridor, as if expecting to be interrupted at any moment. I heard a metallic thrum as the lift rose towards us. Then there was a creaking noise. It had stopped at a lower floor, maybe the one below us.

I could smell her perfume. It was faint, sweet.

'Did you know Alek?'

A flicker of hesitation crossed her face.

'My name's Isabel Sharp. I was Alek's liaison officer at the Consulate. Come on, Mr Ryan. If you don't want to end up like him.'

I felt my back pocket. My wallet was there. I could get another room pass. I was dressed. I had my shoes on.

'OK.'

She moved quickly. My room door closed behind me with a clunk. She was already halfway to a door down the corridor with an 'Exit' sign above it.

She held the door open for me, closed it after I'd passed through.

'I thought I was gonna be met at the airport?' I said, still unsure why I was following her.

'That was a little misunderstanding,' she said. 'But I'm here now.' She started down the carpeted stairs. I followed.

I was going to ask her why she was moving so fast, when I heard a juddering bang above us, as if someone had slammed a door open.

'They're coming,' she said. I barely heard her. A muffled clatter of footsteps echoed from above.

She took the next set of stairs in two jumps.

Someone shouted. Then a crisp popping sound filled the stairwell. It was accompanied by a shrill pinging near me. A rain of concrete chips and dust fell around my head. Something had hit the wall above me!

'Bastards,' she said, in a low voice, as if she was talking to herself. I was barely keeping up with her.

My heart was pounding.

Something struck the metal handrail behind me. It squealed. I jerked my hand away from it.

Adrenaline pumped through me, tingling every muscle. The hair on my body stood up straight. My scalp felt tight.

I was taking three steps at a time, sometimes four. I could feel the rough concrete under the thin carpet as I landed on each step. Then Isabel almost fell. I put a hand under her arm, held her up. She regained her footing. We kept going.

The sound of running feet, voices, wasn't far above us now. They were catching up. I looked behind. All I could see was a shadowy blur coming down.

Isabel's face was pale.

The backs of my legs were straining. Who the hell were they?

At the bottom of the stairwell I overtook Isabel, barged through the fire exit door, held it open for her. The deafening noise of an alarm rang out above our heads.

Then she was sprinting like an Olympic runner down the deserted concrete laneway in front of us. I went after her, my lungs dragging in air. She was heading for a black Range Rover, a giant cockroach resting on oversized tyres.

The Range Rover's lights flickered as we came up to it. For a moment I thought there might be someone in it.

'Get in,' she roared, jerking open the driver's door.

As I slammed the passenger door closed, a sense of security enveloped me. Then I heard muffled shouts. I turned, looked through the back window. Two huge guys, one of them bald, had emerged from the fire exit door. The bald guy lifted his arm, pointed a gun at us.

There was a noise like fire crackers snapping.

'Go!' I shouted.

The engine of the Range Rover growled. I heard a whoosh, fans starting.

We jumped forward. There was a loud ding. I looked around.

The back window had taken a hit. The glass had a star in it now. Then another. But it didn't shatter. We had bulletproof glass.

'Put on your seat belt,' she shouted.

A brick wall loomed. She swerved.

'They'll need a missile to stop us.' She sounded triumphant.

We slid sideways, tyres squealing, onto an empty street. Exhilaration filled me. I was glad to be alive.

'These diplomatic cars are worth every penny,' she said. She was holding the steering wheel so tightly I could see her knuckles protruding through her pale skin.

'Who they hell were they?' I shouted.

'I think a better question is, what the hell have you been up to that they want you so bad?'

'I have no idea,' I shouted. I took a deep breath, released my grip on the armrest, peeled my hand slowly from the plastic.

I'd been holding it way too tight. I stared out the back window. There was no one coming after us. Isabel squealed around another turn. My shoulder banged against the window.

'You better thank your guardian angel I didn't get a taxi tonight,' she continued.

I settled back in my seat, rubbed my elbow. It throbbed lightly. The inside of the Range Rover was a cocoon of black leather and brushed aluminium. A shiny logo sat at the centre of the polished walnut steering wheel. The vehicle was cavernous and it smelled of leather.

We turned the next corner a lot slower. Then, after examining the rear view mirror, Isabel sat back in her seat.

'Do you have any idea what a bitch this car is to park?' she said.

I was still thinking about how close the bastards had come. I looked at Isabel. She had tiny gold studs in her earlobes. They shone as we passed a street light.

She looked as if she'd done this sort of thing before. Only a few hairs had escaped from her ponytail. And they were flying gently in the breeze from the air conditioning.

The Range Rover growled as she changed gears. The steep side street we were on was empty. Pools of darkness crowded around lonely street lights. We bounced through a pothole.

'You're in good shape,' she said, glancing in my direction. 'You live in your gym, right?'

'No. I free dive, run most days, but not usually for my life. Does this sort of stuff happen a lot to you?'

She shook her head.

'No. Mostly I help businessmen and holidaymakers. And I rescue the unlucky from police custody.'

'What do you think that lot were after?'

Her expression hardened, as if I'd insulted her. 'Mr Ryan. This has to do with you and your colleague, Alek.'

'Well, I've no idea why anyone would come after me like that. Has Istanbul gone mad?'

'Not at all.'

I felt an ache in my arm. I rubbed it, moved it in its socket. Nothing seemed to be broken, but it was stiff and painful.

We stopped at a traffic light.

'You obviously can't go back to the hotel. I'll take you somewhere else.' It sounded as if she was going to find a kennel for a sick dog.

'I can look after myself.'

'Don't look a gift horse in the mouth, Mr Ryan. Didn't they teach you that at MIT?' She looked at me, then at the traffic lights.

'No, I was taught to look for explanations. And I still don't have one for what just happened.'

'Mr Ryan, when people get shot at here, it's usually for a good reason, because of drugs or something worse.'

'I'm not into drugs or something worse.'

She didn't speak for a few seconds. 'What about this project you and Alek were working on? Could it be something to do with that?'

'I don't think so. The project's no big deal. There's nothing controversial about it at all. We're doing photographic work in Hagia Sophia for God's sake. That's it. What kind of joker is going to start killing because of that?'

'Well, you've trodden on someone's toes. Those thugs were prepared to kill you. And me, by the way, which I don't appreciate one bit.'

As we drove on, she checked the mirror at regular intervals. My breathing had just about returned to normal, but my leg muscles were tight, as if I'd run a marathon, and my stomach felt weird, all hollow, as if I'd retched, even though I hadn't.

'Are you into antiquities, Mr Ryan? This place is awash with them. Maybe you have something those guys want, something of value.' There was a suspicious edge to her voice.

'You're on the wrong track.' Her insistence that all this was something to do with me was pissing me off.

'We don't deal in or smuggle antiquities at the Institute. I have nothing those guys could want.' I made a show of patting my body.

My fingers touched the USB storage device in my trouser pocket. For a moment I considered not mentioning it, but I decided to take it out, to show her how little I'd picked up in the few hours I'd been here.

I pulled out the storage device, waved it dismissively in the air.

'This is the only thing I've been given since I came here. It was in an envelope with some photos for Alek at the hotel. I don't think they'd try to kill us for this.'

She reached for the USB key. 'We'll be the judge of that.'

I swung it away. 'This is the property of my Institute.' I hadn't even looked at what was on it.

'Give it to me, Mr Ryan.' We were travelling through an obviously poorer district now. The houses crowded in on each side.

'Or perhaps I should drop you here, if you're going to be so uncooperative.' She stopped at a corner, as if she meant to let me out.

'I could outrun them better, without you holding me back,' I said.

'But their aim might improve.'

'Tell me a good reason I should give it to you.'

62

She let out an exasperated sigh. 'Look, beheadings are long out of fashion in Turkey. If they've started up again, there has to be something serious going down. We need to follow up anything that could help us find out why Alek was murdered, and who did it. That requires you to give me your full cooperation. Now please, can I have it?' She held out her hand.

'OK,' I said. 'But I want a copy of whatever's on it. Agreed?'

She hesitated, then nodded.

I handed over the device.

11

Arap Anach stood on the balcony of his suite. In front of him the lights of the buildings crowding around the Golden Horn were cobwebs of diamonds.

The hem of his midnight-blue silk robe wafted in the breeze. There was an angry shout. He looked down beyond the black ironwork balcony. Istanbul in early August was a hot and airless city at ground level. Only those with expensive apartments or hotel suites high up felt the cooling breezes that glided over the rooftops.

Far below, in the thin light of a street lamp, a beggar jerked in the dust. People were gathering. Someone shouted. Malach watched, as if observing the death of an ant.

The sliding door behind him opened with a swish. He turned. Malach came through, bowed and spoke in a quiet voice.

'They failed,' he said. 'The car he escaped in had CD plates. It's registered to the British Consulate. We got photos from his room, and an iPad too.' He handed the photos to Arap.

'Don't turn the iPad on,' said Arap. He held the photos up. 'You didn't get his phone?'

'No. But we know his name. He came from England yesterday.'

'Look for him, but discreetly. And finish the clean up. I want no traces for anyone to find.'

Malach nodded, turned, went back out through the door, closed it with a click behind him.

Arap ran his hands along the balcony, caressing it. Then he gripped it, hard.

Copies of the pictures that Greek boy had taken could be in the hands of the British already. It wouldn't be easy for them to work out where they had been taken, but it wouldn't be impossible either.

But would they understand the significance of what they'd found, bother to follow it up? Maybe. They weren't stupid. All these loose ends would have to be sorted out quickly.

Five years of planning could not be wasted. It had taken too long to get to this point. Everything was almost ready.

He remembered the day he'd started down this road. The day he'd discovered his father's dismembered corpse in the master bedroom of that gaudy villa in Austria.

His father had deserved what he got. Anyone who spent their time on the Cote d'Azur in a drugged haze, squandering their inheritance, deserved a painful end. The only useful thing he'd taught him was a lesson very few fathers thought it necessary to teach their children.

Arap's own tastes had been corrupted a long time ago. He'd known that since he'd raped a girl near his school in England. The local paper had been full of it. Why they'd cared so much about a nobody, an insignificant larva, he still had no idea. The English were far too squeamish.

That slippery wisp of a girl hadn't been his first taste of forbidden pleasure either. He'd lost his virginity when he was ten. His father's friends had laughed as they'd pretended to strangle him on a yacht in the Aegean, as they took pleasure from his body. That had been an experience he would never forget.

What his father told him afterwards had stuck in his mind; *when you've done things that can never be forgiven, you become free, because you can never go back, never undo them.*

And he'd been right. He was free, and about to make his mark in a way his father had never contemplated. He was going to do something such as his ancestors had done centuries ago. His inherited estates and titles going back a thousand years made it all possible. There were few others who had the ambition, money and connections to make this thing happen. His time was coming.

His phone beeped. He picked it up from the marble table. A scrambled message icon was flashing. He pressed at it. Letters scrolled in front of him.

The siren of an ambulance sounded below. He put the phone down, peered over the railing. Shadows were milling around the ambulance. All the powerless larvae.

Everything they'd known was about to change. There were just a few things to fix now, and Malach could take care of those, easily. He'd proved long ago that he enjoyed such tasks.

12

We arrived at one of the British Consulate's guest apartments after midnight, and it was past 1:00 AM before I closed my eyes in one of the spartan, marble-floored bedrooms.

I didn't sleep well. A few hours after drifting off I sat up and looked around, memories of being shot at playing through my mind. I felt angry as the early morning sunlight filtered through the blinds. The air in the room was humid and already heavy. I'd turned off the air conditioning unit by the window before going to sleep.

One question had lodged in my mind. Were those bastards still looking for me?

The apartment had a balcony with a stunning view. Not surprising, I suppose, seeing as how it was on the tenth floor and overlooking where the glittering Sea of Marmara met the choppy Bosphorus channel.

I had a shower in the small bathroom attached to my room. I stayed longer than usual, as the tension of the last twelve hours dissipated into the water. When I was dry and dressed I went out onto the balcony.

The far shore of the Bosphorus, the Asian side of Istanbul, literally another continent, swam far off, in the early morning heat haze. Directly in front of me a variety of ships, freighters and tankers were making their way in two distinct lines, like foam-flecked water insects, travelling into and out of the sun-dappled channel of the Bosphorus.

Isabel had told me the night before that the apartment block overlooked the old Byzantine port of Bucoleon, the sea port that had served the Roman Emperor Justinian's imperial palace. The shimmering sea and infinite azure sky must have been as alluring back then as they were now.

As I was admiring the view, Isabel joined me. She was carrying a tray with croissants, butter, jam, coffee, warm milk and pale brown sugar.

Her black hair was undone, flowing over her shoulders, but she still looked businesslike. And her expression was serious.

'Did you sleep?' she said.

'Sure, every time I get shot at, almost kidnapped, I sleep like a baby.'

'It'll make a good story for your grandchildren.'

'If I ever have any.' I poured coffee for the both of us, then tasted mine. It was strong, black, just what I needed. I ate a croissant.

'What about the police? Are you going to call them?' I asked, as I poured myself some more coffee. I'd been wondering whether we should have reported what had happened already.

'We'll tell them at the appropriate time. What we're concerned about first is your security.'

'Why didn't you shoot back at those bastards last night?'

She was gazing out to sea.

'I don't carry a gun, Sean. I'm not James bloody Bond. This is not a movie.'

I could smell salty sea air as a welcome breeze wafted up to us.

'Having pitched battles in the street isn't the way we operate here.'

'Have you any new ideas about who those guys were?'

'No, and we don't jump to conclusions. Everyone with a grudge is taking their chances these days. Perhaps you have some new idea?'

'You gotta be joking,' I said. 'That was like Grand Theft: Istanbul last night.'

She stared at a giant red oil tanker that had left a flotilla of ships moored out in the Sea of Marmara. The tanker was proceeding slowly towards the channel of the Bosphorus. Isabel sat down on one of the cushioned wicker chairs facing out to sea and pulled her long legs up under her, as if she was about to do yoga. Her black sweatpants and skintight black T-shirt made her look like a gym instructor. I stayed standing, taking in the view.

'Some tankers wait a week to get through these straits,' she said.

We sat in silence for a minute.

'I didn't expect that last night,' I said.

'The Turks are among the kindest people in the world, Sean. They're welcoming, warm and giving, almost to a fault.' She stretched her arms above her head. 'What happened to you I have never seen happen to any visitor here.' She sipped at her coffee.

'We're very concerned, Sean.' She put her coffee cup down. 'Alek's death has been linked to a threat against the United Kingdom.'

'What?' I recoiled.

She stared out to sea. The heat was growing stronger by the minute, as the sun climbed in the sky. Home felt a long way away.

'There's a video clip on the Internet already. It shows Alek's beheading.' She was talking fast now. 'It also contains a threat to bring Armageddon to London.' She paused, as if to give time for what she'd said to sink in.

69

'We've had a lot of this stuff in the past year, what with every-thing that's going on. The nuts like to come out together. So we won't be panicking, but we have to follow up every threat. So I need to know if there's anything else you can tell me, which might help us to find the people who murdered Alek.' She turned to look at me.

I stared back at her. Was this for real? Had Alek gotten him-self caught up in something totally stupid?

'If I knew anything that might help, I'd tell you. I would.'

'I hope so.'

She stood up, went inside. In less than half a minute she was back, holding some photographs.

She placed the prints on the glass-topped dining table.

'These images were on that storage device,' she said.

I bent over, looked at them. There was a page of thumbnails and two images printed out full size. The thumbnails were images of mosaics in Hagia Sophia. I scanned them quickly. The only ones not clearly from Hagia Sophia were the two that had been blown up and the photo of Alek with Isabel.

The two photos she had printed out full size were the ones I'd left in the hotel room, which had been in the envelope. They must have meant something for Alek to have had them printed out. But what?

'Can you tell me anything about these photos?' Isabel pointed at the two prints.

I looked at them closely. 'They're not part of our project. That's all I can say.'

She pulled one of the chairs forward and sat down.

'OK, let's go back to the beginning,' she said. 'Did your project include work in any excavations or tunnels under Hagia Sophia?'

'No, not all.' I was sitting opposite her, facing the sun.

'Then why does this picture look like it was taken underground?'

'I have no idea. Our project is about the mosaics that are on public view. And anyway, we did a lot of research on Hagia Sophia and there are no crypts under it, nothing like this.' I pointed at the pictures. 'There's just a few drainage tunnels. No one has ever found mosaics under Hagia Sophia.'

'So where were these photos taken?'

I didn't have an answer.

She stretched her arms up high, as if she was warming up for a yoga session.

'I think Alek must have gone off and done some exploring, Sean.'

'He couldn't have done it in Hagia Sophia. The place is guarded day and night. It's a museum housing priceless treasures. Their security is tight.'

I took a sip of my coffee, placed the cup on the table and picked up one of the pictures. It was of a floor mosaic, a representation of a Madonna with child in dull blues and pale greens. The faded IH letters near the baby represented the word Jesus. It was a classic and beautiful image, an archetype of Christian art. There was a giant Virgin and Child wall painting in Hagia Sophia, which was like it.

'Did Alek tell you anything about what he was up to? You were friends weren't you?'

'Yeah, we were, but he never said anything about this.' I motioned at the pictures again. 'What about you, did he tell you anything? This is a picture of you, isn't it?' I pointed at the thumbnail.

'We went for lunch, Sean. The Consulate likes to keep itself informed about what's happening in this city. He was a nice guy, but he hardly spoke about his work. And he never said anything about taking pictures anywhere else, before you ask.'

Why hadn't Alek told me he'd met her, and about these odd photos? Was he planning to when he got back? Or was I being naïve?

'I'm sure you have experts who've examined this already,' I said, pointing at the picture in my hand. 'What do they make of it?'

'It's an almost classic representation of the Virgin, so I'm told.'

'What do you mean, almost?'

She moved towards me. I caught a faint lemony perfume smell.

'Look at the Virgin's dress. It should have gold stars. And the colours are wrong too. It needs expert examination.'

'Your people know their stuff.'

'But not enough,' she said. 'We don't know where the photo was taken.'

She was holding something back though. I could feel it.

'In a few weeks I might have an answer,' I said. 'My Institute has access to a lot of people. Maybe we can figure this one out.'

'You don't have to go to all that trouble,' she said. 'The greatest living expert on early Christian mosaics of the Virgin is an Orthodox priest. We're going to contact him, find out what kind of mosaic this is, where it might be found.'

'We'll do our own investigation too.'

She looked at me coolly. 'You'll get a copy of these images, I promise, Sean, but not yet. They're part of our evidence chain. Alek's death was a serious criminal act. We think these pictures have something to do with it.'

I knew where this was going. I'd be lucky if they gave me a copy of these in six months. My best friend had been murdered, I'd been shot at, and I was about to be cut out of what was going to happen next. I felt anger bubbling up inside me.

'Do your superiors know that Alek and you were close?' It was a long shot, but it was worth a try.

'You've got to be joking, right?' Her smile was gone. Her expression was glacier-like now.

I'd met some officials in the last two years who'd tried to protect me, tell me as little as possible, whenever I'd asked about Irene's death. I wasn't going to accept all that this time.

'I bet the British tabloids would love to find out that one of Her Majesty's Consular officials had been involved with a guy who was beheaded. Wasn't there a campaign to discredit the Foreign Office a while back for bungling? I'm sure there's plenty of journalists who'd run with this story.'

She looked calm, unmoved by my anger.

'Alek was a good friend, not just a colleague. I will find out what happened to him. I'm not going to walk away from this. Neither is my Institute. Not now. Not ever.'

She shook her head slowly, indicating I was heading the wrong way. I didn't care.

'We consulted with the Greek Orthodox community when we planned this project. So it won't be hard to find this expert of yours and a few of our own.' I reached for the photo of the mosaic and picked it up.

'And I'm sure the Turkish media would love to know about our research material being confiscated, an important UNESCO project being interfered with by the British government.'

Now she pointed a finger at me.

'I don't like being threatened, Sean. But I'll put it down to what happened last night, for your sake.'

'You can put it down to whatever you like, after I tell the media about this.' I waved the photo in front of her face.

We looked at each other. Her expression was a mask of grim determination.

'Your Institute is involved in something it shouldn't have been,' she said.

'You're talking crap. And you know it. But I don't care what lies you make up about us. This is too personal.' An annoying jingle from what sounded like an early morning TV show came up from the apartment below.

I felt a slight breeze on my skin. It barely alleviated the rising heat.

'You're upset,' she said. 'I'll see what I can do. But I'm not making any promises.' She stood up and went inside.

I waited. It was getting hotter by the minute and it was still only 8:30.

I shifted my chair around. A thick pad of lined green paper lay discarded under the table. I imagined Isabel or her colleagues sitting here taking notes.

She had a frown on her face when she came back half an hour later. 'You can come with me, if you want. Someone thinks it might be a good idea to have you along.'

She sat down opposite me.

'When are you going?'

'You'll see.'

'I love being kept in the dark.'

She spoke slowly. 'I can show you this.' She placed a netbook on the table in front of me. The sound of a car beeping angrily echoed from the street below.

She pointed at the screen.

On it was an English language version of a Turkish newspaper's website. The top of the screen read 'Zamiyete – Breaking News' in big letters.

Below the banner there was a picture of the iconic dome of Hagia Sophia. The headline underneath read:

'Greek Plot to Steal Hagia Sophia's Treasures.' I pulled the screen towards me. The article was about Alek.

It claimed that a shadowy group of Greek businessmen had been trying for years to penetrate the tight security at Hagia Sophia, and that the man whose decapitated body had been found in its grounds was connected to them. It claimed that man had been murdered by fundamentalists who wanted Hagia Sophia to become a mosque again, against Atatürk's explicit wishes.

The man who'd died, the article went on to say, had used the cover of working on an official UNESCO project to conduct unauthorised electronic tests at Hagia Sophia.

The article also claimed that there'd been speculation in the Greek media that the Labarum of Constantine, a banner used to rally the first Roman Christian legions, was one of the artefacts being sought by the Greek businessmen.

'I thought you said your little project wasn't controversial?' She sounded tired.

What concerned me though was what they were saying about Alek.

'I don't know anything about Greek businessmen. And we weren't doing any unauthorised electronic tests. How can they make this stuff up and get it published?'

A horrible sense of déjà vu came over me. There'd been speculation in the press in London too, after Irene had died. Some stories had claimed that she'd been killed by friendly fire.

It had been totally unsettling. It was one of the reasons I'd gone out there.

'You think they made it all up?' Her tone was sceptical. 'You know nothing about this Labarum thing?'

Her arms were folded.

'I didn't say that.' There was no point in denying it. 'Alek told me all about Constantine military standard, the Labarum thing, as you call it. He claimed . . .' I hesitated. The craziness of what Alek had said when he was alive seemed spookier now that he was dead.

'He claimed . . .' Was this how he'd be remembered?

'Do go on,' said Isabel.

I sighed. 'Alek said the Labarum of Constantine would reappear at a time of great change.'

That was enough for her. She raised her hands in the air as if she didn't want to hear any more.

I shrugged. I'd always been a cynic when it came to Alek's crazy theories. This one was only a bit stupider than the rest.

'If he'd found even a part of this banner of Constantine, it'd be worth a mint, right?' she said.

'Yeah, but he wasn't looking for it.'

'Why do you think they're talking about it?' she said.

'It's one of the legends of Hagia Sophia. That's enough reason for them to write this stuff. Some people like stirring things up. It sells newspapers. But whatever they say, there's no way the Institute was part of a search for the Labarum. And whatever you say about him, I honestly don't think Alek was either. He would have told me. We should sue that newspaper.'

She shook her head. 'Not a good idea, unless you like spending a lot of time in hot court rooms.'

'Well, their story is full of crap.'

'So where did Alek take this photograph?' She tapped her finger against the print lying on the table.

'Like I said, I've no idea.'

I shaded my eyes. The sun was way too hot already. My skin was burning.

Despite my insistence that Alek was innocent, I knew I had to consider that there was a chance, if even an outside one, that he might have become involved in something he hadn't told me about. Sure, he valued his job, but what about all the weird stuff he used to go on about?

Had he spread his crazy ideas about Constantine's Labarum? Had someone persuaded him to look for it?

Isabel gazed out at sea. Then she turned to me.

'Why did you go to Afghanistan after your wife died?'

Someone had been digging about me. But it was a question I'd answered many times before. I put my hands on the table, palms downward.

'I went to Afghanistan because the Institute I work for got permission from the Ministry of Education there to do an aerial survey.'

'You're telling me it was a coincidence? Your wife had died out there six months before; then you get to go out there. Come on Sean, I'm not stupid.'

I pressed my palms down on the table. I'd heard this response before too. 'What would you do if your husband was murdered, and no one was ever caught for it, never mind punished, and the whole incident ended up almost forgotten?' I was getting louder, but I couldn't help it, 'If the whole thing is brushed away as if it never happened?

Her voice was softer when she responded. 'I heard you almost got yourself killed. That you were lucky to be deported.'

I stared out to sea. We sat in silence.

'I'm not going to argue with you,' I said.

What she'd said was all true. I'd managed to visit the nearest village to where Irene had been murdered by a roadside bomb. I'd ended up in a room with ten armed men and a nervous translator. I'd been hoping to find out which group had killed her. To get closure. Put a name to the bastards.

An American patrol was called in by a local guy. I was taken into custody, handcuffed, put on a plane out within seventy-two hours. They'd threatened to charge me too, but my visa to get into Afghanistan had been legitimate. I must have had ten people shouting in my face before the plane doors closed. I'd put lives at risk. I had to accept I shouldn't have done it.

I'd also put my own life at risk. But I didn't care about that. My parents were dead. My beautiful wife was dead. We had no children. Who the hell would care if I was history?

I was a hollow human robot with a ghost haunting it. All I did most days were tasks I cared nothing about.

And going out to Afghanistan hadn't cured me. It had just created more problems.

The fact that the Institute was banned from Afghanistan for ten years was one of the reasons I'd had to accept that my role at the Institute was going to to change. I had to get approval from Beresford-Ellis before I went off on any project now, no matter what I thought of him. It irritated me – I'd co-founded the place – but I couldn't argue with the logic of it.

'You've definitely stepped on someone's toes this time too,' she said, softly, after a minute had passed. 'Hagia Sophia is a big deal here. The oldest copy of the Koran in the world is in Istanbul, a few minutes' walk from it.' She went to the balcony.

'Are you ready?' she said.

'For what?'

'We're going.' She shaded her eyes. She was looking along the coastline. A low-flying white helicopter was coming towards us. I watched it approach.

'I've just realised,' she said, turning towards me. 'That's an upside down V.' She pointed at the top corner of the mosaic in Alek's photo. 'That could be the Greek letter lambda, our letter L.'

'L, what does that stand for?'

'It could stand for Luna, the goddess of the moon. Maybe this isn't Christian after all.' She laughed, grabbed the photos off the table. She had a high-pitched laugh.

Her laughter was drowned out by the roar of the helicopter. It was almost level with us now.

'It's a bit noisy, isn't it?' she shouted in my ear.

The helicopter descended towards a patch of grass in front of the building, between the sea and the road.

'Where are we going?' I said.

'To meet that expert I told you about.'

'Is this the way you always travel?' I shouted.

'No, only when people's lives are in danger.'

13

In Whitehall Sergeant Henry P Mowlam was looking at his screen. His hands were curled into fists.

He closed his eyes. Would they listen to him? The raid on the London mosque had led to two riots already. As far as he was concerned, traffic checkpoints in the city should have been in place for at least another two weeks. The unrest in other European cities had continued during the last twenty four hours. All across Europe similar raids on mosques had been conducted in search of terror suspects who'd gone on the run after the escalation in the Middle East. Acting on rumours, looking for scapegoats, was how it had been described by some in the media. The civil rights mob had been having a canary, live on television.

He listened to the drone of the underground control room. Some days it reminded him of a symphony, all that humming and buzzing and heels clacking and coughs and clicks.

'Are you all right, Henry?' a woman's voice whispered.

He nodded, opened his eyes. Sergeant Finch was standing beside him. She always looked so good in her starched white shirt. He pointed at his screen.

A message in a secure window read:
DO NOT PROCEED WITH PTRE/67765/67LE.
'What's that about?' said Finch.

The matter of the checkpoints would have to wait. This was something Sergeant Finch could help him with.

'I am not to place surveillance on Lord Bidoner, despite the fact that he's met two other men we've been monitoring in the past week!'

Finch looked surprised. A troubled look crossed her face.

'That request was playing with fire, Henry. You do know who Bidoner is, don't you?'

Mowlam nodded, shrugged. He closed the message and went back to the video images he'd been assessing.

14

'That was easy,' I said.

The Turkish immigration authorities had only taken our passports for ten seconds. The security check was quick as well. We just walked through a metal detector in a quiet corridor. The diplomatic briefcase embossed with the lion and unicorn crest of the British Foreign Office, which Isabel had carried with her from the helicopter, had probably helped. Now walking across the baking concrete apron towards a white, tube-like executive jet, I felt as if I'd been dropped into another world.

I was looking forward to going back to London. That was where Isabel had said we were going when the passport official had asked her.

The Greek Orthodox community in England was one of the largest outside Greece. I could well believe there was an expert there who could help us track down where the two pictures had been taken.

The shrill sound of an aircraft readying for flight assaulted us as we made our way across the concrete. The smell of aviation fuel, heat and dust filled my nostrils as I climbed the rickety aluminium stairs and entered the small passenger cabin.

What surprised me most was that once I was inside I couldn't stand up fully. The cabin must have been only five foot something high. I had to bend in order to reach one of the royal-blue leather seats.

They weren't your usual commercial airline seats either. These were lower, wider, and far more comfortable. And there were only seven of them.

Isabel sat opposite me. We were the only occupants of the cabin. A large blue cooler bag sat on the floor at the back. Isabel pulled it forwards, reached inside and passed me a bottle of orange juice.

'You're lucky. The last time I did this they forgot to put the refreshments onboard.'

'That must have been a bad flight,' I said. I took the bottle and drank from it. It tasted wonderful.

'You two OK?' a voice called out. The door to the pilot's cabin was open. I could see an expanse of blinking lights and dials. The man who'd spoken was in the pilot's seat, leaning towards us, his hand holding the door open.

'A OK,' replied Isabel.

The pilot gave us a thumbs-up.

A second, younger man, who would be sitting in the other cockpit seat, came into the cabin. He pulled the door to the outside closed. A light above it flashed red.

The engines roared. My seat reverberated as we prepared to taxi.

Then the roar diminished. I looked out of one of the tiny port-hole windows. An all black Porsche jeep was speeding towards us. It had darkened windows. For a brief moment I thought it might be the Turkish authorities looking for me, that my inspector friend was wondering why I was leaving Istanbul so soon. Isabel leaned forward. Her knee touched mine. She reached over, grabbed her jacket, threw it on to the seat behind us.

'We've got company,' she said.

The Porsche had pulled up by the plane. A man got out of the back, strode towards us. He was tall, dressed in a mustard coloured suit. He had that lightly tanned, angular sort of face that reminded me of pictures of celebrities trying hard to look good.

The door opened with a whoosh. Wind and the smell of jet fuel filled the cabin.

'Good to see you, Isabel,' boomed a voice. 'Looks like I got here just in time.' The man in the mustard suit sat in the seat beside her. Both of them were facing me.

'It's a bit tight in here,' he said. 'I hope you don't mind, Isabel.' He patted her knee. Then he turned to me.

'This is the man, eh, Isabel?'

'Sean,' she said. 'Meet Peter Fitzgerald. He works in the Consulate.' As if that explained everything. Then I remembered. This was the guy who'd told me about Alek's death.

'Peter, this is Sean Ryan, from the Institute of Applied Research in Oxford. He co-founded it. He's their Director of Projects.'

Not for long, I thought, after the way this project in Istanbul had gone, but I wasn't going to tell them that. In any case, the expression on Peter's face was that of a wine waiter who'd just been asked for plum juice.

'We spoke on the phone,' he said. 'So sorry about your colleague. What a dreadful death. It's certainly stirred things up here.' He put his hand out. I shook it.

'Alek didn't deserve that,' I said.

Isabel was staring at me.

'I'm sure. What a terrible nightmare,' said Peter. 'And what about you, how are you? I heard you had a difficult night.'

'I'm alright,' I said. I didn't need his sympathy.

I heard scuffling, looked around.

Two leather bags were being loaded into the passageway between the seats and the door to the pilot's cabin. My own small bag, with everything from my hotel room packed into it, had been waiting at the private jet terminal when we'd arrived.

I'd seen, straight away, that my stuff had been rifled through, that some items were missing, but compared to what had happened to Alek, and what could have happened to me last night I felt fortunate.

'Tell me all about yourself,' he said. 'I'm sorry if I was a bit abrupt on the phone the other day. A lot on my plate right now.' He tapped his nose.

Peter seemed to be fascinated by everything I had to say. It was an hour, at least, and we were many miles from Istanbul before the flow of his questions slowed. By then he knew all about my origins, my father's Purple Star background, our life in Norfolk, and in upstate New York, where I started college after my father left the military, and all about my very English mother, my one-year research extension in London, how I met Irene, my first job, how we founded the Institute. Surprisingly, there were things he didn't ask about though. Like what had happened to my wife. Maybe he knew the answers to those questions already.

'Tell him about the mosaic Alek took a picture of,' said Isabel, when Peter seemed to have finished his questioning.

I told him the little I knew. Isabel took the photo of the mosaic out of her bag and passed it to him as I was talking.

'Very interesting,' he said. When I finished, he looked around, as if he was afraid someone might be listening to us.

'And you have no idea where this picture was taken?' He waved the photo at me.

I sat back. 'I told Isabel already, and the answer is still no. Our project is about assessing how the mosaics in Hagia Sophia have changed over the years. It was never about identifying unknown mosaics.'

'Your colleague was working only in Hagia Sophia, correct?' He was staring at me.

I nodded.

'There's a lot of interesting stuff besides mosaics in Hagia Sophia, isn't there?'

'Yes. It goes back a long way. The building we see there now was put up in the 530s,' I said.

Peter's eyebrows shot up. 'It's older than that, I think. Didn't that old treasure hunter, Schneider, find out during the excavations he carried out in '35 that the foundations were from an earlier church?' He knew his stuff.

'The first Christian church on the site was probably built in 351.'

Isabel looked amused.

'Yes,' said Peter, drily. 'Hagia Sophia is one of the foundation churches of Christianity.' His right hand slapped his armrest. 'And it's the best of them by far. Don't some people say it'll be returned to Christianity one day?' He looked at me innocently.

Was he trying to trap me? I didn't reply.

'So you don't go along with all this Christian revival thing, do you, Sean?'

'No.'

'And you don't know anything about the stories in the Turkish papers?'

'No.'

I felt myself getting irritated. Not only was he asking too

many questions, I was also beginning to feel boxed in with his long legs blocking access to the corridor.

'If any of those journalists poked into the dusty corners of your life, Sean, would they find anything . . . smelly?'

Now he was really annoying me. I shook my head, fast. 'Not a single thing. I have nothing to be ashamed of. Nothing.'

'Not that it would be just journalists doing the investigating,' he said, gesturing towards Isabel and himself. His tone was haughty, detached, as if he knew things I didn't.

He looked me in the eye and smiled. He seemed to be enjoying himself.

'There's going to be a lot of interest in this story over the next few days, Sean. It'll blow over, of course, but until then every blogger in Europe will be looking for an angle on Alek's death. I do hope you're not hiding any nasty little secrets.'

'How many times do I have to repeat myself?' I said. 'I've got nothing to hide.' I raised my hands, held them in the air, palms forward, as if I was going to push him and his accusations away.

He rubbed at his trousers, fixed the crease.

'I understand you're upset, Sean, but this story has real legs. I don't know if Isabel warned you, but all the security services, MI5, and 6, and all the rest, they do an under-every-stone trawl in cases like this. And if they do find anything funny, I must tell you, unofficially, they're not beyond a little bit of mild torture, given what we're up against now.' He put his hands together, then braced them on his knees. 'When it comes to defending our country we do get a bit of leeway these days, you know. But I'm sure you've nothing to hide.'

Was he joking? I'd imagined the local police in Oxford going around to the Institute, asking a few questions. Not a platoon of security service types trawling through every chapter of my life.

'I told you,' I said. 'I've nothing to hide.'

The cabin was quiet except for the rumble of the plane's engine.

'So there's nothing you want to tell us?'

'Not a thing,' I said, emphatically.

'Very good,' said Peter. The atmosphere changed from Artic cool to warmish again.

'It's the truth.'

'I do hope so.' He leaned back, drummed his fingers on the arm rest.

He clearly enjoyed playing games with people. I'd never liked people like that. Isabel seemed irritated too.

I looked out the window. I could see snow capped mountains far below. The sun was high in the sky. There was a blue shimmer of sea far off to our right. I got a strange feeling. That was where the landmass of Europe should have been.

What route were we taking?

'Spectacular view, isn't it?' said Peter.

'What mountains are they?' I said.

'Sorry, I'm no good at all that stuff. But they are beautiful, aren't they?'

'Now, about this mosaic,' he said, in a softer tone. 'I have to tell you there's no record of such a mosaic anywhere in Istanbul or in all Turkey.' He stretched his legs out into the passageway.

'Which means it has to be from some undiscovered site. Mosaics were popular in the Roman Empire. They had to find a way to brighten their homes, I suppose.' He sat up straighter.

'I wonder what this old priest will tell us,' said Peter.

Isabel brushed hair from her face.

'Peter's been busy trying to find out who was shooting at us last night,' she said. Her tone made it sound as if she was trying to sell Peter to me.

'Great, any news?'

'A little,' said Peter. 'Somebody's been trying to track the Consulate's Range Rovers. That was what you were driving last night, Isabel, wasn't it?'

Isabel nodded.

'Well, someone went and hacked the systems at Istanbul's Range Rover service centre early this morning. Whoever is after you is serious, Sean.' He was looking out the window now.

'What sort of people do this kind of thing?' I said.

'There are a number of small groups that might be involved. There are a lot of refugees in Istanbul. We've been keeping an eye on them, but it's a big city and things are changing fast.'

He reached over, took an orange juice from the cooler bag and drank from it.

'The Turks are blaming the whole thing on foreigners, of course.' He gestured expansively. 'They're probably right.'

'I'll check what the news sites are saying,' said Isabel.

She pulled a laptop from her briefcase, fired it up, hit a few keys, stared at the screen for a few minutes.

'You don't want to look at this.'

'I want to.'

She passed the laptop to me. The browser window was filled with the BBC News website. The lead story, accompanied by a gruesome, but blurry image, was about Alek. What had happened to him was hitting the big time. I stared at the picture. It felt weird, as if I was watching someone else. This was too crazy.

Alek's chin was down on his chest, his eyes hidden. He was strapped to a pillar. It was a still from that video I'd read about.

I felt an urge to push the laptop away. I resisted. Then there was something catching in my throat. I put a hand to my mouth, kept it clamped shut as the sickening sensation passed. I wasn't going to look away. That would be too easy.

The story underneath the picture read:

Beheading in Istanbul.
No one, so far, has claimed responsibility for the beheading of a Mr Alek Zegliwski, whose body was found in Istanbul on August 4. Turkish security experts are pointing the finger at a radical Islamic sect intent on the re-establishment of the Islamic Caliphate, which until 1924 was based at Hagia Sophia, where Mr Zegliwski was working. Re-establishing the Caliphate is a key goal for many Islamic fundamentalists.

The Arab script in the photo above Mr Zegliwski's head, was, the article said, a threat to bring the war to London. Further on, the Turkish Prime Minister's office had issued a statement saying arrests had been made that morning, and that the Turkish security services were following up a number of lines of enquiry.

'This wasn't supposed to happen,' I said. I passed the laptop back to Isabel.

Peter took it, put it on his knee, read for a few minutes.

Then, he looked up from his screen and said, 'The Turkish police raided known activists. They like to be seen to be taking action. I doubt they'll find the people we're looking for though.' He nudged Isabel's leg with the laptop. 'Did you get a description of your friends from last night circulated?'

'It was attached to my report,' she said.

'Was there anything about Alek's behaviour in the past few weeks that seems odd now, Sean?' Her tone was soft, coaxing.

I thought about her question as the queasy sensation from seeing that image of Alek slowly faded. 'There's nothing I can put a finger on. He was unavailable a few times, but that happened now and again with him.' It was weird talking about Alek in this way.

Peter was drumming his fingers on his armrest.

Isabel looked out the window.

A flash of sunlight in the corner of my eye made me turn and stare out the window on the right. What I saw amazed me.

The glimmer of sea that I'd seen in the distance stretched to the horizon now, where the continent of Europe should have been, and in the sky, flying parallel with us, was a silver-grey jet fighter, no more than half a mile away. It had the distinctive dual tail-fins of the F-35 Lightning.

We were being escorted by a state-of-the-art fighter jet. But why? And where the hell were we?

15

On the rounded top of a salt hill, an outcrop of the Zagros Mountains, a black-cloaked shepherd sat. His flock, fourteen thin black sheep, was foraging among skeletal dwarf oak trees. In the distance a layer of dust and pollution marked the location of the city of Mosul.

The Zagros mountain chain is a natural barrier between Iran and Iraq. It extends from north of the Straits of Hormuz all the way into Turkey. It's a thousand miles long and its peaks are snow-capped. Its foothills resemble the hills of the US South West or the Highlands of Scotland. The city of Mosul, in the north of Iraq on the Tigris river, is near the ancient site of the city of Nineveh, capital of the Assyrian Empire. Uncounted armies have battled in this area.

The shepherd watched the white trail of a plane as it rose from Mosul airport. He thought about the warning he'd heard the night before. The evening star of Ishtar had risen late. The wizened crone who slept in a cave at the bottom of the hill had come into the village square to speak to them for the first time in ten years.

'Not since Jonah warned the Ninevites has such a thing happened,' she'd said in the pale evening light. Then she'd coughed for almost a minute.

Finally she'd continued, 'Remember Jonah's warning.' She'd looked at every face. 'Another great city will be destroyed.'

16

'That's the easternmost corner of the Mediterranean,' said Peter. 'We'll be heading inland soon, now that we've picked up our escort.'

'What do we need an escort for?' I was trying to sound as unfazed as I could. I turned, looked out the window again, just to check the F-35 was actually there.

'We'll be flying near the Syrian border soon, and with everything that's been going on, we don't want to take any chances. Thankfully, air cover is one of the few things we can still rely on here.' He leaned back in his seat.

'I should have told you we were making a stop before taking you to London,' said Isabel, looking at me. 'But I was asked not to.' Her gaze flickered towards Peter.

A list of questions came into my mind. 'Where are we going?' was the one that came out.

'Mosul,' said Isabel.

'Northern Iraq?'

She nodded. 'The expert I told you about – Father Gregory – has been working on an archaeological dig not far from the city. We don't have much choice, Sean, unless you want to wait a month until he finishes up there.' Isabel sounded genuinely sorry she hadn't told me what was going on.

If I remembered right, Mosul had been the scene of a number of bloody battles after Saddam's fall.

'Isn't Mosul still a bit hot for archaeological work?'

Peter closed his eyes. 'Mosul has been hot for a long time. The whole of Iraq is an archaeological minefield. Everyone has a different view about which layer of history is the most important and which you can trample on.' He waved at Isabel. 'Why don't you tell him what we dug up?'

Isabel sat forward. 'Mosul was the earliest Christian city outside what is now Israel,' she said. 'The reason Father Gregory is there is because the Greek Orthodox Church wants him to look at some very old Christian sites, before someone bans them from digging in the country. It's not an ideal time to dig, but when is it around there?

'Mosul has nearly as much history as Istanbul,' said Peter. 'It's not far from the tar pits, which were the original source of Byzantium's secret weapon, Greek fire, which saved their asses from the Muslim hordes. All of us might be worshipping Allah now, if the Greeks hadn't won in 678 with the help of Greek fire.'

Suddenly, we dropped altitude. A gaping hole opened in my stomach. I looked out the window. I could see a range of grey mountains. One, far off, still had snow on its peak. To our right there were bare rolling hills stretching away into a yellowy horizon. Our altitude stabilised after about thirty seconds. Then our escort was alongside us again.

'An evasive manoeuvre most likely,' said Peter. 'Some unknown radar signal must have lit us up.'

I continued staring out the window. Was this for real?

'Can anyone just walk into Iraq these days?' I said.

'You can, if you have the right visa,' said Peter. 'The Iraqi Department of Border Security has a temporary visa programme for just this sort of occasion. And we have friends at Mosul airport. I don't expect there'll be a problem.'

He was right.

'Welcome to the land of Gilgamesh,' was how the green suited senior guard at the airport greeted us. His soft, educated accent seemed out of place after the guttural tones of the Iraqi guards who'd escorted us in a hot, white minibus from our plane to Mosul's concrete airport terminal.

'I lived in London for five years,' he said, before he handed us back our passports.

'Have a nice day!' were the words that echoed after us as we crossed the passport hall.

And it was hot, brutally hot. The air was as thick as oil. There were air conditioning units on the walls of the terminal at various points, but for some reason they were turned off.

I felt a crawling sensation under my skin. There were guards standing around, but few travellers. And the guards were standing well back from us, as if they were waiting for someone to blow themselves up. They were all wearing ill-fitting green camouflage uniforms, with black patches on their arms with yellow lion head insignias on them, and soft peaked caps.

Within a minute of leaving the airport building my shirt clung to my skin as if I'd showered in cola.

We were being escorted towards a camouflaged Hummer by two young guards barely out of their teens, with tufts of wispy hair on their chins. The Hummer was parked beyond concrete barriers about two hundred yards from the terminal building. Peter was the only one of us who was carrying anything. He had a black Lowepro knapsack over one shoulder. Everything else was back on the plane.

The Hummer's door opened as we came up to it. A man in a crumpled cream suit stepped halfway out, waved at us. Then he got back in.

When the Hummer's doors closed behind us I understood why. The air inside was as cool as a refrigerator's. It was like being in heaven, compared to the heat outside. I undid some shirt buttons, let the cool air slip over my skin.

'Got any water?' I said.

The man in the left-hand driving seat who'd waved at us, the only occupant of the vehicle, opened a black refrigerator box that sat in the front passenger footwell. He passed me a bottle of the coolest water I'd ever tasted.

As I took my first sip, I noticed he had put his hand on Isabel's arm. She had climbed into the front seat next to him. She slapped his hand away.

'Nice to see you too, my dear,' said the man. The Hummer started with a roar.

'Sean meet Mark Headsell, one of our…' she hesitated, as if she was debating with herself how to say what he did, '*representatives* in Mosul.' She spat out the word representative. 'He's an old friend.'

'Good to meet you, Sean. Don't mind Isabel. Welcome to the front line'

'I thought the front line was in Afghanistan,' I said.

'We're still busy here, I can tell you,' said Mark.

Isabel was looking out the side window. Peter was outside on his phone. He was standing with his back to us.

He finished his call, jerked the door of the Hummer open.

'How is your personal hellhole these days, Mark?' he said, loudly. Then he slapped Mark's shoulder.

'Wonderful, if you don't mind sewage pipes that back up, gun-toting locals with grudges, and fleas as big as rats.'

'That sounds like progress,' said Peter.

'You're heading for Magloub, right?' said Mark. 'Where that crazy Greek priest is digging?'

'How long will it take to get there?' said Peter.

'Well, if we don't get blown up or have to take a lot of stupid detours, we should be there in less than two hours. It's only fifty miles or so.'

At the exit from the airport there was a checkpoint. It was manned by bearded security guards wearing the same yellow lion insignias. They also had black bulletproof vests on. Mark told us they were from a new Golden Lions security force that had taken over after the last US Marines had left. A sign nearby in English and Arabic read *Deadly Force Area*. After an exchange of words between Mark and one of the guards, we were waved on.

We travelled for a while in silence. I was soaking up the sights outside the tinted windows. The road from the airport was wide and dusty. There were one or two wrecks of houses, but most of the buildings looked untouched by the years of war. There was even some building work going on.

There were small craters on the road occasionally, probably where IEDs had gone off. We passed a big petrol station a few minutes after leaving the airport. It was surrounded by cement walls, except for a small entrance manned by security guards. There was a queue to get into it.

Then we passed a cluster of low houses at a crossroads. Some of them had sandbags piled haphazardly near their doors. One had a cement wall in front of it. They looked deserted.

I was reminded of the village in Kandahar where Irene had been murdered. It was similarly dusty, though the holes in the roads there hadn't been filled in.

I met the officer who'd been with Irene in her last moments. It was the only good thing to come out of my visit to Afghanistan. He'd wanted to meet me, to tell me what she'd said right before she'd died.

And I envied him. Envied him that he'd been with her. And I'd been grateful too, that he'd wanted to see me. In the end though, the words he told me felt like knives plunging into my heart.

'Tell Sean I love him,' were her last words. And I could hear in my mind how she would have said them.

I closed my eyes.

I hadn't thought about her last words in a while. I let them echo, the way they always did, then I sat up straighter and looked around.

The cars were similar here too, to Afghanistan: Japanese mostly, though the traffic was heavier. There were also old Mercedes here that must have had a million miles on them. They looked held together with dust. And there were even some new Toyota 4x4s.

Most of the cars kept their distance from us and some people at the side of the road turned and watched us as we passed.

Were we that obvious? Were Westerners still a target here? Whatever people said about the new Iraq, I didn't feel safe. The chances of someone letting off an RPG, or sniping at us, were just too high.

In the distance there were hazy grey hills. A line of palm trees stood out on a low ridge. The wide tarmac strip we were driving on had dusty poplar trees lining it on both sides.

Mark drove the Hummer fast. Any time we passed through

groups of buildings, an abandoned petrol station, a walled compound with smoke drifting behind it, he sped up. There were concrete slabs piled up at the side of the road occasionally, and stretches where a thick carpet of dirt had blown in from somewhere and never been removed.

Hard-faced men walked by the side of the road; Arabs in *jellabas* wearing headdresses, some more than shoulder length, and lean bare-headed men wearing dark baggy trousers. Other men, with weather-beaten faces, wore red and white checked *keffiyehs* wrapped around their heads. I saw women only once, a huddle of them standing by the side of the road as if they were waiting for something. Long black scarves covered their faces. Their ankle length black dresses must have been a killer in the heat.

Scraggy weeds grew everywhere. After a while we crossed a wide river. The concrete bridge looked as if it had been repaired recently. It had a checkpoint at the far side with guards asking for papers. Luckily the queue was short: two battered, empty flatbed trucks waited in front of us, then it was our turn. We were waved through by a green-uniformed guard as soon as Peter showed him something. These guards had no lion insignias, just black and white badges. I saw other hawk-eyed guards watching us from behind shoulder-high concrete barriers set up beside the bridge.

'You ever seen the Tigris before?' said Mark.

'No,' I said. I watched the muddy sluggish river flowing off into the flat hazy landscape.

Then we were travelling fast again, heading out into the countryside.

'You know who came down this road before you?' Mark asked, turning to look at me.

'No.'

'Only Alexander the Great, a couple of Roman Emperors, Persians, Muslims, Mongols, the Ottomans, English battalions, and the US Marines.'

'Busy little road,' I said.

'Some of the locals claim there are *djinns* – evil spirits – in the hills around here who bring bad luck,' said Mark.

'That's a bit pessimistic,' I said.

'The two sons of Saddam were cornered in that suburb we just passed. Human *djinns* are the only ones they should worry about,' said Mark.

The road narrowed. It was winding up the foothills of the mountains that marked the horizon. On each side there were trees now, pine and oak. They grew thicker and greener the further up we went. The few houses we passed looked older, and they were made of stone and wood, rather than concrete or mud plaster. I saw a shepherd with a flock of fat-tailed dirty-looking sheep.

Finally, after slowing down for some hair-raising bends and turning off on to a rock-strewn single-lane track, we arrived at a flat open area, with stunted oak trees around it. Two yellow Hummers blocked the track. I saw the glint of weapons pointing at us.

Mark got out as soon as we stopped. He put his hands high in the air as he walked towards the Hummers. He'd left his door open. The heat and the noise of birds twittering rolled in. My skin prickled. Sweat broke out. Peter sat up straight.

'Say nothing about why we're here to these guys. I'll answer any questions. You're just along for the ride, Sean, OK?' he said.

Thankfully, there was no need for any explanations. Mark had a few words with a soldier dressed in a bottle-green uniform, who I glimpsed in the door of his Hummer. The man could have been a local – he had a thick beard – but he could have been a European or an American too.

When he returned, Mark didn't say a word. We all just watched as one of the Hummers reversed to let us through.

About half a mile further on, we stopped in a clearing beside a green Toyota pick-up. A mountain was towering above us now, craggy grey peaks, and up ahead there was a cliff of streaked white limestone. The streaks were like tears running down the cliff.

As I stepped out of the vehicle the first thing that hit me was that it wasn't nearly as hot here as below on the plain. Then, on a puff of wind, I caught the scent of something decaying. There was a strange feeling about the place. We all looked around. Then someone shouted. A tall thickly-bearded, black-robed young man was running towards us with his hands in the air. At first I thought he was greeting us. Then I deciphered what he was saying.

'You must go. You must go. No visitors are allowed. This is sacred ground. I will call the escort. You must leave.'

I felt a chill. What a welcome. Mark was the nearest to the guy, a monk, I presumed from the way he was dressed. Mark walked towards him. The monk still had his hands in the air and he was waving them about, trying to shoo us all away, as if we were foxes who'd strayed into his pasture. Peter, Isabel and I walked behind Mark.

'You have been warned. You must go. Go now.' He turned, as if he was finished with us.

'I'm in charge of a project at Hagia Sophia,' I said, loudly. 'I need to see Father Gregory.'

He stopped, turned, peered at me. He must have been six foot six tall, at least. I stared back at him. At six foot one, I hadn't felt small in a while.

'What do you want?' he said. His tone was still far from friendly, but at least he wasn't shouting. His accent was thick. He reminded me of a Greek boy I'd known at MIT.

'Are you Father Gregory?' said Peter.

The monk made a sour face.

'We want to see Father Gregory,' I said, softly. 'We need some advice about something we've found, something that will interest him.'

'I'll find out if he will see you,' said the monk. He turned, walked towards the cliff face.

We waited by our Hummer. Mark took a large blue refrigerated box from the back of the vehicle, fed us with delicious wraps, chunky pieces of chicken, sticky rice, tomatoes and crisp cucumber, all wrapped in what looked like tortilla bread.

When the monk returned he walked straight up to me and said, 'Come with me.'

Peter made as if to block me. 'We're coming too,' he said.

The monk looked at each of us in turn, as if working out what would happen if we all followed him.

'Don't worry, I'm staying out here,' said Mark. 'You enjoy yourselves.' He grinned at me, as if he knew where we were going.

'You're lucky,' said the monk, as we walked past a grove of gnarled pine trees that grew near the cliff.

I could smell their sap.

'Why's that?' I said.

'Many have dreamt of coming to this place, only to die without their dream being fulfilled.'

Up ahead, the cliff of streaked limestone loomed. The rocky path we were on led straight towards it. The cliff shone with reflected sunlight, hurting my eyes.

'Those who are impure of heart fear this place,' said the monk loudly, as he walked ahead. 'Some who come turn back here.'

I shielded my eyes. There was something unsettling about the place all right. I could imagine people turning back.

That was when I saw it. The arched, unembellished entrance to a cave, about eight foot high and the same wide, like a burrow for some monstrous bird. The monk was walking straight towards it. We followed.

Inside was a cave with a blackened roof, a flat dirt hearth at one side near the entrance, thin bones in crevices near it and a tunnel at the back. It looked as if shepherds had been using the place for a long time. There was a bad smell, as if something rotten had soaked into the packed earth floor. We headed for the tunnel. It was high enough to walk upright in.

Its walls were lit every hundred feet by electric lights on thin steel tripods. They beamed a sickly low-watt glow onto the streaked walls around us. It became cooler with each step we took. The walls were smooth as if they'd been gouged clean. As we went on the tunnel sloped gently upwards.

We were walking into the heart of the mountain. The tunnel was definitely not a recent construction. I could feel the weight of rock above us, and a sense of awe came over me, as I thought about how old the tunnel might be.

After walking for about five minutes the tunnel opened into a large cave, the likes of which I had never seen before. Its walls were a shiny blue-grey stone, carved here and there with huge winged creatures like something you'd see in a museum.

The roof was a dome shape with its centre high above. It was totally black. The cave walls curved inwards about three hundred feet away on either side. In the centre of the cave there was a collection of modern aluminium and black equipment laid out on the almost smooth stone floor. The place had a hostile air to it. Beside the equipment stood a gaunt old man in a dark brown monk's habit. He was looking at us.

I walked towards him, leading the group. Our institute's work in Hagia Sophia had to be of interest to him. He shook my hand, pointed at the wall above where we had just entered, as if eager to show the place off.

'See that,' he said, his finger shaking. 'That is the goddess Ishtar, the cruel destroyer. She was an Assyrian deity. Her temples were adorned with the skins of her enemies and pyramids of skulls. They called her the goddess of love. Imagine!' He made a loud dismissive noise.

'Who built this place?' I asked, looking around.

'It was carved by water, young man, by nature. After that, who knows.' He sniffed. That was when I realised there was a smell in the cave. It wasn't strong, but now that I was in the centre I was more aware of it. It reminded me of the smell inside a freezer when something's gone bad.

'I've never heard of this place,' I said. Peter and Isabel were standing beside us. They each shook hands with Father Gregory. He gave them a sickly smile, then drew his hand away fast as if distracted. He directed us to an old, but richly-patterned red carpet that had been laid out at the centre of the cave near all the instruments with their dials and read-out screens. None of them were turned on. I imagined Father Gregory rushing around, as we came down the corridor, turning everything off, in case we might be here to report on what he was doing.

'Why did you come here?' he asked me.

'There's something we want your advice on, Father. Have you got the photo, Peter?'

Peter took out the print of the mosaic from his bag and passed it to Father Gregory.

'This is why we're here,' I said. 'We have to find out where this photo was taken.' Father Gregory examined the print, brought it close to his face.

'The only reason I let you in here was because you told my assistant you were working in St Sophia.' His tone was soft, but totally self-assured. 'Is that true?'

'Yes,' I said. 'In Hagia Sophia.'

'Our great church is St Sophia, Holy Wisdom,' he said, tartly. Then he blessed himself. 'St Sophia is closer to the Divine than anything else here on earth. Its walls once showed the fields of paradise, and in its dome the heavens could be glimpsed.' He closed his eyes, as if in prayer. Then he blinked them open.

'Before we lost it.' He was staring at me, as if I were the one to blame.

'There are many secrets to St Sophia that have not been revealed. You know they want to turn it back into a mosque, and keep us out again. Now tell me, which university are you with?'

'I'm with the Institute of Applied Research in Oxford. These people are helping me. They work for the British government.' I waved towards Isabel and Peter. Isabel's eyebrow arched, but she said nothing. Father Gregory looked at them, as if they were dung beetles.

His eyes narrowed. 'You won the project in St Sophia last year, didn't you?' he said.

'Yes, we're in the middle of it now.'

'Have you uncovered anything?' There was a distinct eagerness in his tone.

106

'We're digitizing mosaics. I don't expect anything revolutionary will come out of it.'

'They're afraid to look properly,' he said. 'All of them.' He nodded his head, vigorously, as if he was agreeing with himself. He leaned forward. His brown habit draped down like a tent.

'We are at a crossroads, you know, and they want to close the path.'

This guy was the original Mr Creepy.

'Do you want to know what I'm working on, young man from an Oxford Institute?' I nodded. Peter was scanning the walls. The other monk was pacing, head down, as if he was praying.

Father Gregory pointed at the wall behind him. The opposite wall to the one with the carving of Ishtar.

'Look, these are demons, the *djinn* they call them. The things concealed by darkness. That is what the word means. These are the oldest images of demons ever found, I am sure of that. They are from well before the time of Mohammad and from before the time of Moses too and all the commandments, for us people of the book.'

The carvings on the wall behind Father Gregory were of winged creatures with horned helmets. It looked as if they had cloven feet. Great. This was exactly what the place needed, something to lighten it up.

'The *djinn* bring war, destruction, disease, like a murmur passing from man to man.' He paused. 'And this is where they were worshipped, until Christians came and then Islam.' He pointed above us. Someone had painted a thin cross above the *djinns*. Near it was a crescent moon. It had writing beside it, a jagged Arabic-type script.

Tell me, why did you need to see me so quickly? What is it that could not wait until I leave Iraq?' said Father Gregory.

'Sean's colleague was murdered in Istanbul,' said Isabel. 'He was beheaded. We'd very much like to find out who did it.' She paused. 'If we can find out where this photo was taken it will help us'

Father Gregory inhaled sharply.

'It is all starting then,' he said.

'What's starting?' I said.

'The *djinn* will be released.' He glared at me. He was being serious.

'You reckon they're for real?' I said. I pointed upwards.

'They take over minds. They twist people.' He seemed genuinely worried now.

I looked around. He was right about this place. There was something unsettlingly weird about this cave, as if it was holding its breath.

'Evil exists, young man. It eats at men's hearts. Don't ever deny it. And it comes from somewhere, as love does. Evil doesn't die either. It renews itself with a fresh face.'

'It's amazing this place survived all these years,' said Isabel. She said it wryly, as if she thought Father Gregory had gone mad down here.

'The locals say this cave is cursed,' said Father Gregory. 'That is why they don't come here.' His voice had a shaky quality to it now. 'They also say I'm here to steal the gold of Sargon. Do I look like a gold digger to you?' He stuck his grey bearded chin towards me.

'No,' I said. I wasn't going to argue with the guy. 'What do you think about our photo, Father?'

I hadn't travelled all this way just to listen to this guy's ramblings.

He waved Alek's photo at me. He was still clutching it in his hand. 'This is Lambda,' he said angrily, pointing to the upside down V in the top right-hand corner of the mosaic in the picture. He sounded as if he was talking to a child.

'We know,' Isabel cut in.

'But do you see?' boomed Father Gregory. I stared at him. What next? Was he going to start pulling his hair out?

'In the old days, people knew about good and evil. They had respect.'

'You're right, Father,' said Isabel, softly.

The monk who'd brought us in was standing beside Father Gregory.

I leaned back as I caught a whiff of stale sweat.

'What do you need to know?' said Father Gregory.

'My colleague took this photo, but we've no idea where. It could have been taken anywhere in Istanbul. If we knew where he took it, we might be able to find out who murdered him.'

Father Gregory sighed. It sounded as if he'd decided to cooperate.

'This photo could not have been taken in St Sophia, but I can't tell you where it was taken. This mosaic is pre-Christian. Christian mosaics have less of a green tinge, less silica. This is an earlier mosaic, a pagan mosaic.' He emphasised the word pagan.

'Even though it has this Christian symbol. That means nothing.' He pointed at the IH letters. 'These signify the Greek word for Christ, but the normal letters on a Christian mosaic of the Madonna are the letters MP OY. This is without doubt a pagan mosaic, which someone has tried to make into a Christian one. It should not have been done.'

'What does the Lambda signify?' I said.

He glared at me. 'Lambda signifies Lampas, the light of peace. This mosaic shows Eirene, the daughter of Zeus. She is the goddess of peace. The Arabs call her Al-Lat. Lambda is her symbol. See how she holds her child.' He tapped the photo.

'He is prosperity, Ploutos, the offspring of Peace. See, he holds his horn. The horn of plenty. This is not an image of Jesus.' We all craned towards the picture. The baby in Eirene's arms was indeed holding a small horn.

'Eirene was venerated all over the ancient world. If this was our Theotokos, the Mother of God, blessed be her name, she would have had a red or wine cloak and her head would be bowed. The earliest Church in Constantinople was named after Eirene.' He stopped abruptly. After a few seconds he looked at me, his face darkening.

He pointed a finger at me. 'Does this have anything to do with the murder in Istanbul, the one they're blaming us Greeks for?'

He was up to date with what was going on.

'That's just in the Turkish media,' said Peter.

'Hah,' replied Father Gregory. 'Until the knock comes to the door. As for your mosaic, it's not Christian, but it's valuable. Is that what you want to know, how much money it's worth?' He looked at me disdainfully.

'No,' I said.

If what Father Gregory said was true, about the mosaic showing the goddess of peace, it was a missing link between the worship of pagan Gods, and Christian veneration of the Virgin Mary. And I'd never heard of a mosaic with both Christian and pre-Christian symbols on it. How had it survived this long? Such mosaics would usually have been destroyed when temples were converted into churches or, if they had survived, later on when images were banned for a time in the Eastern Church.

Then it came to me. There was a place I hadn't considered

yet for where Alek might have taken the photo. It was a place Alek would have loved to investigate.

'The Turkish media claim there's a plot to recover the Labarum of Constantine, Father. Do you think it could have survived this long?' said Isabel.

'The Blessed Labarum was stolen,' said the younger monk, intervening. He seemed angry. 'It could have helped us on that final day. The day our city fell to the Turks. But it was hidden, on the orders of the Pope. No one knows where.'

The assistant's face flushed pink. The Labarum was clearly a touchy subject.

'The Labarum has powers, you know,' he continued. 'It, and our other sacred relics, gave strength to those who believed. It sent Goth, Persian and Arab armies back to their homes with their tails cut off, when it was shown on the walls of Constantinople. One day we shall get our sacred Labarum back, and our city too. I pray it will be soon.'

'I'm not sure the Turks will be too happy about that,' said Isabel.

The assistant snorted. Father Gregory shook his head.

'The Labarum was woven with gold thread and embroidered with precious stones. I doubt it has survived man's greed.'

He stood. The cave felt cold.

'We will go,' he said. His voice was shaking. He glared at Peter, then turned to me. 'We should not talk about these things any more. We have no need for power, for material possessions. That is the way of the demons.'

'Thank you for your help, Father,' I said.

'I will pray for you all.' He glanced at his assistant.

'Great,' said Peter. There was a hint of cynicism in his voice. Father Gregory turned on him angrily.

'You unbelievers, you scoff at everything. See those signs on the walls?' He pointed at the circles, stars and other symbols that ran around the cave's walls, almost at floor level.

'They were written when demons were worshipped here. And remember, every era of mankind has an end as well as a beginning. Don't think you will escape.' He pointed at the tunnel.

'We'd better leave,' said Isabel.

Father Gregory walked towards the tunnel, beckoning us after him.

We followed. I'd been thinking about Alek's mosaic, where he might have found it. My idea seemed more plausible with every passing second.

I didn't look back. I was glad to be getting out of that place. We'd walked most of the way back, when suddenly, all the lights in the tunnel went out.

'Keep going,' said Father Gregory sternly.

His assistant pulled out a torch, turned it on, shone it ahead of us. We were in almost total darkness as we walked.

So, half stumbling, listening to the echoing sound of shuffling feet, we exited the tunnel. Before we reached the end though, I heard a noise behind us which seemed to come from the cave: a murmur, as if someone was still in there. I looked back but saw nothing. I kept going. It was just the sound of the mountain.

Peter made a phone call as soon as we exited the cave. He jumped into our Hummer as we were about to move off.

'You should have gone in Father Gregory's car,' he said to me. 'You two were getting on. We haven't got a lot out of him yet, have we? I'm going to find out where he's staying. I think we should talk to him some more.'

I didn't reply. We were the last vehicle in the convoy. Father

Gregory's Toyota was already well ahead of us. The two Hummers that had blocked our path earlier were positioned one in front and one behind his vehicle.

We'd only gone about four miles, we hadn't even reached the main road, when it happened.

The first thing I knew was a stupendous thud. Then I saw a tall tree bending.

And in half a moment, everything changed.

If you've never been near a terrorist explosion or an IED when it goes off, it's hard to explain the shockwave, the way it hits you all over, the way your chest is pummelled as if from the inside, and your eardrums and skull are buffeted. I'm convinced our Hummer lifted off the ground. And I swear I saw the road buckling. Then something hit the roof of our vehicle as gravel splattered the windows.

'Shit!' someone shouted. We'd all instinctively ducked.

We were extremely fortunate.

An IED had been placed in a pothole. And only the fact that we'd maintained a big gap from the vehicle in front saved us from being skewered with shrapnel. Father Gregory's vehicle wasn't so lucky. It took the brunt of the blast.

We came to a shuddering stop by a ditch on the left side of the carriageway. Two security guards came out of the vehicle in front of us and aimed their guns in a circular motion. A plume of dust drifted up ahead where Father Gregory's vehicle had been. My hands were trembling. I felt anger. Then relief. Then sadness. Poor Father Gregory. Could any of them in that vehicle have survived?

One of the guards on the road started waving our vehicle forward frantically, pointing to the side of the road farthest from the dust, where we could pass.

113

'We have to keep going,' said Mark. 'There could be a follow-up action. We could be under surveillance. They could have RPGs trained on us right now.' His tone was agitated.

The wheels of our Hummer spun as we took off. My heart was pounding. We passed Father Gregory's vehicle. Through the dust which was drifting, I saw it had been cracked open, as if someone had taken a can opener to it. I saw flames too.

'Shouldn't we stop?' I shouted. 'Maybe we can help.'

'Are you a fireman?' said Mark, looking straight ahead.

'No.'

'The security guards know what they're doing. You'll only be in their way.'

We sped on. Two men from the lead vehicle were walking back towards Father Gregory's car. Each of them was wearing an oxygen mask and carrying a canister that looked like a small fire extinguisher, painted green. Maybe Mark was right, but I still didn't like the idea of leaving Father Gregory behind.

We were almost unscathed. Our windows hadn't even been shattered, but a film of dust covered us now, and there were chips and marks on the windows, as if something had been slashing at them. The windscreen wipers cleared some of the dust away.

We drove fast, in silence for a while, the reality of what had happened sinking in. It took a long time for my heartbeat to return to normal. Mark turned on the radio. It was tuned to the BBC World service. All the way back to the airport we listened to Elgar. It helped for a while. Then I hated it. I didn't want to listen to anything. And I didn't want it to be quiet either.

I stared out the back window for ages, long after the dust cloud from the explosion couldn't be seen anymore.

I was lucky to be alive. Father Gregory's ideas kept whirling around in my head; I couldn't seem to think of anything else.

Peter said. 'What a terrible waste. And I was hoping you'd have been able to persuade him to tell us where that mosaic came from.'

'You think he knew?' I said.

'I'm a thousand percent sure of it.'

Henry leaned towards the video screen. He knew the British Embassy in Paris. He'd visited it once in Rue du Faubourg, not far from the Champs-Élysées. Its frontage, in the ornate French Second Empire style, filled his screen, along with the demonstrators surrounding it.

Most of the crowd were simply chanting or waving placards and Islamic flags, but there was a small element who were throwing bottles and cans. The raid on the mosque in London had been portrayed in Islamic online forums as an attack on the right to practise their religion. But the reaction across Europe went far beyond what had been expected. *Why* was the big question. Who was fanning the embers?

It was a question Sergeant Henry Mowlam needed an answer to. The other screen on his desk showed an image of the front of St Paul's, where two of his targets were being tracked by cameras. They looked like they were reconnoitring the area.

He'd switched to watching the scene in Paris only when the alert had sounded that the situation was escalating there. Now he wanted to concentrate on the images from St Paul's, his direct area of duty. He knew that the faces in the crowd in Paris would be scanned and put into the database. Images of the small number of individuals stirring things up would be available on Friday, if any of them showed up in London.

Snatch squads of police officers would pick up the dangerous ones, even before they got to St Paul's. Hopefully before they even left their houses, if the images matched individuals they already had data on. Then they could trace all their connections, online and off, to see if the answers he needed would emerge.

The red warning light blinked on again. He switched to watching the images from Paris. Petrol bombs were hitting the elegant carved doors of the embassy. The petrol was exploding in bright red flames. This was orchestrated. You don't bring petrol with you, just in case. Someone was stirring things up.

And they had to be stopped. This was not a good time for this to be happening.

18

Soon after we arrived back at Mosul airport I turned my iPhone on. I'd been warned to turn it off while travelling around Iraq. Something to do with position triangulation if someone wanted to target us. I saw a few missed calls from Dr. Beresford-Ellis. As we waited for someone to check our passports, I rang my voicemail service. In one message Beresford-Ellis said UNESCO had been looking for explanations on what had gone wrong with the project. He wanted a full report on everything that had been happening in Istanbul and he wanted it as quickly as possible. He did not sound happy. His second message was a more urgent version of the first.

One thing was clear to me; I had to go back to Istanbul. I couldn't just go to London. I had to follow this whole thing through, find out what Alek had been up to.

I thought about telling Peter and Isabel about my hunch. But I held back. What would stop them from checking my theory out before I had a chance to? Nothing. All it would take would be one phone call. Then it would be just like after Irene had died. *Go home, sir. We'll look into it.*

That wasn't going to happen this time.

I could taste dust in the air as we waited. Then an official came, gave our passports a cursory glance and waved us through. Peter and Isabel told me to board our plane. The plan was to take off as quickly as possible. Peter said we would only be making ourselves a target if we stayed any longer. They hurried off to see if we could get clearance for a quick turnaround. I made a phone call, then stretched out in my seat, dozed. Presumably getting clearance wasn't as easy as it might be. I drifted off. It was almost one o'clock in the morning.

A sense of foreboding came over me when I woke. I'd only been asleep for maybe twenty minutes.

Memories of Father Gregory, the flames and the pall of dust after the bomb had exploded played in my mind.

It took about an hour for Isabel and Peter to return. I felt shattered.

'You ready, Sean?' shouted Peter when he put his head in the cabin. A hum of engine fuel wafted in as he entered. A refuelling truck was driving away.

'What took you so long?' I rubbed my eyes.

'Sorry.' Isabel gave me a wide smile as if sleeping was something she didn't need to do.

'Where are we heading ?' I said. It was time to tell them.

'London.' She sat opposite me.

'I want to go back to Istanbul,' I said, confidently.

Peter sat down heavily beside me.

'Sorry. No can do.' They looked at each other.

'You know there's probably a bounty on your head in Turkey?' said Isabel.

'I don't care.' The idea that there might be a reward involved hadn't occurred to me. But other things had. And I'd made that phone call too, while I'd been waiting.

'We are talking about the people who cut Alek's head off, Sean.' She spoke calmly, as if describing a rose bush in her garden that had been cut back.

'There are things I have to do, Isabel. I called a contact in Istanbul, woke him up. He wasn't happy. But he forgave me. He's in the department who commissioned us. He says none of this should disrupt our project, that the media speculation will all blow over. He said if I wanted to come back, he'd see me anytime. So I'm going back to Istanbul, now or later. Why don't we go that way? You can drop me off.' I pointed in what I imagined was the general direction of Turkey, though I could have been pointing towards Cairo or Rome.

'What is your hurry?' said Peter. He sounded suspicious.

'I need to see where Alek was working. I can't do a proper report for the Institute without going there. I have to go back to Istanbul as soon as possible.'

'I don't see the urgency,' said Isabel. She flicked a strand of hair from her face. It was a reasonable observation.

But to answer it I'd have had to tell her how much the project meant to us at the Institute. How much Alek had been looking forward to it. How excited he'd been. How he'd infected us all with his enthusiasm. And how I felt responsible for what had happened. And, more importantly, now that I had a clue as to where he'd taken those photos, how I had to follow it up.

But I wasn't going to tell them that. 'I'd better get off here then,' I said.

'Very funny,' said Peter.

'I don't see a lot of security. What are you going to do, kidnap me?' I looked Peter in the eye. 'My colleague's been murdered. And now you want to take me prisoner. That's some help you're providing. Thanks a lot.'

'Why is it so important you go back to Istanbul now, Sean? We're trying to protect you. If we did detain you it would not be kidnapping anyway. We'd be delivering you home. You do live in London.' Isabel snapped her seat belt closed.

'Is there something you haven't told us? Some other reason you want to go back to Istanbul,' said Peter.

'I've heard enough,' I said. I undid my seat belt. The plane's engines had started, but they were just ticking over.

'Be sensible, Sean,' said Peter. 'Your involvement in all this is over. Think clearly. We do have to decide what level of ongoing protection you'll need back in London. You know I'm concerned about your safety. And you should be too. Now sit down.' His voice was firm. Threatening people was probably something he was very good at.

'I'm getting off this plane,' I said.

'Would your wife have agreed to your being so reckless?' said Isabel. She put her hand up to block me.

I put a hand out to push hers away. Her eyes were wide, as if she was amazed at my intransigence.

'We've got very good reasons to be concerned for you,' she said. 'Your colleague was murdered for God's sake. Wake up, Sean. You're in danger.'

'You assume I give a flying frack about that.' I looked in her eyes, saw a flicker of something – empathy maybe. Or perhaps it was pity.

'Don't try to stop me.' I took a step towards the passageway.

Peter rose, half blocking me. I pushed past him before he could do anything.

'Don't be stupid Sean,' said Isabel. 'You're a material witness to a terrorist incident. We have powers to detain you.'

I pushed Peter's shoulder down hard as he grabbed at me. I made it past him to the door and turned the handle. An alarm went off. I pushed the door open. The plane's engines died.

A hundred yards away, illuminated by the bright lights of the airport building, a green-uniformed guard with a gun was looking in our direction.

'I'm not going back to London,' I said. 'I'll jump out, even if we start moving.' I looked back at them.

'You are one stubborn bastard,' said Peter loudly. But he made no move to get up.

'All I want is to be taken back to where you picked me up.'

'Is everything all right?' a voice called out. I looked around. It was the pilot. He was standing in the doorway to the cockpit.

'It will be,' said Peter. Then he sighed, loudly. 'Maybe we can go back to Istanbul.' He said it softly, as if he was talking to himself.

Isabel looked surprised. Then her head moved, like a metronome, from side to side. 'He should go back to London,' she said, looking at Peter.

'I will, later,' I said.

'Pilot, change of plan. Let's go back to Istanbul,' said Peter. He pointed at me. 'But there'll be a price to pay, Sean. We'll stick like glue to you in Istanbul.'

'I don't need a babysitter.'

'We'll make you stand out like a bandaged thumb, if you don't cooperate.'

I didn't reply. I was thinking.

'How long do you intend to stay there, Sean?' said Isabel.

'A few days.'

'You'll be staying in my place,' said Peter.

I stared into his blue, unblinking eyes. If they flew me to London, I could be on the next scheduled flight to Istanbul in hours. Or I could try to get off this plane. But God only knew what the schedule from Mosul to Istanbul was. I might have to

122

go to Baghdad to fly out of this country. Then they'd follow me around as soon as I got to Istanbul anyway. Maybe I shouldn't even have told them I wanted to go back there. Now it looked like the only choice I had was to work with them.

'OK, I agree,' I said. A worried look flashed across Isabel's face.

'You don't want to go back to your quiet life?' she said.

'No, I have to do this.'

'Close the door, and give me your phone, Sean. We'll put a tracker in it,' said Peter. 'We wouldn't want you getting lost in Istanbul, like your colleague.'

'We're flying to Istanbul, no detours?'

'No detours.'

I passed him my phone.

'It needs a charge.'

He turned the phone in his hand, examining it.

'We'll charge it,' he said, languidly.

I took my seat.

'And I want to know everything that you plan to do in Istanbul,' he said.

'I'll make up a list.' I looked out the window. It was still dark as we taxied to the runway. As we rose high into the sky and turned I saw the dawn far off, a glimmer in the sky beyond the Zagros Mountains like something from a Biblical painting, spreading a golden glow from the east. What time was it back in London? My brain felt too fried to work it out.

Having someone coming around with me was going to make it difficult to do everything I wanted in Istanbul, but maybe it was for the best. I looked at Isabel. She had rescued me from my hotel. I'd probably be lying next to Alek if she hadn't.

A few minutes later Peter went to the toilet.

123

Isabel used the tip of her pointed boot to nudge my leg. 'If there are other reasons you want to go to Istanbul, you have to tell me,' she said. 'I'm on your side. I hope you haven't forgotten that.'

'I haven't.'

'So what's the rush to get to Istanbul?'

'I'll tell you later.'

Her expression became serious. She sat forward in her seat and looked at me. 'Don't play games, Sean. If you know anything that could lead to the arrest of any suspects in our investigation, you must reveal that information or you could be charged with obstructing justice.'

'Why do you assume I won't tell you?' I said. 'And what are you going to do if I don't, torture me? With your shoe, perhaps?'

I smiled, then went back to staring out the window.

'You've got an idea where Alek took those photos, haven't you?'

'Are they all like you where you come from, Miss Sharp?'

'No. I come from a perfect English village, where floral-dressed women go to summer fetes at this time of year and worry about their cake recipes, not who's going to die next.' Her voice broke a little, as she said the word die. She looked unusually vulnerable for a few seconds.

'You didn't have an idyllic childhood then,' I said.

She looked away, then back at me. 'I did, until it happened.' She glanced towards the back of the plane.

'My mother died when I was fifteen. Just when I needed her most. Then my dad cracked up. I had to work two jobs to get through uni. I've never had it easy.'

I spoke slowly. 'Both my parents died in my twenties,' I said. 'That was a bad year. Irene got me through it.'

'She must have been a good person.'

We sat in silence for a minute. Death had affected us both.

'I used to be able to sense storms coming when I was young,' said Isabel, softly. 'I'd get funny prickly feelings. You know I'm getting those now.' She rubbed her arms. She had goosebumps, pale molehills on her amber skin.

'Maybe it's an omen,' I said.

'Maybe Peter adjusted the air conditioning,' she said.

The buffeting of wind on the plane grew stronger suddenly, as we banked, changing direction.

'I don't believe in omens,' she said. She sounded firm, as if she was trying to convince herself.

'Look.' I pointed out the window. A Venusian landscape of angry grey clouds lay below us.

Her face was serious.

'All chummy now, are we?' said Peter as he sat down again. The stubble on his chin was gone.

'Do you believe any of that *djinn* stuff Father Gregory was going on about?' said Isabel, ignoring Peter.

'People used to believe the world was full of evil spirits,' I said. 'They had no other way to explain things they didn't understand. That's my explanation for evil spirits. And I'm sticking to it.'

I looked out the window. We had no fighter escort this time. Below us, the huge carpet of brooding clouds stretched endlessly. Above, the sky was china blue. We'd probably already passed into Turkish airspace.

I thought about Father Gregory again. It was hard to stop thinking about what had happened.

'I managed to make contact with Mark,' said Peter. It was almost as if he'd read my mind, or maybe my face had given away what I was thinking.

'Father Gregory is in hospital, in intensive care. His buddy didn't make it.'

I closed my eyes. I was too tired to take it all in. At least one of them had survived. I needed to sleep. I didn't want to think any more.

When we reached Istanbul, the sky was still a mass of angry clouds. I imagined we'd brought the bad weather with us, as if some jinx was following us.

Luckily, we didn't have to wait for our passports to be checked with the other tourists. Peter knocked on a side door in the main passport hall and we passed through a long white corridor to a large white room. There, a bored-looking official at a polished wooden desk stamped our passports after checking them.

We'd agreed that I would meet my contact, Abdal Gokan, the Director of the Laboratory for Conservation, the following day at the time I'd arranged. Isabel would come with me; I'd be tracked. I imagined MI6 operatives talking into their sleeves, trailing us in packs. What transpired was nothing like that.

A door beyond the room where our passports were checked led directly to the public area of the airport. Peter hadn't given anything away about himself during the whole flight. He was clearly used to deflecting questions, saying a lot while saying nothing. But I had found out that Isabel had worked for the police before joining the Foreign Office.

We were met in the arrivals hall by an unsmiling grey-haired, grey-suited driver. He led us to a Chrysler minivan with blackened windows. We were stared at by three hulking dark-suited characters standing nearby as we climbed in. They looked like they were trying to memorise our faces. Istanbul was hotter, if anything, than when I'd arrived a few days ago, despite the clouds moving slowly over our heads.

Half an hour after leaving the airport we arrived at the tall, wrought-iron gates of Peter's villa. We all needed some sleep, he said. He was right.

The reality of everything that had happened was sinking in like a brick in a pool. During the car journey across Istanbul, Peter had received a call. Father Gregory had died in hospital overnight.

I felt ill, and a sense of foreboding.

Pink roses hung in drifts along the top of the high, white-washed wall, which stretched away on either side of the gates to Peter's villa. This was clearly an upmarket suburb of Istanbul.

Isabel hadn't said a word after Peter's announcement of Father Gregory's death. She looked pale.

The tall gates made a loud grating noise as they opened. An impeccably dressed man in a navy suit stood to one side as our driver pulled into the gravel courtyard.

'Sleep well,' said Isabel, softly. The driver jumped out, came around and opened my door. I took a deep breath as I adjusted to the heat after the air conditioned car.

'You too, old girl,' said Peter, as he got out.

'Safe home,' I said to Isabel. Then I got out.

Isabel called after me. 'I'll pick you up in the morning, at about eight.'

I turned. She gave me a knowing look, then a genuine smile. Her mask had slipped a little on the plane, and I was glad. There was something about her that reminded me a lot of Irene. The way she pushed her hair back behind her ears. Her smile. It was a little spooky.

As the car door closed I caught a last glimpse of black hair.

'I have to go out tonight but my man will prepare dinner for you. We don't want you wandering the streets,' said Peter as we went inside.

I'd made the appointment to meet Abdal Gokan at 9:00 AM, at his offices the next day, Wednesday. It was lunchtime, but all I wanted was a proper bed. I felt like I hadn't slept in days.

I shook my head and said, 'Don't worry, I won't be going anywhere.'

After a quick shower and a snack of soft bread and crumbly white cheese that was brought to me in my spacious all-white bedroom, I paced up and down for a while, my mind still racing, but my body aching to sleep. The window in my room overlooked the front courtyard. The sound of Istanbul's incessant traffic didn't reach the room except for the occasional blast of a distant car horn.

After going through everything that had happened and my plans for the next day, I finally fell asleep. The luxurious feel of the cool cotton sheets was wonderful.

Peter wasn't around when I woke later that evening. Nor was anyone else, except his 'man', the guy who'd met us at the front door.

He was as discreet a servant as I'd ever met. Not one word did I get out of him about Peter. Nothing. Not when he'd left, where he was, when he might be due back. Nothing.

He brought me dinner in my room though, set it on a round table near the window. I had turned on the Sony LCD TV. The BBC World news service was on. I turned it off after he left the room – the endless roll call of the problems in the world was too depressing.

As I listened to the faint hum of the city, still tired, feeling like I wanted to sleep again soon, I thought about everything that had happened.

Where was all this leading? Peter had claimed, when he'd told us Father Gregory had died, that it had been the third such attack on his convoy in as many weeks. Why hadn't he told me that when he'd asked me if I wanted to travel with Father Gregory? Was it just a coincidence?

It took me a long time to drift off and my dreams were disturbed when I finally did. In one of them Isabel was walking away from me and I was trying to catch her. And I couldn't. Something was preventing me.

19

Doctor Brian Osman was the son of an American dentist and a Turkish biologist. His medical practice, in the upmarket Istanbul suburb of Besiktas, was focused on tropical diseases, which Turkish people who travelled all over the world were now picking up in increasing numbers. A recent outbreak of haemorrhagic fever in the Black Sea region had brought a small number of patients to his shiny white door.

That morning, as Dr Osman put his key in the lock of the door that led out of the basement parking area of his building, the last thing he expected was to be knocked unconscious. When he woke, he was lying in the back of a truck and a man with a bald head, a pockmarked face and a cruel expression was kneeling on top of him. The man had a shiny knife in his hand. The tip of the knife was inches from Dr Osman's face.

'Do not struggle, Dr Osman, or I will enjoy running this piece of steel right through your eyeball until it's poking around inside that clever brain. Understood?'

Dr Osman nodded. His heart was beating like a kettledrum.

'What do you want?'

Malach leaned down.

'I have a friend who is sick,' he said. He pushed the knife against the doctor's cheekbone until a bubble of blood appeared.

'She needs you.'

20

A car arrived for me at eight o'clock the following morning. I'd eaten soft bread, olives, some spicy salami and downed coffee and two glasses of orange juice for breakfast. Peter hadn't returned, his man said, after he'd carried my breakfast into my room. I didn't care. I wasn't exactly looking forward to having Peter with us when Isabel and I went to Hagia Sophia.

Isabel wasn't in the car though when I looked into it. The driver said, in heavily accented but perfect English, that he'd waited for her, rung her doorbell three times, tried her phone, but she hadn't come down. So he'd come to get me, as he'd been told to.

My energy was already being sapped by the heat. This was not what I needed to hear. What was she up to?

'You still need me, *effendi*?' the driver asked. He looked distracted.

'Does the Consulate know about Isabel not coming?' I said. He nodded, but looked a little unsure. Had something happened to her?

He took out his mobile phone as if he sensed my anxiety. He pressed some numbers. I waited beside the car.

'She not answering,' he said, holding the phone out to me. I could hear the sound of it ringing. 'Maybe she forgot.' He shrugged.

All of a sudden my memory was a bit hazy about what she'd said before we'd parted. She'd told me a car was coming at eight, but had she said she'd come too? Had she just said I'd be picked up?

Yes, it was a possibility. And it was getting closer to nine by the second – I didn't want to be late for my meeting with Abdal.

'Can we pass by her apartment to see if she's ready?' I asked.

He shook his head. 'No, no. I cannot. I can take you to one place. Where I was told to go, or nowhere.' By the look on his face it was clear I wasn't going to change his mind.

Was this deliberate, or was she flakier than she seemed? I looked at my watch. Why should I be worried if she wasn't here? Weren't they the ones who needed to shadow me? Wasn't it also possible Isabel had decided to let me have my freedom?

As we drove off on our way to the offices of the Laboratory for Conservation beside Hagia Eirene, at the back of Hagia Sophia, I wondered if I should do more to find her.

'Where does Isabel Sharp live?' I said, to the driver.

His only response was a shake of the head.

'When did you see her last?'

He didn't respond to that question. I was on my own now. The only problem was, I didn't have my phone.

Peter hadn't given me my phone back. I'd been too tired, distracted, to ask him about it the afternoon before. If I'd known he was going to disappear with it I'd have demanded it back.

Questions flowed through my mind, as we nosed through the traffic. Was this all a game to them? Were they hoping to find out if I was hiding something? Was I being followed?

I looked around. There were too many cars behind us to have any idea if I was being tracked.

It was certainly possible that they were giving me plenty of rope, to see what I'd do with it.

A minute later I got an idea. I borrowed the driver's phone, spoke to someone at the British Consulate. The driver had the number. The man at the other end didn't sound at all concerned that Isabel had missed her appointment with me. He offered to get a message to her, and assured me that she'd contact me as soon as she could.

The driver dropped me off at the back gate of the laboratory near Hagia Sophia. The laboratory was in a three-storey Ottoman-era building constructed of giant blocks of granite. The entrance was right behind Hagia Eirene in a stable yard, which was paved with slippery soapstone that looked as if it had been new when horses had been the only form of transport.

There was a deserted out-of-the-way feel to the yard.

'No Abdal Gokan. No,' shouted the attendant, shaking his head, when I enquired about him. The attendant had raised his voice when it became clear from the look on my face that I hadn't understood the stream of Turkish that had come from his mouth. He was sitting inside a scuffed wooden cubby-hole that took up one corner of the black and white tiled high-ceilinged entrance hall to the laboratory.

It took me a few seconds to work out that he probably meant that Abdal Gokan simply wasn't in yet.

'I'll wait,' I said.

He didn't reply. He just closed the frosted glass hatch that separated us.

A large gilt-framed picture of Atatürk looking stern was the only image on the walls. Pinned up to the right of the door was an old calendar, curling at the edges, with a Turkish red crescent moon at its centre. I could smell dust. There was a stifling air to the place, as if asking for anything to be done quickly here would be met by utter indifference and then total silence.

I waited.

Every time I heard someone walking in the yard outside, a sense of expectation rose up inside me. I stared at each person who passed through the hall. They looked back at me with undisguised suspicion.

Come on Abdal.

There was a single piece of paper pinned to the wall near the door to the yard. It was in Turkish. I was looking at it when I heard a voice behind me.

'Mr Ryan. How are you?' boomed the voice. I felt a hand on my shoulder. I turned quickly.

It was Abdal Gokan. He looked troubled.

Abdal was a big man, bearish, friendly, with a greying well-tended beard and a thick sixties-era moustache. He looked like an old-fashioned professor from a southern university who'd been bypassed for promotion. His clothes, a limp black linen jacket and a faded black shirt and trousers, hung on him like crumpled curtains. Where he'd appeared from I had no idea, but I didn't care.

'Abdal, great to see you.' We kissed each other's cheeks.

'Has anyone else contacted you? I was supposed to meet a colleague here. She was going to come along with us this morning.'

'I arrive now,' he said. 'Wait, let me see if there are any messages.' He turned and went to the cubby-hole. I stared at the back of his jacket. It looked as if he'd slept in it.

'No messages,' he said, when he turned back to me. 'Come,

you will look at our new laboratories. I want to show them to you.' He had a weary expression, as if he was a gundog who'd seen too much death.

I decided to put the whole thing about Isabel not turning up aside. She knew what she was doing.

He spent the next twenty minutes taking me on a tour through chaotic offices and pristine new laboratories, telling me all about the new researchers and restorers they had working inside Hagia Sophia.

'Everything this year is focused on the main apse,' he said, as we passed a room where tiny pieces of mosaic were laid out on long tables.

'Did Alek work at any other location, somewhere not directly related to our project?' I asked.

'No, he worked where we agreed. There was no reason for him to work anywhere else.'

I was disappointed.

'Come, let's go over there. You can see where he was working for yourself,' said Abdal. His expression had become closed, as if he hadn't appreciated the veiled suggestion that Alek had done something he shouldn't have, and that if he had, that Abdal might have any knowledge of such things.

We exited through a side door. It took about ten minutes to walk around to the main entrance to Hagia Sophia. Abdal walked slowly. I looked, but I couldn't see anyone following us. Had I slipped the net? Or had something happened that I knew nothing about?

I felt a coldness in the pit of my stomach. As I looked at the passers-by an image of the thugs who'd pursued us out of the hotel a few days ago came to me. I scanned the passing tourists – from every country it seemed – and the street vendors selling postcards and bottles of water. Were those evil bastards still looking for me?

Abdal's security card got us past the long queues of tourists at the main entrance to Hagia Sophia. Then, after dodging shoals of them in the long high narthex, clustering around their guides, we went through to the main part of the building, where it was much cooler. This was a space I knew well. Every time I entered it I felt a sense of sanctity, spirituality. Maybe it was the trapped air, the thin dust of marble and ancient brick, or maybe it was the hushed voices, the upturned faces all around, or simply just the sheer size and age of the place, its massive walls reaching up like a fortress of faith.

I'd spent a few days visiting Hagia Sophia during the bidding process for the project. This time however, as it was high summer, the nave was brighter from sunlight pricking though the air from the rows of luminescent windows on the second, third and distant fourth levels. This had been the largest Christian church in the world for a thousand years, its grandeur an advertisement for the success of the empire that built it.

When Abdal had finished pointing out the wall paintings and mosaics that Alek had photographed, he took me to an area cordoned off by high scaffolding around the Sultan's gallery. The tourists circling the central nave – cameras and guidebooks clutched tight – stared at us as Abdal knocked on the steel door that provided access to the shuttered area. The door was opened by a white-haired older man. Beyond him, I saw two other men kneeling at the thin pillars that supported the gallery.

'Is it possible that someone took Alek somewhere else to look at mosaics? There was talk of other interesting mosaics nearby,' I said.

Abdal looked at me as if I'd insulted his family.

'That's not possible,' he said shaking his head vigorously. He sounded irritated. 'This is where the interesting work is.' He pointed at where the men were working.

'I only ask because I wondered if someone took him underground. Some of the tunnels and cisterns have been opened up recently, haven't they?'

He shrugged.

'Your colleague worked where we told him to. We are very strict about such things. Your project included work in the public areas only. I pointed all those out to you.'

Someone behind Abdal called out in Turkish. Abdal turned and shouted something back. A man in the far corner had risen to his feet. He came forward, waving his hands. Abdal turned to me. He didn't look pleased. When the man arrived beside us, a rush of Turkish poured from Abdal. I heard my name somewhere in the middle.

'*Merhaba*, Mr Ryan,' said the man who'd come over, solemnly, when Abdal had finished. He bowed slightly. He was small and had a thin black beard and leathery skin. Another archaeologist, I guessed. He was wearing a red Polo T-shirt and cream pants. He looked concerned.

'My name is Bulent,' he said. 'Abdal tells me you are a colleague of Mr Alek.' Before I could reply, he continued, 'It was a terrible thing that happened to him.'

He shook my hand for a long time, gripping it tightly, as if he was trying to comfort me. Then he kissed me on both cheeks. His skin was smooth.

Abdal looked at him disapprovingly. His colleague ignored him.

'Your Mr Alek, he was crazy for his work. He stayed here late every night. And he start in the morning before everyone. He wanted to know everything.' He gestured at the golden-veined dome high above us.

'Alek always worked hard,' I said. Talking about him in the past tense made me feel uncomfortable. It didn't seem right.

'He was a good man.'

He looked down, held his palm to his chest, as if he was praying. 'It is too bad, Mr Ryan. He didn't deserve such a thing to happen to him.'

'At least he was doing what he loved in his last few days.'

'You are right. He loved this place.' He looked a little teary-eyed.

'He said to me that people in ancient times knew more than us about sacred geometry, about how a space like this can help us come close to the divine.' He gestured again at the dome high above our heads.

'He was a clever guy,' I said.

Alek had told me about his sacred geometry theories about Hagia Sophia. He'd dug up some weird facts about the place. He'd claimed Basilides, the philosopher who inspired the architects of Hagia Sophia, had learned the secrets of sacred geometry from the first followers of St Peter.

Bulent nodded in agreement. Abdal looked as if he couldn't wait for the conversation to end.

'Mathematical harmony is a true reflection of the divine, Mr Ryan. A clue to the master plan. It'll survive us all. But I must go.' He bowed his head.

'I'm glad we spoke,' I said. Abdal looked relieved.

'Did Alek do any work outside Hagia Sophia?' I asked Bulent quickly, as he started to turn away.

Bulent paused before answering. 'He talked about a lot of things. He had some crazy ideas.'

He looked at Abdal, who seemed furious now.

'Mr Ryan, enough. I have to get back to my office. I have showed you where Alek was working. I have answered your questions. I have done what I promised. I can do no more. We are all sad about what happened, but I can assure you, it had nothing to do with his work here. Our police tell me it was bad luck. He was, how you say, in the right place at the wrong time?'

I didn't bother to correct him. His colleague held out his hand. I shook it.

'*Güle güle*,' he said.

Abdal ushered me out through the steel door. His colleague went back to work.

'If you need more help, email me from England,' said Abdal, as he shook my hand.

Then he was gone, and I was alone with the tourists. I walked fast across the patterned marble floor. The heat of the day, even well out of the sun, lay heavy like a blanket. It made it difficult to think. And I definitely needed to think, to work out what I should do next.

One thing was sure; they wouldn't want to hear about sacred geometry back in Oxford. Alek should have been collecting digital images, not superstitions. But what had annoyed Abdal so much?

An odd sensation came over me. I could smell, ever so faintly, the smell of death from Father Gregory's hidden cave, as if it was clinging to me. Outside, I stopped a man selling bottles of water and bought one.

And then I was in the brilliant sunshine and ahead, across the wide open area in front of Hagia Sophia, were the minarets and giant dome of the Blue Mosque, the four-hundred-year-old Islamic mirror of Hagia Sophia, designed, it seemed, to demonstrate that Islam could equal the magnificence of any Christian edifice.

I heard a voice saying my name.

'Sean.'

I looked around, but couldn't see anyone who might be calling me. Just streams of people moving this way and that. They were all around me. I headed across the flag-stoned, open area in front of Hagia Sophia, intending to look back as soon as I was away from the crowds to see if I could spot anyone.

Then I felt a hand on my shoulder and I spun around.

'Mr Sean, wait.' It was Bulent. He guided me out of the way of some passing tourists.

'I'm glad I found you,' he said. He was breathing hard.

'Abdal sent you?'

'No, no, not Abdal. He's an office man. He hates anything that interferes with our schedule.' He pumped my hand, kissed me on both cheeks again.

'I am Professor Bulent Athangelos. Abdal didn't tell you who I am, did he?'

'No, Professor. He didn't.'

He nodded, waved a hand dismissively. 'Abdal wants us all to be anonymous. Now, please, call me Bulent. Will you come for coffee with me?' He coughed and smiled, showing his yellowing teeth.

'Sure.'

'Let's go then,' he replied.

We walked at a brisk pace. Bulent was clearly in a hurry. His pants flapped at his ankles.

'Did Alek tell you he was taking pictures in other places?' I asked, as we waited at a signal to cross the road and the tram tracks leading up from the Golden Horn.

He shook his head, looked around furtively.

'Not here.'

We crossed the road. The heat was sapping my energy. We headed down a side street, entered an ancient looking café. The building it was in was leaning a little, as if its shoulders were curving with age. Inside, the place had white tiles on its walls and rows of solid wooden tables. Down one side ran a long deli-style glass case. I felt a delightful blast of cold air from the air-conditioning unit above the door. Apart from these two concessions to modernity, the place looked as if it had been the same for a hundred years or more.

We received only a few curious glances; most of the customers were busy with their companions. The buzz of conversation grew around us as we moved through the room.

We made our way towards a table in the far corner. The cool air, after the heat outside, made the place an oasis. My shirt was damp with perspiration, not only under my arms, but down my back too.

'Turkish coffee?' said Bulent.

'Yes, please.'

'This place was a favourite of Atatürk's, you know.'

'Really?' I tried to look impressed.

He put his hands face down on the table and leaned forward as if he was about to say something important.

'I will pray for you,' he started, shaking his head mournfully.

'Why will you do that?'

'You have no security guard.' His hands were in the air now.

'I don't need one.'

He tutted and waved. 'If they catch the dogs who killed your friend, you know what they will do?'

I shook my head.

'Send them all to hell.' He pointed a finger at his forehead and imitated a gun going off. Was this why he'd followed me, to tell me that Alek would be avenged?

A waiter approached. I ordered coffee, and an invitingly thick slice of chocolate cake I'd seen on the way in.

'You came from London?' he asked.

'Yes.'

'There are problems there, yes?'

'A few.'

'Tolerance is dying,' he said matter-of-factly. 'When Mehmed the Conqueror ruled this city, almost half its population was Christian. We all lived in peace. He said the different peoples in his empire should live as one.'

I'd heard about Mehmed's tolerance after he'd captured Istanbul.

'These days, we are going backwards,' he went on. 'When Islam first appeared, it reduced taxes, banned usury and slavery too. Did you know that?'

'No.'

'Well, it's true.'

I studied him. The skin on his face was deeply grooved. He looked kind, but worried. His red T-shirt was pristine, as if it had come out of its packaging only that morning.

The coffee arrived. My cake tasted even better than it had looked in the glass case. It was silky soft, with a crisp layer of chocolate on top. Irene had always liked chocolate cake. She would have enjoyed this one.

'Your friend, he met a most terrible death. It is hard even to imagine such a thing,' said Bulent.

My imagination had had no trouble in serving up bloody images of Alek's death since I'd seen his body. Those images were ghosts haunting me, becoming clearer if I tried to escape them, as if my mind wasn't under my control.

I looked at my cake. I'd eaten enough.

'Did Alek say anything to you about his interest in other places, like the Blue Mosque or Hagia Eirene or anywhere else?' I asked.

'He said nothing about the Blue Mosque. I told him Hagia Eirene is closed. It opens only for concerts, recitals, things like that. There are pictures of the interior in our Archaeological Museum. I told him all this. He did ask about Hagia Eirene.'

At last, we were getting somewhere. 'Did he ask about any other place?' I picked up my coffee, pushed the remains of the cake away.

'He wanted to know about the old Imperial Palace, Constantine's Palace – everyone does these days – and how the Senate project is progressing. He had lots of questions.'

'He had an idea that there was a temple to Aphrodite on the site of Hagia Eirene, before Constantine turned it into a Christian Church,' I said. 'Did he ask you if you'd found any proof that it existed?' It was a theory Alek had spoken about only once, and it was hard to see how it could have led to his death, but I had to ask about it.

'We have been studying everything,' said Bulent. He looked around the room, as if he was looking for someone.

'Might there be crypts under Hagia Eirene?'

He put his coffee down and waited. The buzz of conversation in the room got louder.

'There are underground areas on most sites near here, the old Palace, the Senate building, the Hippodrome, everywhere.'

Which one Alek had decided to investigate was the question.

'It was not unusual for early Christians to take over temple sites. St Paul's in London was a temple to Diana, was it not?' he said.

'I don't know.'

He smiled briefly, then looked pensive again. His bushy black eyebrows hooded his eyes.

'Some of the Greek temples were centres of prostitution.'

'Really?' I replied. 'That must have been a sight.'

'It was a disaster, Mr Ryan. I wrote a paper on the subject.' He paused. His expression darkened. 'It hasn't been published, yet.'

'I'm sure it will be,' I said.

'Hagia Eirene was my project. Mine. The wrong people are working there these days.' He looked around. He seemed afraid.

'They are better connected than me, *effendi*.' He examined the dregs of his coffee. 'Us researchers on the Hagia Sophia project, we know nothing about their excavation plans, nothing. Can you believe that? It's crazy! We don't even talk to each other!' He stopped, pressed his lips together, as if he'd said too much already.

'When did that project start?'

'I'm sorry, Sean.' He shook his head.

'What's wrong?'

He bit his lip. His eyelids drooped further. 'I cannot say any more.' He was closing down on me.

'My Institute could support your work, Professor.' It was true. I could get good projects onto the Institute's agenda. Our grants weren't that big, but often a little went a long way. 'Perhaps we can help each other.'

He eyed me suspiciously.

'Why don't you tell me what's going on in Hagia Eirene? I'll owe you.'

He looked at me for a minute before he responded. I could see him thinking, going through the benefits of having a director of an Oxford Institute in his debt, wondering what I really wanted.

'Alek didn't tell you anything?' he said.

I shrugged. 'Nothing would surprise me about Alek.'

'I am sorry,' he said. 'I cannot talk any more about this.'

I sat forward. I was close to finding out something important. I could feel it. But my chance was slipping away.

'Alek was up to something and he told you all about it. You've just confirmed it.' I looked around. 'Maybe I should tell Abdal Gokan about this. He might be able to help me.'

I stood. He looked shocked. Then he glanced around.

'No,' he said.

'Tell me more then.'

He looked up at me.

'You must not tell people you got anything from me,' he said quickly.

'I don't want to get you into trouble, but I have to find out what happened to Alek. I need to know what he was up to.' I sat back down. 'Tell me what's going on in Hagia Eirene.'

He sighed, like a ball deflating. 'Not in Hagia Eirene. Under it. Since Alek's death they've been working there every day, every night for all I know.' He was speaking in a whisper. 'You know what I think, Sean?'

I shook my head.

'They want to steal my idea.' His voice rose an octave. 'I was the one who found the doorway. But they got the permission to open it.' His hands held the air, as if he was holding a weight up. His fingers were spread wide, his frustration clear. 'My life's work is being stolen.'

He shook his fist in front of him. 'It is wrong. Whoever publishes this find will have a triumph, medals, awards, everything. They are thieves.' He spat the word out.

'Did you take Alek to Hagia Eirene?'

His head moved up and down, a nodding dog in the back window of a car. 'Can you show me where you took him?' This could explain everything. Alek had interrupted someone on a secret dig.

Bulent looked away. He rubbed his forehead unhappily.

'No, no. I can't get involved.'

'How did this group get permission to work there?'

'They have people with the best credentials.' He waved his hands. 'That is what I was told.' He leaned forward. 'I asked them not to let a private dig take place in Hagia Eirene. But they say the people have all the proper letters, permissions, that they were doing a simple site survey for a larger project. I don't know, maybe it's true.'

'You can take me there?'

He shook his head fast. 'No. No. I have a wife, two children.' He pulled out his wallet, showed me a photo of a plump woman with black hair pulled back, her arms tight around two smiling children, a black-haired boy and girl.

'They are beautiful,' I said.

We looked at the picture. Bulent was nodding sadly. I knew what he was trying to tell me.

'I go now,' he said softly.

'Why can't you at least tell me where you took Alek?'

His expression hardened. 'I can't help you any more. I answered your questions. You must leave me alone.'

'You can explain where you took him.' My voice rose. I wasn't going to give up.

He patted the air between us, trying to get me to quieten down. 'You have to forget all this. Where I took him is guarded, *effendi*. They've put a security camera on the door. I will not take you there.' He clamped his mouth shut.

'Give me something more.'

His eyes narrowed. '*Effendi*, I will tell you one more thing. Then you will stop all this.' He leaned close to me. 'The people who are working there, they come and go through a side door in the courtyard in front of our office. That's all I can tell you.'

He stood. I got the impression he wanted to get away quickly. That he'd decided meeting me hadn't been a good idea. I stood as well.

He held out his hand. 'I'm sorry, I cannot help any more.'

We shook hands. He headed for the door. I sat back down for a split second, then raced after him. He turned as he reached the doorway and looked at me enquiringly as I came up to him.

'One last question.'

His eyebrows shot up. 'No, no more, please.'

I took my chance. 'What hours do these people work under Hagia Eirene?'

He shook his head. I stood my ground. His eyes darted towards the street. His attitude had changed. He looked really scared.

'It's a small request. Tell me for Alek's sake, if nothing else.'

He closed his eyes for a few seconds, opened them, then pushed his face towards mine.

'OK, *effendi*, friend of Alek who won't give up, if you want to see them, to see what I say is true, I will tell you this.'

He gripped my arm. 'At four every afternoon two men exit into the courtyard. That's when they finish their shift under Hagia Eirene.'

'How will I recognise them?'

He snorted dismissively. 'Their overalls are covered in dust. You will know them. They are the only ones who use that exit. So now you know this and you can see with your own eyes that what I say is the truth. And you know what I think?' His hand gripped my shoulder. 'Why Alek died?'

'Why?'

'He was mixed up in something before he even came here. I don't think it had anything to do with all this.'

And then he was gone.

I went back into the café. Two waiters, young men with slicked-back hair, and an old, grey-haired man behind the counter, were staring at me. I took my seat. A party of tourists at one of the other tables was looking at me too. I'd attracted a lot of attention. It was time to go.

Within minutes I was in a taxi, heading for Peter's house.

I wanted to find out what had happened to Isabel. Why hadn't she turned up? The lack of anyone following me had made me think again about what her and Peter were up to. Was I supposed to let them know what I'd found out?

The taxi driver looked at me in his mirror, as we shunted through the late morning traffic.

If Isabel was at Peter's villa, I might tell her I was going to Hagia Eirene at four. And if she insisted, she could come along too. It would probably be a good idea to have her with me. At the very least I'd be sticking to the deal I'd done with her and Peter.

As I waited for someone to open the gate at Peter's villa I walked up and down. When at last it opened, the first thing

I did was ask Peter's man if Isabel had come round. I surprised myself at how quickly that question came out.

'No, sir, but Mr Fitzgerald is back,' was his reply.

He led me through the house to a small courtyard. It had a froth of pink rose bushes climbing up three of its whitewashed walls. Peter was sitting at a coffee table, talking on a phone. He waved at me to sit down on a thickly-cushioned high-backed chair near him. It took him a couple of minutes to finish his call. Arrogance came off him like heat from a fire. It wasn't just the way he sat, or the expression on his face, it was everything put together. I stood up and started pacing.

'Sean, what have you been up to?' he said, a moment later.

I told him about Isabel not showing up, about Bulent and about Hagia Eirene. Almost everything, in fact. I only kept one piece of information to myself, and even that I nearly told him, but something held me back.

Isabel not showing up was still annoying me, but he didn't seem worried about it at all.

'We can take it from here, Sean,' he said condescendingly, when I finished my story.

I stared back at him, glad I hadn't told him everything. What a total dick. I'd figured out where Alek had taken those photos, and it seemed like all this guy wanted to do was get rid of me.

Then, abruptly, he excused himself. As I waited for him to come back, I thought about what I should do next.

'You weren't thinking of going to Hagia Eirene by yourself, were you?' he said, when he rejoined me a few minutes later.

Going to Hagia Eirene was exactly what I'd been planning to do.

'I thought Isabel might like to come along.'

'We've a lot of experienced people out here, Sean. They're

trained for this sort of thing. You really don't have to get involved with this. If these are the buggers who killed your colleague, we'll find them. Be sure of that.' He put his hands together, turned his fingers into a steeple, then touched his forefingers to his lips and stared at me. 'You've done enough.'

'What's happened to Isabel?' I said.

'Don't worry about Isabel. She'll be alright.' His expression remained unreadable.

He just wanted me to walk away from it all.

'Do you know anything else that might be useful to us, Sean?' Had he guessed I was holding something back?

'No.' I kept my voice flat.

He didn't break eye contact. 'Then leave this to us. I'll organise your flight home.' He folded his arms as if he'd made my decision for me. Then he gave me one of his perfect fake smiles.

'You're not getting rid of me that easy,' I replied. 'I came here to find out what happened to Alek, and I still don't know. If I go back to London, you guys will never tell me anything.'

'You really must think of your safety first, Sean. You've found out a lot already. You've done well. There's really nothing more you can do now. It's time for the professionals to take over.'

'You can't stop me from going to Hagia Eirene. I want to see these people for myself. And you can't change my mind, so don't even try.'

There was no way I was going to give up. All that sorry sir, we'll keep you informed sir bullshit. I knew the routine. I'd hear nothing for weeks. Then months. Then before I knew it a year would have passed and the case would be ancient history. If I was lucky, I'd receive the odd letter regretting things, telling me they were still working on the case. Maybe I'd get a brief meeting, if I pressed hard for it, with the same end result.

I had nothing to lose any more – no family, and my best friend was dead. 'I'll be going to Hagia Eirene this afternoon. I'll see you there, if you can make it.' I forced a smile.

He looked surprised, or maybe he was faking it. I didn't give a damn.

'I suppose I should credit you for perseverance,' he said. 'What do you plan to do?'

I kept my voice level. The heat was getting to me. This was the hottest day by far since I'd arrived. It felt almost as hot as northern Iraq had been.

'I want to see these people for myself. That's it.'

'Well, if you insist, we'll take you there, no problem at all.'

'But,' he paused. The catch was coming, 'you'll do what you're told, no more, no less, or we will not be responsible for what happens to you. Don't forget how your colleague died.' His tone was measured, his words cold.

He turned his head. His man was standing by the door to the corridor that led to the outside world. He nodded at him.

'I think it's time for lunch,' he said.

21

'Stupid bloody demonstrators. They've got a cheek,' said Lord Bidoner, as he wobbled up the wet granite steps leading to the shiny black door. 'We're at war. Don't they know it?' He sniffed. 'Good to see you could make it, Arap. Just in time too.'

'Good to see you too, sir,' said Arap Anach. His limousine driver was holding a cavernous black umbrella above his head. He waited for Lord Bidoner to move up the steps.

The pavement was deserted. At the end of the street, traffic inched past along Haymarket heading towards Trafalgar Square.

Above them, monsoon-like August rain streamed down the creamy plaster frontage of the elegant London mansion. When Bidoner reached the top of the stairs the gleaming door set between white pillars opened. The red eye of a security camera stared down at them from a bronze lion's head, set above the door. An expanse of hall, floored in white marble, beckoned beyond the doorway.

Gilt-framed portraits of people in wigs or top hats dominated the walls. A black marble staircase, which would not have been out of place in an old Hollywood musical with Fred Astaire, led up to the gallery level.

You could smell tradition and money. It wasn't just the lavender perfumed polish, like a whiff of expensive aftershave, or the scrubbed servants or the hush that descended as the front door closed behind them, it was everything together. And Arap liked it. This was his world.

The double doors on the far side of the entrance hall creaked as they opened. A head peeked out, then pushed the doors wide. They passed inside.

The room was a long hall with white pillars along each side. Well-dressed people in dark suits filled rows of plush, red-upholstered chairs facing a podium. Beside the podium, on a stand, stood a large, thin LCD TV. The room buzzed with chatter. Arap moved to a free seat near the front and sat down.

Lord Bidoner moved to the podium. After a minute spent talking quietly with an elderly gentleman who was standing next to him, he tapped the microphone.

'Today,' he began, dispensing with any opening pleasantries, 'the Muslim faith is the fastest growing of all Europe's religions. By some projections, within some of your lifetimes, it will be the faith of the majority, given the comparative birth rates. An Islamic Europe may not aspire to tolerance, either. It may well be fundamentalist. And they don't usually take kindly to dissent. When they offer your granddaughter a *burqa*, she may have to put it on.'

Arap had heard it all before, but he sat through it. Lord Bidoner was the only man he trusted in England. And he had personally vouched for each person in the room.

'So what are our plans, you ask me?' Lord Bidoner paused, and scanned his audience.

'Some of you ask about population control. You tell me that mother nature will inevitably check the explosive growth of humanity. But it is our job to ensure an orderly reduction.' He coughed.

'We cannot allow our country to be destroyed. And we will not, I promise you.' He wagged a finger at the group before him. It was as explicit as he got, which pleased Arap. Only the inner circle could know more. Everyone else would just have to content themselves with believing in coincidences and bad luck.

When the speech was over, applause broke out. It lasted for two minutes, at least. The queue of people waiting to talk to the speaker diminished slowly. Malach waited, standing to the side.

'A well crafted speech, sir,' he said, when everyone had gone. 'Let's go for our little meeting, Arap.'

He nodded. Within minutes he, Lord Bidoner, and three others were sitting around an emerald-green baize card table in an adjoining oak-panelled room.

Lord Bidoner was the first to speak.

'You know we can trust this chap.' He nodded towards Arap. 'He's proven that. The advance notice he gave you all about those riots last week was spot on. I vote we give him what he asked for the last time he came here.' He turned to Arap.

'You have something to tell us?'

Arap's expression was rock steady. 'I do, Lord Bidoner. My view, as you all know, is that a resurgence of pneumonic plague is likely to break out soon.' Everyone looked at him expectantly. These men wanted to know what was going to happen, but they also wanted to be kept at arm's length. They weren't a big group, but they were influential. And their objectives were the same as his.

'I expect that mass protests and overcrowded transport systems will result in the virus spreading fast. As for outcomes, in Fiji, in 1875, one untreatable measles outbreak killed 25 percent of all Fijians. 80 percent of Hawaii natives were killed by similarly untreatable epidemics. Modern man thinks such things are in the past. But antibiotics are losing their potency. Untreatable epidemics can produce similar mortality rates in western populations, focused mainly on the groups in which the infection will arise.'

'You and yours will be safe, gentlemen, but it's time to head for the country.' The faces around him were gloomy, but determined.

'I have only one more thing to say, Lord Bidoner,' said Arap.

'Yes?' Lord Bidoner's tone was flat.

'If things go as expected, we will all have a lot to thank you for.' Arap smiled, like a pike in front of its prey.

The others nodded.

A new country would emerge, Arap knew, when the crisis was over. Great changes had occurred the last time the plague devastated England. They would happen this time too. New leaders would be needed. And the changes at the very top in the UK would be mirrored elsewhere. The men in this room had plans for when the time came. Plans that would introduce a new system, without the ridiculous compassion of the past.

There could be no turning back now. Malach would tie up the loose ends in Istanbul with his usual precision and soon nobody would care about a few people losing their lives. Access to a working vaccine would be all that people cared about. He took the box of white vials from his satchel and began handing them around.

'Your oaths of silence will soon be rewarded,' he said.

'The change is finally coming.'

22

'Shouldn't we be going?'

It was five after three. The lunch plates hadn't even been cleared yet. The salads had been delicious, lemony and sweet, but all I'd done was pick at mine. Peter was acting as if this was a normal day.

I looked at my watch.

'You are such a worrier.' Peter smirked.

I wanted to shout at him. But I didn't. It would probably have amused him.

'Do remember, if you feel you want to, at any time, you can always go home.'

'You wish. I don't run away that easy.'

A few minutes later he stood up, motioned for me to follow him.

We climbed in the back of the Range Rover parked in front of Peter's house. There were two men dressed like tourists, wearing flowery shirts and brightly-coloured shorts in the front seats. A shiny sat nav screen glowed on the console serving the back seats.

I leaned against a leather armrest. The vehicle was similar to the one Isabel had driven, but better equipped. On the front it had a large bull bar, which extended about a foot above the hood line.

'We're going to stick out like an elephant at a wedding in this,' I said.

'Not a bit. A lot of locals drive these as soon as they can afford them. You'd be surprised who likes these.'

'Are you going to put a British flag on each corner?'

Peter ignored me. He exchanged some indecipherable comments with the men in front. Then he turned back to me.

'There's been a demonstration in Taksim Square against the mosque raids in Europe. Nothing to bother us, though. We'll be going in another way.'

'Great.' I felt calm, ready for anything.

Peter was looking at me funnily, as if he thought I wasn't taking the demonstrations seriously enough.

'You do know what happened in London last Saturday?' he said.

'I couldn't have been closer to it.'

His gaze flickered as if being anywhere near that riot implicated me in some way.

'Bastards ruined my night,' I said.

We sat in silence as we crossed a wide bridge over the Golden Horn. There were long banners on the railings on each side welcoming us to Istanbul in English, German and French. Similar banners hung from lampposts.

'What's with all the banners?' I said.

'Turkey loves its tourists,' said Peter.

The people on the streets seemed poorer in this older part of the city. I scanned faces. Many were permanently grooved with wrinkles from the sun.

'Nearly there,' said Peter. He peered at the sat nav system. It showed a 3D map of our location, the buildings boxy and yellow on each side of the street. A tiny red dot was blinking in the middle of the screen.

'We can track anything with this,' he said smugly, pointing at the sat nav. The red dot was moving. He pressed one of the keys. The dot became a block of pixels as we zoomed in. The pixels became the black roof of our Range Rover.

I could see people moving around the car. The image was clearer than any commercial sat nav system I'd ever seen.

'This city is bursting at the seams,' he said. 'I swear you can feel the explosion of the worldwide Muslim population through this city, as if it was a pulse point. You know Istanbul has a larger influx of immigrants each year now than New York?'

I didn't say anything. Some people thought I'd end up hating Islam, after what had happened to Irene in Afghanistan, but I'd just ended up wanting to know more about it, to understand it.

I could see the dome and minarets of Hagia Sophia up ahead now. Clusters of tourists were making their way up the hill towards it, fanning themselves in the heat, looking pink, par-boiled. Shops selling carpets, blue-patterned tiles, post-cards and sweating Turk Kola bottles lined the street. A high sun-bleached brick wall came into view. The road was cobbles now, so worn they were shiny. This part of Istanbul had a medieval feel, side streets zig-zagging between worn-out four-and-five-storey buildings, all leaning against each other, like rows of geriatrics lining up for a photo.

We turned into a steep narrow lane with restaurants and an art gallery. The outer wall of Topkapi Palace was on our left. It must have been at least forty foot high. It was made of bleached stones set in layers: first larger ones, boulders really; then long bricks; then more boulders; then a layer of shale; then bricks again; then a crenelated top. For almost four hundred years generation after generation of sultans had ruled most of the Muslim world from the palace beyond this wall.

We were at a junction with a side road to our right. The road ahead was blocked by two-foot-high white iron bollards. A security guard in a blue uniform with VP Security in white lettering above the breast pocket came towards us. Our driver rolled down his window and waved at him. The security guard waved back and moved the bollards so we could pass.

On the right side of the lane there was a white iron railing set into a low wall. Beyond it loomed massive stone piers reaching towards the sky, the back shoulders of Hagia Sophia.

On our left there was a row of three-storey houses all of the same style, reminiscent of clapboard houses in America. I caught a glimpse of an ash-coloured dome, surmounted by a spike with a golden crescent on top. It looked like a jewelled cocktail stick coming out the top of a faded cherry. It was Hagia Eirene.

I looked at my watch. 3:45 PM. We had fifteen minutes to get to the other side of Hagia Eirene. Plenty of time. As long as the gates through the walls of Topkapi Palace were open.

The gateway we need to go through was the Bab-i Humayun, the Imperial Gate. It was constructed by Mehmed the Conqueror six years after he conquered the city. It had a large Arabic-script panel above its arched entrance, and it jutted out from the palace wall in a gatehouse block that was as deep as it was tall. The heads of those who defied the sultan used to be displayed there, to discourage rebellion.

When we arrived at the gate, an ultra-modern bus was plugging the entrance, like a bread roll stuck in the jaws of an over-eager dog. We were losing precious time.

We were hoping to follow the bus through the gateway. But it didn't move. This was bad news.

'Let's see what's happening on the other side,' said Peter, tapping at the sat nav screen. 'This gate isn't supposed to be used by buses. But it is wide enough for them to get through. I've seen them do it. We shouldn't be here long.'

The sat nav screen showed the front part of the bus poking through the gate, and the tree-filled open area beyond where people were milling about.

Peter tapped at the screen again and dragged his finger across it. The image we were watching, of spindly treetops and white paths moved to the right, then forwards. The dun-tiled roof of a building appeared. The building moved down the screen. I saw a courtyard and immediately recognised the entrance to the Laboratory for Conservation and Restoration that I'd visited that morning. It was getting very close to 4:00 PM.

'There's gotta be another way in,' I said. 'That courtyard's only two minutes from here.' I needed to see those people, to verify what Bulent had told me with my own eyes.

'Don't panic,' said Peter. 'You won't miss anything.'

Now knots of unhappy tourists were milling nearby too. Not only could no vehicles get through the gate into Topkapi Palace, pedestrian traffic, which used the same arch, was blocked too.

'Why the hell are they going in that way?' I asked no one in particular.

'Perhaps we should go round to another gate,' said Peter calmly.

'Christ, you could have damn well suggested that five minutes ago. We've probably missed them now.'

'I don't think so.' He jabbed a finger at the screen. 'They can't hide from this. The weather in Istanbul makes real-time satellite surveillance easy. Believe me, I can track every beggar their PM gives alms to after visiting his mosque on a Friday if I want to.'

I didn't feel comforted by his little speech.

'Hold on,' said Peter. 'Look at them. I'll bet that's our lot.'

Two small dark shapes, like planets with rings, were moving on the sat nav screen. They were crossing the courtyard, and had come from one corner, exactly as Bulent had described. Each of them seemed to be carrying something.

These had to be the bastards we were waiting for. And I'd missed them.

'This is a total disaster,' I said.

'Not yet,' replied Peter confidently.

He tapped at the screen, moved the cursor that appeared with the tip of his finger and tapped one of the shapes. The screen focused on the slowly moving object.

Then the image was obscured by what looked like the tops of trees, but after a moment's hesitation it continued tracking the object as it moved.

'They're the people we're looking for,' said Peter.

He tapped the screen again. It zoomed in on the shapes. My mouth was dry. The coldness in my stomach had returned and was hardening into a ball. The hair on my arms were standing up. The shapes on the screen were clearer now.

I could distinguish shoulders. Were those dust-coloured overalls they were wearing?

Whoever they were, they were heading along the path that led directly towards the gate we were stuck at. They were coming towards us! Would they wait, pass close to us when the bus eventually got moving? I glanced at it, willing it to move.

'Pull out,' said Peter abruptly. 'That way.' He pointed to the right.

Our driver, whose head was smooth and pink and almost bald, manoeuvred us with a jerk towards the road that ran alongside the high stone wall of Topkapi Palace and down towards the Bosphorus. A silken sheen of blue water sparkled in the distance.

'Where are we going?' I said. I peered at the sat nav. Suddenly I knew why we were moving. The two people we were tracking were heading down a tree-lined road. They were heading away from the blocked main gate, moving parallel to us, but on the other side of the Topkapi Palace wall.

But we were moving slower than them. The cars ahead of us were inching along. Then, about a hundred yards on, we stopped at a junction. The traffic was ridiculous.

Peter was sitting back, almost uninterested now. Our air conditioning seemed to be struggling to cope. From the street I heard a shout. We stopped again.

I could feel my frustration getting to me. Peter was so laid-back, not only about following these bastards, but about everything.

We moved forward another inch.

'You don't give a damn about what's just happened, do you?' I said.

He looked at me, his disdain barely disguised. 'That's not true.'

'These guys could be anyone.' I pointed at the screen, trying to keep my voice even.

'Let's just follow them and see where they're going.' He tapped a button on the side of the sat nav. The resolution on the screen improved. Then the image broke into blocky digital squares before becoming smooth again.

We watched as the pair turned left into a bus park with white-roofed buses in one corner, like dead larvae lined up in a row. The men passed though the bus park and continued down another tree-lined avenue. Did Peter have people on the ground inside that part of Topkapi waiting for them? Was that why he was so nonchalant?

We reached the bottom of the hill where we had to wait in line at a T-junction that led onto a dual carriageway. It ran alongside the Bosphorus, glittering in front of us. Peter instructed our driver to turn left, towards the Golden Horn. It amazed me how bored he sounded.

Then the sat nav screen went blocky again. Peter pressed a button on the bottom edge.

The screen went completely blank.

I raised my hands in disbelief. 'We're going to lose them!'

Peter pressed another button on the sat nav. The screen stayed dead.

Then he pressed a third button on the top. The screen lit up with a menu. It took him over a minute to refocus the screen on the bus park. By that time, there was no sign of the two men. We'd lost them and we were still stuck in traffic.

'Sorry,' he muttered. He didn't seem one frigging bit sorry.

I sat back, my fist pressed against the door. The Range Rover inched forward again, then stopped.

'You should throw that system in the garbage.'

'We're following up on a lot of leads regarding your colleague's death. This is only one of them, Sean. You need to be patient. It's no good getting emotional. We can't go rushing around like headless idiots.' He paused, then continued more slowly, as if he wanted to drive home a point. 'Why don't you go back to London? This really isn't your business any more. I'll keep you informed, I promise.'

I gripped the door handle.

'Don't promise,' I said. 'I've heard too many promises.' The driver looked at Peter in the rear-view mirror. His hand was moving towards a button on the dash.

I knew what was going on. They were going to detain me, maybe take me straight to the airport, send me back to London. I yanked at my door handle. It moved. The door opened. I heard a click. Just in time.

Peter looked at me disdainfully.

'Where do you think you're going?' he said. He reached towards me.

I pushed his hand away roughly. His expression changed. I'd done two years of martial arts in college. I was rusty, but I knew what to do. The most important thing was to move fast. It wasn't rocket science; you just had to take your chances. And this was mine. The car wasn't moving.

I rolled sideways, pushed the door open, jumped out of the Range Rover. A wall of roasting air hit me

I raced around the truck that stood right next to us and ran for an alley. When I reached the end of it, I glanced back, my heart pumping all the way up into my neck. The guy who'd sat quietly next to Peter's driver, observing everything, was in the alley coming after me fast. I wasn't that far ahead of him, but a surge of confidence shot through me. If there was one thing I was good at, it was running.

I turned to the right, crossed a road and sprinted into another alley. It was a long one. I put my head down, ran, then crossed over to the next alley. Someone shouted at me in Turkish. A car horn beeped. I ran on. At the next junction I turned, stopped running, crossed the road and walked straight into a café.

It was busy. A waiter was handing out plates of food. He looked at me, then looked away when I nodded at him, as if I knew him. I walked to the back, then into a corridor, praying that I'd find a toilet there.

I did – it was clean, of the old-fashioned French variety with just a hole in the floor.

Unfortunately, the window in the toilet was too small to climb out of. Bad luck. I went back into the red wallpapered corridor and walked to the door at the end. I thought I heard a noise from the other side – perhaps this door led to the kitchen?

I reached for the handle and turned it, but it was locked. I looked back along the corridor. My pursuer hadn't arrived, but it was probably only a matter of seconds before he was outside. The thumping in my chest became insistent.

I knocked on the door loudly. No one came. I knocked even louder. One thing I was sure of: I was being jerked around by Peter. He'd probably turned that sat nav system off deliberately.

Well, I'd had enough.

I heard a banging noise, a pot falling maybe. Then the door opened. An old woman, built like a chunk of iron, but with a friendly face eyed me suspiciously.

'Hi,' I said. I motioned to move past her. She shook her head firmly. I put my hands together as if I was praying.

Her eyes widened. Then her gaze flickered over my shoulder. I reached for my wallet. She waved fast, indicating that she didn't want money. Then she opened the door wider and stepped aside.

'Thank you,' I said.

Beyond the door, there was a small kitchen with shiny pots and pans hanging from the ceiling. She was the only person in the kitchen. A radio played jangly Turkish music. I could smell spices, the aroma of cooking.

The room was dominated by a long steel table, on which

a pile of onions sat waiting, half chopped. I went around the table and headed for the door beyond.

I stepped out into a narrow rutted lane. Houses backed onto it. At intervals in each direction, streets cut across the lane. I didn't run. I walked fast. I turned at the first junction, my heart slowing in my chest at last. To hell with Peter and his stupid games. He didn't give a damn about what had happened to Alek, about finding out who'd killed him. I knew what I had to do.

I had to talk to Bulent again.

I used the lanes and side streets to make my way back to Hagia Sophia. It was seriously hot, even in the shade. The sun was a furnace in the sky. I had to stop to buy water. I splashed half the bottle on my face, my head.

When I arrived back at the gate into Topkapi, the bus that had been blocking the way was gone, but no one was going through the gate. Its three-storey high iron-studded wooden doors were closed. Topkapi was closed and it was only four thirty. I hurried around to the front of Hagia Sophia, a two-minute walk away. When I reached the main entrance it was closed too. No late opening for museums in this part of the world

I waited by a busy stand selling guidebooks near the main entranceway to Hagia Sophia. Mottled, sick-looking pigeons squawked around, fighting for crumbs.

I watched the stragglers coming out of Hagia Sophia. I knew Bulent might still be in there.

And even if I didn't catch him now, I'd come back in the morning. One way or the other, I'd find him.

I stood. Someone who looked just like Bulent was walking across the street about fifty feet away, by the tram tracks. I walked towards him, squinting, with the sun in my face, trying to check if it was him.

166

It wasn't. I turned away in disgust, found a bench in the shade that allowed me a clear view of Hagia Sophia. I was keeping an eye out for Peter's Range Rover too. If I saw it I'd have to move fast. God only knew what kind of stunt he'd try next.

The minutes crept by. The number of tourists had dwindled now. The street vendors were packing up. I bought a few postcards from a persistent boy. I felt briefly like a tourist.

And then I saw Bulent driving past.

I put up my hand.

He recognised me, waved and drove on.

23

'Did you know that the young Count Dracula visited this city before it fell?' asked Malach.

The doctor shook his head, straining at his gag. His hair was wet with sweat. He was trembling. His gaze was fixed on the long black-handled knife in Malach's hand.

'A Serbian legend says the Count learned his tricks here. The Byzantines were renowned for their cruelty to prisoners in the years before the city fell. Skinning spies alive was one of their specialities.' He put the edge of his knife close to the doctor's cheek. The doctor flinched. A vein pulsed in his forehead.

'I studied his technique for skinning victims. He always started at the neck, to allow the skin to be removed almost completely from the body, while the face remained untouched.'

The doctor was trembling uncontrollably now. They were parked in a truck in a tiny unmanned car park behind the main street of the Istanbul suburb of Bebek. The Bosphorus was only a few hundred metres away, as were the busy restaurants and shops that lined the main Bebek drag.

'We have a job for you, but before we start, I want to make sure you know the penalty for making trouble. You understand?'

The doctor nodded, eagerly. Then he was crying. Not loudly, quietly.

24

Bulent was driving a dirty green Renault Espace, one of those older models with the big bumpers. The car was badly in need of a wash. I ran straight after it.

A dog barked madly. People turned and stared. I pounded on. The beggar boy I'd bought the postcards from ran after me. I had no idea why.

Then he whistled. The sound that came from his mouth could have penetrated steel.

I shouted 'Bulent!' as loud as I could.

The whistling and the shouting must have made him look in his rear-view mirror.

He stopped, then reversed to meet me. The boy had his hand out and a big smile on his face, as if we'd won a medal.

'Give him nothing, Mr Ryan, *bey*,' said Bulent, from his half open door. He called the boy over and passed him something. The boy looked disappointed. Bulent made an exasperated noise. The boy ran back to me with his hands outstretched. I gave him the smallest Turkish note I could find in my wallet. He ran off gleefully. Bulent's face was a picture of disapproval.

'Boys like that make more money in the summer than is good for them, Mr Ryan. Now how can I help you? I have no more information to give you. I have told you that already.'

'We have to talk. There's something crazy going on. And I'm

169

going to keep coming back until you see me.' It must have been the tone of my voice that convinced him. I wasn't angry, just determined.

He looked around, then told me to get in the car. Ten minutes later we were in the basement of a restaurant near the Grand Bazaar. Outside, above our heads, the narrow street was packed with people, like a down-at-heel cinema audience shuffling its way out of an auditorium. I'd never seen such a narrow street so jammed.

The elaborate gold arched entrance to the Grand Bazaar, the greatest bazaar in the whole world, so Bulent said, the forerunner of all our modern shopping malls, was only a few yards up the street. All I'd seen of it though was a blue-tiled tunnel of shops, and sacks of multicoloured spices outside the nearest one.

Below ground, where we were, a fan languidly stirred the air above our heads. It wasn't very effective, but I was still grateful for it.

'This place is owned by Armenians. It's quiet at this time of the day, but it won't be for long,' said Bulent, as we eased ourselves into the high-backed wooden chairs around a table in a corner of the room. Aside from us, the room was empty. Bulent did not look happy.

A waiter poked his head down the stairs. Bulent snapped at him, '*Iki* Nescafé.'

'Why don't you give up with this?' he said, turning to me. 'Your friend is dead.'

'My father told me never to give up. It was one of the last things he ever said to me.' It was true. It had been a few weeks before he'd died, but I'd never forgotten his words.

'My father is dead too,' he said, softly.

The yellow light bulbs hanging in brown plastic shades from the ceiling, and the ancient nicotine-coloured walls, gave the place an old-fashioned feel, as if we were spies in some cold war movie. The muffled footfall of passers-by and the occasional cries of street vendors could be heard above our heads.

He put his hands on the table, as if the place was his personal office. 'OK, so what's so important you have to see me again?'

'You've helped me, Bulent, and I'm grateful, but I need to know who's running those excavations under Hagia Eirene. I have to find out before I can go back to London.' I paused, took a deep breath, then continued, 'And I will find out.'

His face remained impassive.

'And I'll go as soon as I find out. This is one last favour, that's all. What harm could it do?'

'What harm?' asked Bulent, sharply. 'I think Alek would know about that.' He looked at the stairs, as if he was expecting a troop of terrorists to come marching down any moment.

'You know nothing, *effendi*. Nothing about how difficult it is to operate while being watched. Nothing about the people who want Hagia Sophia to be a grand mosque again. Nothing about the others who want concerts there, like they have in Hagia Eirene, but bigger. Can you believe it?' His rolled his eyes. 'They have a Wagner concert there tonight. Some people think we're going to have Wagner in Hagia Sophia soon, or maybe a concert of Christian carols? Can you imagine?'

I waited. He stared glumly at the chequered red-and-white tablecloth. It was faded, but clean.

'All I need is a name, an address, an organisation, Bulent. Something I can go back to London with.'

He shook his head emphatically. We sat looking at each other, playing who-blinks-first-loses.

'If you want the dig to stop you should tell me. I know people in UNESCO. I can find out if they have all the right approvals for the work they're doing. If they don't, it can be exposed. Somebody has to protect Turkey's heritage, Bulent, find out if they're a bunch of crooks.'

We listened as a street seller above our heads called out in a sing-song voice. Finally, he spoke.

'I will do this for my country,' he said, while pointing a finger at me. 'Because these are our sites.' He paused, rubbed his forehead. 'Have you been to Büyükada?'

'No, where is it?'

'Büyükada is one of the Princes' Islands in the Sea of Marmara. It's only twenty miles from Istanbul, forty minutes on one of our ferries. Byzantine emperors and princes used to be exiled there. Sometimes, after their eyes had been gouged out.' His face was impassive, his cheeks pink and glistening.

'Not much of a retirement.'

'It was worse than that for some.'

'Rough justice.'

He leaned back in his chair. He looked every inch a professor about to give a lecture.

'Yes, and I'll tell you a story. The year before Islam first took Jerusalem, 638 by your calendar, Atalarichos, a son of the Byzantine Emperor Heraclius, predicted his father was going to let Islam take Jerusalem, and that Christ could not return if that happened. For saying that, his eyes were gouged out, and his limbs cut off. Afterwards, Jerusalem was taken by the Prophet's army, just as he'd said.'

'How did he know Jerusalem was going to fall?'

'Maybe it was planned, as he said, or maybe Heraclius underestimated his enemies. His son certainly did. After we

172

took Istanbul in 1453, the Princes' Islands became a refuge for Greeks, Jews and Armenians. These days it's a suburb of Istanbul, and not its furthest point.' Bulent downed his coffee.

'Ask for the Villa Napoleon. The people who work under Hagia Eirene take everything they find there. That's all I know. I do not know their names.'

'How did you find this out?'

He looked around. 'I saw the papers for their application to investigate under Hagia Eirene. I was asked for my opinion. Can you believe it?' He shook his head, sorrowfully. 'I said it shouldn't be allowed, but who listens to an old man?'

If the people working under Hagia Eirene were based at the Villa Napoleon, I could go there, see what I could find out, discreetly. Then I could put in a request to UNESCO to see who these people were, if they were approved for this type of project.

Was I getting close to uncovering what had happened to Alek? It certainly felt like it.

'The villa was a gift from the French government, Mr Ryan, but the Ottomans never took possession of it. Monsieur Napoleon stepped on too many Ottoman feet, I mean, toes.'

'Thanks, Bulent, I mean it. You won't regret this.'

It crossed my mind I might be proved wrong about that, but I dismissed the thought.

A few minutes later we left the restaurant. Soon after, I was in a taxi.

As it barged its way through the streets heading down to the Golden Horn, I felt a sense of expectation. What would I find on Büyükada?

We passed through a narrow street and I saw an old man sitting on a step in a suit that looked like it belonged in the fifties.

He had white bathroom scales, of similar vintage, in front of him. Was he weighing people for money? If he was, he didn't have a lot of customers. But he continued to sit there, with a morose look on his face, as if he had no other choice.

Some of the buildings around us looked five hundred years old at least, and so beyond renovation that they would either have to be torn down or converted into museums.

This part of Istanbul was an ancient warren. I opened the window of the taxi. The air conditioning was useless. The smell of fresh bread and a heavy windless heat greeted me. Even the slightest breeze was a blessing here.

Bulent had told me it would be easy to find somewhere to stay once I got to Büyükada. Apparently there were lots of small hotels there. I would stay the night, find out what I could and come back to Istanbul the next morning.

My taxi pulled into a feeding frenzy of vehicles beside the slapping waters of the Golden Horn. 'Büyükada, Büyükada,' said the driver, pointing at a two-storey red catamaran that was out at sea, but heading towards us. All around people were hurrying towards a pale cream Ottoman-era ticket hall with a tiled roof that sat at the entrance to the short jetty. I paid the driver.

When I reached the ticket window I offered the man behind it one of my Turkish notes.

I didn't understand what he said, so I just smiled in answer to his questions and hoped he didn't take that as an agreement to purchase a season ticket.

The people in the queue behind me were getting restless. The ferry was sounding its whistle, as if it was about to depart. The ticket seller passed me back a ticket and some coins.

Fifteen minutes later I was seated in a brightly-lit indoor cabin, like an ultra-wide airplane. The rows of seats all faced forward, fourteen abreast, and there were two narrow aisles, one on each side. The windows, scratched oval portholes, were sealed.

Through the glass of a porthole, I watched flecks of phosphorescence flashing by on the surface of the purple sea. In the distance, twinkling lights covered the long ridge of hills on the Asian shore of the Bosphorus.

Though the ferry was far from full, there was a great chatter, people smiling, going home after a day out in Istanbul. I was a zillion miles away from roadside bombs and beheadings.

Two hours after that I was sitting in a café awash with light. Its location, at the bottom of the tree-lined street on which the Villa Napoleon stood, made it the perfect place to enjoy a beer and keep an eye on the villa. I'd picked a table outside. Most of the patrons of the café were inside, so it didn't take much effort to ensure I got a seat facing the long pink brick wall that extended from the front of the villa all the way down the steep street to the café.

In the previous hour, I'd booked a room at a tiny run-down hotel a block away, and after receiving directions to the villa, I'd walked all the way round the rectangular block it dominated, until I'd found this café. Shadows were lengthening and people were emerging from their houses as I passed. The wooden verandas and the creeping swathes of pink honeysuckle and drifts of purple wisteria on some of the houses gave the place the feel of a nineteenth-century holiday town. I could smell the tingle of ozone from the sea too.

All I'd seen of the villa so far was a glimpse of its ochre-tiled roof, as the brick wall that surrounded it must have been twenty feet high.

Horse-drawn buggies, phaetons, that was what a leaflet from the reception of my hotel called them, jingled along the street every few minutes. The leaflet claimed that no cars were allowed on the island. The only other noises were the occasional tinkling of cutlery, and a low murmur of voices emerging from the open door of the café.

Jasmine and wisteria peeked over the brick wall opposite and further up the street. In one garden I'd glimpsed tall pine trees and apple and apricot trees heavy with fruit. A tendril-like sea breeze gave welcome, if intermittent, relief from the evening heat.

I took a sip of my beer. Maybe it was time to contact Isabel again, find out what her excuse was for not turning up this morning.

I stood up and looked inside the café. There was an old public telephone on one wall. I went in, rang the Consulate number from the card Isabel had given me. After waiting for what seemed like ages, a woman with a north of England accent answered. She couldn't tell me anything about Isabel, or whether she'd picked up her messages at all, but she did promise to leave her another message for me. I told her to simply tell Isabel that I'd rung. I walked back to my seat.

The café was full of families with parents and their children playing around the tables. Near the back, an olive-skinned girl with a mane of sun-bleached hair was laughing. There was something idyllic about the place.

In the previous two years, I'd always thought of Irene in situations like this and sadness would come over me, which I'd battled against. But that night it didn't happen. So much had been going on.

I caught a reflection of myself in the mirror at the back of the café. My shirt collar was up and I clearly hadn't shaven in far too long. I looked a lot rougher than I'd imagined.

I ordered another beer. Perhaps I'd eat soon, ask the waiter about the villa. Somebody was sure to know something about the place.

The TV, high up on a shelf in the far corner of the café, was switched to a news channel. As I stared at it, the newscaster was replaced by an image of St Paul's. Then a video of the crowd rioting on Oxford Street played for a few seconds. The camera lingered on smashed shop fronts. The implication was clear. Something might happen at the demonstration planned for St Paul's.

The distant clatter of a helicopter intruded on my thoughts. It grew louder, as if it was heading in my direction. I scanned the sky and saw only faint stars.

Then the racket grew louder. My paper napkins flew across the table. Suddenly, flashing red and white lights appeared, no more than a hundred feet in the air. The helicopter was coming down. And it was heading for the villa.

A waiter came out of the restaurant to see if I needed anything. He raised his eyes heavenward and shook his head resignedly as the noise slowly faded.

Did the helicopter have something to do with the people who were digging under Hagia Eirene? If it did, they were certainly well funded.

But why all the secrecy about the dig? The possibility that they were Greeks, looking for the 'blessed' Labarum of Constantine, as Father Gregory had called it, couldn't be discounted. It would be a sensational find. And it was something Alek would definitely have been interested in. Knowledge of the banner's whereabouts had been snuffed out when the Ottomans stormed Constantinople in 1453.

Hundreds of monks had died as Ottoman soldiers, fired

up by danger and tales of hidden wealth, had pillaged the city. All the monks with knowledge of the Labarum's whereabouts could easily have been killed in the slaughter. Was this why Alek had been murdered, because he'd stumbled on a group searching for the Labarum?

But if that was the case, why were jihadists filmed beheading him and why had the video been released onto the internet?

It was raining. At first, it was only a few drops. Then it became intense. Water was soon rushing down the gutters and bouncing off the thick canopy above my head. Thunder crashed. A huge crack of lightning split the sky. I shifted my seat further under the canopy, away from the rain, and watched it pour.

I thought about the secret dig. If underground tunnels, like the one in Alek's picture, existed under Hagia Eirene, they might have been a hiding place used by the Orthodox clergy or by the Byzantine ruling families when the city fell. And maybe there was more than the Labarum down there. Maybe there were a lot of other treasures down there.

When the Turks rushed the gaps in the landward walls created by the largest cannon then in existence, on that fateful Tuesday, May 29th 1453, some of the greatest treasures of Christianity were gathered in Hagia Sophia. They were used in the last Christian ceremony ever held there, in front of thousands of monks and devout citizens, all praying for a miracle.

What treasures had been gathered in Hagia Sophia? The list was long. Sacred icons that had protected the city many times, fragments from the true cross, the lance that had pierced Christ's side, many of the earliest books of the Bible.

The Orthodox hierarchy would surely have known that most Christian artefacts would be destroyed as the city was captured. But what had happened to them? If something like the Labarum had escaped the city, someone would have spoken about it, announced its arrival wherever it had gone. No, there was a good chance that some of these treasures were still here, in Istanbul.

So what would happen if long-revered Christian treasures suddenly reappeared?

The arguments would begin, that was for sure. If the Labarum reappeared, Catholics and Orthodox Christians would both claim it.

Others would say the Labarum had been lost because of the wickedness of the unreformed churches. Some would, most likely, claim its reappearance was a sign that God was on the side of Christianity, as it had returned when the conflict with Islam was reaching a head again. They'd say it had mystical powers.

There were a heck of a lot of reasons for keeping the reappearance of long-lost sacred artefacts secret.

A tall magnolia tree with shiny leaves and creamy flowers stood at the side of the road where the wall of the villa began. Beside it there was an entrance to a small lane. Rainwater was rushing from the lane and cascading into the street.

I watched it. Then, out of the corner of my eye, I saw something that made me forget everything else.

25

'Only two days to go and they're late. Unbelievable,' said Arap Anach, under his breath. He pushed his coffee cup away. It rattled, almost fell over. The Turkish coffee was too sweet and too strong for his taste, but the café belonging to the Syrian exile had few other options. It wasn't even officially open that evening. He slapped at a fly that had been circling the cracked sugar bowl. He hit it. It fell to the table. He swept it away.

Arap looked through the door to the street beyond. The yellowing blinds were pulled down halfway. He exhaled hard in a low growl. There was no one in the room to hear him. The owner was in the back somewhere. He was unlikely to appear again.

When the door to the street finally creaked open a few minutes later, his smile lasted no longer than a millisecond. The two young Arab men passed the rows of plastic tables and chairs and stood opposite him. Both looked like diligent university students in their jeans and long white collarless shirts.

Arap Anach stood and bowed. '*Salaam aleikum*,' he said. Peace be with you.

'*Aleikum salaam*,' they replied. And also with you.

Arap sat and reached down to the black plastic shopping bag he'd brought with him. He pulled out two bricks of English currency. The two men sat, glanced at the money and then looked away as if they weren't that interested in it. But their faces, pink with anticipation, gave them away. It was unlikely they'd ever seen so much money at one time before. It was also unlikely they'd ever imagined getting it could be so easy.

Hatred is such a simple thing to harness.

'Distribute it wisely, *effendi*. Make sure that many of our brothers and sisters join the demonstration on Friday. I told you I would pay for their tickets and I am a man of my word. Soon the flag of Islam will fly over England.' He bent forward, for the important bit. 'If you keep your vows.'

They nodded eagerly. Each of them picked up a brick of money. One man's hand trembled slightly.

Arap smiled thinly.

'When you leave, go in different directions.' He bowed, kept his eyes closed. They were devout, these men – that was their strength – but he was about to use it against them.

This payoff, and his recent recruit, an insider in the British security services, were the final pieces of the puzzle.

There was no way this plan could be stopped now.

26

I waved, then rose from my seat.

Isabel was walking towards me with her head down. She was holding a black umbrella above her head. It was half shielding her face, but there was no doubt it was her. She'd emerged from that lane halfway up the hill in a rush. She'd pass by on the other side of the street in seconds if I didn't attract her attention. I put a few Turkish notes under my glass and ducked out from under the awning.

Within seconds I was drenched.

And then, for a moment, I thought I was mistaken, that it wasn't Isabel, but as she came nearer I knew I'd been right. But what was she doing here? She owed me an explanation, at the very least.

The rain was beating down on me but I didn't care.

When she was a few feet away she looked up and gave me a wide amazed smile.

'What are you doing here, Sean?' She stopped in front of me.

'Enjoying the weather. Lovely, isn't it? What happened to you this morning? Sleep late, did you?'

'Didn't Peter tell you?'

I should have guessed. She seemed genuinely disappointed that I hadn't been told too. Either that or she was an Oscar class actor.

'Peter said I should go back to London.' I put my hand up to shield my face.

Her hair was tied up. She had two big black pins sticking through it at the back. They looked like antennae.

She moved her umbrella so it partly covered me. 'I told him to tell you to go on. That something came up.'

'That's it?'

She stared at me, pursing her lips as if she was deciding something.

'I still have other work to do, Sean.'

I put my hands up. 'OK, OK. But why didn't Peter tell me? He had lots of opportunities.'

She looked pained. 'I don't know, honestly. Peter is a law unto himself. I'm sure his intentions were good. I spoke to him only a little while ago. He told me you asked about me. He's concerned about you, Sean. He told me you pushed him aside, ran off. What are you doing here?'

'Having a beer.'

She let out a sigh. 'Look, we're the good guys, Sean. Peter's off with the birds sometimes, but he's on your side. You shouldn't have run off.' She looked over her shoulder. 'Come on, walk with me. We can't stand here like idiots getting wet.' We walked down the hill, side by side in the rain.

'You know who's working under Hagia Eirene, don't you, and about Villa Napoleon?' I said. 'That's why you're here, isn't it?'

'I don't know what you're talking about, Sean.' She stopped at the top of a long flight of stone stairs. 'And please don't get paranoid. I'm trying to help you.'

'If you know who's working under Hagia Eirene, why don't the Turkish authorities raid the place? What are you covering up?'

'We're not covering anything up.' Her face was an inscrutable mask.

'Sure.'

She frowned. 'Sean please, put yourself in our shoes. We can't go around making accusations about people until we have evidence. And we can't believe every conspiracy theory we hear. We just can't. Otherwise we'd end up chasing our tails all day. Please, trust me.' She went down a step.

I didn't move. I had a funny feeling about this. And I didn't like being led by the nose.

She stopped, turned and came back up.

'What's wrong?'

'Where are you going?' I said.

'Back to Istanbul.'

'I've booked into a hotel here.'

'Do you actually want to die like Alek?' She looked in my eyes, as if she was searching for something. Her voice was softer now. 'Don't you understand why Peter keeps saying you should go back to London? Your life really is in danger.'

'I've booked in under a phony name. I'll be OK.'

'Trust me about this at least, Sean. No Westerner stays at a hotel on this island without everybody knowing about it. What's more important to you, the price of a room or your life? How do you think we knew you were here?'

I took a step back. She came towards me.

'Please Sean, you're compromising a surveillance operation right now. If you stay here, you're going to make our job even harder. Is that what you want?'

'No.'

'Then come with me. There's something I want to show you. I was going to show it to Alek, but I never got the chance.' There

184

was a note of excitement in her voice, as if she really did have something interesting to show me.

'What is it?'

'Wait and see. I think you'll enjoy it.'

'It better be good.'

The ferry terminal building was jammed tight with waiting passengers when we arrived. They stared at us as we ran in dripping from the rain. Other stragglers, also soaked, were coming in behind us.

The rain was belting down like a storm of arrows now. Then a toot-toot sounded from a huge catamaran as it pulled up to the narrow jetty. People milled around, pushed forward as one. Although no one queued properly, the press to get on the boat was surprisingly orderly.

Within minutes everyone had boarded. Then, with a longer toot, we departed Büyükada.

'So what were you doing all day?' I said, turning to Isabel after we sat down.

'Looking for someone.' She pressed a finger delicately to her lips, then glanced over her shoulder. There were people sitting all around us.

She curled into her seat, her head almost touching my shoulder.

'I need to rest,' she said.

The catamaran bounced through the waves, heading for the far-off gloom that was the European shore of Istanbul. A thuddering passed through the ship constantly as if we were in a vibrating machine designed to extract badly-implanted fillings. The short twilight was long gone now, and the cabin was brightly-lit and sealed like a fluorescent tube. All around us people were stewing in their damp clothes.

After a while, after a particularly vicious wave, Isabel rose, went to a counter in a corner and returned with Turkish coffees. I noticed a woman at the end of the row staring at us. There were some other women in *chadors* and a few in *burqas* in a group near her.

'I didn't know they'd taken up the *chador* here,' I whispered.

'Those are tourists,' said Isabel. 'They come here from Iran and Saudi these days to cool off in the summer. The islands are a big draw.'

Nearby there was a young, bearded man in a plain white shirt talking into a phone. He'd been glancing at us every now and then.

Isabel followed my gaze, spotted the man.

'This is why Peter wants you to go back to London,' she said. 'You have no idea how complex it is here. We can't guarantee your protection.'

'I'll go back when I'm ready.'

'We honestly don't want to see what happened to Alek, happen to you, Sean.' She turned, looked out the window. There was a scar below her right ear, I noticed. How had she got that?

'You must have to deal with a lot of crazy situations,' I said.

'Too many to talk about.' She touched her forehead, then tucked her hair behind her ears.

'Have you worked out where Alek took those photos, Sean?'

'I thought you'd have figured that out by now. You probably have a hundred people working on it.'

She gave me a deadpan look, as if we were playing poker. 'Maybe we have, but I doubt it. There's been cutbacks.'

'Yeah, right.'

'Yeah.' She said it with a straight face. Then a smile flitted across her lips.

I hadn't held much back from Peter, only a few little things, like how I'd recognise the place where Bulent had taken Alek. I wasn't about to tell her about it yet though. The way she'd appeared out of nowhere was a bit weird. If I did tell her everything, and she told her boss, as she'd have to do, they might have me sent back to London in a diplomatic box with a few air holes in it. She mightn't even be able to stop them.

Peter would probably seal most of the holes himself after the way I'd pushed him aside.

As our ferry approached the dock at the entrance to the Golden Horn, the noise in the cabin grew louder as people called to each other and arranged bags and children. Then the muffled sound of the engines changed pitch and we swayed vigorously as our progress slowed and the waves shook us. The atmosphere in the cabin was expectant now.

'What a day this is turning out to be,' said Isabel. Then she stretched.

I looked out the window. The rain had stopped and the dock was bright because of arc lights set up on tall steel poles. There was a wall of faces jammed up against the fence that surrounded the dock waiting for people to arrive. And a throng of late commuters heading for this ferry could be seen through the long windows of the terminal building. The passengers were better dressed than most Istanbulers. Their clothes were more fashionable, their haircuts better, their handbags more designer store than market stall.

Isabel scanned the crowd, as if she was looking for someone. The people seated nearby moved into the aisle. Isabel stayed put.

'When are you going to tell me everything you've figured out?' she said.

'Maybe when you start doing the same.'

The cabin was nearly empty now – our fellow passengers had wasted no time in making their way out.

Isabel came close to me. 'Alek went off on a one-man-mission.' She gripped my arm. 'I just hope you're not planning to do the same.'

'I don't think the Turks would take too kindly to me poking around.'

'Peter said the same thing.' She looked concerned.

An announcement in Turkish blared out over the speakers high up on the walls of the cabin. Then, the same female voice announced in English, 'Last stop, please take all your belongings.'

As we came out of the cabin Isabel shivered under the thin black windcheater she was wearing. I still felt wet from the rain. My clothes were damp, only half dried. We must have looked like a couple of bedraggled refugees coming off the ferry.

We were the last two people to leave the catamaran, and as we stepped off the gangplank, Isabel scanned the dock.

'Dry land at last,' she said.

The squawking of hungry seagulls filled the air.

We were behind a group of waddling Turkish mothers herding some excited teenagers towards the terminal building. Isabel walked beside me.

'You must have been very close to Alek to care so much about what happened to him,' she said.

'We were close. And he certainly didn't deserve what happened to him.'

'There are usually taxis this way,' said Isabel, pointing to the right.

'Wait a second,' I said. I stopped, bent down to tie the laces on my brown suede loafers. The smell of fish was heavy in the air.

'Can we wait another minute for the crowd to go?' I said, looking up at her.

I never thought I'd have to use the stuff my dad had drilled into me, about how to defend yourself, how to deal with urban dangers, things he used to go on about until I was totally pissed with it all, but I was glad he had now.

'Watch out for crowds, was one piece of advice I remembered.

As I finished with my laces, an attendant opened a side gate and a stream of people rushed out onto the dock heading past us towards the ferry.

Isabel bent down. 'We're being watched,' she said.

'You think?'

'That guy from the ferry. You can't miss him. He's holding back, waiting for us.'

I didn't bother to look around. We had to get off the dock. I stood up, took Isabel's arm and guided her to the side gate the incoming passengers were coming through. Then I pushed past them. They looked irritated.

I kept smiling. The attendant on the other side of the gate shook his head, but let us through into the waiting area beyond. Moments later, we were exiting through a side door and heading for a group of taxis, their snouts pushing up against the brick walkway in front of the terminal.

'Let's go,' I said, as we sat in the back seat of a cramped yellow taxi.

Isabel said something in Turkish to the driver. He set off immediately. When I looked back I saw nothing unusual, just people milling about.

We changed taxis at Taksim Square, a vortex of cars, trucks and pedestrians coming from all directions. The square had one saving grace: a half dozen major arteries intersected there.

The honking flow of vehicles provided a perfect opportunity to lose anyone who might be following us.

'Wait and see,' said Isabel, when I asked her again where we were going, after we got out of the first cab.

'No English from now on,' she continued, as a cab pulled up the second she put her hand in the air.

We didn't talk again until we got out of the second taxi in a busy café-lined street, in a suburb I found out later was called Bebek. Isabel had given the driver directions in Turkish. It probably looked like we were sulking in the back, we were that quiet.

Each time we stopped at a traffic light, I had to resist looking around. I felt like a criminal who'd just broken out of jail and had to know if he'd made it to freedom.

The idea that people were actively looking for me, were out to kidnap or kill me, still seemed weird, but I couldn't ignore that it was true. What had happened in my hotel had been a lucky escape. I mightn't be that lucky the next time.

The upmarket Istanbul suburb of Bebek was on the European side of the Bosphorus, down the hill from Taksim Square but further east, out towards the Black Sea. It had a mixture of Ottoman-era buildings, restaurants, shops and modern apartment blocks. The main road through Bebek twisted along the shore of the Bosphorus like a snake.

Marinas and jetties jostled one another on its outskirts. The small bay that most of Bebek sits beside was lined with sleek powerboats and expensive yachts.

The taxi driver barely let me close the cab door before he shot away to find another fare.

'Back in a second,' said Isabel, ducking into a shop. She came out with a bag of fruit and asked me if I was hungry.

I took an apple. It was crunchy and juicy. She scanned the cars and people around us for a minute, then we moved off. We walked past a newly painted clapboard style hotel with people coming and going from it in smart outfits. Then we turned into a narrow alley. It ran up the hill behind Bebek. Other alleys branched off at regular intervals. This was where the older buildings of Bebek were. Ancient-looking doorways punctuated twenty-foot high walls on either side. The walls were crumbling in places.

We turned into a smaller, dark lane, then into a passageway, so shadowy in places, I could barely see where I was putting my feet. A weak street lamp halfway along provided just enough light to give us something to aim for. Above our heads, an occasional star glittered through a thin orange haze. The noise of the traffic was well behind us and fading fast, as if we were leaving the 21st century behind. I glanced back. This wasn't the sort of place I wanted to get cornered in.

'Where the hell are we going?'

'Trust me just a little, Sean, OK?'

She turned to me when she reached a doorway set at a lower level than the alley. Steep, rough narrow stone steps led down to it. Bunches of stone grapes, smoothed by time, barely visible in the half light, were set into the wall around the door. We were at a doorway to another age.

'We're here,' she announced. 'This is where an empress started work at the age of thirteen.'

'Doing what?'

'I bet you'll never guess.'

I looked around. A square of wooden planks covered part of the wall beside the door. Otherwise, the place looked unexceptional.

27

Doctor Osman bent over the girl. He was holding the front tail of his shirt over his mouth and nose. She was lying on a low steel bed, covered by a purple cotton sheet. The bed's faded yellow paintwork was badly chipped. The girl couldn't have been more than twenty. She was dark-skinned, looked Indian, and was wearing dark threads around her right wrist. Apart from that, she was naked.

Her symptoms were obvious. She had yellowish swellings all over her body and a black tongue, which made her look like she'd been sucking coal. She was sweating too, and her breath, which rasped, stank. That meant the delicate tissue of her lungs was dissolving. He'd seen enough.

The girl had some type of pneumonic plague, most likely, a truly virulent and feared airborne variety. And he knew what she needed. Urgently.

He turned to the man who'd brought him to the basement room.

'This woman must be taken to a hospital. At this stage she has a fifty percent chance of survival, no more, if we can get her treatment quickly. She'll die if we don't.'

The giant with the puckered skin and bald head blinked. Then he pulled out a finger-sized glass vial from a thin aluminium case from inside his pocket. He was wearing a white hospital mask.

'Take a sample from one of the pus sacs, doctor,' he said. His mask moved in and out as he spoke.

Doctor Osman saw the other item in the aluminium case. It was one of the permission forms he used when he needed to request a specimen test. The Florence Nightingale Hospital in Sisli, a twenty-minute drive away, where most of his tests were done, wouldn't accept the form without his signature. The sample would be tested for Yersinia pestis, the plague bacilli. Plague bacilli express a unique protein.

The difficult work would be identifying which family the bacilli from this case were from. The great fear among doctors who knew about these things, was that a natural mutation would emerge in the plague virus, which was resistant to all antibiotics. No one in their right minds would cultivate such a mutation. Or would they? He looked at the man holding the vial.

If someone wanted to, and God forbid they succeeded, they might even produce airborne bacilli that would be resistant to even the latest antibiotics. Such a virus would be unstoppable, unless you knew the pattern of mutation. People who weren't treated by someone who knew what they were dealing with would suffer from multiple organ failure. The only question would be how long they'd last, and which of their loved ones they'd infect before dying a painful and traumatic death, while bleeding from all orifices.

'Has she been taking antibiotics?'

'Do as I said. And sign the form.' The man lifted the edge of his jacket, exposing the black knife sheath under his armpit.

'This woman will die if she isn't treated,' said Dr Osman. Could he appeal to the man's humanity?

Malach pulled the knife out of its sheath. He held it up, stepped forward. The doctor put his hands up.

193

When he was finished, he placed the vial in the aluminium case and signed the request form. He noticed an unfamiliar email address – it was his name on the form, but the email address that the test report was to be delivered to wasn't his.

'How long will it take for her to die?' said Malach, as he put the case back in his jacket pocket.

'I don't know. I can't answer that. She needs treatment.'

The door of the room closed with a bang.

'You can't leave us down here,' the doctor shouted at the top of his voice. 'Come back!'

He was hoping someone else might hear him, but the resounding echo of his voice and the memory of the two flights of stairs they'd come down to reach the room made him certain that his efforts were in vain.

He heard a coughing sound and turned. Wine-dark blood was oozing from the girl's mouth. He backed away. That wasn't right. It was happening too quickly. This was a death sentence. His hand was at his mouth. It was shaking, violently.

28

Isabel bent down and pulled at a brick in the edge of the arched doorway. With a bit of wiggling it slid free. She put her hand inside the cavity, pulled out a shiny brass key, then put the brick back, stood, went down the stairs and inserted the key in the door. Then she stepped inside and reached for a light switch.

A single bulb came on. It was dangling on a thin white wire from the centre of a ceiling at least thirty feet above the floor. The bulb and wire looked totally out of place in what appeared to be the entrance hall to an ancient church.

Wall paintings, so stained they were almost totally blacked out, covered the walls and faded into shadow above our heads. The paintings had jagged pieces missing, but I could still make out thin figures standing – they looked like saints. The floor of the hall was made of black and white geometrically patterned tiles, which someone was restoring. Small stacks of tile pieces were stacked in a corner where the restoration work was still ongoing. There were seven wooden doors around us. All were closed.

'This is one of the oldest Byzantine buildings outside the original city walls of Constantinople,' said Isabel, as she closed the door behind us. 'It was part of a monastery before the conquest. After Mehmed conquered the city, it was closed down. During early Ottoman times the place was a storeroom. Amazingly these

Byzantine wall paintings were just plastered over. They were all there when we stripped the layers away.' She looked up at the walls, and turned slowly on her heel.

Faded paintings covered each wall. I could imagine what the hallway must have looked like a thousand years ago, when oil lamps and candles were all they had.

The hallway must have witnessed some amazing sights. Byzantine officers, clerics and merchants must have walked through it, all of them long dead now.

'I think we've lost anyone who was trying to follow us,' said Isabel. She was gazing up at the mosaics, as if she was still awed by them, no matter how often she came here.

'Very few people know about this place,' she said. 'Istanbul still has a lot of secrets.' Her voice echoed.

'It's incredible. Who owns this place?' I was expecting her to say some institution.

'A friend of mine. He's turning the building into an upmarket townhouse. He's persuaded me to do a bit of freelance work for him. I started restoring mosaics when I first came here. I needed something to keep me sane. I went on a course not far from here. I love this place. I always feel safe here.'

The six-inch thick wooden door we'd come through certainly looked as if it could hold back an army.

'And we've discovered a layer to this building that blew our minds.'

'What layer?'

'We found this phallic symbol etched into the wall outside. It was covered in layers of plaster and a layer of brick, but when all that came off it was as clear as day.'

'That's what they found at Pompeii, isn't it? Doesn't that mean there was a brothel here?'

She nodded. 'And it gets more amazing. This guy called Procopius wrote a secret history of the Empress Theodora, the wife of Justinian the Great, the guy who commissioned Hagia Sophia.'

'So,' I said, 'what are you saying?' I'd read about Theodora's reputation.

'Procopius claimed that Theodora started out as a low-class prostitute who danced naked in a brothel for all to see.' She was still turning, looking at the walls around us as she spoke.

'He even named the brothel she worked in. It was called the Lair of the She Wolf Number VII. They all had numbers back then, licences too.'

I felt an odd sensation, as if the layers of the saints' paintings around me were coming off and I could see licentious paintings and a hall full of customers and prostitutes.

'You're not going to tell me you've discovered Theodora's brothel.'

She nodded. 'That's what we think. Above the phallic symbol there's an image of a she wolf etched into the wall with the number VII beside it. It couldn't mean anything else.'

'I can't argue with you.'

'They say Theodora started by servicing fishermen and sailors living outside the city, that she moved on to aristocrats who didn't want to be seen in the brothels in central Constantinople. In the end, she caught the eye of the young Justinian. She ended up saving his imperial crown too, when the Nike rioters tried to overthrow him. She ordered his general to slaughter them all.'

'Why did they call brothels the lairs of the she wolf?'

'Some say it's because she wolves are rapacious, others say that a good she wolf can lick you all over.'

'I see.'

'Procopius says she turned all the brothels in Constantinople into monasteries near the end of her life. She died in 548. That was probably when this building was turned into a monastery.'

She moved to a large arched doorway to our left and went through it. I followed her up a tightly-winding stone-flagged staircase. Its walls were covered in faded ochre and indigo geometric shapes.

'I've never seen patterns like this,' I said.

Isabel didn't answer. The air around us was heavy, thick with a damp, musty smell. I could hear the distant sound of a car horn beeping, then a squeal of tyres, but the noises were muted. The modern world was being kept in the distance here.

'What did Peter say when you told him about the secret dig under Hagia Eirene?' she asked, as we continued climbing.

'Not a lot. He wasn't that interested.'

The stairs were lit with low watt bulbs dangling intermittently from the roof. It was going to take a lot more work to finish the place properly. We stopped on a deeply shadowed landing with a stone archway leading off it. On the other side of the arch was blackness. Isabel pressed a switch dangling loose from the wall.

A string of bulbs came on high up, illuminating the most breathtaking hall I've ever seen. The walls were alive with paintings, many of them of warrior angels. The floor was a riot of cracked and broken black and white tiles. Many of the wall paintings were only partly visible because of soot. The effect was captivating.

I imagined shaven-headed Byzantine monks praying here while these life-sized frescoes looked down on them.

'They're a militant looking bunch, aren't they?' said Isabel. 'See, that one. That's St Michael.' She pointed to an angel holding a faded, but fiery sword. 'There's St George. They look like real people, don't they?'

The ceiling was almost totally black, except for where a section was missing in one corner and grey roof beams could be seen.

'This looks newer than the entrance hall down below,' I said.

'Yeah, we think so too. We reckon this was an upper area, maybe a tavern, which was rebuilt into a chapel. Have a look at this altar,' she said. 'I was thinking of it when we were talking to Father Gregory. This is really what I wanted you to see.'

At the far end of the chapel was a dining-table-sized block of yellow marble. The mosaic floor pattern around it was even more elaborate here. Someone had been working on it too. Piles of a chalky mixture lay around it.

'Is this your work?' I said pointing at the floor.

'Some of it.'

I bent down to look at it. Gaps in the mosaic had been filled in with a neutral colour that let the mosaic stand out.

'This is amazing. Irene would have loved this. She used to paint. She'd have gone mad for this place.'

Isabel looked pensive, as if she was weighing up something. Her black hair shone in the golden glow from the bulb dangling above our heads.

'I can't imagine what you must have gone through, losing your partner like that.' She sounded genuinely sympathetic.

I didn't answer her. It was a part of me that I preferred to keep locked away.

'How did you get through it?'

I shrugged. 'Most people go through tough times – divorce,

their parents dying, losing jobs, illness. Nobody escapes,' I said.

'You're right.' She paused.

I got the feeling she wanted to tell me something else, something personal.

'When my marriage broke up,' she went on, slowly. 'It took me a year to get over it, maybe more. He was one hell of a cold fish at the end. It really got to me. But I still don't think that was on the same scale as what happened to you.'

'What is it they say, if it doesn't kill you, it can only make you stronger?' I touched the marble table with one hand. It was ice cold.

'A lot stronger.'

She walked around the altar to the other side.

'You'll like this,' she said softly. 'They used to believe that an altar like this could ward off evil, that it held healing magic. Put your hands on it, Sean, flat like this.' She put her hands on the altar, splayed out.

I did what I was asked. It certainly couldn't do me any harm. The altar felt cold, but it wasn't unpleasant. I didn't feel any magic though.

'We discovered so much stuff about this place, when we were researching it.'

'There's more?' I took my hands off the altar and put them to my forehead. They felt amazingly cool.

'You know the story of Hansel and Gretel?'

'Sure.'

'Did you know it's based on real events, children being abandoned in forests during the Middle Ages in Europe?'

'Why would anyone abandon children?'

'In the fourteenth century, the Black Death and the famines

that followed it struck people down from Egypt to Scotland. England's population crashed by more than half – from five to two million. Image the impact of something like that. The rules of society crumbled. Some people couldn't look after their children. They were dying themselves. Children were taken into forests and abandoned. People thought they were doing the best for them. Maybe they were.'

'Crazy.'

'Remember Father Gregory talked about evil returning in cycles.' She shivered, put her arms around herself.

'Yeah, but he believed in evil spirits. I think we've moved on from there.'

'The monks here in Constantinople predicted cycles of evil, of famines and plagues. We found references in some archives that mention this monastery. Apparently this place had a continent-wide reputation for its predictions.'

The air in the chapel seemed colder now than when we had come in. There was a lonely feel to the place too, as if it was waiting for tonsured rows of monks to return.

'The fourteenth century was the last time anything truly threatened the social order in Europe. Estates were taken over by servants. Cities were abandoned by the ruling classes.' Her voice echoed off the walls.

'It was the worst century in Europe for seven hundred years. The monks here claimed they'd discovered a pattern. It's mentioned in two documents. One of them is in the Fitzwilliam Museum in Cambridge.'

I did a quick calculation. 'So this coming century is going to be fun too.'

'God knows. Apparently the monks here warned the Byzantine emperor at the time that the plague was on its way.

Monks from this monastery had also predicted the famines and wars of the early seventh century. They happened just before Islam appeared and stormed the Middle East.'

'How did the monks make their predictions? What were they doing, reading the stars?'

'We're not sure. It's all a bit mysterious, dark arts stuff. When the monk's predictions came true in 1314 they were praised for warning people. Later they were accused of being in league with the devil. Shooting the messenger is what we'd call it today.'

'Yeah, I can see that happening.'

'Then things got very bad. In 1347 three quarters of the population of Constantinople died from the plague. A lot of people thought it was the end of the world. Riots overran this monastery. Some of the monks were burnt to death.'

'Lovely. That must have been because of those dark arts.' I ran my fingers along the top of the altar. It felt smooth, well-worn.

'Apparently the monks here were trained in astrology. That was what this place specialised in. There wasn't any distinction back then between astronomy and astrology. Monks used the stars to decide the date of Easter, to tell people when to plant crops, when to reap, all sorts of stuff. It's not surprising they were involved in predicting famines and plagues too.'

She pointed down.

'We think this altar had something to do with their predictions.' She spread her hands over the top of the altar, touching it gingerly, as if it was alive.

'It's the only surviving example of a Byzantine oracular altar. We think it was made in the sixth century. We believe it's a copy of the altar in David's temple in Jerusalem.' She was speaking reverently, emphasising each word. 'It's made of quartz. And it's totally unique.'

'Do you think there's anything in this seven-hundred-year cycle of evil stuff?'

'You know what worries me, Sean?' She looked around, as if checking the place for intruders.

'Go on.'

'The people who try to make these things happen, like a self-fulfilling prophecy. Some people want to stir things up, deep things, forces like hatred and fear.'

She sighed, then leaned over the altar.

'Look at this top stone.' She pointed at it. 'It's an inch thick. It must be the finest piece of Madagascar quartz in the whole world. And we've no idea how it was shipped here. My friend found it in a flooded shaft over there.' She nodded towards a corner of the chapel.

I bent towards the quartz. The slab sparkled close up, as if it was alive.

'See these markings?' She traced her finger along a thin silver line on the top of the slab. There were other lines too, inlaid threads of silver all over the top of the altar.

She traced her finger along one line.

I peered closer. Far off, I could hear a wailing siren. Then it stopped abruptly.

'This looks like the outline of a shape,' I said.

'It's the evening star, we think.' She ran her finger over the lines. I could just about make out lines joining together at the top of the altar.

'On that side,' she pointed to where I was standing, 'there's a pair of scales with a sword across its pans. That's the symbol of the Last Judgment.'

I could see her breasts rising and falling beneath her T-shirt.

Something scuttled across the floor.

'What was that?'

She looked around quickly. 'The place is riddled with vermin.'

'Thanks for telling me.'

She stepped back from the altar. 'What did your professor friend say to you today?'

I told her what I'd told Peter. That I believed Hagia Eirene was where Alek had taken the photos. I also told her there could be all sorts of treasures in any underground areas of Hagia Eirene, if they hadn't been opened up for centuries.

I told her about the group digging there. That there were some suspicions about them. I didn't tell her everything though. I had one last ace. I was keeping that face down.

When I was finished, she said, 'Peter thinks there's no need for you to do any more.'

'I'm sure he does,' I said. 'What's that noise?'

Music was thumping through the walls of the building, distinctly Turkish music, fast, lively, with a whirling gypsy quality. It suited my mood.

'That's Fasil music, Turkish nightclub music.'

Something Bulent had said came back to me. And I knew in a moment what we should do next. 'You know there's a Wagner concert in Hagia Eirene tonight.'

'And?'

'We should go there, have a look around, say we're autograph hunting or something. It's a great excuse to be there. Hagia Eirene will be open, people will be milling around.'

She looked at me with her mouth half open. I could almost see her brain working, turning over her options, whether she should try to stop me. I smiled at her. I'd been thinking about

204

going to Hagia Eirene the next day, but this would knock a few birds dead with one stone.

The people digging there might well have been spooked by everything that was going on. They might close the place up if they were up to no good. And I'd find out if Isabel could be trusted, or if all this sympathy was just a game to get me to open up. If she informed her superiors what I planned to do, and they tried to stop me, I'd know what she'd been up to.

There was a loud banging noise. It seemed like it was coming from somewhere below us.

The banging grew louder, echoing through the room, as if someone was trying to break in. Isabel reacted as if she'd been stung.

'Come on,' she hissed. She ran towards the far end of the chapel. I ran after her. There wasn't a doorway down there, or anywhere for us to go. What was she thinking?

When she reached the corner of the chapel she pushed something in a section of the wall that looked like it was made of brick. As I came up beside her I saw that the section wasn't made of brick at all. It was a painting of bricks. A *trompe l'oeil*.

I heard a low thud. The banging stopped. It was replaced with deathly silence.

'What's back here?'

'Give me a hand,' she replied. She was pushing at the wall. I pushed too, though I wasn't sure what she was expecting. Was the whole wall going to move?

'You think it's the people who tried to kill us?'

'I don't know,' she said. 'But I'm not hanging round.' She glanced back at the door to the stairs.

With a low groan a door opened in the wall where we were pushing. It was only five foot high, but it was big enough to get through. There was no way I'd have known it was there if she hadn't shown it to me. Cool air washed over me.

'I thought it wasn't going to open,' she said, as she went through. 'Come on, push the door behind you.'

I closed it gently after I went through. Then I looked around. There was a small window high up at the end of the tall and narrow corridor we were in. Moonlight lit the corridor. Slowly my eyes adjusted to the gloom.

It would take a long time for anyone who didn't know this place existed to find us. But where did the corridor lead? Would we be trapped?

'Is there a way out?' I said. There was a stale smell in the corridor. I could still hear the Turkish music. It was louder now.

'This was totally blocked when we found it,' said Isabel, as she moved up the corridor. 'The rubble in here was five hundred years old. This corridor was barely big enough to get down. It leads to a back door.'

'I thought you said we weren't followed.'

'Shsssh, did you hear something?' she whispered.

'No.' I looked around. I couldn't see anything.

We went on. At the end the window above stood guard over the tightest stone staircase I'd ever seen. At the bottom of it there was another door. It took a minute to find and then open the two locks that held it closed. The door opened with a grinding noise. Luckily we had, so far, heard no more sounds from above.

We stepped out into an alley that had a modern feel, compared to where we'd been. We pushed the door closed. When we reached the end of the alley, where it connected with the main street, the traffic was bumper to bumper, barely moving in both directions. It was still steamy hot. I was sweating.

'What the hell was that all about?' I was looking over my shoulder every few yards.

'I've no idea, but I'm not going back to find out.' She didn't look too shaken. This was one glacier-cool lady.

Pedestrians were criss-crossing between the cars. People were laughing, gesticulating. I'd heard about Turkey's booming economy, the way it had turned around, but this was the first time I'd really experienced what that meant.

'Is this what Istanbul's like every night?' I looked at my watch. It was 10:30 PM.

'Bebek's crazy seven nights a week these days, sometimes a lot crazier than this.'

Not far away, a muezzin began his call. Everyone seemed to ignore it. We pushed through the crowds, like friends on a night out.

We walked past a couple of restaurants and shops. We were both silent.

Then I asked, 'How often do they have concerts in Hagia Eirene?'

'Every few weeks in the summer. There was hardly any security there the last time I went.'

We passed a shop selling TVs. Its window was full of the latest super-thin screens. On one there was a picture of a man whose face looked familiar.

'What the hell,' I said. 'That's Bulent. The guy I met this morning.'

Isabel stopped walking. The shop had closed, so we couldn't hear anything, but I felt a sense of deep foreboding. Had something happened to Bulent?

The image of Bulent's face was replaced a few seconds later by a picture of the Golden Horn at night, with Hagia Sophia lit up in the background. That was replaced by a video of an ambulance racing through traffic. Then the picture of Bulent came back on the screen. There were two dates below the picture, 1955–2012, and Professor Bulent's name.

Isabel spoke matter-of-factly. 'He must have been pretty important to get on to the news.'

'This is totally crazy. I was with him this afternoon.'

Some tether had been cut inside me. I felt as if I was floating. Memories of what had happened to Alek, to Father Gregory, came rushing back. I saw the picture of Bulent's family in his hand. His poor wife and children. I felt a rush of nausea. Then anger.

I put a hand to my face. It felt hot. I took a step back. If I hadn't gone to see him, maybe this wouldn't have happened. Images of basketball players suddenly filled the screen. Now I felt cold.

'Let's keep going,' said Isabel.

We walked on. Twice I tried to say something, but the words didn't come out.

Then I realised what I really needed to say. 'We've got to find out what's going on,' I said. My voice sounded odd. 'Before one of us is next.'

Isabel put her hand on my arm, squeezed it.

'Are you OK?' she said.

I stopped walking. It was time to get a few answers.

29

Sergeant Henry P Mowlam was reading a memo from the Home Office Security and Counter Terrorism unit. He wanted to scream.

What the hell was wrong with them all? Having Muslims from all over Europe come to London to demonstrate against the raids on mosques, the new restrictions being placed on them all, the *burqa* bannings, was not a good idea.

The UK was one of the few countries where Muslims were free from the worst xenophobic excesses, but that didn't mean it should become a rallying place.

A huge Muslim demonstration outside St Paul's would be like Arsenal supporters holding a meeting outside Chelsea's football ground.

Who had approved this? It went directly against all his advice. Was someone trying to gain favour with the Muslim community? He had heard on the grapevine that someone high up had ordered that the right to peacefully demonstrate would be honoured in the UK, to show the world how these things should be handled.

The flight information, private bus bookings, ferry passenger lists and every other piece of data he'd seen in the last few hours pointed to hundreds of thousands of Muslims coming together.

The largest gathering of Muslims in Europe was what the organisers were aiming for. And it was going to happen in London in less than forty-eight hours. And it made him very very uneasy.

30

'There's one thing I want to know before we go any further,' I said.

Isabel turned and looked at me.

'Why was Peter playing games with me this afternoon?'

She shrugged. 'Sean, I'm not telepathic. I have no idea what Peter was up to.' She had her hands on her hips.

'So, why don't you tell me what you do know, like who's using Villa Napoleon? You were very keen to get me off that island.'

Her tone was plausible when she answered. 'Look, if we find evidence that there's something going on at that villa, we'll tell the Turkish authorities. They'll listen to us. They'll have to. And then they can take action. But we need evidence, something real. All we have right now is your theory that Alek's death was linked to Hagia Eirene, and then to that villa. I hurried you off the island because I thought you'd be interested in what Father Gregory had been talking about, that cycle of evil stuff.'

'I am interested,' I said. 'What do you think I'm doing right now, if it isn't looking for evidence?'

I turned to see if anyone was coming after us. The traffic was inching along, but mostly not moving at all. I scanned the pedestrians. No one was looking in our direction.

'Does your phone have a camera?' I asked, as I turned back to her.

She put her hand into the front pocket of her black trousers, took out a credit-card-sized phone and held it in the air.

'This has a 16 megapixel camera, and a Carl Zeiss lens. Is that good enough?'

'Maybe, wait here,' I said. We were near a large brimming-with-goods general store that was still open. It had everything from boxes of fruit to washing powder on its shelves, which extended into the street. It took only a minute to find what I was looking for. As I paid for the items, I peered through the grimy shop window.

A minute later we were at the taxi stand. As we left Bebek behind, two chunky SUV police vehicles passed us, speeding in the opposite direction.

I turned to look at the police cars, until the traffic obscured them. I was half expecting them to turn around and come after us.

The road we were on ran parallel to the Bosphorus, curving along the shoreline. We were heading back towards the centre of Istanbul. On the far side of the water a billion tiny lights sparkled below a deep purple sky. Boats, all lit up, were plying the waterway and families were out walking along the tree-lined path by the shore.

Isabel rested her head on the back of the seat. 'I was hoping to bring my father to that chapel before he died.'

'Your dad would have liked that place?' I said.

'Yeah, he was the reason I volunteered to come to Istanbul.' She sounded sad.

'He used to go on about Constantinople, about all the secrets that must be buried here. I really wanted to show him what we'd found.' She stared out the window at the streams of headlights passing by, a wistful expression on her face.

She said something in Turkish to the taxi driver. The cab's engine whined as he accelerated into the outside lane.

'If we get there too late, the concert will be over,' she said.

We passed a group of women at a bus stop. There must have ten of them, all wearing full Islamic dress, their heads covered, slits for eyes. Nearby, a pair of mangy dogs went at each other's throats.

'This place is changing,' said Isabel.

'Alek reckoned religion is on its way back in the world,' I said. I turned, looked out the window. Nobody seemed to be following us. But how would I know if they were? Any of the cars behind could have been tailing us.

Isabel turned to me. 'You do know Islam is very similar to what early Christianity was like?' she said. 'All the fasting, open prayer halls, veiled women.'

'I'm sure some people would dispute that.'

'They'd be wrong.'

I wound down my window. Warm air, exhaust fumes and the smell of salt water slid into the car. We passed a crowded two-tiered restaurant with wide balconies facing on to the Bosphorus. Booming disco music assaulted our ears. I was struck by how multi-faceted Istanbul was. It was a sleeping giant with millions of parts, which could swallow you whole. The way it had swallowed Alek.

The wind was whipping Isabel's hair across her face. Her cheeks were glowing and there was a band of sweat on her forehead.

We passed over the Golden Horn. Ahead, on the top of the hill, the oldest part of Istanbul stood out against the night. The dome of Hagia Sophia was lit up by spotlights. It was easy to imagine how the city might have looked two thousand years before, when it was an ancient Greek city with an Acropolis and temples lit at night by torches all around them.

Near the dome of Hagia Sophia was another smaller dome, Hagia Eirene. It was lit up too, though not as brilliantly as Hagia Sophia. And it had no surrounding minarets.

The cab driver said something in Turkish. I didn't understand a word.

'One question is one too many for me,' said Isabel. She said something in Turkish to the driver. He tilted his head to one side and pressed the accelerator.

'I told him we're going for a romantic walk by the Bosphorus and to hurry up.' She smiled at me.

We were driving in light traffic along a dual carriageway. On our left was the Bosphorus, on our right was a three-storey-high stone wall. Beyond the wall a hill loomed like a dark shadow, crowned with the glowing lights of Hagia Sophia and Hagia Eirene. As we approached a break in the barrier between the carriageways, Isabel leaned forward and asked our driver to pull over. It would be a good place to cross over, if we were planning a walk along the shore line.

We'd just passed a small bus park on our right. Two dust-smeared ancient buses sat in a corner of the bus park. They looked as if they'd be lucky to move again. There were a couple of down-at-heel looking men by the side of the road near them. They seemed to be waiting for something. There was nobody else about. Traffic was light.

A cropped-haired, sad-eyed young soldier in olive green, ill-fitting military fatigues was leaning against the wall further along, near a wooden gate. Once our taxi was gone we headed towards him. As we came up to him Isabel began talking excitedly in Turkish. She sounded angry. She pulled her identity card out from her back pocket and waved it in front of the boy.

He let the butt of the cigarette that had been dangling from his mouth fall to the ground. He mumbled something, then turned and with a bow ushered us through the gate he'd been guarding. He saluted as we passed.

'What did you say to him?' I asked, as we started up a dark lane. It headed straight up the hill in front of us.

'I told him our taxi broke down and the driver dumped us here, instead of at the main entrance.' I could see the white of her teeth. 'He said it'd be quicker if we go up this way. Turkish army boys are always so nice.'

My eyes adjusted to the dark. The path stretching out in front of us had a brick wall on its left side, which could have easily been a thousand years old or more. On the right was a high wire fence holding back a row of drooping and dusty pine trees. Up ahead old street lamps from the earliest days of electricity cast small circles of light on the hard earth laneway, which became steeper and steeper as the hum of the dual carriageway faded behind us. The sweet smell of pine trees was all around us.

'Have you ever been inside Hagia Eirene?' said Isabel.

'No. I'd no reason to.'

'When I went to that violin concerto last year, we had to go down a ramp to get into the nave. It has a great stone floor, tiers and tiers of arched windows, and a very high domed roof. There's a giant cross in outline in black, on the half-dome at the end of the nave. That's the only decoration in the whole place. If that mosaic Alek took a picture of was from before the eighth century, as Father Gregory said, there's no way it's in any of the main areas there.'

I looked over my shoulder. No one was following us. Up ahead, the laneway was in shadow between the street lights. The wind rustling through the tall pine trees blew stronger as we made our way up the hill.

'The Byzantines thought icons had magical powers,' she went on. 'One empress, Zoe, believed an icon changed colour to predict the future just for her. Most people who lived here thought icons protected Constantinople. The city had been saved so many times after icons had been paraded on its walls. Enemy armies had just faded away. You can't argue with that.'

'It was a different world,' I said. 'They were certain of a lot of things.'

'I'd have loved to have been here in 330 AD, when Hagia Eirene, and this whole city, was dedicated by Constantine to Christianity.'

I could barely hear her above the rustle of the trees.

Then she stopped walking, looked back down the lane, put a hand in her pocket and pulled out her phone.

'I have to make a call, Sean.' She tapped at the screen and put the phone to her ear.

Was she going to tell them what we were up to?

'Isabel Sharp here,' she said, looking at me. 'Anything for me?' She listened for at least a minute, then gave directions to the chapel in Bebek, asked for the place to be checked out, to see if anyone had broken in there.

'I'll call again soon,' she said. 'And send that picture through to me.'

Then she hung up.

'There's something I have to ask you, Sean.' Her tone was more officious now.

'Ask away.'

Her phone beeped. She looked at the screen, then showed it to me. It was filled with a picture of a naked girl lying crumpled inside a large white plastic sack, the type that holds hospital refuse.

It was a sickening image. The body was streaked with blood. I wanted to look away, but I couldn't. Isabel took back the phone.

'That woman was found in a waste chute at your hotel.'

Something slotted into place inside me. I'd only seen the girl's chin, a bruised cheek, her matted blonde hair, but the chill of recognition that ran through me was unmistakable.

'Do you recognise her, Sean?'

'I think it's the receptionist who was on duty when I checked into my hotel.' I felt bile rise in my throat. The poor girl didn't deserve this.

'You're right. It is.' She paused, then flicked a strand of hair away from her eyes. 'The problem for you, for us, is she disappeared the night you fled your hotel, which doesn't look good, not good at all. The Turkish police have been in touch with the Consulate, asking questions about you.'

Was I the one under suspicion now? The world had gone totally mad. A blast of wind bent the tops of the trees above us.

'They know she called your room before she disappeared.'

'This is ridiculous.' I was struggling to keep my anger in check. I was annoyed, but not just for myself.

'She tried to help me. Those bastards who came to my room must have killed her. You saw what they were capable of.' I felt a pressure on my chest. This was a nightmare that just kept getting worse.

'Maybe, but if the Turkish media find out you've disappeared from that hotel, they'll love it. Foreigners being involved in this sort of thing is manna from heaven for the press here. Considering that Alek died in mysterious circumstances, it's going to be sensational if all this comes out as the next instalment.'

I closed my eyes, took a deep breath, held it. The picture of the blood-streaked receptionist was etched in my mind. It wouldn't go away. Whoever had murdered her, left her like that, was nothing less than pure evil. A chill was winding its way around my stomach.

'There's something else too.' I opened my eyes. Her chin was up, as if she was on parade.

'What's that?' I was ready for anything now.

'Alek's phone records show he spoke to someone on the Turkish security services' watch list last week, someone Greek.' Something heavy inside me sank.

'I have no idea what that was about, before you ask,' I said emphatically.

'I'm sure you don't, Sean. But it doesn't look good. If the press here find out there's proof of a Greek connection to both these murders, there'll definitely be trouble. We'd have to consider issuing a denial on behalf of your Institute.'

'As far as I'm concerned this just makes it more important to see exactly where he went,' I said. 'This is not going to put me off. No way.' I started walking up the hill to the next pool of light. A few seconds later she was beside me, our forearms almost touching.

'You can't get away that easily,' she said with forced brightness.

Up ahead, two elderly bearded men in long Islamic tunics were walking towards us.

'Smile,' she said.

'You too,' I replied. But the last thing I felt like doing was smiling.

She took my arm as the men approached. It felt good to have her hold me, even if it was only a pretence.

Both men nodded at us in the dim yellow street light.

'Nice people, Turks, very friendly,' she said in an upbeat voice. 'It's an amazing place, Sean. You know they were using forks here when most Europeans hadn't even heard of them?'

'Alek may have come this way,' I said, 'when he took those photos. But doesn't it seems strange to kidnap and murder someone for taking a few snaps?'

Isabel gripped my arm. 'It is strange. Alek's kidnapping didn't follow the normal rules at all, Sean.' Her tone was low, cautious, as if she wasn't sure how I'd react.

'There are rules?'

'Almost. Most terrorist kidnappings follow a pattern; demands, threats, deadlines. There was none of that in his case. There was no waiting at all. They killed him within a few hours. It's all very strange.'

'I hope to God he didn't suffer.' It was hard to imagine his last moments, his fear as the knife approached.

There was silence for a while as we walked. I thought about Alek and that poor receptionist. I looked behind. The orange and white lights from the far side of the Bosphorus were reflecting eerily off the thick cloud hanging above the Asian shoreline. The rain clouds that had battered Buyuk Ada were following us, reaching out over the Bosphorus.

We crossed a lane, passed a bus park on the right. The glow from the dome of Hagia Eirene was visible up ahead.

The prison-like courtyard wall of Topkapi Palace was on our left. This time we were inside it. Up ahead, a red and white barrier pole blocked the road. Two guards in green uniforms stood behind the barrier. Both of them were cradling black machine pistols, their barrels pointed upwards. They didn't look as innocent as the conscript who'd been at the entrance to the lane we'd come through.

The sight of the guards brought home to me what we were planning. I felt a tingle of anticipation, and a strong sense of determination. This was for Alek, whatever happened.

'Keep smiling,' I said.

'That's my secret weapon,' she replied. 'Didn't you know?'

We strolled up to the grim-faced guards.

One of them put a hand up to stop us.

'We're going to the concert,' I said. I moved forward another step.

He put his hand up close to my chest. I stopped, looked at it. I was tempted to swipe it away, but his buddy had his weapon pointed at us now.

He said something in Turkish, then, in English, he said, 'No entry.' He was grim faced.

I clenched my fists. We didn't have time for this.

Isabel had taken her phone out of her pocket. She stabbed a number into it. I could hear it ringing. 'Wait, Sean,' she said to me. She put a hand on my arm.

The guard said something in Turkish. He didn't sound happy. She held her hand up, as if she wanted to attract attention to herself. The guard looked at his buddy.

'Is this a good time to make social calls?' I said.

The other guard said something rather loudly. Isabel raised her hand higher, as if to silence him.

The guard's mouth closed. He was deciding what to do next, contemplating getting nasty, probably. Isabel took a step towards him and held the phone out in front of her. The other guard took a step back and adjusted his machine pistol. We all listened to a faint ringing noise, an electronic cricket sound, emanating from the phone.

For one long painful moment it seemed as if no one was going to answer. The guard took a step forward.

'*Merhaba*, Cem!' said Isabel loudly as the phone was finally answered by what could only be described as a grunt. She put the phone to her ear and began to speak rapidly in Turkish. The guards listened to her. After a brief conversation she passed the phone to the one nearest her.

He said something brusquely to his colleague over his shoulder. Then he took the phone, said something in Turkish, listened and a moment later stood to attention. It looked as if he was about to salute. He handed the phone back to Isabel and muttered something under his breath. It sounded like an apology. He and the other guard stepped aside, raised the barrier and waved us forward.

'What was that all about?' I asked, as we walked up the steep sloping lane.

'It helps to have friends in high places,' she said.

'You're a useful person to bring along. Who did you call?'

'A friend. A new Turkish general. He taught me some beautiful verses from the Koran.' She had a fond smile on her face.

As we crested the hill, the main gate of Topkapi, the one the bus had got stuck in, appeared to our left. Guards stood to attention near the gate in coal-black uniforms, with highly visible round white helmets. A high pale stone wall loomed behind them.

Hagia Eirene was a hundred yards ahead beyond some thin trees. It was all lit up. Golden light blazed from tiers of arched red brick windows and from a circle of skylights that surrounded the raised dome. A few guests in evening wear could be seen milling around the far end of the building to our right. Was the concert over? Then I heard some music faintly.

Hagia Eirene was looming in front of us, rearing up like an ancient fortress. The hair on the back of my neck stood up. The arched, leaded windows of the great church had golden light pouring out of them.

Between the church and the path around it was a deep, twenty-foot-wide moat.

'After the conquest this was one of only a few Christian churches not made into a mosque,' said Isabel.

'Anyone know why?' I said.

'Supposedly Mehmed the Conqueror was into the Kabala. Apparently he received mystical warnings about Hagia Eirene.'

I looked up. The sound of distant laughter and a bus revving filled the air.

'If Eirene was the Greek goddess of peace,' I said, 'why didn't they change the name of the building when they made it into a Christian church?'

'Don't ask me,' she replied.

I was peering down into the moat. It was a mess of ancient half-broken walls and tumbled stones.

'The Greek temple that was on this spot before it was a church was probably a den of prostitutes. That could have been why Mehmed didn't want the place,' I said.

'It goes back a long way,' she said, looking up at the walls.

'You better believe it. Alexander the Great came here, I'd say. And that was six hundred years before Constantine. The Greek town that was here was even part of the Persian Empire for a while. We can only guess what went on on this site when it was one of their temples.'

We kept walking. I still hadn't seen any sign of a doorway with a recently installed security camera, my big clue from Bulent, the ace I'd been hiding. It wasn't that much of a clue, but I was hoping it would be enough.

'So how do we find the place Alek took those pictures?' she said, as if she was reading my mind.

'Patience, patience.' I was examining the moat. The bottom of it was about fifteen foot below the level of the path. We walked to the right, to the end of the building, then turned left alongside it, staying with the path. People were milling around here. The concert had ended.

I was grateful for them being there. It meant we could have a good look at the building without attracting attention.

Hardly anyone gave us a second glance as we walked as far as we could, right up to the main entrance where the high doors stood open. A stream of concert goers were drifting out. Security guards in black suits were hanging around the entrance.

Maybe we could claim we had to go back inside, to find something we'd left behind. What was the worst they could do, stop us?

'Where to now?' said Isabel.

'Let's check back all the way around as far as we can go.'

'What exactly are we looking for?' There was a definite note of frustration in her voice now.

'I'll tell you when we find it.'

She groaned. We retraced our steps.

There was only one possible door that I'd seen so far. It was near the main entrance, almost under it, down at the level of the moat, which might have been what we were looking for, but, although there were steps down to it, there was no security camera near it. Was there a similar door on the other side of the building?

We walked back alongside the moat to the spot where we'd first approached the building. Around the next corner, turning right this time, the moat-like area became wider.

There was nobody else in this part, between the high outer wall of Topkapi and the looming red brick south wall of Hagia Eirene.

Trees and giant weeds grew in the wide moat here, a steep walled area of ancient foundations, much of which was in shadow and about twenty feet below ground level.

Then I saw it, in a corner of the exposed foundations: a recent addition, a wooden walkway, with steps leading down to a wooden platform. We walked off the path towards it and looked down. There were more steps leading down again, disappearing from view.

I went down to the first platform. Isabel followed me. I could smell fresh wood.

My thoughts were racing. Was this where Alek had been? And if Alek had died because he came this way, were we being stupid by coming down here?

But I didn't care. I had to do this.

I looked up at the wall of Hagia Eirene looming over us like a brick cliff. If you wanted a building to survive seventeen hundred years near an earthquake fault, in one of the most contested cities in the world, this was the way to build it – squat and heavy.

I went down another flight, rounded the corner of the stairs and stopped as if I'd met a glass wall.

Isabel was beside me in a second. The light streaming from the windows of Hagia Eirene way up above us was enough for her to see why I'd stopped. My heart was thumping. This was it.

'Kiss me,' she demanded.

31

Arap Anach reached into the pocket of his midnight-blue Armani blazer. He pulled his phone out, glanced at the screen. A text message had arrived. He'd read it as soon as he got a chance. An usher was leading him through the wood panelled corridors of the House of Commons. The bustle of the parliamentary staff and visitors pushing past him was annoying him.

The usher stopped at a long stuffed-leather sofa outside a tall brass-handled door. An ivory plate on it read PRIVATE. The sofa looked as if it had been new in the 1920s. There was a lemony smell of polish in the air.

'Wait here, sir,' said the usher, motioning towards the sofa. The man Anach was meeting didn't have his own office. He was using an out-of-the-way meeting room. All this would change soon. Anach sat, looked at his phone, tapped at the screen.

A decrypted message from Malach popped up a few seconds later. Malach had done well. *Diagnosis confirms faster outcome than anticipated*, read the message.

He imagined the girl slipping into a coma, the look on the doctor's face when she died, and then... the doctor's terror at feeling a headache come on, then the lumps growing. He'd know what his fate would be. That would be the worst part.

Many who were about to die would have no idea what was coming for them. They'd line up in hospitals and doctor's surgeries and pharmacies convinced that modern medicine would save them. And then they would die. And the world would be a better place.

Man, the intelligent animal, was about to prevent his own natural extinction before he reached the point where he'd used up all his planet's resources.

And then the changes could begin.

The door he was waiting outside creaked open. A young woman bulging out of every part of her black suit came out. 'Lord Bidoner says to go in, Mr Anach,' she said. Then she walked off.

32

A drum was beating in my head. I hadn't kissed a woman properly in years. Even if this was a trick, because of the security camera above our heads pointing down at us, the reality of kissing Isabel was more exciting than it should have been.

And there was something achingly familiar about it too. A memory of my first kiss with Irene swirled through me. The smell of Isabel's skin, her touch, it was all so similar. I pulled away.

'Sean,' she whispered.

Our bodies were touching; we were pressed together. Hers was warmer than I'd expected.

'Don't get too excited.' Her tone was playful.

I looked up at the shiny security camera above us. There wasn't a speck of dust on it. It looked as if it had been put there only last week, at a position where it could observe both the stairs and whatever was below us. And if the camera was on, someone must be watching us.

A new security camera was exactly what I'd been looking for. Now the question was, what would whoever was watching us, if someone was watching us, make of us being down here?

If they were the ordinary security guards for this part of Topkapi Palace, we'd probably be OK. We'd get into trouble for trespassing, sure, but that would be it. But, if it was someone else, the people who'd taken Alek, and they realised what we were up to, we would be in a very different class of trouble.

A kiss was a good excuse for us coming down here. But what Isabel did next was inspired.

She shook her finger at the camera, as if she was admonishing whoever was watching for snooping on us. Then she ran down a few steps, to a point where she was just below the camera, and reached up. It was clear she wasn't going to reach it.

'Boost me,' she whispered. I went down, lifted her at the waist and boosted her up. I couldn't believe how light she was. Maybe it was the adrenaline pumping through me.

She wrenched the camera to one side, pointed it at the wall.

'We've got a few minutes, no more,' she said, as she dropped down beside me.

'They'll think we're making out and send someone to investigate. They'll probably hope to catch us at it if they can. We better find out what's down here, and fast.'

At the bottom of the stairs was a heavy, out-of-place looking, red steel door set into the wall of Hagia Eirene. Its only embellishment was a small keyhole set into a brushed steel plate. I pushed at the door. It didn't budge.

My pulse was still drumming from the memory of that kiss. The knowledge that we had only minutes before someone turned up didn't help calm me.

I looked back up the stairs. Stars were glimmering faintly. I heard a woman's voice, high pitched, in the distance.

Isabel had taken her phone out of her pocket. 'No signal down here,' she said. 'I won't be able to call for back-up if I get this open.'

'You think you can open it?' I pointed at the door.

'It shouldn't be too difficult,' she said. She pulled out a set of keys from her pocket and held them up. There were two long bent pieces of wire on one of the rings. They looked like ornaments. She picked one out, held it up, straightened it a little and undid it from the key ring.

'If I can see what I'm doing.' She bent down. I watched her back.

'How often do you do this sort of thing?' I said.

'Once or twice a year. We learned all sorts of stuff before we were sent out here. Now sssshh.'

I craned forward to see what she was doing, but aside from her poking methodically at the lock, there was not much to see.

She grunted.

'It's a German lock. This is not going to be easy.'

'What's wrong with German locks?'

'They have wafer tumblers.' She turned and looked at me. The whites of her eyes were visible. 'Are you going to watch out for the guards or just stare over my shoulder?'

I had to go up two flights of stairs before I could see the path again. Thankfully, there was no one in sight. Maybe the camera was switched off.

A few souls were walking away from Hagia Eirene in the distance. Had we gotten away with this?

I thought about that kiss again, the sweet smell of Isabel's perfume, so faint, so tantalizing.

The last time I'd kissed a woman was at a party a few months ago. I'd pulled away then. It had felt all wrong, as if I was being unfaithful to Irene. How crazy was I? How can you be unfaithful to someone who's been dead for two years? It had felt almost as if her ghost was stopping me.

But I hadn't felt like that this time. It had felt right. Or was I just going crazy?

My heartbeat was almost normal again. I felt detached as I watched the paths leading towards us, as if someone else was doing all this. What was beyond the door?

A distant crunching noise echoed in the warm night air. Something gripped at my insides. I scanned the paths. There! Coming towards us from the main gate, heading straight in our direction, was exactly what I didn't want to see; a phalanx of maybe ten determined looking security guards. They were still quite distant, but they were approaching fast.

The guards were dressed in olive-green uniforms, which was a good thing. They looked like official Topkapi Palace security guards. But it still felt as if someone had dropped a weight on my chest. Maybe we weren't going to get decapitated by this lot, but getting arrested didn't seem like such a good idea either.

The urge to just stare at them approaching, like a rabbit caught in headlights, was strong. But I snapped out of it and with a jerk of my head, turned, and leapt down the stairs hissing Isabel's name as I went.

As I came around the last bend, it was disappointingly clear that nothing had changed. Isabel was still poking at the lock.

Did she have any idea what she was doing?

'Security guards are coming, Isabel. You've about thirty seconds. Maybe less.' My words came out fast.

'Don't rush me,' was her reply, as if we had all day.

I wanted to shout at her. Instead, I let out a short nervous laugh and looked back up the stairs. Everything seemed so serene. All I could hear was the scratching sound Isabel was making and the distant hum of the city. For one long endless moment I thought I must have been mistaken. That the guards were on their way somewhere else. It was possible, wasn't it?

I listened hard.

I heard the rattle of stones.

Go on, pass by.

But a voice called out in a hard Turkish accent. Someone was calling down to us. I had no idea what he was saying, but it didn't sound friendly. Then there was a great clattering noise, the sound of people moving on to the stairs above us.

Pebbles skittered wildly. One bounced in front of me. The noise of boots reverberated. Would Isabel be able to get through the door if I held them off for a while? It was time to act. I turned my head quickly.

33

The ambulance driver shivered. This was a bad omen. He waved at the police car blocking his path. Its flashing blue light was spinning fast, filling the driving cabin with its electric glow.

He had worked for the Istanbul municipal emergency ambulance service for two years and he had never had to carry such a load before. If he told his wife, she would curse their fate.

No, he would not tell her anything, he decided, as he inched between the police cars, then out of the lane and up the concrete ramp into Taksim Square. No, he would deny he'd found the second beheaded man discovered in the city in less than five days. And he'd claim no knowledge of what he'd overheard that inspector say – that the man was an Iranian biologist who specialised in virus mutation. He didn't want to know any more. He wanted to go home, to see his children, to eat meatballs and watch game shows on TV.

He didn't want to know that the dead man had worked with strange viruses.

Everyone knew the Iranians were likely to be developing biological warfare agents. But why had this one been murdered in Istanbul?

Was it an omen? He shook his head. No, it wasn't. It couldn't be.

34

The steel door was open. The brick passageway beyond was lit by a low-intensity yellow bulb. The passageway looked vaguely familiar.

Isabel had stepped inside. I followed her. Cool air passed over me. My skin prickled. Would we be able to get the door closed in time? Would it hold them? It seemed impossible. The clattering was close now, and loud. They were about to turn the last corner on the stairs.

I closed the door behind me. It clicked softly. There was a handle and a round knob above the lock. I turned the knob, heard another soft click. Then I turned it again. It clicked again. At the same time, Isabel was putting the piece of wire into the keyhole, bending it, pushing it up and in. Then she flattened herself against the door.

'Do you always leave things right to the last second?' I whispered.

'Shssssh,' she replied softly.

There was a reverberating bang. Someone or something had hit the other side of the door. It almost bounced on its hinges. We both moved away from it. Then a shout rang out. It sounded as if the person was right beside us. I leaned against the passageway wall and tried to calm my breathing. The door shook again. Would the lock, Isabel's little piece of wire, really hold them?

Muffled voices echoed. Someone banged on the door again. Harder this time. Knocking.

I totally expected it to jump open at any moment. Once the lock was open, that would be it. We'd be prisoners. What would we say? Stick to our story. I could hear my breathing, Isabel's too.

Something sharp struck the door. It rattled. There was a scratching noise like a key being inserted into a lock. Isabel was kneeling in front of the door with her hand up at the key-hole holding the piece of wire into it. Could that hold them? Surely not.

Any moment now.

My desire to pursue this was about to be punished. Even if these guys were only Topkapi Palace security guards, breaking into this kind of place was a serious offence. It had to be.

Isabel held her hand at the key hole. Her hand turned a little. I could see the wire moving in her fingers.

Suddenly there was a shout, as if someone had yelled in frustration. Something banged against the door. It could have been a hand. The wire in Isabel's hand moved again, twisted. I held my hand on hers, pressing lightly. I felt her hand move once more as someone tried to turn the key again. This wasn't going to hold them.

But it did. The door didn't open.

There were more shouts, more rustling, more shuffling. Then more scraping. I had no idea what was going on on the other side, but I could guess. Different people were trying the door. Then there were shouts that sounded like threats, then more scratching. Isabel's wire was bent, but it had stopped moving, as if it had jammed in somewhere. There was banging again. The door rattled.

It remained closed.

Then there was a rushed clattering, as if everyone on the other side was heading back up the stairs.

We'd done it. I leaned against the wall, relaxing a little for the first time since we'd come down the stairs. I could breathe again. Isabel bent down and looked through the keyhole.

Then she stood and whispered. 'This gives us maybe twenty minutes. There aren't too many locksmiths open in Istanbul this late, but I expect they'll find someone. If they catch us in here, we'll be in serious trouble. We've got to find another way out.'

She looked at me with an expression that was almost pleading.

'We'd better have a look around,' I said. I moved down the passage, walking fast.

'This was your idea,' she whispered, as she came up behind me.

'Lets stick to the story that we wanted a bit of privacy,' I said.

'Sure, but I don't think they're stupid.'

That was when I noticed the block of faded yellow marble set into the wall halfway along the corridor. There was an Arab inscription on the marble. The hair on my neck stood to attention.

'That's the Janissaries' motto,' I said, stopping at it. '*I place my faith in God.*'

I looked back. There was no one coming through the door.

'That was in one of Alek's photos. He was here,' I said.

The bulb above us flickered and a long forgotten memory came rushing back. As a boy, when I'd behaved very badly, I'd been locked in a basement storeroom. The room had been lit by a faded yellow bulb, just like this. It had flickered. The smell was weirdly similar too, damp and earthy. I'd hated that place.

We continued, moving fast down the gently sloping, brick-lined corridor. A hundred feet further on the corridor turned back on itself. The next section ended in what looked like a storage corridor.

In the far wall there was a rough door-sized opening in a solid brick wall. The opening looked recent. There were dust and brick fragments all around.

Who had broken through this wall?

I looked back over my shoulder, then stepped through the opening, moving fast. The wall that had blocked the passage had been over two foot thick, enough to deter casual investigations. Chunks of loose rubble lay to one side in the next section of the passage.

The walls here were made of pale brick too, but they were cleaner, as if this lower part of the passage had been used a lot less over the centuries. It ran straight, and away from Hagia Eirene.

I had a feeling we were heading in the direction of Hagia Sophia.

Then, without warning, the yellow bulbs hanging from the walls went out. I stopped. A curtain of blackness engulfed us. The darkness felt primitive. Prickling sweat broke out all over me.

'Wait a second,' I said, as calmly as I could. I reached into my pocket and pulled out the torch I'd bought in the shop earlier. A shaft of brilliant white light popped out from it, illuminating everything in its beam.

'Always be prepared, that's what my dad said.' I waved the beam around.

'Not in my eyes, please,' Isabel hissed. She pushed the torch to one side.

I swung the beam over the faded brick walls around us, the arched brick ceiling above and the shiny stone passageway sloping down in front of us. A red electric cable ran along the bottom of one wall. Someone was working down here.

'No wonder geo-phys surveys of Hagia Sophia never find anything,' I said. 'Reliable readings in this type of ground go to a depth of twenty feet, maybe a little more. We must be thirty feet down already, and we're not even near the bottom of this.' The beam of light from the torch illuminated the corridor up to about a hundred feet away. After that everything faded into gloom. Behind us, black shadows pressed in.

'Thank God for the wonderful Mr Maglite,' I said, as I set off down the passage. I was walking fast. 'I wonder where the hell this goes.'

'I just hope there's a way out,' said Isabel.

There were no sounds now, just the noises we were making – the sound of our footsteps on the stone, the rustling of our clothes. The air was cool down here.

I shone the torch beam over the walls as we walked on, looking for anything interesting.

'This place gives me the creeps,' said Isabel.

'It's amazing, isn't it?'

She put a hand on my arm. 'Let me have a go.'

I passed her the torch. We walked on, moving fast. The next section of the passageway sloped even steeper.

Then, up ahead, there was no wall on the right. I held my breath as we came up to it. I knew what was happening. The passage was turning into a ramp going down one side of a large underground hall. My notion of space was suddenly inverted. We were above something now, not below it. It was weirdly disconcerting.

Isabel played the beam into the hall below us as we came down into it. The hall was massive, maybe twenty feet high and a hundred square feet, at least. It reminded me of the underground cisterns in other parts of Istanbul. But this space was not built to hold water.

Its most prominent feature was a large door, maybe fifteen feet high and the same wide, in the centre of the far wall. Isabel directed the torch beam onto the door, then moved it around the walls as we came down.

There was an unnatural quiet here, as if the walls were listening, watching.

'This is something else,' said Isabel. 'And I usually hate being underground.'

'I hope this isn't the entrance to a plague pit,' I said.

'A plague pit, you're joking, right?' She shuddered.

'It's got to be a possibility. Istanbul was the first city the Black Death hit in Europe. One summer in the sixth century, five thousand men, women and children were dying of the plague each day in this city. When it returned in the fourteenth century it was even worse.

'This was a Christian city back then. The clergy looked after the sick. They buried the bodies in crypts under the churches first, then in pits. Later there were so many bodies they just threw them into the sea. Large crypts, catacombs in some places, were dug out under churches all over Europe. They were sealed up afterwards. I'm sure they would have done the same here, except on a bigger scale. Remember, Constantinople was the biggest city in Europe then.'

'The Black Death, that's just what I want to hear about right now.' Isabel groaned.

'You have to be careful in places like this, that's all I'm saying.'

'Where's the way out then?' She shone the torch around the room again. There was no obvious way out except through the big door in front of us. She shone the light on the floor.

'Where's this plague pit?'

'I don't know.' I shrugged. 'And we haven't got time to look. Come on.'

Isabel was turning the torch on different parts of the underground hall. The walls were alive with frescoes. They reminded me of Pompeii. The faded mosaic floor was like an exhibit at a museum.

She let the beam of the torch linger on a wall fresco.

'Look!' She held the beam steady on a painting of an old man, seated, with a halo around his head. A younger man in a toga was kneeling in front of him, writing something on a roll of parchment with a long pen.

'St John,' I said. 'The guy who dictated the Book of Revelation.'

'What the hell is St John doing down here?'

'I don't know, but he isn't going to help us find a way out.'

'Did you hear something?' she said.

We both stopped moving. There was nothing but silence.

Isabel moved the beam around the room. On the floor, in one corner, was a mosaic. A Madonna with Child. Debris littered the area around it.

'That's Alek's mosaic,' I said. 'It's gotta be.' It was good to have found it, but unsettling.

I ran over to the mosaic. It looked, if anything, more vivid than in Alek's picture. There was a low scaffolding platform near it, as if someone was planning to remove it completely.

I heard a far-off sound, a distant thud. My ears strained for something more, but nothing came.

We had to go. Isabel was pointing the torch beam at the great door. There was no other way forward.

The door was an impressive piece of work. Isabel walked slowly up to it, shining the light on the floor in front of it. The electric cable from the corridor ran straight under the door.

'Look at that,' she said, pointing at scrape marks near the door. 'They're recent.' She turned the beam on to the door again.

It was made from thick planks running vertically, all so grey with age, they appeared to have turned to stone. Foot-wide veined black marble pillars stood on each side of the door. They were surmounted by globes the size of a human head. The pillars had bands of Greek letters carved into them.

'Whoever built this was preparing for the end of the world,' I said. 'Sacred inscriptions used to be carved in marble to ensure they'd survive the fires of the apocalypse.' I stepped towards it.

'Let's see if it opens.' I pulled one of the two handles. Nothing happened. I stopped and listened for more noises.

'Wait a second,' said Isabel. She passed me the torch, took out her phone and took a picture.

'We haven't got time for that,' I said.

I pointed the beam at the door handles. They were metal rings that had blackened with age and were just about big enough to put my hand through. There was one near the centre of each door. I passed her the torch, gripped them properly this time with both hands and gave them a proper tug. They had to open.

Nothing happened. I looked for a lock. There was none.

'Let's pull them together,' I said.

'I knew I was going to come in useful,' she said.

'Just pull.'

We pulled together. Nothing happened.

'Turn your handle,' I said. 'Make it straight.' It was at a 90-degree angle to the one I was pulling.

'It doesn't move,' she said. She yanked at it, pulling hard, jerking it each way in frustration.

I tried turning mine. At first it didn't turn. I tapped it with my fist. It creaked loudly, then turned. Both handles were at the same angle now. We pulled again.

There was a low grinding noise. A welcome crack of light appeared. We pulled together. The doors moved slowly, but they moved. Bright light flooded into the room.

I stopped and squinted, unable to believe my eyes.

35

Sergeant Mowlam paused the stream of text messages flowing across his screen. The one he was interested in had two red stars against it. The first indicated it was related to a current threat. The second indicated that a fatality was involved.

He clicked on the link. Another screen opened. He began reading a translated summary of a Turkish Interior Ministry emergency warning notice.

NOTICE: 24-9006734456C – CONFIDENTIAL
INTERIOR MINISTRY STAFF ONLY
WARNING: INTERNATIONAL RELATIONS IMPLICATIONS.
VICTIM: DR SAFAD MOHADAJIN.
CAUSE OF DEATH: BEHEADING
COMMENT: DR SAFAD WAS A LEADING BIOLOGICAL SCIENTIST
BELIEVED TO BE WORKING ON THE IRANIAN BIOLOGICAL
WEAPONS PROGRAMME. HIS DEATH IN ISTANBUL CAUSES
GRAVE CONCERN AS HIS REASONS FOR BEING IN TURKEY
ARE UNKNOWN. DR MOHADAJIN'S SPECIALISATION WAS VIRUS
MUTATION AND DNA EXTRACTION.

36

'What the hell is this?' I said. Musty air flowed over us.

The space beyond the door stretched away into a gloomy distance of dark shadows and evenly spaced columns holding up the roof. This wasn't just a room. This was a vast underground cavern, similar to the Basilica Cistern not far away, used all the way back to ancient times for storing water. But there was no water here.

Bright bare bulbs were suspended crudely from the ceiling near where the door was, but further away there were no lights at all. This space looked even older than the one we'd come through. It's ceiling was lower too and the thin pillars gave it a crypt-like feel.

I looked down. The floor was a faded mosaic with an endless chequerboard pattern. It stretched away into the distance between the red marble columns. They were about twenty foot high and six inches thick and were spaced equally, maybe twenty feet apart. It was like looking into a wood of young trees.

'This place is the find of the century,' said Isabel.

Nearby, on a metal table, was a small black-and-white LCD screen. It was turned off. It had one red switch on its front panel. I pressed it. The screen came on.

The image on the screen was a view of the stairs from the security camera we'd turned away from us only minutes before.

The camera angle was weird too, not straight, as if whoever had moved it back had positioned it wrong. I couldn't see the door we'd come through, but I could see polished black boots and baggy black trousers. A guard was standing to attention on the stairs. They hadn't arrived with the locksmith yet.

Then something struck me. Did the fact that the guard was wearing black trousers mean that he wasn't one of the ordinary Topkapi security detail I'd seen earlier? Was this guy connected with the people doing the exploration work down here? If he was, our chances of experiencing Alek's fate had just risen by a factor of a hundred.

'Let's close this door,' I said.

We grabbed the door and pushed it closed.

Isabel's skin was shining like a mannequin's in the yellowy light.

'Someone's gone to a lot of trouble to keep all this hidden,' I said.

'I wonder why,' she said.

The unease I'd felt since I'd seen that guard was growing. We had to get out of here, and quickly.

I started walking towards an open area straight ahead, about the size of a tennis court. I was hoping we'd see a far wall beyond it, another door.

Through the columns I'd seen aluminium tables. I ran towards them. Isabel followed.

The tables were bare. There were four of them. One was upside down. It looked as if someone had cleared the place out.

Beyond them, at the centre of another open area, there was something on the floor. I ran toward it. It was a zodiac circle pattern in a three-foot wide grating made of interwoven bands of black and white marble.

'There was a lot of blood to be washed away in old temples,' said Isabel.

'Messy,' I said.

'I wouldn't have liked to be a slave cleaning this place up.'

I could see a red brick wall now, about fifty feet further on. It was almost totally in shadow. But there was no door.

I headed towards the wall, running now. Was there another way out? The pillars in the row in front of the wall were thicker than the others, maybe a foot across. Something about them looked familiar. Unsettlingly familiar.

Then it hit me. The photo on the Internet from the video of Alek's beheading was coming alive in front of me.

I reached the thicker pillars. I didn't want to be here, but I was being pulled forwards, like iron to a magnet. I felt cold.

The only sound I could hear now was my own breathing. I looked along the row of pillars, saw a dark stain below the next one along. Was this where it had happened? I walked over to it, bent down and touched the stain. It was bone dry and crumbled a little as I rubbed at it.

Images flooded my mind. I saw Alek lying in the morgue, blue-veined, his head oddly distant from his body. Then I saw Irene in her coffin, the top of her head covered by a cream veil. Then that picture of the poor receptionist. So many deaths. So much evil. I wanted the images to go away. But they wouldn't.

'They usually drug them before...' Isabel's voice trailed off. Her hand was on my shoulder.

'They mustn't give a damn, leaving a stain like this,' I said.

'They probably haven't finished cleaning up yet.' She gripped my shoulder tight. 'Come on, Sean. I can get the Consulate involved now. I've got pictures. It's the proof we need. The

Turkish authorities will go berserk when they find out what's been going on down here, right under their noses.'

I could feel malevolence all around us, as if it was alive.

'Which way should we go?' she said.

The forest of pillars ran away ahead of us into darkness. There was no visible way out. We could follow the wall, see if there was another door somewhere, but which way should we go, left or right?

A low creak echoing through the hall answered my question. It only took a second to work out what it meant.

'Someone's coming,' hissed Isabel.

Her face was pale. 'What do we do?' she said.

'You won't like this.'

Her eyebrows shot up.

'Follow me.'

I ran, crouching, to the marble grating in the floor. A low grinding noise echoed through the hall. They were pushing the doors open. We had seconds.

I reached down. The marble grating reminded me of a man-hole cover. I pulled at it. It wouldn't budge.

'We're going to go down here,' I said.

The marble cover was cold. I pulled, bracing my knee on one side.

'What's down there?' she hissed. She pushed a pebble through one of the holes. I didn't hear it hit anything.

'Just help me,' I said. My fingers were covered in slime. I pulled again, harder this time.

Isabel went to the other side.

'There's a catch. There's gotta be,' I said. 'See if you can find it.' I moved my fingers under the edge of the grating, felt around. The slime on the underside was thicker in some places than others.

'Found it.' I pushed at something sticking out.

We pulled again. I half stood. The grating moved. We slid it sideways. The grinding noise had stopped. They wouldn't see us straight away, but it wouldn't take them long if they were searching.

The hole looked like a well. My skin crawled as I thought of what might be down there. There was a sour smell coming out of it too.

'Look, handholds,' I whispered. 'Come on. You go first. I can pull the grating back.'

'I can't,' she said softly. 'It's horrible.'

'Go on,' I said. 'It's not that bad. I'm not going to watch you being beheaded.'

I looked up. I'd heard a noise. I couldn't see the door we'd come in by, because of the pillars, but I could see the tables. When they reached them they would see us.

She put her legs over the edge, reached down, grabbed the handholds. She looked terrified, her eyes were wide, but she swung herself down.

I glanced in the direction of the tables. There was still no one there.

I pulled the grating halfway over the hole as noiselessly as I could. Then I swung my legs over, and took a deep breath.

I went down. The sickly smell was stronger suddenly. A rotting sourness engulfed me.

Isabel had turned the torch on and was pointing it downwards. The beam of light bounced around the encircling brick wall. I had an awful feeling I was being sucked into something which wouldn't be easy to get out of.

'Turn it off,' I whispered quickly, leaning down.

She did.

My head was parallel with the floor. I slid the grating forward, pulled it over on top of me. For one horrible second I thought the grating might tip over into the hole. But then it slid into place with a little snap. As my reward, most of the light went out. It felt as if a thick shroud had been thrown over us.

And the rotting smell just got worse with each step I went down.

37

The exclusive St George's Hotel, on Park Lane in central London, looked from the outside like a large top-of-the-range townhouse. Inside, however, once you got past the punctilious English butler and deferential Spanish housemaids, lay a haven for the platinum class.

Once a guest had been ushered in to their self-contained suite, they'd never even have to see another guest if they didn't want to. It was like having your own Mayfair townhouse, with a two-lane swimming pool, a marble jacuzzi, a canopied balcony overlooking a private garden, a chef, a driver and a personal masseuse – Thai or Swedish – all to yourself.

Arap Anach was well used to such simple pleasures. Having recently arrived, he was sitting alone in the main reception area of his suite watching a wall-mounted LCD TV.

The channel he was tuned to, Al-Jazeera English, was showing images of a riot. He had the sound turned down. On the screen a veiled woman was running towards the camera. She was screaming. Blood was streaming down her face from a deep cut in the centre of her forehead. Behind her a line of black-scarved and hooded rioters was throwing stones at a distant police line. Arap sat back in his chair. It was all going exactly to plan, better than he could have expected.

The riots and demonstrations against the mosque raids in London and Paris were producing the desired effect. It was easy to stir things up if you knew how; to incite hatred if you had the right connections.

A buzzer sounded. Arap stood, walked to the desk, picked up the electronic tablet that came with the suite and pressed a button.

An image popped on to the screen. It showed the hallway of the hotel. A man was being helped from a long navy overcoat.

The butler turned to the camera and bowed. 'Your guest has arrived, sir.' The microphone he spoke into was on a stalk running from his ear to his cheek.

'Show him up.'

The butler nodded.

Arap reached out for a slim laptop that sat on a long walnut cabinet. He tapped the screen. An image flashed onto it; two faces side-by-side, passport photo sized, a man and a woman.

Images of people who'd soon be dead.

He flicked his fingers over the mouse pad. The images of Isabel and Sean grew larger. The discovery of their bodies might not even be noticed once the events on Friday reached their climax, but even if their deaths were covered in the media it would send a perfect signal.

Peaceful co-existence was no longer an option. New policies were needed. And they would be implemented, once the change had taken place.

38

I gagged at one point, the smell was so disgusting. I stopped, took a slow breath and looked up. So far, nothing. I imagined the grating above us being opened at any moment. I needed to cough. I suppressed it. Seconds went by.

The grating above me, a bright criss-cross, didn't move. After the wave of silent gagging passed I kept going down.

Then I heard someone shout in Turkish. It sounded as if they were right above us. Isabel turned the torch off. I stopped, absolutely sure that the grating above would be moved aside, that we'd been caught. But the seconds turned into a minute, and only silence followed.

In the stinking dark, gripping each handhold as tightly as I could, my hands like claws, I moved down one rung at a time. And the deeper I went, the smellier it got, until something slapped at my foot and I almost shouted.

'Careful,' Isabel hissed. She pinched my ankle. I moved up a rung. How was I supposed to know she'd stopped? All around there was only shadows. The only light was a faint glow from the grating far above.

I was scared now, and nauseated by the smell. A tiny part of me almost thought it might be better to go back up and face whoever was up there.

Then I heard another shout, and a moment later louder voices, different voices, someone angry.

Shoes tap-tapped across the grating above. The light dimmed, as if there'd been an eclipse. A vein throbbed in my neck.

Then the light dimmed more and I distinctly heard a match being struck, and the tiny sound of something dropping onto the grating.

Someone was standing up there. And they were smoking. Maybe they were looking down at the grating. Did they know we were down here? Were they doing this deliberately?

Looking up, I thought I could make out the shape of boots cutting the light out. This was it. Any second. It were over.

I thought about Alek, what had happened to him up there. Something tightened inside me, as if a cable was being pulled. I wasn't going to give up. They'd have to come down here and get me.

Then there was another distant, excited shout. The shadow moved. A sprinkling of dust fell on my face. I closed my eyes. Something touched my leg. I jerked, shook it. An image of a giant rat pawing at me flashed through my mind.

'Stop,' whispered Isabel.

I put my foot back on the rung.

'There's a passage down here. Maybe we can use it.'

She switched her torch on, her hand covering it almost completely, making the light dim and red. Slimy grey brick appeared all around. I looked down.

When Isabel had said passage, I'd imagined a walkway we could stand up in. What she'd meant was a brick-lined pipe about four foot high, running off horizontally from the drain we were descending. Its slope must have been only a few degrees.

The pipe's entrance was next to the rung Isabel was holding on to. I had serious doubts about going into it – we'd have to crawl – and God only knew what was in there.

'What's it like?'

'It looks dry at least,' she said, softly. 'I'm going in.'

'Excellent,' I whispered. 'That means I'm coming after you.' I don't think she heard me.

I moved down another rung. Maybe it wasn't as bad as I imagined. I could see a little bit of the passage now. It didn't look slimy. In fact, it looked inviting.

And it would be a good idea to be out of this shaft, if they opened that grating up above.

Isabel had disappeared into the passage.

'Sure glad you found some use for my torch,' I whispered. I was in almost total darkness. Then, just for a moment, she shone the torch beam back through the pipe, so I could see enough to pull myself into it. She must have heard me that time.

In the pipe, all I could see of Isabel were the dark soles of her runners. There were long fingers of green slime embedded in them. She pointed the beam in front of her most of the time, illuminating the grey bricks all around us as she moved forward.

The smell was different now. It was more clayey, less rotting water. And I could feel the enormous weight of the earth above us, because of the way the tunnel bulged in places, as if it had blisters, as if it might burst.

As I moved forward I scuffed my hands on pieces of brick lying on the curved floor of the tunnel. Who or what had put them there?

'Can you go a bit faster?' I said. I wanted out of the place, and to stand up.

After about fifty knee-scraping feet, I stopped. It was stuffy now. Sweat was prickling my brow. My head was ringing too. The ear-splitting explosion in Iraq had left me with a dull headache that came and went at odd times. I could ignore it in the open air, but down here, with walls pressing in around us, it was coming back for another shot at the title.

I closed my eyes, took three deep breaths, held each of them and released them slowly. I'd done a course in Pranayama yogic breath control, where I'd learned to control my breathing, the summer before as a way to improve my free diving times and to help me feel calmer. As I slowly let out the last breath a distant voice came to me. Was I imagining it? I opened my eyes. I couldn't hear Isabel moving anymore. She must have stopped. And she'd turned the torch off. The darkness had enveloped me completely. It felt as if I'd been swallowed.

I took another deep breath.

Then, just ahead, as my eyes adjusted, I saw a faint light, dancing about twenty feet away, playing on the floor of the tunnel like an apparition. Then a shadow blocked my view. Isabel was moving forward again. I followed her, slowly, my hands and knees scraping on the brick under me.

As I came closer to it, I saw the light was a faint beam streaming down from a pipe heading up into the roof of the tunnel. For a brief moment, hope surged inside me as I imagined a hole just wide enough for us to escape through. When I came closer though, I saw, to my disappointment, that the pipe wasn't even a foot wide. Isabel was beyond it. I could hear her breathing.

I looked up the pipe when I reached it. There was a grating at the top, maybe fifty feet away, tantalisingly close, but sickeningly far. The grating was casting a pattern in the shaft of light streaming down.

I pulled back. I could just about make out Isabel's shadow now beyond the beam of light. The light gave the tunnel floor a ghostly sheen. A feeling of being trapped, buried alive, rose up in me as I looked up the pipe again. It felt as if the walls around me were tightening, moving in slowly.

Then I heard the voice again. It was clearer this time. It sounded as if whoever had spoken was only a few feet above us. The man had only said a few words – 'Have you found them?' – but unsettlingly I knew the voice. Could it be?

Our heads banged softly as we both peered up towards the grating. I rubbed mine, pulled back to let her look up.

Isabel moved back after a few seconds. I looked up again. Through the grating above, as my eyes focused on it, I could make out an arched brick roof. That was all.

Then the voice spoke again.

'She didn't tell us she was coming here.'

My suspicions were confirmed. I don't know how close Peter was to the grating, but the sound of his voice had travelled down clearly to me, as if he was only a few feet away.

I said the word 'Peter' softly to Isabel. I could just about make out her expression. Her gaze was fixed on something in the middle distance. She blinked and nodded.

We heard Peter's voice again, but it was more distant, indistinct now. He was moving away.

I put my hand on Isabel's shoulder. She'd moved a little closer to the beam of ghostly light and was looking upwards into it. She seemed to be about to fall towards me, she was stretching forward so much.

'What's he doing up there? Why is he talking about us?' I asked.

256

'Don't jump to conclusions.' She sounded angry, and her expression was as dark as a storm.

'We simply heard a conversation. It proves nothing.'

'So who's he talking to?'

'Honestly, I don't know.'

'What the hell's he doing here? He's walking around up there as if he owns the place.'

She didn't reply.

Thoughts were racing each other through my head. If Peter knew about this dig, was he also involved with the bastards behind Alek's murder? Was that too crazy? But why else would he be up there, talking like that? Then something clicked, like a lock opening. This was why he was being so weird, why he hadn't told me that Isabel wasn't going to meet me, why he wanted me out of Istanbul quickly.

He was working with them, the people who'd murdered Alek. It would certainly explain a lot.

I felt stupid. I shouldn't have told him anything.

'We gotta keep moving,' I hissed. 'Look for another way out. I'm not hanging around here.'

'Can you hear water?' said Isabel.

'No.' The thought of water down here was not pleasant. I imagined slimy, unrecognisable creatures living in it. At least with a dry tunnel you knew what you were dealing with.

'I can hear water,' she said. She turned the torch on, pointed it ahead and crawled on.

When I caught up with her, she was sitting on the far side of a three-foot wide circular opening in the floor, shining the torch beam down into it. Below, an arm's length away, I could see water. I felt a sinking feeling as I looked at it. This could well be a way out of here, but there was almost definitely something disgusting down there too. I just knew it.

'I wonder if we're still under Hagia Sophia?' I said, glancing around.

'No idea, but this has to go downhill. It's flowing. There has to be a way out for all this water.'

'I'm going to put you forward for the Nobel Prize for Observation for that.'

'Stop, Sean. Feel this. It's marble.'

She had her hand below the opening. I put my hand in the same place. Our fingers touched. She gripped my hand. I could just about make out her troubled expression in the torchlight reflecting back from the water below.

'I hate this place,' she said, softly. Her grip tightened. I felt her shiver. 'I hate it so much. Don't ever bloody leave me down here.' She sounded angry again.

'I won't. I promise. What makes you think I would?'

She paused before answering. 'I was left behind before. It was the worst thing that ever frigging happened to me.'

I looked into her eyes. 'It won't happen here.'

She released her grip on me. 'The bastard said he'd come back.' I could hear her take a deep breath. 'But he didn't.'

'Who?

'Mark. My ex. The guy you met in Mosul. I was married to him once.'

'Why the hell did he leave you?'

She looked into my eyes, as if assessing whether to tell me more. Then she looked down at the water flowing below us.

'There's not much to say. We were with a British building contractor in Kurdish Iraq. The guest house we were staying in was attacked. Mark went out the back door, left us. That's it.' She shrugged. 'I waited with this big Scottish businessman who'd actually shitted himself. We were lucky. The attackers fled after they shot the place up a few times.'

'Mark didn't come back?'

'He said he wanted to, but the Iraqi police unit he found detained him. The next time I saw him was in a police station in Kirkuk. He was full of apologies. But things were never the same between us.'

'I can definitely understand that,' I said. 'And I promise you. We'll find a way out of this together.' I was trying to be positive for the both of us.

'This has to run into one of the old underground cisterns. They had them all over the city for when they were besieged. They had the best aqueducts here, the best water management system in the whole Roman Empire. We're probably near a way out.'

A smile crossed her face. She looked down at the water. It was black, unpleasant looking.

'This is very scary, Sean.'

'It's only water,' I said.

'The odds of dying underground are a million to one, right?'

'Unless you're underground already,' I said.

'Thanks.'

There was a salty fishy smell in the air. It was coming up from the water.

'Can you smell salt water?' I said.

She sniffed. 'A little. Is that good?'

'The Bosphorus is very salty. We can't be that far from it.'

The light from the torch became dimmer. Now it was only about half the strength it had been when I'd turned it on. Why hadn't I bought extra batteries? Beyond the beam of fading light, the darkness pressed in, like an animal that knows when its prey is faltering.

If we were going to do this, we had to get moving. 'I'm going down to have a look,' I said.

The torch beam became weaker.

'I won't be able to pull you back up,' she said. There was anxiety in her voice.

'Don't worry, I can wedge myself against the sides if I have to.' I peered down. It looked doable, just. 'I have to check this out, Isabel. We could be near an exit.'

That was the optimist talking again. I'd definitely have preferred to stay in the dry tunnel. But if anyone came after us they'd probably come through the tunnel first, before going down into this water. Going this way would buy us time.

Then I felt something fall on my shoulder. Something heavy.

'Uuuhhhh.' I jerked and brushed frantically at whatever it was. Something black fell in front of me. It was the biggest spider I'd ever seen. It had hair like an old hippie's. It scuttled away into the darkness. I shuddered, half stood, banged my head against the roof, sickeningly hard, bent down quickly and rubbed it.

'Are you OK?' said Isabel.

'Sure. No problem. I just love it down here.'

'Look, a fish,' she said. She pointed upwards. A fish shaped sign had been carved into a brick above our heads. 'Amazing.' She traced her finger over the sign in the jaundiced light from the torch.

'You know a Byzantine emperor, Alexius III, was supposed to have escaped this city through a tunnel under Hagia Sophia just like this?' I said.

She shook her head.

'That's what they say. He got away in a fishing boat waiting for him in the Bosphorus. He fled with his mistress, a Serbian princess, and his daughter the night before this city was taken during the fourth crusade. A wonderful crusade that was. That was about this time of year too.' I leaned over the hole.

'You know if those crusaders hadn't sacked this city, Constantinople might never have fallen to the Ottomans. And then Christopher Columbus would never have raised enough money for his expeditions.'

The torch became fainter.

'Time to go,' I said. The water looked darker now, ripples twisting on its surface as if it were alive.

'All that water's gotta go somewhere,' I repeated, hopefully. It was true though. The tunnel we were in might just stop somewhere, but a tunnel with moving water in it had to have been built to exit into the Bosphorus or the Golden Horn. This had to be our way out.

There was a gap of maybe four feet between the water and the roof of the tunnel holding it. I looked at Isabel. She had a gaunt look on her face, as if she were looking at a ghost.

My chest tightened as I thought about the water. I had to fight off thoughts of what might be down there – worms, eels, snakes, leeches – all the slimy things in the world. I clenched my fists. Maybe they weren't here.

'I'm sure we'll find a way out.'

She nodded.

I dropped into the water.

A loud splash echoed. A fierce iciness engulfed me. The current tugged at me. I was in a pipe-like tunnel similar to the one I'd just dropped out of. But this one was bigger, and half full of water. And for a few seconds, I couldn't get to my feet, the bottom of the tunnel, under the water, was so slimy. I looked up. Isabel was leaning down precariously, shining the torch along the tunnel roof in the direction the water was flowing.

Then I steadied myself, found my footing, stood. I was wet all over. My hair was dripping down my back.

'Can you see a way out?' she said.

I'd banged my ankle and my elbow. But the water was only up to my thighs.

'No,' I said. The tunnel just went on and on like the one up above.

A violent shiver came over me. My earlier optimism seemed totally unrealistic.

The water was a lot colder than I'd imagined. And my trousers felt heavy, as if they were dragging me down. This didn't seem like such a good idea any more.

I stood up straighter, shook myself like a dog, took a long breath, held it. I wasn't going back. This water had to have a way out. And we had to follow it, no matter how bad it seemed. I wasn't giving up.

'I can stand. And it's big enough to wade down,' I said. My words echoed in the darkness. 'The water isn't that deep.'

'Hold this,' said Isabel. I looked up. She leaned down and passed me the torch.

Then she dropped into the water beside me with a huge splash. I closed my eyes, and wiped the water off my face. Then I held my hand out to help her steady herself.

'Great fun, isn't it?'

She held my hand tight. I passed her the torch.

'Turn it off for 30 seconds, Isabel, the batteries need a rest. When you turn it on, do it only for a few seconds at a time.

We've got to conserve power. I don't know how long this tunnel is. When we need light, we'll need some power, OK?'

She turned the torch off.

'I bet you're glad you came along tonight,' I said into the darkness.

'You are a barrel of fun,' she replied. I heard her teeth chattering.

She blinked the torch on, briefly, then off again.

The water was freezing, but the rate at which it was flowing gave me hope. We'd done the right thing.

Suddenly rock-hard goose bumps broke out all over my legs, arms, and on my back. It was a weird feeling, but I had to concentrate on the positives. The torch was still working. Neither of us was injured. We'd be out of here soon.

We began wading. I led the way. Above our heads bricks seemed to spring forward every time the light illuminated them. Their solid construction was reassuring though. If they'd lasted this long, they were definitely going to last until we got out of here.

And then something thick and slithery touched my calf, moving with the current.

I went rigid. What the hell was that – fish, eels?

An instinctive terror gripped me. The sinews in my neck tightened. They felt like wires. I wanted to scream, but my mouth was clamped tight. Isabel didn't need to know about this.

I raised my hands towards the roof, controlled my breathing again. Whatever had touched me had passed. It was gone. Hopefully for good.

Isabel flicked on the torch. 'Are you OK?'

'Sure,' I lied.

She flicked the torch off. We moved forward with the flow.

I was shivering almost uncontrollably now. I thought about everything we'd seen, everything we'd heard, the fact that we'd found the place Alek had been butchered in, that we'd heard Peter. We had to get out of here. We had to tell someone what we'd found.

We waded on.

The next time the light turned on, I noticed that the gap between the roof and the water was closing slowly, but inexorably. The walls seemed to be tightening around us too. I looked back quickly.

The level of the water hadn't changed dramatically, but it had changed. It was almost up to my waist now. And I could sense more than ever the millions of tons of rock above us, pressing down.

Then suddenly, there was a sloshing noise. I had no idea what it meant. And then a groan echoed down the tunnel. Isabel flicked the torch on.

'Something touched me,' she said. Her voice was defiant, but shaky.

'It's nothing,' I said. 'Don't think about it. We'll be out of here soon.'

The surface of the water looked alive every time Isabel turned the torch on now, a black skin shifting languidly as if something was moving fast beneath it. We waded on. I was shivering and every second I expected something slithery to touch me again – or worse, to take a bite.

And then I saw vertical bars looming, blocking our way. Maybe I should have expected them, but I hadn't, and seeing them there, blocking us, felt like a disaster.

This tunnel could be a trap. They'd have had to have been pretty stupid not to put bars in. And the Byzantines were anything but stupid. Thieves and enemies could have easily gained access to the palace, or Hagia Sophia, if they waded up this way.

'I don't believe this,' said Isabel.

The water was rushing faster now, pulling at my trousers, at my feet. We stood there staring at the bars. There was no way we were getting through them. They looked completely solid.

'Just once in a while,' I said, 'It'd be cool if ancient engineers hadn't been so damn efficient.' I waded forward, touched the bars, held them with both hands. They were ice cold, and hard as steel. I kicked at them. Yes, they went down all the way. There wasn't even a gap of an inch at the bottom.

'Well, this proves one thing,' I said. 'We're nearly outside.'

'I'm getting very cold,' said Isabel. Her teeth were chattering audibly now.

I pressed at one of the bars near where it went into the roof. Maybe, just maybe, the mortar and brick might have worn away with time.

But the bar was as unyielding as granite. Isabel turned the torch off. I shivered in the dark. I felt angry with myself. I should have guessed these bars would be here. We were trapped.

Something slithered over my ankle. My worst fears came alive.

Because this time, the slithering didn't stop. A shoal of eels or giant worms was passing through my legs. Every sinew in my body said move, get out of here, but I couldn't.

I was paralysed. I stood still, my eyes wider than I thought they could go, just letting it happen, letting the slithering go on and on.

Isabel turned the torch on. By the look on her face, I knew she felt them too, whatever they were.

Revulsion gripped me. Hot bile came up into my mouth. My stomach was a ball of hard muscle.

Then something gripped my calf, and another wave of fear passed through me.

Isabel reached out to me. She kept the torch beam on, even though it was really faint now. We gripped each other's fingers tightly.

Then the beam dimmed again and she turned the torch off.

And something bit me in the thigh, right through my trousers. Its teeth were needles.

39

Sergeant Mowlam was working an extra shift. It didn't happen often, only in emergencies. The situation in Spain was deteriorating.

Local bloggers, Twitter addicts and radio journalists were providing a fuller picture of what was going on than TVE, the Spanish state television station. But what his superiors needed to know was, were agitators fermenting the violence, as some were claiming?

Sergeant Mowlam was watching images from security cameras at the edge of the Plaza de los Cortes. The live images were usually available for car drivers to assess the level of traffic in central Madrid, but the public feed had been turned off. A separate security services feed had replaced it. The feed showed a neo-classical pillared and pedimented building with bronze lions guarding the wide steps leading up to its entrance.

The image also showed a mob of about five thousand men and women milling around in front of the Congreso de los Diputados, the Spanish parliament. The mob was pushing up against a line of Spanish police from the Cuerpo Nacional de Policía. The riot police were equipped with padded body suits, transparent shields and futuristic helmets. What they clearly weren't prepared for though was the anger of the crowd.

And there weren't enough of them either. A raid had taken place on a small new mosque in the city. But why this reaction to such a minor provocation? He looked at the screen to his right. Twitter, Facebook and other messages were moving fast up the screen mentioning Madrid, Plaza de los Cortes or other key words. There were a lot of them.

The ones rated as inflammatory by the automated word checking system, the ones that encouraged violence, paused for a few seconds in the centre of the screen, before disappearing to the right to be stored for further processing. But there weren't that many of them, that was what was surprising. He'd only seen two in the last five minutes.

So who the hell was stirring these riots up? And why?

40

Whatever had bit me moved on, leaving a stinging sensation on my thigh.

But what if more of them started biting, all together? My breathing was quick, shallow. And I couldn't feel my feet anymore. All around was the deepest dark I'd ever known.

And still the eels or water snakes or whatever they were wriggled through my legs, around my thighs. Some were biting like rats at a feast now. Only the pressure of the current kept them from latching on for too long, or maybe the taste of my cotton chinos wasn't to their liking. Among them there were rough-skinned giants, whose skin felt like sandpaper even through cotton, and whose bodies were as thick as my arm.

Isabel let out an echoing yelp. 'It's biting me!' She sloshed up and down, splashing frantically, sending waves into me.

'Stop moving,' I said softly. 'It'll go away.'

She blinked the torch on, stopped splashing. I could hear her breathing.

'I don't think that Alexius guy came this way. Royalty wouldn't put up with this,' she said, quickly.

She looked pale, like the next victim in a horror movie. The one who knows what's about to happen to her.

'Is it gone?'

She shook her head. The torch light was fading. She turned it off. That took a lot of courage.

'I'm coming.'

I waded towards her, pushing my feet against a writhing mass as I tried not to think about them. I put my hands into the water and ran them down her legs quickly. My chin was barely above the water at the end. I kept breathing slowly. There was indeed something thick and unpleasantly slimy attached to her bare ankle.

I straightened up, pushed my foot down on it slowly and pressed my weight hard on it. Whatever it was, it held for another moment, then slithered away.

'They'll all be gone in a minute,' I said confidently. It seemed like the right thing to say. Something my dad would have said.

'Can this get any bloody worse?' she roared. Her voice echoed.

'It could,' I said.

'How?' she screamed.

I didn't answer. My head was throbbing. I leaned a hand against the roof. It was slimy. I'd been OK while we'd been moving forward. I'd been concentrating on what I was doing, focusing on moving ahead. But now that we were stuck there was time to think. A memory of Irene came to me. She'd looked pale sometimes, like Isabel right now.

One thing was sure. Irene wouldn't have wanted me to die down here. She'd have wanted me to fight. To live.

There was one option left.

I gripped Isabel's shoulder. She flicked the light on again. 'We're going to get out of here,' I said. 'Just be still. They'll move on.'

She nodded, and as soon as the beam faded, she turned it off. The darkness flooded back.

A few seconds later, whatever had been slithering and biting us passed. This was our chance.

'I'm going to dive down to see if I can pull out some of the bars at the bottom. They've gotta be worn away down there.'

'Do it quick, Sean, please. The next lot might be hungrier.'

There was still an occasional slithering past my legs, but I tried to put it out of my mind.

Suddenly, I could feel Isabel's breath on my cheek, warm and invigorating.

'You can do it, Sean,' she whispered near my ear. My teeth were chattering. I clamped my mouth shut. She was trying to encourage me, I knew; I also knew she'd been incredibly brave already, coming down here, risking herself to be with me.

Now it was my turn.

I took a breath, held my nose and dropped down fast. The icy water hit my face like a vicious slap. The bars were rough in my hands.

Isabel turned the torch on. Its light filtered down milkily, as if I was in some ghostly Hall of Mirrors. I pulled myself down further into the icy gloom, my fingers numbly pulling at the pitted bars.

A tendril brushed my face, tingling at my cheek. An angry thumping had started inside my left rib cage. I kept my eyes open, trying to pick out anything in the watery gloom, hoping Isabel would be able to keep the torch on for as long as possible.

Then my foot hit the side of the tunnel. I let go of a bar with one hand. For a moment I didn't know which way was up. I touched Isabel's legs, kicked for the surface. My head broke out of the water.

'Yeuch,' I said, spluttering, gulping air. I rubbed the water from my eyes.

She held out her hand and squeezed my shoulder. It felt warm, encouraging.

'Are you OK?' she said.

I was shivering, almost uncontrollably so, but I nodded.

The torch faded. Its light was a thin yellow mist. Now, I could only see the sheen of black water. It seemed higher than it had a few moments ago. Isabel turned the beam off.

I breathed in, held it. A reliable sign of early stage hypothermia is fast breathing. It was time to get out of the water. Instead, I had to go down again. This time in the dark.

'Maybe we should go back, Sean?' There was a shiver in her voice.

I didn't answer. I took another deep breath, permeating my blood with air, and went down, a needle-sharp determination pushing me on.

My hands went straight into the slime at the bottom of the bars this time. I dug frantically, found something round, hard. It felt like a leather bag that had solidified into a ball around its contents

I yanked it from the mud, headed for the surface and held it up in front of me like a prize. For a moment I imagined it might be a bag of gold coins that that guy Alexius had left behind. Isabel turned the torch on as water dripped from me.

'My God,' she shouted. 'What did you bring that up for?'

I blinked. My prize was the top part of a skull covered in oozing mud.

It made a soft plop as it hit the water. I was grateful the flesh was long gone, eaten by only God knew what.

'Don't bring that up again.' Isabel looked really frightened now.

'You weren't the one holding it.'

I reached forward in the darkness, found Isabel, held her arm tight. She gripped me back. I wanted to hug her. I hadn't felt such a protective instinct towards someone in a long time.

That skull could have belonged to someone who'd died where we stood. How long had that taken? Probably not *that* long in this cold.

Isabel pulled me to her. 'When we get out of here, I want to lie in the sun for a long time,' she said.

I imagined lying beside her.

I squeezed her shoulder, took a huge breath and dived in for the third time.

I could feel where the bars met the bottom now that the skull was out of the way, though I couldn't see anything at all in the blackness. But I'd been right. They were worn away a little. One was not even connected to the floor of the tunnel any more. There was a chance. I pulled at the bar. It didn't bend.

I broke the surface, shivering. Isabel turned the torch on for a moment. Her expression was hopeful.

I nodded. I couldn't smile. The bar had been too solid to give much hope. She turned the torch off.

The last thing I saw as I filled my lungs with air was Isabel's half smile. It reminded me of Irene's, the memory of which had been fading, until her face had become a dreamlike vision; her sitting by the window in our bedroom, getting ready to go out, smiling as if she had a surprise for me. That part of my life, all that happiness, was so distant now.

I dived in again and made my way quickly down to the bottom of the bars.

This time I would check the bottom of the other two bars.

Isabel turned the torch on briefly, as I went down. Its light held steady for a few seconds, then went out. I used my hands to feel my way down.

My fingers were almost totally numb, but I pushed them down into the silt.

And a surge of hope poured through me. One of the other bars was also worn away at the bottom, deep in the mud. I felt for the last one. There was something hard and square wedged against it, buried in the mud. I pulled at the obstruction. It held fast. I pulled harder. Whatever it was, it was definitely manmade. It had corners. It seemed to be a box.

And then it was free in my hands. I kicked for the surface. The torch went on as I splashed into the air.

'What about this?' I said. I passed the object to Isabel. She turned it over in her hands.

'But the best news is, two of the bars are worn away down there. If I can bend them enough, you might be able to slip through.'

All I could hear was the silky rush of the water as it went past, the drips falling from me. Isabel turned the torch off.

'I'm not leaving you,' she said. 'If you can't get through, we'll have to find another way out.'

'I want you to go first,' I said.

'No, I won't. If someone as big as you can get through, don't worry – I'll be right behind.'

She turned the torch on for only a second and winked at me. It warmed me. And then, despite the freezing cold, my chattering teeth, the salty, rancid smell, I laughed as if we weren't buried under tons of rock, as if we were free, in the middle of an open field.

Then I took a deep breath, slipped under the water and made my way to the bottom. I wedged my feet against the other bars and pulled at one of the ones which wasn't connected at the bottom. It moved, shifted a little. Slowly at first, but then more quickly. I went up for air, then back down again.

This time I pulled at the other bar. I had to bend two high up enough for me to be able to get through. It wasn't easy, but I felt it give, just a little, then a bit more. Now there was a gap at the bottom. It might just be big enough. But I didn't want to get stuck down there.

I gulped more air, dived back in, pulled at the bars again. They bent some more. Now I'd try it. I pulled myself forward and down.

It was a tight squeeze, and for a truly horrible moment I thought I was going to get stuck, that my belt had caught, but then I was through.

I came to the surface. 'Come on,' I shouted. A surge of exhilaration ran through me as if I'd won an Olympic medal. We were through!

Isabel flicked the torch on, let out a whoop, passed it through to me and dived down into the water. A few seconds later she was beside me.

We started wading, fast.

The roof of the tunnel was flat from that point, and the water was up to our chests, but thankfully the level didn't change any more. As we waded forward I noticed there was a difference in the atmosphere too. It was warmer, as if we were closer to open air. We moved fast, shivering and mostly in darkness, but occasionally with the torch light on for a few seconds. My chin was still chattering, my feet and hands numb, but I knew we would find a way out now.

After another fifty yards I heard a hissing noise that sounded like heavy rain. Then I heard a car beeping distantly, like the toot of a far off train. It was a wonderful sound. The sound of humanity. I had to stop and savour it.

The walls had barnacles on them now. And there was a faint phosphorescent glow up ahead.

Then, in the distance, I saw the most amazing sight – sparkling diamonds. It was the distant Asian shore of the Bosphorus, with its thousands of building and street lights glittering against velvet blackness. We were emerging, wet and shivering, at sea level at the bottom of the hill that Hagia Eirene and Hagia Sophia crowned. And we were alive.

We'd done it. We'd got out.

I turned to Isabel. She was waving the object I'd pulled from the water. It looked like a bundle of disintegrating leather rags.

'You've still got that?' I said. She smiled widely, as if she'd won a rollover on the lottery.

Rain blew into my face as we came into the open leaving the brick pipe we'd been stumbling through behind. The feeling of space, lightness, airiness was wonderful. So much so that the rain on my face was a total pleasure.

'We did it,' she said. The rock we were standing on was flat, not very wide and the Bosphorus was lapping at its edge. It was right beside where the water from the pipe was pouring out. She hugged me. A surge of warm feelings for her ran through me. But I wasn't going to tell her. I had no idea if it would last, even if it felt this real. I almost hoped they would go away. They made things too complicated.

'God only knows the last time someone escaped this way,' I said. Then I pulled away from her, looked around, up the steep rocky shore behind us. It wasn't going to be easy climbing up. The rocks were large and the angle was almost like a cliff.

'We've got to be careful. They're probably still looking for us. Your boss, that is.'

'Don't jump to conclusions, Sean, please. There's an explanation for what we heard, for him being there.'

At that moment I didn't care enough to say any more or to wonder why she was still sticking to the party line. We'd escaped. Every moment after this would be a gift. I sampled a heavenly lungful of air. There was a wonderful freshness to it, as if it was a meadow I was standing in.

I closed my eyes and turned my head up towards the rain. I'd never ever wanted to do such a thing before. Raindrops hit my head like a waterfall of ping-pong balls.

I heard Isabel moving to my left, where the incline of the rocky wall looked a little less steep. I followed her. We must have looked like giant half-drowned water rats. My teeth were still chattering. And there wasn't any easy way to go up.

And then I heard the music, and maybe twenty feet from the shore, a line of fairy lights appeared, gliding towards us like an apparition. As they grew brighter, a surge of anxiety ran through me. Who the hell was out on the Bosphorus in the middle of the night?

Then I recognised the music. It was one of those upbeat remixes of an old jazz song, which had been popular back in the States a few years ago.

A second later a searing light shone in our faces. I was completely blinded.

Then a voice rang out. The accent was American.

'What the goddam hell are you up to?'

'We had an accident,' I called back. 'Help us out here, buddy.'

'For a fellow American, no problem. Hold on. I'll throw you a line.'

41

The sound of the pane of glass being removed from one of the back windows of Sean's house in London was as loud as the noise of a suction cap being removed from a jam jar. The window had an alarm attached to it, but only went off if the window was opened.

A man dressed in a dark-navy tracksuit and trainers slipped a thin piece of metal – an electric current generator – between the two parts of the alarm and opened the window. A minute later he was working his way through the rooms. He was mostly interested in Sean's office. Once he found it, he closed the curtains, turned on the lights and began photographing. He took pictures of everything that might be of interest. He photographed the cover pages of the academic journals beside Sean's desk, the covers of the novels he was reading, his mobile phone bills, his bank account statements, his birth certificate, pictures of him with the swimming and boxing medals he'd won in his first year at university. He also photographed the two newspaper articles on Sean's escapade in Afghanistan, which were tucked under a picture of his dead wife.

It took two hours in all. There was a lot of stuff about Sean available on the Internet and from computer records, but getting the juicy stuff, what he held close to his heart, was best done by searching someone's home. Before the thin-faced man fixed the glass pane back in place, he ran a tube of quick drying plaster along the edge of the window. Only the most minutely observant would know what had happened.

42

'You guys really should come up with a better story than that,' said Kaiser.

We were sitting in the curved seating area in the main cabin of Bobby Kaiser's Sunseeker motor yacht, bobbing at anchor in the heavy rain. My relief at having been hauled out of the Bosphorus and back into the 21st century was draining away fast under the glare of his cynicism.

He'd let down the anchor soon after he'd picked us up. The cabin was wonderfully warm, smelled of coffee, and was panelled in teak like the inside of an oil billionaire's Bentley. But we still had problems.

We'd been trying to convince Kaiser – that was what he insisted we call him – that we'd been forced down the rock wall after being robbed. Now I wasn't sure if coming on board had been such a good idea after all.

'You don't expect us to believe that lame story, do ya?' He turned to a slim, unsmiling Arab with a round well-fed face, his assistant I presumed, who was perched halfway up the steep aluminium stairs that led up to the deck.

Kaiser had one of those pumped-up bodies I associated with lots of time spent in the gym. Both he and his Arab friend wore black T-shirts and jeans. Kaiser's clothes fitted loosely.

His assistant was either wearing clothes meant for someone much thinner, or he liked the skin-tight look.

'The bull's piling up tonight, Tunjai,' said Kaiser.

The Arab stared at us with blank eyes.

A tic in my cheek started beating.

'Come on, guys, spill it. What were you doing in the Bosphorus in the middle of the night? And where did you find this?' He pointed at the wet square parcel that sat on the shiny, curved teak table in front of us, surrounded by slimy pieces of decaying leather.

'I told you. We found it among the rocks,' I said confidently. I stared at him. Isabel continued to dry her hair with the fluffy white towel Kaiser had given her. The plain black T-shirts and baggy pants Kaiser had given us were exactly what we'd needed. My trousers had a thick coating of mud.

'Bull, bull, bull,' was Kaiser's reply. He ran a finger over the clasp at the centre of the belt keeping the parcel together.

I'd been as keen as him to see what the parcel contained, but when he'd employed a tooth brush to clean the clasp, and revealed a ruby-coloured stone at its centre, I think we were all surprised. Within moments the atmosphere in the cabin had changed, cooled to icy. What we'd found was clearly valuable. All eyes were on it now.

'Make another one up, guys. That one smells. I don't know what you're up to, maybe you're as innocent as Mother T, but I don't think so. You never found this in any rocks.' He pointed his thin knife at the parcel.

The wet and oily looking leather skin was slowly drying in the cabin air. A squall of rain smashed onto the deck above us. The cabin lights flickered. The tic in my cheek started up again.

I felt as if I'd run a marathon. Maybe two.

Isabel was her usual classy self, despite the fact that she was wearing items meant for someone a few sizes bigger than her. Kaiser had been friendly up to this. If the parcel hadn't been sitting there between us, we'd probably have been reminiscing about Broadway shows by now.

Kaiser's Arab friend had gawped at Isabel when she'd reappeared after changing in the low-roofed cabin under the steep stairs that led up to the deck. I'd decided then that I didn't like him. The air of watchfulness he'd adopted since didn't help either.

'So what about you? What are you doing out here in the middle of the night? Fishing?' I said.

'No way, man. I wouldn't eat the giant eels they pull outta this place.'

'Eeuuu,' said Isabel. She shivered, then looked at me. Something was different now that we'd made it through that tunnel together. I knew I could rely on her.

Kaiser made a sucking noise. 'You seen 'em?'

'We saw something in the water. It could have been eels.'

'Fortune slips through the fingers, like the eels of the Bosphorus,' said the assistant. His voice was rough, like gravel after a rake had been hauled over it.

I remembered the tunnel, the dark, the slithering. I rubbed my calf. I'd found a long puckered break in the skin when I'd taken off my wet clothes, a triangular red weal, with blood near the surface, where an eel had been sucking on my flesh. We'd come far too close to becoming their dinner.

'So what are you doing out here?' asked Isabel.

The atmosphere in the room chilled a few more degrees. Kaiser wore a rock hard expression now. His assistant had stopped fidgeting.

Then Kaiser placed the knife he was holding on the table and spun it around. It stopped, pointing at me. His gaze remained fixed on it.

'OK, honey, seeing how y'all are so curious, I'll tell you what we're doing.' He paused, then pointed at Isabel. 'Then maybe you'll do me the favour of doing the same.'

I shifted on the curved high-backed cream leather bench. What the hell should we tell him?

'We will,' said Isabel. She sounded positive, but her eyes whispered something different.

Kaiser began talking. It sounded as if he was giving a well-practised description of his activities.

'We got a permit to map the floor of the channel here. We're using the best sediment-penetrating radar you can get your hands on,' he said. 'We scan by night, to avoid interference from the day-time traffic. This is the busiest sea lane in the world, you know. 60,000 ships pass through these straits each year, honey. We either work at night or we don't work at all. Any more questions?'

'And if you spot something on the sea floor, you report it?' said Isabel.

He nodded.

I leaned forward. 'Are you looking for the lost Ottoman Treasury? The Hazine mother lode?'

Isabel smiled at me and pushed her damp hair back from her face. She looked very calm for someone who'd just escaped death.

'No, mister smarty pants, we aren't.' Kaiser spun the knife again.

'When I was in the army,' he continued, 'they taught me a few things. Knowing when someone is hiding something was one.'

The next few seconds of silence were as tense as the two main cables on the Golden Gate Bridge.

'I thought most of you guys were sick of this region after all the extended tours,' I said.

'Must be the chicks,' he replied. He glanced at Isabel. 'They're real different out here.'

'Feminism doesn't travel well,' said Isabel.

He shrugged. 'At least they show a bit of respect.'

'Where did you serve?' she asked.

'I'll give you name, rank and serial number, but you're gonna have to torture me for more.' His hand lay cupped over the knife.

'Now, you gonna tell me about this little bundle?' He lifted the knife, pointed it at the parcel.

'We found it a few minutes ago,' I said. 'That's the truth. And right now we know as much about it as you do.'

'OK, so let's open it together then.' It was a statement, not a request.

Kaiser picked up the leather parcel. He had an irritating proprietorial grin on his face.

I leaned forward, was about to reach out and snap it from him, when Isabel gripped my arm tight.

'Sean,' she whispered. I glanced at her.

Her gaze was fixed on Kaiser's Arab friend. He'd moved from his perch, had come down the stairs and was only a few feet from us. He looked as if he was expecting a fight.

I pointed a finger at Kaiser. 'That doesn't belong to you,' I said.

'Don't worry, I ain't gonna steal your precious parcel,' said Kaiser. He put the parcel down, took pink rubber gloves from below the table and pulled them on. 'I just want to look at it. I can help you identify what you've found, OK? I'm just naturally curious, I swear.'

I had to admit I was curious too. And my suspicion of Kaiser was blunted by tiredness.

The parcel was about eight inches wide, eight long and four thick. There was a faint rotten fish smell coming from it.

Kaiser placed a white plastic board on the table. He put the parcel on the board and with all of us around him, began poking at the crumbling leather inner layer with what looked like a dentist's steel probe. As he picked away at it he examined what was being revealed with a large magnifying glass with a built-in light. He pulled some of the leather away. The process of pulling away the layers was like peeling the skin off an onion.

As he went deeper, I could see that whatever was inside was wrapped in a yellowy waxy material.

'That looks waterproof,' I said.

'Full marks, buddy,' said Kaiser. 'And it looks old too. Fifth Avenue was an Indian trail when this parcel was wrapped up. Pre-Ottoman, I'd say, just by the smell of it.' He put his nose to the parcel and breathed in deeply as if he was smelling an old wine.

'Did you know when Mehmed the Conqueror was supervising the building of his palace up on that hill, he spent a whole year searching for things like this?' he said.

He held the parcel up, turned it. The rain was beating down on the roof above us. The noise was getting louder, reverberating through the cabin.

'Mehmed met with the fishermen who worked these parts,' he went on. 'He got 'em to drag the seabed here with their nets for anything the Byzantines lost in the Bosphorus as they escaped the city.' He stuck the knife in a corner of the yellow waxy material, and with a slow movement, cut along one side, slicing through multiple layers.

'You know what bugs me?' he said. He looked at Isabel. 'I didn't get a single parcel sent to me during my three tours.'

He sliced along another side of the parcel. A second, more buttery yellow animal skin wrapping was revealed underneath the first. This skin was totally undamaged and sealed on one side with a blood-red wax seal.

'Did you know this city is where the Shroud of Turin came from?' he said, as he laid the parcel down with the seal visible on top.

'And that's one heck of a seal,' he said. Impressed into the wax was a stylized eagle with two heads. The wax was dull and faded, but the eagle was still impressive looking.

'That's the old Byzantine Imperial seal. There could be anything in this,' he said.

He shook the parcel gently. Tiny yellow fragments fell off.

'You know there's layers to this city that you wouldn't even believe.' He raised his knife, cut the seal, pulled the yellow skin off. All eyes were on the parcel.

I heard an intake of breath from Kaiser's assistant. Inside the parcel, in perfect condition, was the oldest book I'd ever seen. Its cover was a mottled coffee-brown colour. It had a stylized eagle in faded black on its front. The cover looked to be made from thin wood covered with leather. It was unlike any book I'd ever seen.

Kaiser, without much delicacy, cracked the book open. Its pages were stiff parchment, animal skins, dried and stretched. They had faded writing on them. The pages looked frail, but they still turned.

He let them fall on top of each other. Each page was different, frayed a little at the edges. He closed the book, turned it around, examined it from every angle. The pages were jagged, the back bare. Its binding was a visible, thin leathery cord, which passed through each page and was tied at the back. It looked more like a collection of bound documents than a book. What had we found?

I put my hand out. For a moment I thought he wasn't going to give me the book. I straightened, pushed my hand out further.

The atmosphere changed again. It felt as if we were heading for a confrontation. I moved my hand another inch towards him.

He grinned and passed me the book.

I gave him an equally insincere smile. Then I turned my attention to the book. A dark stain covered one corner. It looked as if the stain had been old long before the book had been lost.

'You guys made a real find,' said Kaiser. His assistant was standing beside me now. I could smell tobacco on his breath.

'Looks like it,' I said.

'You could wait a lifetime for something like this.' He was still smiling.

I put the book down on the plastic board and cracked it open using the thin dentist's probe that lay nearby.

I let the yellowing parchment pages fall on top of each other until the last page was revealed. Each page had writing on it. On the inside back cover was a large square in faded but still clear red ink. I thought of Father Gregory. This was exactly the kind of find he'd have loved.

The square was hand drawn and it had small double-headed eagles at each compass point, north, south, east and west. A line connected each double-headed eagle to make the square shape. Other lines, one each from the east and west eagles, and one from the south, connected straight to the north compass point in an arrow shape. It was an arrow facing upwards in a square.

Each small double-headed eagle was a faded colour. The top one was black, the bottom white, the east one green, the west red.

At the bottom of the inside back cover was a pale red inscription in what appeared to be Latin. I could just make out the words *fame ad mortem*, then further on *semel quisque* and later, very faded the words, *novus semita*.

Justinian the Great had moved the Byzantine Empire from Latin to Greek. This could well have been from his time, or from before.

'That looks like a Kabbalistic symbol,' said Kaiser. He was pointing at the square. His finger moved to point at the Latin inscription underneath.

'This could be anything, a prayer, an invocation, a magic spell. The Byzantines were into the occult big time. Cryptic signs, charms, evil eyes, and all that. I saw a symbol like this on a coin once, from Knossos. 5th century, I think it was. It means something, that's for sure.'

'It looks like a prayer to me,' I said. 'I wonder what library this manuscript came from.'

Above our heads, the rain was hissing loudly on the deck. Kaiser was staring wide-eyed at the book, as if it was an invitation to meet the Queen.

'If it's a library book, you can pay the fine, Sean,' said Isabel. 'You found it.'

'That red ink is worm scarlet. It's from a Middle Eastern tree insect – the coccus ilicis,' said Kaiser. He peered closer at the square.

'Where exactly did you find this?' he said.

'In the water, near where you picked us up,' I said loudly. Anyway it was true, relatively speaking, if you stretched the meaning of the word near.

Kaiser turned his head and looked up at the roof as if he'd heard something.

'We gotta get outta here at zero three thirty.'

'How come?' I asked.

'That's when the Turkish Coast Guard comes by, to check that we're gone. If we're not, they board us. It gives 'em something to do. We get a two-hour window each night. After that the ferries start up.' He looked at the shiny brass clock high up on the wall. It read three ten.

'We got a few minutes,' he said.

Isabel patted her pockets and retrieved her phone. I was amazed she still had it. She shook it. A little water dripped from it. She wasn't going to be calling up the cavalry any time soon.

'Anyone know how to fix wet phones?' she asked. 'I'd like to take some photos.'

'Sorry, honey,' said Kaiser. 'But don't worry. I'm gonna take all the shots we need.' He took a sleek black Leicon camera with a hooded lens from a shelf above the table, and began taking shots of the manuscript. He closed it so he could get a shot of the cover. I took a step sideways. His Leicon was similar to the one Alek had bought recently. There was a red light flashing on its side. It reminded me of one of the camera's best features.

'You'll get some good shots with that,' I said. I came up behind him, right up beside his shoulder. 'Good camera.'

He nodded. 'Only the best, man.'

I'd seen what I'd wanted to see, so I stepped back.

290

He turned the pages of the manuscript. A few of the pages were clearly letters that had been sewn in with other pages. They had seals at the end of the page, folds and headings at the top. Some of the letters had multiple seals. His camera whirred.

Most of the text was tightly packed and hand written. Some pages were decorated with a single ornately designed letter with spirals or corkscrew shapes around it in faded colours. Some of the pages were in Greek. A few were in Arabic. Kaiser stopped taking pictures.

'The Greek parts are Koine Greek. 5th to 7th century, I'd say. You can tell from the thin strokes,' he said. He bent closer. His nose was almost touching the page.

'The Arabic text is early Abjad, from that time or a bit later.' Kaiser peered at the page, then moved his head back.

'That's the word Mohammad,' He pointed halfway down a page. There was a word written in faded red. 'This page must have been written after Islam appeared.' He turned the book to face me. His finger traced the words without touching the parchment.

A gust of wind rattled the hatch at the top of the stairs. Isabel looked as if she was about to say something. Then the lights flickered.

'The Islamic history nuts are gonna love this. Nothing like this has been discovered for years, no – centuries,' said Kaiser.

'We'll have to get this examined properly,' said Isabel. 'I'd love to see it translated.'

'Books in this city were pretty important,' said Kaiser. 'There's a story that the original Book of Revelation, the one written by St John himself, used to be kept here.'

'This isn't the Book of Revelation,' said Isabel.

Kaiser waved his hand towards the book. 'I can get this translated, dated, we can see exactly how old each section is. I know this expert on Byzantine symbols. He works here in Istanbul. And there's another guy I know who's written a bunch of papers on early Arabic. Their university will know what to do with this.' He paused, put his hands up. 'I'm just saying, that's probably the best thing we can do, get the academics involved. Do this right.'

Next, he'd be asking for me to leave it with him. 'Thanks for the offer, buddy, but we'll take it from here,' I said.

'Hold on,' he said, leaning towards me. 'I'm part of this now.'

We stared into each other's eyes. His were cold, blue, determined.

I didn't blink. 'Thanks for the offer, but like I said, we'll take it from here.' I wasn't going to put up with any bullshit from this guy.

We stared at each other.

Then the shrill wail of a siren split the air. It was so loud it seemed as if someone had let it off right on top of us. Isabel's head jerked upwards. Kaiser's eyes rolled.

'Goddamn coast guards. They're way early. What's got up their ass?'

He hurriedly placed the manuscript back in its inner wrapping.

I wondered if we should hide it.

As if he'd read my mind, he said, 'We never deceive these guys. It ain't worth it.'

Within seconds the hatch at the top of the stairs swung open. Along with a gust of wind and rain, a rapid burst of Turkish poured forth.

'Come on in, get out of the rain, guys,' shouted Kaiser in reply. He added something in Turkish.

Dripping coast guard officers with see-through, plastic-covered, white-peaked caps filed down into the cabin.

Kaiser's hands were already raised in greeting. 'Hey guys,' he said. 'Welcome aboard.' His tone was friendly.

One of the officers said something to him in Turkish. Kaiser replied in Turkish. Isabel said something. I heard the words British and Consulate. The officer shook hands with her.

'They're gonna bring us in,' said Kaiser, angrily, as he turned to me. 'They say they're looking for someone.'

I didn't reply. There was a chance they were looking for someone else, but if they were looking for us, at least we were in the hands of the Turkish authorities, not some private gang hired by whoever was in charge of that place we'd escaped from.

Trespassing couldn't be that big a deal here, could it?

Then one of the officers who was standing beside me looked down at the leather package.

A few minutes later, as I stepped on board the coast guard vessel, I turned and watched the same officer, who was still on Kaiser's yacht. In his hand, pressed into his body, was the manuscript, back in all its layers of animal skin and in a see-through plastic bag. It was an evidence bag and he was carrying it as if his life depended it. I'd tried to bring it with me, but my request had been met with a lot of shaking heads.

For a chilling moment, I thought he might drop it into the Bosphorus as he came on board. Was it going be lost so soon after it had been found? I looked around, tried to get a bearing on where we were. The rain was still beating down, but the sea was calmer. Before he stepped onto the short gangplank between the two vessels the officer put the plastic bag under his jacket.

'You know, in some places, they still kill people because of books,' said Kaiser breezily, as we went down into the gleaming grey bowels of the coast guard vessel.

He was right, of course.

43

It was 1:25 in the morning in London. Arap Anach heard the front door of his suite close. Lord Bidoner had taken his time with all his stories and plans, but Arap knew better than to interrupt him. Lord Bidoner would be the public face of a new United Kingdom.

He looked at the LCD screen, where thirty minutes ago they'd watched images of the rioting across Europe. Everything was ready. Years of work were about to be rewarded. The world needed a new beginning. And before rebirth came death. It was the natural order of things.

Europe, the western world, had been in the ascendant for five hundred years, since Christopher Columbus had discovered America. But its inhabitants had grown weak from not having to defend their borders in recent centuries. Military ascendancy could easily be lost in the next one hundred years if things didn't change.

People had to realise that compassion had run its course. The distaste for outright war which had permeated the West since only the Second World War had to end. Europe's elite, fearful of being overrun, should use the weapons at their disposal. Soon the West would be on top again.

The new Black Death, about to be unleashed, would kill enough people in Europe to help make fear more important than compassion, as it had always been. Deaths would be in the millions, but they would all die for a good cause. What were their lives worth anyway? The future of humanity was at stake. The resources of the earth would last a lot longer now. And the quality of life would improve for the survivors. The reality of declining birth rates in Europe, and a Muslim population explosion, would be tackled too.

Humanity would be saved from itself.

All the West needed was a little nudge every now and then to keep its destiny on track, and the people who knew how to do it. People such as him. The current generation of leaders had lost the will to be strong. New leaders were needed, new figureheads too. And blood would flow to make it happen. When every family in the land had lost half its members things would change.

44

Despite the hour, the police station near Taksim Square where we were taken was as busy as an anthill. I saw my first drunken Turk in a corridor there, and two Russian hookers. Both had thick flaxen hair, purple marks on their faces and the vacant expressions of long-time drug users.

We were, it transpired, under arrest.

I was pissed off. Not only had they transported us like everyday criminals in the back of separate police cars from the wharf, they'd kept me waiting in a bare corridor for what seemed like ages without even bothering to tell me what was going on.

'What do you know about this book you found?' was, surprisingly, the first question I was asked after being escorted, alone, to a windowless interview room. It had exactly the same dirty blue tiles on its floor as on its walls. The room had a foul nicotinic air, as if it had been used in the past to interview a troop of chain-smoking mass murderers.

'Not a lot,' I replied. We stared at each other.

'Mr Ryan, I need you to cooperate.' He leaned forward. His English was very good, though heavily accented. 'This is a serious matter. People are in prison for less.'

'I haven't done anything,' I said. 'And I don't expect to go to prison for looking at something. I'm not a smuggler.'

'Let me remind you that our prisons are not holiday camps.

If you tell me everything, I will make sure you are dealt with quickly,' he said.

'I appreciate that,' I said. I gave him a thin we'll-see smile.

'You admit you found this book we discovered on Mr Kaiser's boat, yes?'

He wore a uniform similar to the policemen who'd brought us here, but he had stripes on his epaulets and more badges. He was older too, tanned, and had thinning black hair brushed over an egg-shaped head.

A security camera in a metal box high up on one wall observed the two of us.

'Yes, I did. I found it, in its wrapping, at the shoreline. We were robbed at gunpoint. I gave them my camera. We were forced down the rocks to the Bosphorus to give them time to get away, I expect. I spotted the parcel. We got soaked retrieving it. That's all there is to it.' The policeman stared at me with his head to one side.

He did not look impressed by my story.

'That's not what your friend is telling us.' He paused to gauge my reaction.

I stared at a point low down on the far wall. There were shouts from outside the room. One of the drunks was letting off expletive-laden steam.

'You know the penalties for smuggling artefacts from Turkey, don't you?'

'We haven't smuggled anything. Are you not listening?' I looked him in the eye. How crazy was this going to get?

'But you were planning to, no?' He had a triumphant look on his face as he drummed his fingers on the tabletop.

Sweat ran down my forehead. It was hotter here than in a sauna on Coney Island on the fourth of July.

'The Directorate of Monuments Investigations Division have been contacted, Mr Ryan. They told us your name is known to them, that you are involved in some work in Hagia Sophia. Is that correct?'

I nodded.

'So, tell me the truth. You found the artefact in Hagia Sophia, yes?' His eyes were gleaming.

'No,' I replied, forcefully. 'Now when can we go?'

He shook his head. 'The artefact in question is incredibly valuable, is it not?'

I wondered what would happen if I asked him to open the door, so we could get some air. I smiled grimly to myself. I knew the answer I would get.

'Do you find this funny, Mr Ryan?'

'Yes, I do. It's funny that my colleague gets murdered here, but I'm the one that ends up in a police station. Wouldn't it be better if you were trying to find out who killed him?'

'We know all about your colleague, but right now we want to find out about this artefact.' He paused. 'Did your friend Kaiser help you find it, Mr Ryan?' He shifted towards me, placed his elbows on the metal table that separated us, and crossed his arms. 'Is that not the truth?'

'How about you tell me what progress you've made on Alek Zegliwski's case?'

His mouth was set in a thin line. He did not look pleased.

'Christians aren't the only ones who believe in justice, Mr Ryan. We too believe God will send evil doers to their doom, and the righteous to their reward in heaven.' He leaned closer to me.

I could smell his sweat. The tic in my cheek, which had been coming and going since we'd been arrested, started up again.

I slapped the side of my face. The tic stopped. My interrogator looked at me as if he thought I'd gone mad. Maybe he thought all westerners were mad.

'That's good,' I said. 'Then we're on the same wavelength.'

He leaned closer, as if he was getting to the nub of his questions. 'Do you know about the speculation about some Greeks wanting to reclaim Hagia Sophia?'

I shook my head.

'Are you working with the Greeks, Mr Ryan? You had better tell us if you are. We will find out, you know, and if you haven't told us, I promise it will be worse for you.'

I shook my head slowly. Talk about being obsessed, fighting previous wars over and over.

My interrogator looked pained, as if he didn't believe me, and didn't like what he was going to have to do next. 'We know all the tricks, Mr Ryan. I promise you, you will regret not telling us, if you are hiding something.'

I stared at him. Did he really think I was working with some crazy Greeks? I'd expected to be quizzed about trespassing at Hagia Eirene, not about some far out conspiracy theory.

I raised my hands. 'Look, honestly, I had no idea what was in that package when we found it. You came up on us right after we opened it. Surely that says something. You've got all the wrappings. Ask Kaiser or his friend. Now, I'm tired. I haven't had a wink of sleep. Let us go. I'm not being charged with anything, am I? Doesn't that rule apply here?'

My brain was slowing and my exhaustion was making me even more irritable than usual.

The policeman let out a knowing laugh. He shook his head. 'You'll be released when we are ready. And yes, that rule does apply here, unless you're a terrorist. You're not a terrorist, are you?'

'No,' I said, indignantly. 'Do I look like one?' I raised my hands.

He shrugged. 'Who knows, these days. Are you sure there's nothing else you want to tell us? This is your last chance to come clean. We will be reasonable.'

'I'll tell you this.' I paused. 'I need to sleep.' I put my head on my arms. The policeman said nothing. After about a minute he stood and went to the door. As he opened it, he said, 'Don't get too comfortable.'

I picked my head up and replied, 'Where's the book?'

'Where is it? It's already been taken by someone from the British Consulate. We received word from our Ministry of Culture that we should hand it over to them. The best place to verify what it is is in England. It will take some time to do that, I'm sure. I doubt you'll be seeing it again soon.'

The door closed with a bang behind him. I put my head back down on the table. Bastards. We'd found it, they'd taken it.

I could smell a lemony disinfectant from the table as I lay my head down on my arms.

Was I going to be charged? Was this how it would all end, with me in a Turkish prison?

I moved my head, tried to get comfortable. I was almost overcome with exhaustion, but it was difficult to sleep.

One thing was sure, if Father Gregory had been alive he'd have been a help in deciphering what we'd found. He'd probably have known straight away what that symbol at the back meant, and what those letters towards the middle were all about.

I slept fitfully. And the interview room was hotter and even more airless when I woke. I felt as if I'd been beaten up, then put into an airtight container. My eyes were stinging, a muddy taste filled my mouth, and my body had aches and pains I didn't even know were possible.

I was angry. When were they going to let us go?

I got a cramp in my right calf. I stood and pressed my foot down hard. Slowly it went away.

'*Gun eydin,*' said a woman's voice.

I looked around. The door to the interview room was open. A slim Turkish police officer was standing in the doorway, holding a clipboard. She was fidgeting, as if she had enough nervous energy for the two of us.

'My name is Adile,' she said. A rush of cool air had come into the room.

Hope and anxiety poured through me as if I'd been injected with them. I kept my expression as blank as I could.

'You are released, Mr Ryan. The British Consulate is taking full responsibility for you, because you were with a member of their staff.' She stepped to one side.

A surge of relief flowed through me. I looked past her. Isabel was standing down the corridor, looking in my direction. She was still wearing the black T-shirt and trousers Kaiser had given her. She gave me a restrained wave.

We were escorted by the lady police officer to the exit. I didn't even have to sign anything. We walked out into the busy car park. It was wonderful to be out of that interview room, to be in the open again.

'I had to wake up our chief security officer in Ankara,' said Isabel. 'He wasn't happy.'

'I'm glad you did.'

'It's my neck on the line. Did you keep to our story?'

'Would they have let us out, if they knew where we'd been?'

She shook her head. 'No, and the last thing we need is the

local police to be stumbling around where we were. Trust me, I know how they do things here.'

She glanced back towards the police station. 'They had one hell of a bee in their bloody bonnet about antiquities smuggling. '

Was this the right time to tell her about Kaiser's camera?

I rubbed my hands through my hair and groaned. I was almost too tired to think.

'Are you OK?' she said. There was real concern in her voice.

She was right beside me. Our bodies were almost touching. I was acutely aware of her presence, the glow of her skin, her curves. I hadn't felt so attracted to someone in a long time.

I pushed away the feelings. I was just tired. We'd been through an emotional wringer together. I had to get a grip.

'Do you know what happened to Kaiser?' I said.

She shrugged.

That was when it happened.

We were only a few steps from the police station. I had just turned my head to check if we could cross the road, when something needle sharp, which made a phttt noise, stung me on the cheek. Dust spurted from the wall, as if it had exploded. I could taste gritty concrete. At first, I thought something had happened to the wall.

Then dust splattered again. I grabbed Isabel's arm. 'Get down.'

We ducked and scuttled across like crabs towards a shiny new black BMW parked by the curb. My brain was alert again. Amazing, isn't it, what fear of imminent death can do.

But where were the shots coming from? The only people on the street I could see were two couples, a block away. Neither of them was even looking at us. I could hear cars rumbling, a horn blowing. Then a rotten smell reached me, as if there was something dead in a drain nearby.

I turned my head. The tree-lined street looked completely safe. I couldn't see anybody with a gun. Maybe it was over. They'd sent their message.

Then there was another... phttt. Isabel yanked hard at my arm, pulling me further down.

In the polished black sheen of the BMW, I saw a dark streak on my cheek. I put my hand to it. It felt wet. I caught the scent of iron as I pulled my fingers away. What the hell? I shivered hard, as if I had a fever.

Then that noise again, like an over-excited bee, and a bullet hit the pavement by my feet, digging a crater into the ground. I tasted more grit, felt it in my throat. Someone was trying to kill us. Or me, at least.

I pushed Isabel down, tried to cover her with my body. I could feel her warmth under me.

As I listened for that noise again, I looked under the car, tried to see across the road, to catch whoever it was that was coming to finish us off. Then I looked around and saw them.

'Help!' I shouted. I raised my arm, started waving frantically at a group of police officers standing in the station car park, no more than a hundred feet away.

As they turned to see who was shouting, it was like watching people reacting in slow motion. First, they all stared at us. Then, after a cloud of dust skipped into the air near us, two of them pulled guns.

What followed was a cacophony. An alarm went off, and in a display of real courage two Turkish police officers raced out into the street, guns raised.

Someone began screaming. A woman carrying a mop and bucket in the police car park had noticed what was going on.

The next thing I heard was the sound of a motorbike. I peeked around the side of the BMW. In the alley directly opposite where we were hiding, a motorcyclist in black leather was speeding away. The bike turned a corner and was gone. I looked at my hands. They felt sticky. They were covered in something red.

45

Henry Mowlam read the article on his screen again. This was not good. Not good at all.

The Iranian scientist who'd been found dead was a bigger fish than he'd thought. He looked closely at the paragraph. The Iranian was one of the world's leading scientists in the field of chromosome mutation. The fear among Henry's colleagues was that this specialisation could be easily applied to virus mutation. If a scientist had access to a source of smallpox or ebola or some variant of the plague, God forbid, and could mutate it at the chromosome level, he could develop a virus that was not only resistant to antibiotics, but might even feed off the most powerful of them.

Such a possibility was enough to get the Ministry of Defence Biological Warfare Unit to open a file on the case. And that meant that every Whitehall department would be briefed within twenty-four hours on the steps they would have to begin taking to protect UK citizens.

The big question was, had a new virus already been produced, or were they all just in danger of overreacting?

Because if they were facing a new, mutated virus, contingency plans would have to be implemented, not just talked about.

'You should be well soon, sir, but we strongly recommend you stay here for a few days, get some rest. If you leave, we can't be held responsible,' said the doctor in the New International Hospital, as he watched me signing my release forms.

I passed the signed forms back to him. He looked through them, shaking his head.

I'd been lucky, really lucky. I knew that, but the last thing I wanted to do was to stick around in an Istanbul hospital, resting.

Someone wanted me dead.

Did I want to entrust my life to a smiling security guard, or even two of them?

My right cheek had been nicked by a bullet. If I hadn't turned my head when I had, I'd probably be with Alek in the morgue right now, getting colder by the minute.

The reality of being shot at was like being at a fairground in a nightmare: everything seemed brighter, people were smiling, but way too much.

My paranoia had risen another notch. I could hear sounds I wouldn't even have noticed before, doors closing far away. And it felt as if my senses had become sharper. Suddenly I was noticing things I normally took for granted. Like breathing.

The muscles in my chest felt tight too. And my head felt

weirdly hollow. I had no idea if this was due to the two injections they'd given me or simply a result of the shock I'd got, but I still wanted to get out of that hospital. And I still needed to figure out why someone was trying to kill me, and more importantly, how I could stop them.

'The Turkish police have offered us an escort to the airport,' Isabel said, when she arrived back at my room, after checking in with her superiors. 'They don't want you shot dead in Istanbul.'

'That's good news. I agree with them on that. But what's happening about Peter?' I said. What we knew about him was the best reason I could think of for someone wanting me dead right now.

'We have to go back to London, Sean. That's where he went. We can't do anything from here.'

'What about Villa Napoleon, shouldn't it be raided? What about that amazing place under Hagia Sophia?'

'The Turkish authorities have already been tipped off to search both locations for whoever killed Alek.'

'What happens if both places are empty, if Peter's tipped them all off?'

'We have to let the authorities here do their job, Sean. This is their country. And from my experience they don't like anyone interfering.'

So that was it. We had to go back to London. Peter had been with the people under Hagia Sophia. He had to be confronted.

We headed for the exit.

'How do you know he's in London?' I said.

'I asked at the office. He's gone back there for a few days.'

'Surprise, surprise.'

She ignored the sarcasm in my voice.

'Doesn't it make you crazy that someone you work with might be a traitor?'

She turned on me angrily, pointed a finger at me. 'We don't ever use that word, Sean, not until we're 100 percent sure,' she snapped. 'This isn't some stupid game. Lives are at stake.'

'Yeah, mine and yours,' I said. We stepped out into the hospital car park. Waves of heat hit us. Going to London was looking like a better idea every minute. There were people there who could help me blow the whistle on Peter too, if Isabel wasn't prepared to.

A black-windowed Mercedes 950 Jeep sitting yards away jerked to life, then moved towards us.

'Our ride,' she said.

I peered around. A twinge of anxiety passed through me as I remembered the last time I was out in the open. Was there someone waiting to take another shot at me? I followed Isabel into the car quickly. It was going to be a long journey to the airport through the Istanbul traffic.

The Mercedes purred off. The driver was a young smiling Turkish police officer. He pointed at the sky as we left the hospital driveway. Then a few minutes later, he gesticulated at the sky again. I looked in the direction he was pointing and saw it. A police helicopter was hovering above us. Were the police giving us air cover too?

We ran a red light with our siren on, our blue lights flashing, then we turned into a car park and sped up the ramp towards the roof with squeals echoing as we rounded each bend. I could smell hot rubber. Walls rushed past in a blur. It didn't take a genius to work out what was going on. If the Turkish police were taking such precautions, they must have concluded that whoever was after me would most likely try again.

The juddering of the helicopter went through to my bones as we came up the last ramp. When we emerged into the blinding sunlight it was waiting for us, its blades twirling fast, in a corner of the roof car park.

'Who organised this?' I shouted.

'We've still got friends here,' she replied.

The helicopter was a Sikorsky 340X, so it said on its side. Seconds later we were strapped into its black bucket seats. It rose up fast with a stupendous roar, then banked and sped, nose low, towards the airport.

I rubbed at the bandage on my cheek. My skin felt itchy, as if I'd been stung. The doctor had said I'd be left with a small scar, but that was the least of my worries right now. I was lucky not to have a hole in my head.

I held on to a rubberized handhold on the wall of the helicopter. It vibrated hyperactively, as if it was directly connected to one of the engines.

'Bloody desk jockeys,' Isabel shouted over the noise.

'Who?' I roared. The smell of jet fuel was getting stronger.

She shook her head.

I kept staring at her. She looked cute in the helmet the pilot had given her, if a little pale. I wanted to reach over, whisper something to her, hold her.

I looked away and shook my head, like a dog shaking off water. I was going soft, like an addled teenager. It had to be the shock. I stared out of the window.

After what must have been a minute she said, 'I spoke to the office a little while ago. They told me off for not filling in some stupid request form.'

I caught the look of fury on her face. It was replaced a second later by her standard issue poker expression. She had to be feeling the pressure too, though she was probably better at handling it than I was.

Straight ahead was the concrete expanse of Atatürk airport. Planes were ascending and descending like mechanical insects. Below us, a metallic snake of cars queued from the motorway. All around, a blue-tinged haze hung over Istanbul. On the horizon, to our right, the skyscrapers of Levent, Istanbul's Manhattan-like northern suburb, poked steel and glass shards of modernity upwards.

We landed by a hangar. Within minutes of disembarking we'd been given the once over by a neatly uniformed Turkish immigration official who came out to greet us. He seemed to know Isabel. He whispered something in her ear. I almost envied him for a second. I looked away.

Then he came over to me and asked me for my passport. It had dried out, but looked more battered then I'd ever seen it. He didn't say a word. When he was finished with it he waved us through.

Then we were back on the same private plane we'd been on only forty-eight hours ago.

There was a mobile phone on the seat beside Isabel. She picked it up and made a call on it. She opened the call with, 'We're on our way, sir.' Then she went quiet as she listened to the person on the other end.

'I'll write it all up as soon as I'm back in London, sir,' she said. 'We'll be in the air in five.'

'Say goodbye to Istanbul,' she said to me, as the city disappeared behind us, and our plane accelerated into dark rolling clouds.

'I could get used to this,' I said.

'Don't, I had to push my luck to get this approved. If I hadn't claimed I had a strong lead to the threats against London, we'd still be in the queue for passport control at Atatürk airport.'

'Peter is a strong lead?'

She looked me in the eyes. 'Yes, Sean.'

47

Sergeant Mowlam was looking at a laboratory report from the Florence Nightingale hospital in Istanbul. The report was the result of a blood test on Dr Safad Mohadajin.

The report confirmed the existence of a Yersina Pestis bacterium in the doctor's blood. That fact alone would not be enough to ring warning bells. Every year many thousands of cases of plague ended up being reported to the World Health Organisation. But the next piece of information was certainly cause for concern.

The variant of Yersina Pestis in Dr Mohadajin's blood was not only compatible with strain KIM, but also with strain CO92. That fact alone, that this form of plague had multiple genetic characteristics, was so noteworthy that the laboratory technician had run the test twice.

No identified strain of the plague, variants of the Black Death, had ever shown this characteristic before. Dr Mohadajin had been beheaded, but the logical conclusion of him being infected was that he had acquired the infection while working on a mutated plague virus. He may have even infected himself. But did that mean there was an imminent threat to the United Kingdom? It was a possibility. He would pass the information on straight away to the Ministry of Defence Biological Warfare Unit, and hope to God they would know what to do.

Because if a mutated strain of the plague had been created along the lines that had been feared, and it did get loose, its impact could be devastating. It might even be considered an act of war.

'We've been attacked before, my dear. The 29th December, 1940, for instance. That was the day the bloody Luftwaffe dropped 100,000 fire bombs on us. The buggers caused the second Great Fire of London.'

Sir David Simon, Member of Parliament, advisor to the Privy Council, sat back in his overstuffed leather armchair and stared glumly at us. He had the appearance of someone who was confused about the way the world was going, though in reality he had a better grasp of what was really going on than most.

A waiter in a white coat placed our coffees on the long polished coffee table we were sitting around. The room, which had been converted into a bar for MPs in 1845, was the size of two tennis courts. The waiters, in their short black jackets with brass buttons, looked like extras from a Victorian-era light opera, as they darted between the nests of armchairs and low mahogany tables.

I'd never been invited for drinks to the MPs' bar at the Palace of Westminster before. The nearest I'd ever been to the British Parliament was gawking at Big Ben from Parliament Square. Dark wood panelling rose halfway up the walls and red wallpaper, in a busy fleur-de-lis pattern, covered every inch of what remained.

I was feeling far from relaxed though. It wasn't just the surroundings. It was the reason we were here.

'Do you know that the Second World War was the first time anyone used bigger artillery shells than were used to breach the walls of Constantinople in 1453?'

I shook my head. He turned to Isabel.

'I have to tell you, young lady, the Palace is definitely interested in this. There's a certain Prince with a military background you might have heard of.' He paused. His face was stern, his cheeks red, as if he was about to bark orders. 'Well, I'm the one tasked with keeping the Prince up to date about important intelligence matters.'

He stared at us for a few seconds to let what he'd said sink in. His gaze shifted from me back to Isabel.

'And after all that's gone on these last few years, I think he's absolutely right to do so. We need to be vigilant.' He finished his visual examination of Isabel.

She was dressed in a tight-fitting black trouser suit. Under her jacket she wore a lacy black bra, which revealed itself when she leaned forward, which she was doing right now.

'The next few days are critical, as I'm sure you know,' he said. 'We have some big events coming up. The last thing we want is someone stirring things up.' His hands came together, his pudgy fingers interlocking. Light reflected from his almost bald head. The patches of black hair he had left, above each ear, were slicked down. His face was jowly.

He leaned towards Isabel. 'No disrespect, my dear, but you're not even MI6. Don't get me wrong. The Foreign Office is wonderful. King Charles Street spits out reports like an overexcited photocopier, but I must tell you, we expect this sort of news to come through the official channels. Appearing in person is not how things are done any more.' He waved a hand in the air, as if swatting a fly.

Isabel opened her mouth. Then she shut it again.

He pointed his finger at her. 'But I do give people a hearing. Too often, some say. Now do keep in mind, young lady that I know quite a bit about Turkey. The place is at a crossroads. Has been for a while, in my view. Atatürk pointed them in the right direction, but that was a long time ago.'

He paused. When he continued, he sounded calmer. 'Now, Miss Sharp, tell me all about this manuscript you've found.' He looked at her expectantly.

Isabel told him everything.

I let her handle it. He was her contact. I looked down at my hands. Both had deep scratches on them. I had a nasty purple bruise above my right wrist too. And another one on my knee.

All Isabel had told me before we got here was that we were going to visit a sympathetic MP, a man who sat on top-level committees, someone who'd be able to pull strings, someone at the heart-valve of the old boys' network. More especially, someone who could have Peter investigated and arrested, if indeed he was a traitor. It was the way she had to do it, Isabel had said, if we wanted to get results and be discreet. Knowing how things worked in England, where who you knew was still a valuable currency, I believed her.

I would have liked to have rolled up the sleeves on the crisp white shirt I'd purchased at Harrods on the way in, but I didn't. This wasn't the time for good old American informality. Instead, I sat back and tried to enjoy the luxury of the deepest leather armchair I'd ever sat on. In the heavy air and hushed atmosphere I could feel the power that resided in the rooms and corridors around us.

I'd slept for ten hours the night before in an emergency room at a less-than-busy holding centre in the Northolt Government Airbase west of London. Isabel had suggested I stay there for security reasons. Whoever had tried to kill me could well be watching my house in Fulham, she'd said.

The next morning I woke up wondering if I'd missed the action; if they'd arrested Peter already

'Don't be absurd,' she'd said, when she returned for me at nine in the morning. 'I can't have people arrested because of a conversation I overheard. Accusing someone of being a traitor is a very serious thing. I have to approach this carefully. I have to report what we've heard to the right person. There's a right way to do these things.'

'Did they find anything in that cavern under Hagia Sophia? There's evidence down there, I'm sure of it.'

'It was raided by Turkish special forces yesterday. The place was empty. Even the tables we saw were gone. Whoever was working down there must have cleared it out right after we escaped. The safe house on Buyuk Ada they were using was empty too. Our leads are drying up.'

'We still have one,' I'd said.

'Yes, we do.'

Which was why we were here. Why I was here. I was a witness to what had happened with Peter.

'You're really up to your neck in it, old boy,' said David Simon, turning to me.

I nodded. 'Runs in the family, sir.'

'I'm sorry about your colleague. Frightfully bad form about him being beheaded. Do you know why it happened?'

'It seems his curiosity took him to the wrong place.'

'And you have doubts about our man, Fitzgerald, isn't that right?'

He looked at me searchingly. I wondered for a second about what I'd heard with my own ears. Perhaps there *was* an explanation. Then I felt sure again. Peter was working against us. I'd overheard him scheming. He couldn't have known we could hear him talking. I wasn't going to deny hearing him.

'I remember every word that came out of his mouth,' I said. 'And I think Isabel should be listened to.'

'That is exactly what I am doing.' He sounded irritated.

'If you'd been there, you wouldn't have any doubts,' I said. 'This guy is involved with the people who murdered my colleague. At the very least he's covering up what he knows. These people threatened to bring Armageddon to London, Sir David.'

'Please, just David. And there's a lot of people who threaten us, old boy. Most of them are delusional.'

He sniffed loudly. 'What about this manuscript you found? What do you think about that? Is it a fake?'

Isabel's face was blank.

'No,' I said. 'It would be a very odd place to put a fake.'

He looked at me intensely, as if he was trying to figure something out about me.

'Well, it's quite a find, that's for sure. I did a bit of digging after your call this morning, Ms Sharp. An old friend of mine from Cambridge filled me in on a few things.' He looked up, stopped talking as a group of people passed us on their way out.

'He said the Eastern Roman emperor at the time of the Prophet Mohammed was rumoured to have converted to Islam.' He put his hands together.

'You do know a manuscript, perhaps this one, sparked an attempt on that emperors's life?'

I nodded.

'That manuscript was believed to include letters from the Pope in Rome, and from Mecca. The Emperor was, supposedly, trying to mediate between the two sides. If what you've found is authentic, and the letters inside it are what we think they are, they could cause a sensation. So we have to be truly careful. This is not a good time to go upsetting apple carts.' He looked around the room, nodded at a group of aged, rumple-suited men in the far corner.

'This was the genius who lost Jerusalem to the Muslims?' I said.

'Indeed, Jerusalem was a Christian and a Jewish city back then. That was the golden age for Christians in Jerusalem. All that ended when the city fell to the Muslims. Heraclius, our mediating emperor, was blamed. What you've discovered could answer a lot of questions. But we have to wait and see what the academics say, and not just our lot either.' He paused.

'Do you have pictures of what you found?' I had the feeling he wanted to know if we had access to what was in the manuscript.

'There's some photos on the Internet,' I said. 'Do you want to see them?'

Isabel looked surprised.

I leaned towards her. 'Kaiser's camera uploads every image it takes to a website,' I said. 'All you need is the camera's serial number to be able to access the images. We used the same website at the Institute last year.'

'You have the serial number?' said Isabel.

I smiled, enjoying the moment.

'You should have...' She stopped herself.

'Pass me your iPhone,' I said.

320

She passed me her phone. I opened the web browser and went to the site.

David moved forward in his chair. The screen on the new iPhone was ideal for showing photos.

I logged in, scrolled down and looked at the images for a few seconds. Then I held the phone up for David. He stared at it. Isabel nudged me gently with her foot. Her smile said don't-leave-me-out-of-your-show.

I put the phone down on the table so we could all see the images. Then I flicked through them with my finger.

Not only were all the photos there, some of them had been split up and then blown up. Some even had other analysis done on them, revealing lines and shapes.

There were shots of the front cover, first page, last page, a few inside pages; then, a close up of one of the letter-type pages. It had a seal at its bottom that I hadn't paid much attention to the first time I'd been looking at it.

I stopped on that image.

'That looks like a papal seal,' said David. He sounded angry. 'This material shouldn't be so easily accessible. It has to be studied, verified, before the public gets hold of it. These could be scurrilous forgeries.'

Isabel held her hand out. I passed her the phone. She looked around, as if she wanted to verify there wasn't anybody watching us.

'These images won't be made public, sir.'

'They better not be,' he said. 'But I'm not exactly brimming with confidence. You didn't even know where these photos were stored until a minute ago, young lady.'

She gave me a withering look.

'They're on a private site,' I said.

'That's not the point. Look, I'm going to have a word with someone about your Peter Fitzgerald chap. Wait here. You're not in a hurry, are you?'

'No,' I said.

Isabel nodded in agreement.

'Good,' he said. He stood up, ambled over to a table nearby, directly under one of the giant gothic-style windows that dominated one entire wall. Beyond the windows, blue sky beckoned.

I sat back. With sunlight streaming through the windows, the room looked more like a chapel than a bar. I wasn't going to get too many opportunities to take in the laid back atmosphere of a place like this.

I watched David Simon. He was speaking to some people at a table in the far corner. He turned and waved us over.

'I'd arranged to meet these people for lunch. Why don't you wait with them until I get back,' he said as we joined them. Sitting at the table was a shiny-faced pensioner. With him was a smiling woman with huge, bushy blonde hair. She was wearing a black-and-white houndstooth suit. It made her look like a retired Hollywood star. A whiff of spicy perfume hit me.

'This is Lord Enniskerry,' said David, introducing the man sitting down. Enniskerry half stood as he held out his hand. 'How he wangled his way into this place, I'll never know. And this is Gülsüm, the famous fortune teller. She'll cheer you up. Did you let Enniskerry in, Gülsüm?' He gave the lady sitting beside Lord Enniskerry a grave look. She laughed, a high-pitched friendly laugh. We shook hands.

She smiled, as if seeing me meant she'd won the lottery.

'Delighted,' she said. She sounded French or Egyptian.

'Why don't you do an old friend a favour, Gülsüm, and read these people their fortunes while they wait for me?'

'Only for you, David,' she purred. She waved at him as he departed.

There was an awkward silence as we sat down. Having my fortune read didn't interest me one bit. I was about to decline the offer, but Gülsüm had already turned towards me, and before I could speak, she said, 'Are you in trouble, Sean?' Her tone was low, conspiratorial. Her gaze flickered over me, as if taking in every part of me.

I looked at Isabel. Her lips were pursed. Say nothing, her expression said. She was sitting as far back as she could on the leather armchair to my right. Gülsüm and Lord Enniskerry were on the opposite side of the coffee table.

'No,' I replied. White porcelain coffee cups and saucers emblazoned with the crowned portcullis emblem of the House of Commons sat on the table.

'Let me order you chaps some coffee,' said Lord Enniskerry. He waved a waiter over.

A few minutes later, Gülsüm was quizzing Isabel about her job in Istanbul. Isabel spoke at length, without giving anything away. She'd make a good politician.

I was hoping David would come back soon.

I looked out of the window. I could just about see the top of the London eye. I imagined the queue of tourists waiting to view the city from 440 feet. Despite everything, London was still full of tourists.

My reverie was interrupted when Gülsüm suddenly sniffed loudly and said, 'Do you smell fire?'

I crinkled my nose. She was right. There was a burning smell. 'Yep,' I said. I looked around.

49

Arap Anach looked out of the tinted window of his night-black Maybach 62S. The Bose sound system was playing *Ride of the Valkyries* low, just how he liked it. The climate control system was purring. The electro-transparent partition between the driver and the rear compartment was up. The twin-turbo V12 engine was as loud as a distant breeze. All would have been right with the world, if the speedometer in the rear compartment wasn't reading 0 MPH.

He pressed his fist into the black pigskin seat. He was going to be late. He hated being late. It was all the fault of this new security cordon in the City.

At that moment the in-car telephone system buzzed. Arap stabbed a finger at the control button.

'Yes.' His tone was imperious. It displayed nothing of his desire to see the cars around him vaporised.

'The packages have been delivered.' Malach sounded eager.

'Very good,' said Arap. He closed the connection.

The final step would be easy now. He smiled. He didn't care about the traffic any more. It was all so close, and no one had any idea what was about to happen.

50

'I hope it's not serious,' said Gülsüm.

I was out of my seat, looking around

An alarm rang out loudly from the corridor outside the room. As it did, David appeared in the doorway waving at us languidly. It would take a lot more than a fire alarm to make this guy panic.

'All out,' he called.

We trooped out of the room, everyone letting everyone else pass by in front of them with a great show of very British politeness. A lingering acrid smell drifted in from somewhere.

Like children after the Pied Piper, our little group traipsed after David. He led us into a small wood-panelled room. It looked as if it hadn't been used since the Second World War, so old were the iron radiators and the two wooden desks that almost filled it. He led us on through a small door in the back of the room, and down a long panelled corridor of the same vintage.

My mind was racing as I brought up the rear. Was this about us, about what we were doing here, or was I just being totally paranoid?

Some people brushed past us going the other way. More alarms competed with each other. I could smell smoke at one point as we passed a grand stairwell, like something from a

Gothic castle. The smell was stronger now. Lord Enniskerry called out for us to hurry up.

The sense of security I'd felt since coming back to London had evaporated.

Finally, we reached an old-fashioned elevator in a bare hallway. It looked like something the ordinary staff of the building might use. We took it to the ground floor and a few minutes later, after passing through a narrow concrete corridor, we exited through a four-inch-thick steel door into a vast steel hall, the battleship-grey lower concourse of Westminster Underground Station. Straight in front of us dull steel escalators loomed.

'This way,' said David. 'I know a good spot for lunch.'

'Don't you want to find out what's going on?' I said.

'I'm sure good people are looking after it all. Our job is to keep going,' he said, loudly.

Lord Enniskerry declined the invitation, shook hands with us, then kissed Gulsum's hand before disappearing into the crowd.

There were no alarms ringing in the station, but by the time we reached the eastbound Circle Line, two levels below, it was jammed full of people lining the platform five deep, elbow-to-elbow, all waiting quietly. The atmosphere was tense, but as usual on the Underground eye contact was avoided. Even after we'd boarded the train, conversations were hushed.

'This was the Old Bank of England once upon a time,' said David, fifteen minutes later, as he ushered us into a large high-ceilinged pub.

We'd got off the Underground at Temple Station, two stops from Westminster, and had walked along Fleet Street among the oblivious lunchtime crowds of King's College students, city office workers, and pale-faced lawyers from the various Inns of Court. Now, the four of us were ensconced in a private alcove in the pub's large basement restaurant.

The room had a vaulted wooden ceiling. It was decorated in burgundy upholstery, and had shiny brass handrails, rose-shaped lamps, which looked more like gaslights, and polished wooden tables and chairs as dark as a night in any of Dickens's orphanages. Around us, waiters hovered, as well-paid business and legal types lunched with colleagues or entertained clients on expense accounts.

'Nothing disturbs the flow of money,' said David, passing us menus. 'The terrorist threat level has been raised, you know, but it's business as usual down here.'

'They should all be given medals,' said Gülsüm, beaming broadly. 'Or flowers. I do love London.'

She'd been smiling at me all the way from the House of Commons. When I looked at Isabel, I got the distinct impression, from her frosty expression, that she didn't like the woman.

'Did you find out what happened back at the House of Commons?' Isabel asked David.

He'd made a call while we were walking down Fleet Street. Isabel had made one too.

'Nothing to worry about, my dear. A little problem in the kitchens,' said David. 'Everyone a bit twitchy today. For good reason too. You do know about the demonstration the Muslims are planning this afternoon, don't you?'

'I thought someone would have banned that after last Saturday,' I interrupted.

'The free speech lobby won out, old boy.' He waved a hand dismissively in the air. 'We don't want them complaining they can march after prayers in Cairo, but not here.'

'Even at St Paul's?' I said.

He nodded. Gülsüm patted David's arm, then looked at me, her brow furrowed. 'Should I do that reading now, Sean?' she asked.

She was a persistent lady.

'Do you believe in this stuff?' I asked David, gesturing towards Gülsüm.

'I write columns in the *Evening Standard*, and I hate to tell you this, but last year more people read their horoscopes than all my bloody opinion pieces put together. It's a parlour game really, a harmless diversion.'

'But you like it when it comes true, David, don't you?' Gülsüm gave him a cool stare.

'Please, pick a card,' she said, turning to me. 'Just one card.'

She'd spread a yellowing deck in a semi-circle face down in front of her. I could argue, and I might have done a few days ago, but what the hell, I'd come close to death. Let's see what it says.

Without thinking much I pointed to a card. She turned it over with a flourish. It showed a woodcut image of a robed angel holding a trumpet up, with a cockerel at its feet.

'Aah, the Judgment card,' she said, softly. She placed two fingers over each of her eyes, as if she wanted to see something in her mind.

'Something's about to change,' she said, softly. Then she removed her fingers from her eyes and looked at me solemnly.

I smiled. She was good. But if she'd told me what was going to change, I might have been more impressed.

'I have a confession, people. I brought Gülsüm along for another reason too,' said David.

'Which is?' said Isabel.

'When I enquired about that manuscript you found, the FO sent me an image of a symbol. I sent it to Gülsüm. It's a square with an arrow inside it. Quite a simple thing. Did you see it?'

I nodded. Isabel was staring at David.

Gülsüm shifted in her seat, put her cards away. Then she put a hand on the table, as if steadying herself. We were all waiting for her to speak.

'The symbol has multiple meanings, David,' she said, matter of factly. 'First, it has mystical meaning. The square is the earth, the triangles fire. This is simple. Anyone can see that.' She moved her hands across the table as if arranging something.

'And it is also a Byzantine board game. You have to see what new shapes you can make when you move the pieces around.' She stopped moving her hands.

'And hidden beneath that is something else. A Byzantine astrological chart.' Her hands fluttered in the air. 'The symbols are in the right order for a reading. The only thing I cannot say is, who or what the chart was written for.'

'Who or what?' said David.

'Yes, it may have been made for a person, for a voyage, or a city even. I would need to see any other writing or symbols that were near it.'

David leaned back. 'No need to trouble yourself any more,' he said.

'I hate to interrupt,' said Isabel. 'But I was wondering if you'd made any progress on our friend, David?' Her tone was taut. She clearly wanted to move the conversation on.

Sir David shook his head. 'It would be a lot easier if you had evidence, my dear.' He obviously wasn't enjoying being the bearer of bad news.

An awkward silence followed.

On the wall at the far end of the bar, straight in front of me, a jumbo LCD television was showing a satellite news channel. A familiar face came on the screen. At first, I thought I was mistaken. I looked away. Then I looked back. I felt an overwhelming sense of déjà vu. For the second time in 48 hours I saw someone I knew on the TV news.

It was Kaiser, the American. We'd last seen him as we'd entered the police station in Istanbul together.

I stood, mumbled an excuse, and mesmerised, crossed over to the TV, hoping the sound would be on.

As I got closer, I saw that there was a text caption running along the bottom of the screen. It read: American archaeologist discovers long-lost manuscript.

I felt as if the ground was falling away. What the hell was Kaiser up to? Then, as I came closer to the TV, I could hear his voice.

'... we discovered it in the Golden Horn. It's from the time of Mohammad. If it's what we think it is, it's the only document from the period that mentions him by name, and explains what the emperor at that time decided to do about him.'

Behind him, a blurry image of the cover of the book we'd found appeared.

Kaiser smiled like a fox who had found his way into a hen house.

The sneaky bastard!

The news presenter asked, 'Where is this book now, Mr Kaiser?'

'It's under lock and key, for security reasons.' His expression darkened. 'Of course, it still needs to be properly translated.'

In a corner of the screen there was a medieval woodcut depiction of a double-headed eagle. I felt someone at my elbow.

330

'Not much chance of keeping a lid on this now,' said Isabel.

'What have you translated so far?' asked the interviewer, in an excited tone.

'All I can say,' said Kaiser, 'is that we will be publishing what we know at the earliest opportunity.'

I could hear Isabel letting her breath out.

'Well, viewers, that's all we have time for right now,' said the presenter. 'But stay tuned for more after this.'

The TV news moved on to a story about the demonstration being planned for central London that afternoon. Apparently 250,000 people were expected now.

I was about to turn away when I heard the presenter say, 'The group organising the demonstration this afternoon, after Friday prayers, is called the ECP, the English Caliphate Party.'

I felt as if I'd been punched in the stomach.

For weeks after Irene had been butchered, I'd searched for this elusive ECP group. They'd been holding a march in London against the war in Afghanistan on the day Irene's bus had been bombed in Kabul. It was obviously a coincidence, but I wanted to meet them. I think my mind had been warped by grief. An anti-terrorist officer, who'd visited me soon after, had warned me off even talking to them.

But I'd spent weeks reading notices in every Islamic bookshop and mosque I could find in London, and on every English language Islamic website, hoping to uncover where the ECP met. After scouring and scouring, without finding even a single mention of their name, I'd abandoned my search. That was when I decided to go to Afghanistan.

But why had they reappeared now?

I walked back to our table. Isabel was already sitting down.

'You look in the horrors,' said David.

I stared at him, memories of that time searching for the ECP swirling through my mind, all the grim places I'd visited, the sickening despair I'd felt. How I'd imagined it could never end.

'The people organising the demo,' I said, slowly. Something caught in my throat. David looked puzzled. I coughed. 'At St Paul's. They're the guys who held a demo in London the day my wife was murdered.'

I sat.

'How odd.' David's half-smile was sympathetic, but clearly well practised.

I'd felt people's pity hundreds of times in the past few years. And I hated it.

Why were the ECP back?

David was staring at me.

'There's a lot of these groups,' said Isabel. Her tone was placating. 'They demand the right to demonstrate, but they don't want to allow free speech for their critics.'

'Do you know anything about who's organising the demonstration this afternoon?' I asked David.

'It's all above board, or so I'm told. Apparently, whoever's organising it, has no record of any terrorist connections. There must have been no incidents at their last demonstration either. That would have been important.' He put his hand out towards me.

'What the hell was that other thing on the news?' he said. 'Was that something about your manuscript?' He pointed in the direction of the TV.

I nodded. Then I told him who Kaiser was, what he'd said.

'We'll have to get someone to talk to him, and quickly.' David's face was red, almost purple.

I put my hands on the table. 'He better stop spreading lies,' I said.

'The world's going mad,' said David. 'And this is certainly not going to help.' He waved towards the TV, then settled back in his seat.

'I have to go,' said Gulsum. 'All this excitement is too much for me.' She stood, shivered theatrically, her shoulders hunching up, then bent down and kissed David on both cheeks. She did the same for Isabel and me. As we kissed, she whispered, 'Be careful, won't you?'

Isabel must have heard her because she replied curtly, 'He's well able to look after himself.'

Gulsum simply hummed in reply. A second later she was gone.

'What did you make of what she said about that symbol?' said David, turning to me, 'all that stuff about mystical board games and astrological charts?'

'I can't argue with her,' I said.

'You didn't show her the text below the symbol,' said Isabel.

'No. It was in Latin,' said David quickly.

'I'm sure you've translated it by now,' said Isabel. 'I think I remember most of it. Fame ad mortem was in there somewhere, famine and death, cheery stuff.'

David looked at her for a few seconds. 'I suppose there's no harm in telling you. We haven't figured out what it means yet.' He glanced towards the stairs, the way Gulsum had gone. 'I didn't want to tell Gulsum about it until I found out what she thought of the symbol on its own. One of our people thought it was an astrological chart too.'

'What did the Latin translate to?' I said.

He took his BlackBerry out, tapped it for a few seconds.

'What new path must you make, if you go from famine to death, yet wish to take each path, and each once only. That's it, apparently.' He spoke slowly, reading from his BlackBerry, then looked at me.

'There's a bit of debate about whether path should stand for destiny, but that's all it says.'

'The Greeks liked a good riddle,' said Isabel.

David nodded.

That was it. Some ancient riddle wasn't going to solve anything.

'What's going to happen about Peter?' I said, turning to Isabel.

'We need evidence,' she said tiredly.

'It sounds to me like you're not going to do anything about him,' I said.

'Calm down, Sean. Things like this take time,' said David.

I'd had enough. We were getting nowhere. David's attitude to Peter looked to me like the establishment closing ranks, putting things off until they were forgotten about. I should have known.

David glared at me, then continued.

'I'd have thought that coming from an academic background you'd have learned a little about patience.'

His phone rang.

It played *Rule Britannia* as he extracted it from his pocket. A one-sided conversation followed. When the call ended his face was even more flushed.

'That was the Minister,' he said. His eyes were fixed on Isabel. 'Apparently, they know all about your friend. He said to thank you for coming forward.' He gave her a weak smile.

Isabel looked defeated.

'That's it?' I said.

David stared at me. 'Mr Ryan, we're monitoring over three thousand terrorist suspects in London alone. That's not a state secret. We're up to our eyes in threats this year. You might say there's a lot hitting the fan right now. I told you, we need evidence, not just hearsay.'

'I have to go,' I said.

David looked troubled. 'What about lunch?'

'You eat for us,' I said.

I stood. Isabel got up as well.

David held out his hand, motioned to Isabel to come towards him. As he shook her hand he pulled her down to him and whispered something in her ear. When he was finished she moved away from him. I shook his hand a moment later. He didn't smile.

As we headed out into the heat of the afternoon Isabel glanced from side to side, then turned left. The sky above was a dark grey haze. There was a lid of cloud on the city. The tightness in my stomach was still there. Our effort to get Peter investigated had turned into a total disaster. And Kaiser was on the TV claiming our manuscript was his.

'What did he whisper to you?' I asked as I caught up with Isabel.

'He said I shouldn't be involved with you.'

The boy was only twelve, but his father decided to bring him. His son was going to go to university. He was showing great promise already. And this was going to be the biggest demonstration ever by Muslims in the United Kingdom. This would be the moment when English people sat up and took notice. The time for the shadows and the ghettos was coming to an end.

The house they lived in was only a short ten-minute walk from Tottenham Hale station. It was a walk the boy knew well.

As they entered the station, the boy saw a pile of *Evening Standard*s lying on the grubby grey-tiled floor. His father bent down to pick one up.

The boy saw the headline. It filled the front page.

NEW PLAGUE IN ISTANBUL

The picture underneath was of a bearded man. It looked like a passport photo. The boy read the story looking over his father's arm.

Two people had died of the plague in Istanbul in the last twenty-four hours. A hundred others were in quarantine. The plague was classified as airborne. It had resisted all the normal treatments, including high-strength antibiotics. The World Health Organisation was sending a team to Istanbul.

The father grunted, put the paper under his arm. They waved their Oyster cards at the turnstile. As they boarded the train, the boy noticed a lot of people had the *Evening Standard* in their hands.

It was good to be in London, far away from such nightmares.

52

'You're going to give up,' I said.

'We have no evidence, Sean,' she responded.

'You *are* giving up.'

'Don't look at it that way.'

She stopped, stood facing me.

'Sean, it's over. You've done everything you could. Go home. Watch some TV. We'll organise protection for you. We've warned people about Peter. What more do you think we can do?' She turned and walked on, as if she didn't give a damn whether I replied or not or even whether I followed her.

I watched her walk away, disappear into the crowd. She didn't turn her head. Not once.

I wanted to go after her, but I was angry with her. How could she give up?

And then I knew. She was trying to protect me. I ran.

The street was full of people. Was everybody taking long lunches in London these days? Where was she? It was hard to tell the tourists from the office workers.

Then I saw her. I called her name.

She turned, and on seeing me, hurried on. She'd reached the next corner before I caught up with her.

'What's your rush?' I said.

'Go home, Sean.'

'You're not going to get rid of me that easy.'

She was standing with her arms folded in the middle of the pavement, passers-by diverting around us.

'Don't you get it?'

'Get what?' I said.

She looked pissed. 'You have to let it go.' Her hand cut through the air between us.

'Why?'

She walked under the awning of a barber shop. I followed her. She turned her head, checked that no one was standing behind her before continuing.

'This is not about you any more, Sean.'

'It was never about me.' I said. 'It's about Alek. It's about not giving up. Not walking away. I thought you'd understand that.'

'I do.'

She folded her arms.

'No you don't.' I pointed at her. People were staring at me.

'If you think I'm going to slink away, you don't get it. If you think I'll let this go, you don't have a clue. And if you think I'm going to let you take the next steps on your own, you don't know me at all.' I paused, took a breath. 'Don't force me to do something stupid, Isabel. I mean it.'

She looked me straight in the eyes. 'I know you do, Sean. That's the trouble.' She stepped towards me, put her hand on my arm.

'But this isn't your job. It's mine.' Her eyes were begging me to listen.

'It's mine now too,' I said. I spoke calmly. 'You'll have to shoot me to stop me.' I pointed two fingers at my forehead.

A girl bumped into me. Seconds ticked by. A bus beeped.

'You're crazy. And I respect you.' She bit her bottom lip, shook her head. 'You know, you're the first man I've said that about in a long time.'

I raised my eyebrows.

She smiled at her admission. 'Yeah, it's true. I rang a friend last night. I told her about how you wouldn't give up under Hagia Sophia. How you wouldn't leave me.' Her eyes widened, as if she was thinking about it. 'That meant a lot to me, Sean. I've known a lot of spineless idiots in the past.' She closed her eyes, shook her head as if throwing off a bad memory.

'Did I thank you properly for not leaving me?'

I shook my head, wondered what properly meant.

She leaned towards me. And I was sure, for one heart-squeezing moment, that she was going to kiss me. I could almost feel her lips on mine.

But she didn't. All she did was whisper, 'Thank you, Sean. I mean it.'

Then she stepped back, before I could reach out for her.

I looked away. I wanted to reach out, hold her, but something held me back. Maybe it was Irene's ghost. Maybe I wasn't as ready as I'd thought.

'I won't give up,' I said. 'No matter what you say. Even if I have to follow you in a cab or run after you in the Underground. I know you're up to something. This means a lot more to me than just exposing Peter, you know that.'

She groaned. 'You are so pig-headed, Sean.' She turned her head away, put her hand to her mouth. A few seconds later she turned to me again.

'OK,' she said. Then she pointed a finger at me. 'You can come with me. I'm going to see Peter. But I'm going to keep it simple with him. I just need to ask him a few questions.'

I breathed out. 'I have a few too,' I said.

'I'll be asking the questions,' she said, sharply.

But there was a softness in her eyes, as if she was happy I'd pressed hard to go with her. She wasn't going to make things easy, but she wanted me to come along.

And I wanted to go with her.

'Where is he?' I said.

'Not far.' There was an urgency to her answer that took me by surprise.

'We're going to see him now?'

'You bet.'

'There's something going on you're not telling me.'

'This is all you need to know, Sean. I'm going to ask Peter a few questions, face to face, right now.'

'OK.'

Her hand shot up. A black cab screeched to a halt beside us. The driver was a skinhead with an angel tattoo on his forearm. He had a wide smile.

'Where to, love?' he said.

'St Paul's,' said Isabel.

The driver gave me a grin as I squeezed in beside her. There was an *Evening Standard* on the seat. Isabel picked it up and looked at it. After a few seconds she dropped the paper back down. Outside, ball-bearing-sized drops of rain were falling. In seconds the street was a stream. People were dashing under awnings and into doorways. A flash of lightning reflected into the cab, a momentary neon glow. A crack of thunder echoed. The weather was weird for August, that was for sure.

Isabel was staring out of the window at the traffic.

I picked up the *Evening Standard*. The front page was about people dying in Istanbul of the plague. What the hell? Had I

341

come and gone out of a city with a killer disease without knowing anything about it?

I shivered, turned the page, then the next. Where was the story about the demonstration this afternoon? I flicked on through the paper. There wasn't anything about it.

'Did you see this?' I said, holding the front page of the paper in front of her.

She glanced at me. 'It's a nightmare, Sean. They're thinking about closing the airports there.'

'We got out just in time,' I said.

The taxi pulled over. ''Ere you are, love, can't get you any closer, that demo's blocking half of bleeding Ludgate Hill. You better get home early too, love. I heard this crowd will get a lot bigger.'

We paid him, got out into the rain. A hundred yards away, up a road lined with five- and six-storey office blocks, curving gently up towards St Paul's, was an eight-foot high sheet-steel barrier. It was painted yellow. The barrier was just beyond a Pret A Manger sandwich shop. It blocked the road from side to side except for a passageway at its centre. Were they worried about suicide bombers? Was the plan to allow the event, but heavily restrict it?

The barrier had the Metropolitan Police logo emblazoned on it. Beyond the barrier, the dome of the cathedral reached up into the sky. A small orb glistened at the top of the dome, like a golden cherry.

I turned up my collar. Rain trickled down my face. It had eased, but it was still uncomfortable, seeping into my clothes, making everything damp. We ran into the doorway of a book shop.

Despite the rain, throngs of people were moving through the barrier towards St Paul's.

'Where the hell are we going?' I said.

Isabel's hair was sticking to her forehead. In the distance I could hear the slow beat of a drum. It sounded more like a call to war, than something you'd hear at a demonstration.

'Peter's place is in St George's Tower, near St Paul's,' said Isabel. 'This is the easiest way to get there.'

'I'm looking forward to seeing his face when we tell him why we came,' I said.

She leaned towards me.

'I've agreed to this, but I hope to God you don't make me regret it.'

'You won't, but he better have a good explanation,' I said.

There was a sense of anticipation around us – people were walking fast, talking to each other. When she spoke again, she changed the subject.

'There have been wild claims on the Internet that Allah's going to perform a miracle today. That he's going to convert London,' said Isabel. She raised her eyebrows.

A bolt of lightning split the sky above the chalk-grey dome of St Paul's. Its tiers of pillars and statues of saints, peering out expectantly, were lit up for a moment as if by a giant spotlight.

'It's certainly the right weather for miracles,' I said.

As I watched people passing through the barrier, I felt a sense of expectation grow inside me. I was about to pass through an ECP demo. Should I say something if I met one of the organisers? But what? Do you know anything about a bomb two years ago in Afghanistan? Sure, I was going to get an answer to that question.

The rain lashed the road.

'Come on,' said Isabel. She led the way, her head down.

We passed through the steel barrier along with a group of four-foot-something women dressed all in white, their heads covered. On the other side of the barrier, white police vans lined each side of the street. A large truck had 'Incident Unit' in red lettering on its side. Policemen in white shirts and armoured vests were sitting in rows in the vans.

'They're worried that someone might attack the demonstration,' she said, as we walked together, heads down, towards St Paul's.

'That's not going to happen,' I said

She replied in a soft voice. 'I hope not.'

Just up head, across a small triangular piazza, was the high-Baroque citadel of St Paul's, its wide grey Portland stone steps glistening in the rain. The tiers of wedding cake style Corinthian columns and twin towers on its west front looked like time travelling relics from the 17th century.

Some of the people around us were waving black banners now. Some were holding up see-through plastic covered placards with 'Repent or Prepare' written on them. They were prepared for the rain anyway.

As we came onto the piazza in front of St Paul's, the crowd grew thicker. Still, there was little sign of any organisers or stewards marshalling everyone. There were simply knots of people standing around in the rain, waiting for something to happen. Looking up at the cathedral I felt its timeless majesty. It reminded me of how I'd felt looking up at Hagia Sophia.

That was an older, darker edifice, but the feeling of being in the presence of something sublime and brooding was similar. If anything, I felt it more distinctly here. This was the place where British pride began, where Arthur drew the sword from

344

the stone, where England's great heroes, Nelson and Wellington, had their crypts.

We wove our way through the crowd, headed towards the buildings on the left, the northern side of the piazza. In places, the clumps of bearded men and penguin-like huddles of black-cloaked women were too thick to penetrate. Many of the crowd had umbrellas too. We had to detour around them. The rain was easing. I felt damp right through. I had goose bumps on my arms. Even my shirt cuffs felt damp. In the distance, thunder rumbled, as if there was another storm on the way.

We walked under the awning of a coffee shop. Isabel took her iPhone out, tapped at the screen for a few seconds. Then she put her phone away.

'I had to send a text,' she said.

I heard a huge noise, looked up. Two Royal Air Force jets, dart-like new Eurofighters, flying low, roared straight overhead. Each of them was trailing an amber glow. For a moment, the hubbub of the crowd in front of us died as everyone looked up, followed the jet trails. Then, after executing a tight turn, the planes came roaring back over us.

That was when I noticed that people nearby were staring at us. We weren't obviously Muslim, and I hadn't felt unwelcome, up until now, but an uncomfortable feeling of wariness crept over me.

'What time is all this kicking off?' I said.

'Soon. They're going to have some ceremony in front of St Paul's, by the statue of Queen Anne. That's all I know.'

To our left, stone and glass office buildings reared up like a prison wall, their rows of rectangular windows staring implacably down at us. Two passageways provided a way between the buildings. Isabel pushed through the crowd and headed for the smaller of the passageways. At the end of it, after making our way against a stream of demonstrators, we crossed a street empty of vehicles, but full of people heading for St Paul's.

It felt like we'd met a crowd going to a football match, except that we were wearing the wrong colours.

We crossed the street, made our way towards a shiny steel gate set into the granite wall of a keep-like building. There was a keypad at shoulder height on the wall, which reared straight into the sky. We were supplicants at a castle gate.

Isabel jabbed at the keypad. Nothing happened. She pressed two of the keys again. People passed behind us, looking at us. Finally, an accented voice called out from a speaker somewhere.

'Who is it?'

'It's Isabel, for Peter.' She waved jauntily at the camera embedded in the wall beside the keypad, as if we were there for a party. There was no reply.

The gate had slits in its metal surface. I could see a stone flagged passage beyond.

There was a dim patch of artificial light at the other end of the passage. What else was down there was far too indistinct to make out. The rain began to beat down again. Some people on the street began running to find shelter.

Isabel gave me a nudge.

'Nice place, ain't it?' she whispered. 'There used to be a hospital on this site, a long time ago.' She looked over her shoulder.

'You'd think they'd have something better to do on a wet Friday afternoon,' she said.

We waited. More demonstrators rushed past us, squelching loudly.

I pressed the bell. 'We're not going away, Peter,' I said. 'We just need to ask you a few questions. Then we'll go.'

We stood there. I was sure he wasn't going to let us in. I asked Isabel for her phone.

'Who are you going to call?' she said.

'If he doesn't let us in, I'm going to call a journalist I know, tell him everything I overheard in Istanbul. He can get a TV news crew here in fifteen minutes.' It was true that I knew a journalist at the BBC. He'd be surprised to hear from me, but he would listen if I called him.

'I can tell you his name, if you want,' I said.

Seconds later, there was a metallic click from the gate. I pushed at it. It opened. The curved roof and walls of the passage beyond were constructed from centuries-old brown bricks. As the gate closed behind us, the light grew dim for a moment.

'Welcome to St George's,' said a disembodied woman's voice. Lights embedded in the wall lit up. They were blue, tiny, and ran in two inch-apart lines. They drew my eye to the far end of the passageway.

As we walked on I saw the wall on our left was no longer brick. It was made of smoky glass. I could see something moving beyond the glass too. A woman in a long alabaster dress was walking parallel to us. It felt weird, as if we were being shadowed. I stopped. So did Isabel. So did the woman on the other side of the glass.

I'd heard of apartment buildings with electronic concierges, but this was the first time I'd seen one. We'd stepped into a private world of privilege.

'Follow me,' the woman's voice said. She smiled through the glass, turned and walked on. If I didn't know better, I would have assumed she was smiling at me.

'This isn't your average crash pad,' I said.

The door at the far end slid open with a low shusssh, revealing an enclosed circular courtyard that must have been a hundred feet wide, with tiers of reflecting windows in rows above us, and unmarked cream doors at the main compass points.

I looked up. The building surrounding us had six storeys. High above, a white roof like a spider's web separated us from the sky. A square, smoky glass pillar about six foot high stood in the centre of the courtyard. The pillar had the same blue lights around it as the wall in the passageway.

Isabel led the way, walking briskly. When we'd got about halfway towards the pillar, our feet crunching softly on white gravel, I heard the voice of the concierge woman again.

'You may view information about this building here. Please say 'yes' as you pass, if you would like to know more.'

As we approached the pillar I said yes.

Isabel turned and rolled her eyes.

The blue lights dimmed and became an embedded video screen. A scene of dark water close up, a lake in winter, played on it.

'The first recorded use of this site was as a temple to pre-Christian gods — nature deities,' said the voice. 'The foundations of a man-made pool were uncovered here when the complex was being constructed. Because of this, water pools are a feature in each building.'

Isabel passed the pillar without looking at it and walked down the path to the right, towards the doorway at the end.

As I passed the pillar, the video changed. A hand holding a black-hilted sword appeared out of the water, dripping. I slowed to look at it.

'Before the first Christian church was constructed in the early 6th century nearby, where St Paul's is today, there was a temple to the goddess Diana, the huntress, on that site. When the time is right, so the legend says, when he is needed, the once and future King will again come to prominence in this area.' There was a brief pause. 'To learn more about this site please say 'yes'.'

I didn't say anything. The water scene disappeared. The square pillar became a pillar again.

'They really overdid the marketing hype here,' said Isabel, as I came up beside her. 'Only a few of the apartments have been sold, you know. I think Peter still has this whole building to himself.' She pressed a silver button on the wall by the cream door. I could feel anticipation rising within me.

The door slid open, to reveal a long, dazzlingly-white, high-ceilinged foyer. Along the walls, on each side, there were four six-foot-high stones that looked as if they'd been brought straight from Stonehenge.

We walked inside. The door behind us shushed closed. At the far end of the foyer were lift doors and an opening that appeared to be a stairway heading down.

An aluminium sculpture, a criss-cross of wires, was suspended inches above a pool of dark water, which dominated the centre of the foyer. At the end of the pool was a cream reception desk, with a man standing behind it.

This was a real show-off space, a way to tell people you could afford all this, just to make your entrance look interesting.

The guy behind the desk was bald and was wearing a tight

black short-sleeved T-shirt. He had the physique of a body-builder who'd been overdoing the steroids. His skull was slightly elongated at the back. And he looked familiar. Then he raised a hand, motioned us forward.

'Come,' he said, in an accent so rough it seemed loaded with gravel. I had no idea where he came from. Eastern Europe, maybe the Middle East.

We passed the pool.

'Peter is not available,' said the man, as we came closer to him.

He was looking at us as if we were interlopers trying to gain entry into his high-class nightclub. His head was down, his chin low, his gaze moving between us restlessly.

We stopped a few feet from him. I wasn't just being paranoid. This guy gave me the creeps.

'You are?' said Isabel. She sounded suspicious. 'I thought this place didn't have any security staff yet.'

The guard looked at her. His face twisted into a sneer. There was definitely something wrong.

'Is Peter here?' I said.

'I told you, he will not see you. You can email him, make an appointment. Now you must go.'

'This is a national security matter,' said Isabel curtly. 'I need to see him now. You have no authority to prevent me from going up to him.' She pulled an identity card from her pocket and held it out in front of her.

Then she started for the lifts.

I moved between Isabel and the guard. If he was going to try and stop her, he'd have to go through me first. He turned and raised his hand to the side, as if he was a bus conductor trying to stop people from getting on a bus.

'This is your last warning,' he said. 'You will stop now or you'll be considered intruders.'

He moved swiftly from behind his desk. I had a sudden sinking feeling. He was holding a black metal truncheon in his left hand. There was an electric blue glow at its tip.

53

The screen on Henry's left showed the exterior of a Turkish Ministry of Public Health laboratory. Henry was waiting for an official courier to appear. The man would be carrying a signed and stamped report from the forensic pathologist, Dr Illiyc, who worked on the building's third floor.

The practice of hand delivering pathology reports of special significance dated back to an earlier period, but was still in use, despite the availability of computer networks that could transmit the information in nanoseconds. There were still cases where a state prosecutor, senior police inspector or government department simply didn't want a report transmitted electronically.

The practice was limited now, used in very special cases only.

This was such a case. The forensic pathology report for a new plague victim, an ambulance driver who had been within feet of a victim, and in his community for the last two days, had just been completed. What Henry needed to know was if this driver had died from the new plague virus too.

Because if he had the Turks were going to have to quarantine a lot more people. Otherwise, this virus was going to spread like fire in a tinder-dry forest.

54

I felt stupid. Real stupid. Of course he'd be armed. I could feel the blood draining from my face. Isabel turned and clasped her hands in front of her.

She was pointing something that looked like a gun at the guard. It was a gun.

'Stop now. Put your hands above your head,' she shouted.

The guard grinned.

The end of the device he was pointing at me was glowing brightly. It did not look pleasant. I wasn't scared though. I was angry.

Then, one of the elevator doors behind Isabel opened soundlessly and I struggled to grasp what I was seeing: it was Peter, holding another of the blue-tipped devices. The gears in my mind turned slowly. This would be no polite confrontation. He was a traitor. He could do anything now.

He stepped out of the elevator. My mouth opened to warn Isabel, but as her name came out, an arc of blue lightning reached from Peter to her, and she crumpled like a rag doll, twitching spasmodically as the blue light flickered around her like ball lightning.

Peter was smiling. The bastard!

Isabel was jerking, as if she was having an epileptic fit. Her gun fell from her hand. I did the only thing I could think of.

I raced towards the security guard, my fists up. If I could only knock that taser from his grip.

He must have heard my thoughts, because he lifted the taser just at that moment. A blue flash filled the air.

And all my thoughts disintegrated. There was just pain. Muscles contracting. Cramps. Shock.

Then I was lying on my back, jerking, stabs of agony piercing me. The taser had turned my muscles into burning jelly.

I heard voices, felt my legs move. Someone was binding them together! I tried to kick out to stop them. Instead I jerked convulsively, my muscles cramping. Dread raced through me. What was going to happen?

I felt hands turning me on my side. I saw Peter wrapping black tape around Isabel's arms, pinning them behind her back. She was mouthing something I couldn't hear. Then I was pushed over. I couldn't see her any more.

'You deserve your fate,' said a man's voice. My arms were being taped. I was being dragged by my feet, my muscles still jerking. Where was he taking me?

To the pool!

I made a desperate attempt to kick my assailant. But my foot just jerked in the air again. And before I could think of what else to do, I was at the edge of the pool. The water had a sickly, ozoney odour.

'You do it, Peter,' said a gravelly voice.

'I will.' Peter's voice was firm, as if he was agreeing to make tea.

I turned my head. Hatred boiled inside me. How could that bastard have betrayed Isabel like this? He must have been in on Alek's death. I wanted to knock the smug expression right off his face.

But he was standing over me, looking down at me. And I was all trussed up.

'You should have drowned under Hagia Sophia,' said Peter. 'Now you will drown here.'

Like being in a car crash, time slowed. I knew what was coming, knew it was going to be bad, and that there was nothing I could do about it.

He put a sticky plastic tape over my mouth. I could taste the glue. I tried to jerk again, but my head dropped back on to the marble floor. I actually saw stars. Then I opened my eyes. The ceiling seemed strangely near. I was breathing way too fast, through my nostrils. My chest was heaving in and out.

I could feel the edge of the pool against my left shoulder. I needed to roll back. I turned my head. The rest of my body wouldn't respond. Then it jerked. Then it stopped.

I looked around, wildly. My eyes weren't focusing properly. Then I saw Isabel was on the ground, trussed up near the desk. She was staring at me. Her eyes were wide and wild. She had black masking tape over her mouth too. Her body had stopped jerking. I saw horror in her eyes. She knew what was about to happen.

My head turned again. All I could see was the glistening blackness of the water, a great beast with a dark mouth waiting for me.

The initial effect of the taser shock had almost worn off. My muscles had stopped jerking. But with my hands pinned behind me, and my legs strapped together with tape, and someone pushing me in the side, all I could do was jerk spasmodically. And I did, even as my body turned slowly towards the water.

And then a vision filled my mind. My body lying on a shelf in a morgue, the way I'd found Alek, cold, blue-veined. I tried to shout, scream, plead. Then I stopped. There isn't much you can scream with tape over your mouth.

'You should have stayed away,' said Peter, bending down over me. The next push he gave would send me into the water. 'You should have given up. I warned you.'

I breathed hard through my nose, filling my lungs. Then again. Peter smiled at me. I looked away. I could feel the dark presence of the water.

I turned my head. Isabel had rolled on her side. Our eyes met. Her expression said *I'll get the bastards if I can.*

'Do it,' came a voice. Not Peter's. 'We have to go down.'

He pushed me. I tumbled over.

There was an enveloping splash as I fell into the freezing black water. Terror raced through me. I shook and rolled until I didn't know which way was up. All I knew was a mind numbing fear.

The icy water closed over me like a door and I sank into a grave-like darkness. And I still hadn't found out why Alek had died. What had he seen that he had to be killed for? That I had to be killed for?

There was a rumour going around London that afternoon. It quickly became a trending topic on Twitter. A man, whose sister was a Special Constable, had told his fellow drinkers in a bar at lunchtime that all police leave had been cancelled that day.

It had something to do with the demo at St Paul's.

The authorities were right to be nervous.

MI5's A4 London security team was at that time actively tracking one hundred and twenty-four known high-category terrorists, including twelve far-right targets. On the ground, officers had orders to shoot on sight, if any suspect they were monitoring was believed to be a grave danger to the public.

Such blanket orders were given only a few times a year, when there was a credible threat to large numbers of people.

The BBC News site recorded an all-time record ten million page requests per second at 4.27 PM, when an article about the size of the demonstration near St Paul's went online.

The article speculated on the significance of the event.

56

'You really shouldn't have brought him with you, Isabel,' said Peter loudly.

Malach pushed Isabel roughly down the last few stairs. She stumbled, almost fell.

'I warned you, but of course you wouldn't listen. You could have stayed in Istanbul, like I told you to, but oh no, you know better. Well, there's nothing I can do for you now – or for him, so don't beg.'

'You are some sick bastard,' shouted Isabel. Her voice was trembling.

'My, my, you weren't growing close to him, were you?' said Peter. He shook his head. 'How very unprofessional of you.'

Malach pushed her forward at the bottom of the stairs. Isabel stumbled again, then steadied herself. They'd tied her hands behind her back, but her legs were free. She was able to walk, though the prospect of falling was ever present as she couldn't reach out to hold onto anything.

The passage ahead was lit by recessed lighting. About fifty feet ahead, it ended at a stainless steel door.

When they reached the steel door, Peter punched a code into a panel set into the wall beside it. The doors slid open. Malach pushed Isabel forward. There was a strong smell of polish, as if the elevator they were in had recently been cleaned.

It moved down with a barely audible whuuussh.

'Wonderful, isn't it?' said Peter. 'If you've got the right codes, you can go anywhere.'

He looked at his watch. 'I'm sorry we had to leave Sean to die, my dear, but it should be over now. At least it was quick. Well – relatively quick.'

Henry's jacket was off. His sleeves were rolled up. There was tension in the air. In front of him, video feeds from locations across London played on a semicircle of five LCD screens. He looked up for a second as his screens blinked, glanced at the curved brick roof above his head. He had to wait a few seconds before he made contact again.

Henry was in MI5's London Control Centre, the main threat monitoring unit for central London. This was the room he enjoyed working in most, despite where it was. He could feel a real connection with his long-dead father here. He'd been part of the first team to work here after the war. And he'd told Henry a little about it.

In early 1942, eight deep-level bomb shelters were dug out in central London. At between 123 and 155 feet deep they became the deepest wartime shelters ever built in Europe.

One was located beneath Chancery Lane tube station, now part of the Central Line of the Underground, between St Paul's and Holborn stations.

The shelter, originally 1,200 feet long, was designed to have two floors, and was constructed with a twenty-foot thick concrete roof. It was still considered to be impregnable. When his father worked here it housed the Special Operations Executive's central London monitoring unit.

On one occasion his father had taken him to see the entrance to the facility, a reconstructed brick 'pillbox' structure at street level. He'd also told him about the floor-to-ceiling metal turnstile, located on a rarely used part of the lower concourse of Chancery Lane station, the other entrance to the facility. This was the entrance Henry mostly used now.

These days both entrances had biometric entry panels, and wall mounted voice recognition systems that would have amazed his father.

In the main control room on the lower floor of the facility, where Henry was sitting that afternoon, a mosaic of LCD screens covered one wall. Henry's desk was the second from the right in a row of five.

When he exited the station, Henry looked like any other middle-aged commuter in a rumpled silver-grey suit with a copy of *The Times* neatly tucked under his arm, folded open to reveal the crossword page.

The resources Henry had access to would have amazed the early occupiers of the facility. He could watch multiple live video feeds from thousands of central London security cameras, including some mounted on helicopters.

Despite all the expensive equipment though, Henry had lost one of his targets. He was waiting for a field team to check in.

And he'd waited long enough.

'A41,' he said, brusquely, into the stalk microphone on the desk in front of him. 'Anyone in that passageway?'

There was a piercing crackle from the earphone in his left ear.

'No, sir,' came the reply.

'Bugger,' said Henry loudly. The tracking device he'd been relying on had been out of range for two minutes. He picked up a sleek black handset.

The controllers on his left and right stopped what they were doing and looked at him.

He spoke quickly, listened, then put the handset down.

He looked at the main screen in front of him and pressed some keys on his curved keyboard.

An image of two people, a man and a woman, the targets he'd been tracking since they'd left the House of Commons, filled the screen.

He watched as his system replayed a stored video of the couple heading towards the St George's building.

'Sorry, A41,' he said into his microphone. 'Stand down. We've had a direct order.'

He switched his main monitor to a feed from a camera overlooking the front of St Paul's. A bearded man in a loose white shirt was standing halfway up its main steps. He was holding a fat black microphone and addressing the crowd pressing in around him.

The man had moved from when he'd started his speech. Most likely because of the size of the crowd.

But that was not what made Henry's eyes widen. Behind the speaker, at the top of the steps, the main door of St Paul's was cracking open at its centre. That wasn't supposed to happen.

Someone was opening the door from the inside!

His gaze shifted to the live news feed from the BBC service. The text banner at the bottom of the screen read: 'Speaker at Muslim rally at St Paul's claims London will become an Islamic city'.

The image above the text changed. People in the crowd had noticed that the doors were opening. Some began to rush forward.

'What?' said Henry. 'Are they going to take over St Paul's?'

He let out a deep breath.

The desktop speakers beside Henry's screen fizzed with a light static. The hum from the equipment all around him gave the place the feel of a beehive.

'Should we come back to base, sir?' came a calm voice in his ear.

He licked his lips. They felt like sandpaper. He had a bad feeling, down deep in his gut

The small red phone on his desk rang. The only time that ever rang was when there was trouble.

He picked it up.

'Yes, sir.'

After listening for a few seconds, he placed the receiver down. All eyes were on him.

The speaker on his desk squawked.

'Are we back to base, sir?' came the same male voice.

Henry pressed some buttons on the keyboard to his left. One of his two screens blinked, went white, blinked again. An image appeared, moved.

An officer in a police uniform came into the field of view. The body armour he wore was hidden under a bulky yellow jacket. He was accompanied by four others who were similarly dressed.

Henry looked up. On every desk around him, one screen was showing the same image he was looking at. There would be other screens around the country watching this feed too, Downing Street included. He sat up straighter.

'Has the security system been cut?' he said.

'Not yet, sir,' came the reply from the speakers.

'Change in orders. Proceed. Code green,' said Henry.

The image on the screen changed, bounced. The camera moved back. A handheld battering ram could be seen. It moved. The side of the door buckled.

But it didn't open. Most doors would have.

This was going to take longer than expected.

He turned to the keyboard at his right, began typing. He noticed the red timer on the top of his screen. It told him how long it had been since the tracking device he was following had gone out of range. '4:05' it read.

58

'Soon we will all be tested, that's what they say, isn't it?' said Peter, as they made their way down a spiral staircase in a shaft of chocolate brown brick, the type you'd find in a Victorian Underground station. The walls pressed in around them. There was a musty smell too.

'You're in a good mood,' said Isabel. 'For a traitor. You won't get away with this, you know that, don't you?'

'Do you want your mouth taped again?' said Peter.

Isabel didn't reply.

The lower they went, the mustier the air became. Isabel was behind Peter, a little ahead of Malach.

She was taking each step slowly. A fall down these stairs would be seriously painful. Malach had warned her not to delay them, but she still went down at her own pace.

When they reached the bottom, Peter stood in front of an old-fashioned steel fuse cabinet and pulled its prominent black Bakelite handle upwards. He then yanked it forwards and upwards again. The whole dull grey unit moved towards him in the dust, on hinges, as if it was a door. Behind it, there was a dim corridor with an arched brick roof. This was a medieval corridor many generations older than the spiral staircase they'd just come down.

And it was barely wide enough for two people to pass,

and too low for Malach to stand upright in. He had to bend his neck. The air in the tunnel left a dusty taste in Isabel's mouth. There was a foul smell, as if dead rats had been left to rot here.

'Lovely down here, isn't it?' said Peter, as they entered the passage. He reached out to a round black bakelite switch on the wall to their left. Lights came on along the corridor, which stretched far into the distance. Peter closed the door behind them.

'Originally, this led to the old Fleet Prison,' he said. His voice echoed in the passage. Isabel stood silently, arms behind her, a little way on.

She was looking at the packed earth floor.

'Come on,' he said. 'You better keep up.' He prodded her to follow Malach, who was striding ahead.

They passed a wooden door made from grey timbers with a small rusty grill at shoulder height. The yellow light from the mesh-covered bulbs set at regular intervals along the tunnel's walls flickered.

'You're following a long tradition, Isabel. Some important prisoners were brought this way.'

Malach had stopped and was waiting for them. Peter prodded Isabel in the back again.

They passed another door and turned left into a side tunnel. There were no roof lights in this section until the tunnel branched again, a hundred yards further on. The light from that end of the tunnel lit only part of the section in between.

As they walked into the gloom a cold fear gripped at her. She'd been taught how to suppress her feelings if she was kidnapped, to think about ways to escape, but she was struggling to remember much more of the advice.

Her thoughts were jumping too fast.

She bumped into Malach in the middle of the gloomiest part of the tunnel. He grabbed her shoulder and pulled her to him.

She turned her head in revulsion.

He laughed. 'Good,' he said, in a tone that left little doubt that he was enjoying himself. He pinned her to his side.

She tried to wriggle free. He held her tighter. Icy lumps of fear passed through her veins.

He pushed at a door in the wall, just where it was gloomiest. A heavy damp smell hit her, and suddenly there was light.

She had to close her eyes, it was so bright. When she opened them, Malach had released her. She was looking into a space the likes of which she'd never seen before. It was one... two... three... four... no, eight-sided, and its black-timbered ceiling angled steeply up from each wall towards a point, high up above the centre of the room.

Peter closed the foot-thick door as soon as the three of them were inside. There was no way anyone would hear her scream down here.

'Amazing, isn't it? This place goes back to the 1640s,' said Peter. He walked slowly around the room.

'Part of it was used in Roman times as well, as an underground temple. The sort of place where they taught divination and magic, that sort of thing.' He pointed up at the roof.

'That hole up there points to the North Star,' he went on. 'Or it did, once.'

Malach was locking the door.

There was a rough stone mound in the centre of the room. It looked like the top of a huge ball, age-blackened and ten foot wide, protruding only inches above the floor. Near it there was an oak table, its edges worn soap-smooth from use. On the table, lying open, was the manuscript they'd found in Istanbul. Isabel moved towards it. Peter didn't stop her. It was open at the last page. The symbol stared up at her.

She wanted to ask how he'd got the book, but she didn't. She wasn't going to give him the pleasure. Anyway, someone had to be coming for her. They'd be looking for her already. The only question was, how soon would they find this place?

A deep sadness filled her up every time she thought about Sean. Poor Sean. Tears threatened every time she thought about him, but they didn't come, like a storm that wouldn't break.

'Can you hear something?' said Peter. He was standing behind her.

There was a distant rumbling. It might have been water. It might have been an underground train. She looked up at the roof.

'That's the River Fleet,' he said. 'It's directly above us.'

There was a cold slick of sweat all over her now, but her mind was floating, as if she was observing a nightmare happening to someone else.

'This place became the Star Chamber for a time in 1641. Charles I used it. The Puritans who founded America were fleeing his regime. It was abandoned and then sealed up. Come and see this.' He pointed at the mound in the centre of the room and walked towards it.

When she came near it, she saw there was a six-inch gap all around the mound. When she looked into the gap she saw it ran down into the earth and grew wider further down. And in the crack, a few feet down, there were grey bones. Lots and lots of them. They could have been animal bones, she wanted them to be animal bones, but the human skulls here and there in the thick lattice of thighs and cracked ribs and brittle arms told her something different.

The protruding ball shape looked like the top of a skull to her now. A skull bigger than any she'd ever seen. And the top of the skull, or whatever it was, was blackened, as if fires had been lit on it long ago. Around the protrusion, about six feet away from it, were four circles, smooth stone lids, set into the stone floor. Each of them was two foot in diameter, and equidistant, as if they'd been the base points for four pillars that could have held a roof or a canopy over the mound.

'Do you want to see more?' said Malach. He was standing behind her.

Isabel shook her head.

'Open one, Peter,' said Malach.

Peter took a short iron pole, about as long as his arm and coal-black, from a hook near the door and went to one of the stone lids. Slowly, he prised the two-inch thick lid off and moved it aside.

He looked inside the hole and motioned Isabel towards him. She didn't respond. God only knew what was in there. Malach walked towards her, pushed her shoulder.

Isabel went to the hole and looked inside. The space was about the size of a coffin. The smell from it was rancid, as if it had once been a latrine, or someone had died in it. There were no bones in it, but the sides were black, as if there'd been a fire in it.

She backed away.

'What's happened to you?' she said, looking at Peter. She wanted to say more, but her tongue felt thick and her throat was constricting.

He stared at her for a long moment before he answered.

'It's all about results, Isabel. The end always justifies the means.'

'You're a psycho,' she said.

He shook his head and pointed at the mound. 'Do you know what that is?' he said.

She shook her head, quickly, as if she didn't want to know.

'That is where Mammon was worshipped, the god of greed and pride. They knew about human nature back then, better than we do with all our science.' He put his hands out, as if he was basking in something emanating from the mound.

'This is a place of power. You must feel it, Isabel. When I brought our friend here, he recognised at once that this was the right place for his needs.'

'Do it. We don't have a lot of time,' said Malach. His grin was a sadist's leer.

Isabel was shaking now, as if she had a fever. She'd guessed something bad was going to happen, that she'd get no sympathy from Peter, but her imagination was running wild now, thinking about what her fate might be. And her last hope was gone. Sean was dead.

And that knowledge alone was crushing in a way she hadn't expected at all.

'Do it,' said Malach. His voice had all the charm of a hissing snake.

Peter poked Isabel in the side, pushed her towards the hole. She stumbled, but managed to steady herself. Having her arms bound behind her back didn't help.

She took a step back. She wasn't going to make it easy for them.

'Shouldn't you send the message?' said Peter. He was looking at Malach.

Malach took out an iPhone from the front pocket of his baggy black trousers. He peered at the screen.

'There's no network, Peter. What happened to great signal booster?' He was angry.

Peter looked perplexed. He pulled his phone out, looked at it, held it out towards Malach. 'Use mine. It switches to a landline. There must be something wrong with the mobile network. Maybe it's overloaded.'

Malach took the phone.

'Send it now,' said Peter. He looked at his watch. 'Aren't your friends expecting it?'

Malach stared at Peter.

'Then you can have your fun.' He glanced towards Isabel.

59

When I was a boy I imagined I could see in the dark.

I used to walk around my grandmother's house in upstate New York after everyone had gone to bed and the lights had been switched off. I was looking for my father. He went to war when I was seven.

There are similar types of darkness. There's the darkness of a clapboard house at midnight, when starlight burnishes doors and windows with silver. And then there's the darkness underwater, if you're deep enough.

When the officers came to tell me about Irene, a numbness stole over me. I'd seen my eyes in a mirror after they left. They were wide, looking at something that didn't exist anymore.

I'd felt as if I was suffocating. Just like now.

But this time nails were being driven through my chest.

Surviving even two minutes without taking a breath would be a feat most people would be incapable of, but for someone who free-dived, who practised breathing control regularly, three minutes was a good, but not top class, achievement. Four minutes was. What makes holding your breath a real test though, is when you don't know if you'll be able to breathe again, once you've reached the limit of your endurance.

You have to fight both fear and pain, while knowing your fear is most likely going to be your fate.

And I kept fighting, distracting my mind with effort, turning, moving, trying to get on my knees, on my feet, hoping to stand. But the water constantly pitched me forwards then back.

Finally, I got on to my knees. My lungs were bursting. The nails were going deeper. But I knew I was near the air. All I had to do was push, push up. And I did, and for a second or two my head was out of the water and air rushed into my lungs. Then the water churned around me, rolled me down again.

But I knew now how to survive, how to get out. And confidence flooded through me. All I had to do was move to the side of the pool, stand, but for longer this time. And I knew, suddenly, the mistake they'd made. I was bound at the thigh, but I could use my feet, at an angle, to stand. That was a mistake Peter would pay for.

The policeman who jumped in, a few minutes later, and dragged me out of the water, as I was leaning on an edge of the pool, a trussed-up half-drowned water creature, was Sergeant Smith. His nametag was the first thing I saw after he pulled me out.

I'll never ever forget it.

It took me all of three minutes, coughing and spluttering, with Sergeant Smith cutting my bindings, to tell him what the hell was going on. All I wanted to do was find Isabel. I didn't have time for explanations. And frustratingly, he wanted more details. More and more. I rattled through answers as fast as speech would allow.

The only reason his senior officer let me accompany them into the bowels of the building, down the brick stairs, was because I swore I knew where Peter had taken Isabel. I swore it three times, louder each time.

And it was a lie. All I'd heard was that they were heading down somewhere.

As I stood there waiting to be told to leave, Sergeant Smith handed me a thick black bulletproof vest. I put it on quickly. It weighed less than I'd imagined.

Then I followed the team down to the basement. And unbelievably we couldn't get the lift to work, apparently because we didn't have the right password. But eventually someone overrode it, a young officer with blonde hair and an East End accent.

And then, the lights went out in the staircase we found.

And as we went on, torchlights flashing, another officer asked loudly why I was there. Sergeant Smith told him that I was showing them where Isabel Sharp had been taken.

I didn't say a word.

'You alright, sir?' asked Sergeant Smith, as we continued down the seemingly never-ending staircase, while torches illuminated brick walls in swiftly moving arcs, as if there were giant bats flying around us.

'No problem.'

I think he understood me, my need to be there.

As we went down it felt as if we were descending into some sick version of hell. There wasn't much air down there. I broke out into a sweat and was shivering slightly. The fact that I was still wet didn't help.

Then I saw scars on the bricks. Gouges made by some beast.

When we reached the bottom of the stairs, all we found was an old electricity substation with a black Bakelite handle. Sergeant Smith pulled the handle upwards, then forwards. The unit opened to reveal banks of old fashioned fuse boards. Great.

The expressions on the policemen's faces around me, as they

peered at the yellow porcelain fuses, were as bleak as stones on a mountaintop in winter.

An order was shouted up the stairs to stop more people coming down into the confined space.

'We'll have to look somewhere else, sir. And I think there's a medic above who wants a word with you.' The look on Sergeant Smith's face was one of pity now. He pointed at the stairs. 'Shall we go?'

The other policemen went up, until only Sergeant Smith and I remained.

As he was waiting for me to go up the stairs I had a thought. Why had they built this staircase? They didn't have to go this far underground to connect to an electricity cable, did they?

'Can we check behind this?' I went over to the ancient-looking cabinet.

Sergeant Smith lifted his bulletproof jacket off his shoulders with his thumbs. His face was strained. Sweat had matted his black hair to his forehead.

'Is that a crowbar?' I said, pointing to the long tool hanging from his belt.

He handed me his torch.

'All right, we'll have a look.' He placed the end of his crowbar against the back edge of the fuse cabinet. At first it wouldn't move. Then it moved an inch free of the wall. I saw only brick. We pulled at the crowbar together.

The opening behind the cabinet was the size of a small doorway. This was where Isabel was. It had to be. But why had they brought her down here?

'Well done, mate,' said Sergeant Smith. He slapped my shoulder.

It took a few minutes to call some of the other members of

his team back down, and to pull the fuse cabinet far enough from the wall to get through the opening, but no more than three minutes later, Sergeant Smith and I were standing in an ancient looking brick-lined corridor. It was way too narrow to be modern, but it was different from the tunnels in Istanbul too. Here the bricks were bigger, darker.

Then a hollow thud sounded from somewhere further along the tunnel. What the hell was that? A silver-haired officer poked his head through the gap we'd just come through. He looked worried.

I started walking down the corridor. Then I broke into a jog. I tried to ignore the fact that my head was pounding and that my damp clothes were sticking to me like drying glue. I was going to find Isabel. God only knew what those bastards were doing to her.

'Not so fast, sir,' someone hissed.

I glanced back. Sergeant Smith and some other officers were right behind me, their armoured vests making them look like giant termites in the narrow tunnel. I kept going, but more slowly now. I think one of them would have tasered me if I'd made any noise.

As I approached a branch in the tunnel, I stopped.

A hand grabbed my shoulder. Sergeant Smith was breathing hard, almost in my ear.

'Stop,' he whispered. 'Be careful.'

I shrugged, looked around the corner. I didn't care what happened to me. I saw a closed door, I ran towards it.

In seconds, if I wasn't careful, Sergeant Smith's friends would throw me to the back so they could go in first. I couldn't have that. Even if I ended up becoming a hostage myself, I didn't care. I had to find Isabel.

The door in front of me looked like it belonged in an old monastery. It had been designed to keep people with axes out. Its surface was stiff with rough markings cut into the wood in rows of symbols, crosses, moons and stars.

'Stand back, sir.'

One of the officers was carrying a long black box. It looked like something you might keep your lunch in. The man took out a silver microphone from the box and held it to the door. Its six-inch wide circular base was flat and intricately webbed. The officer put earphones in his ear and listened for a few seconds. Then he gave Sergeant Smith a thumbs-up signal.

'I recommend we break through now,' he said, softly, motioning at the door.

Sergeant Smith leaned towards me, and said, 'There's people in there. There's something going down. You shouldn't be here, as it is. I'll get a bleeding reprimand for allowing you to come this far. You better go. We'll get her out.'

'No, I can help. You'd still be chasing your tails upstairs, if you hadn't brought me along.' I could smell the damp on him, from him pulling me from the water, and a minty smell from his breath. He'd been chewing gum.

He shook his head, then shrugged exasperatedly.

'We didn't have this conversation, alright?'

He motioned for me to stand back, muttered something to his colleague. The man went to the door, took out a device the size of a cigarette-box from the black metal case he was carrying, removed some thick silver tape from its side and stuck the box near to the door's handle.

Sergeant Smith pulled me back around the corner, where the tunnel branched. He put his hands over his ears. I did the same.

We waited.

The officer who'd put the device on the door pressed a button on a tiny remote control.

Nothing happened.

Then a noise exploded out of the tunnel and a wave of smoke and dust blew around the corner. The noise pounded my chest with the intensity of a hammer, even through the vest Sergeant Smith had given me. And as it died I ran into the dust of the corridor though my eyes stung and I was blinking rapidly.

I raced for the door. There was a police officer already there. He had a black helmet on, which covered his face. He threw something into the gaping hole that had appeared where the door had been. I reached him, heard a double-barrelled blast, weaker than the last, but loud enough to rattle my brain in my skull. I actually felt something move inside it.

I should have stopped, I heard a shout behind me, but I kept running. I was only a few feet from the smoke filled doorway. I thought about Alek, of the stupidity of his life being over, of that beautiful receptionist, the terrible end she'd met, of Father Gregory torn apart. And of Irene too. And I ran on.

60

The boy let the *Evening Standard* slip from under his arm. It was wet already. He'd used it to shield himself from the rain, but he didn't need it anymore. His father was lifting him high in the air. The crowd around them was silent. The only noise was the faint sound of rain falling, and a low hiss from the speakers that had been set up around the venue, as if the rain was affecting them.

A whoosh sounded over their heads. The Air Force jet passed over them again. The crowd's heads moved as one, tracking its progress.

There were men around him, Arabs and Europeans, Muslims from all over the world. There were some women too, but mostly at the back.

Rain dripped down into his neck, but he didn't mind. He'd never seen so many Muslims in one place in England. It was exhilarating.

He felt proud, at home at last.

The voice that crackled through the speakers was one he had never heard before. The next few words electrified him. Was this why they were all here?

61

When I jumped through the jagged hole in the door, the scene was surreal. Curtains of smoke and dust hung in the air. A throat-clogging smell hit me. My ears were pounding. I heard a shout from behind me, though I couldn't understand what was being said. It was probably Sergeant Smith telling me to back off. But I didn't. I couldn't. Near a mound in the centre of the room were some people lying on the floor.

Two of them were getting up.

One I recognised instantly. It was the big guy who'd taken Isabel. The other person was Isabel. She was pushing herself up with one hand. I ran fast towards her. The bastard had something in his hand. A silver gun. Peter was lying on the ground a few feet from him.

He pointed the gun at Peter. I thought he was threatening him or that he was trying to get him to stand up. Then a shot rang out. Peter's body jumped an inch in the air. I saw a thin trail of smoke slide from the gun.

Then he was turning it towards me. I swerved, watched in slow motion, wondered if he'd fire it, wondered if I should dive for the floor. But I kept going. I didn't care what happened to me. And I knew what was going to happen next. And the reddish-yellow flash wasn't a surprise, nor was the thump, like a horse's kick, in my side.

And I kept going. I had my fists up. Even if he pumped holes into me, I was going to smash his stupid face.

I had ten seconds at most, before a ton of adrenalin poured through my body and the shivering started, if the bulletproof vest hadn't done its job.

A series of loud snaps filled the air. Reverberations echoed.

More flashes bloomed from his gun. But these weren't aimed at me. He was firing at someone behind me. Then his arm came up to ward me off.

My heart was hammering out of control. A sickly smell of cordite filled my nostrils. I could taste it.

I reached the bastard. I knew what I had to do. I grabbed his gun with both hands, jerked the barrel upwards, even as a flash emerged from it pinging away somewhere, burning my fingers as if I'd grabbed a flame.

Then it felt as if someone had punched the side of my face. He'd head butted me! I swung my knee fast with every bit of force I could muster towards his groin. I connected.

He grunted. His face was inches from mine. His lip trembled. That was the only indication that I'd hit him. He was six foot six, at least and his skin was pale and flaky in places, except for the back of his hand, which was holding the gun. There it was black, as if the skin had been burnt repeatedly.

I could smell steaming sweat now and in his eyes I could see an arrogance that held no possibility of compassion and a promise of instant death if I failed to hold him.

My arm muscles were shaking. Had the adrenaline kicked in? Were my guts falling out? He jerked his hand back. His gun was still in it but I was still holding it, and he was pulling the barrel down. I pushed it hard to the side, jerked it fast away from me

Then a loud pop came, then another and another. A red and black hole opened in the centre of his chest. As his body jerked my hand fell from the gun. I didn't want to get shot too, by holding him too close. He had to be dead.

My knees wanted to buckle. I wouldn't let them.

He fell back onto the mound, spread eagled on top of it. Blood oozed fast from his chest, over his black T-shirt and onto the black stone below. There was blood pumping out of his face too. He had a wound in his cheek and a pulsing flow of blood that slicked his lips and barred teeth.

My breath was coming in giant gasps.

And then, as if he was a force beyond nature, his head came up and his hand, which still had the gun in it, rose slowly. It was pointing in Isabel's direction. Unintelligible shouts echoed from multiple voices.

Without thinking I stepped forward, kicked out and connected. The gun spun in the air. Then there were more snaps, like nails being banged into a wall. Malach's head – I discovered his name later – spurted blood in four or five places. Reddish pink craters opened in the side of his forehead. They pulsed slickly. Blood poured like gushing oil onto the stone. He was gone. He had to be.

Then Isabel was hugging me. It was the hug of someone who'd been reborn. I hugged her back.

'Were you hit?' she said, softly.

I touched my side carefully. The armour felt rough at one point, but unbroken. I slipped the vest off, felt all around under my shirt. Such relief. I was bruised, but there was no blood.

I shook my head.

She went over to Peter. He was lying perfectly still, as if he was resting. But there was a small red hole in his pale blue shirt, in the centre of his chest.

'You bastard,' she said, as she bent down over him.

'I hope the world finds out what he did,' I said.

An officer with a red armband, who I hadn't seen before, was kneeling beside Peter, taking his pulse. He turned to Isabel and shook his head. Then he stood.

My heart rate was retuning to normal but my breath was still coming in gasps.

And I was glad Peter was dead.

'He got what he deserved,' I said, as I knelt down beside her. She was as pale as chalk.

She stood. She was surprisingly steady. She walked over to a table on the other side of the mound. I followed her. On the table was the manuscript we'd found. Sergeant Smith was beside us as she peered down at it.

'This item is supposed to be in the custody of the Foreign Office,' she said. She looked at Sergeant Smith. 'The Turkish Government owns it.'

'Forensics will tag and bag everything, Miss Sharp. You can put in a request for it.'

'We will, don't worry. And don't lose it. It could be the most valuable thing you'll ever put in a bag.'

Sergeant Smith looked at it. 'I'll make sure I don't drop it then,' he said. He had black rubber gloves on. He placed the manuscript into a plastic bag another officer was holding open beside him.

He looked at me. His face looked carved out of marble.

'We have medics waiting for you both,' he said.

'I'm glad you were behind me, Sergeant.' I said.

'You're lucky to be alive, mate,' he replied. He shook his head.

Amazingly though, I felt calm.

It wasn't until an hour later that I realised how close I'd come to dying, but I was still elated. I suppose part of the reason was that I was just so happy to see Isabel, and that I also knew we'd probably caught one of the bastards who'd been after me in Istanbul. One of the bastards who'd killed Alek.

I'd looked down at Malach as I was being hustled out of that chamber, and I knew why he'd seemed familiar when I first saw him. His build, his bald head. I'd only seen the guy for a few seconds, but it looked like the bastard who'd chased us when we'd fled my hotel room. And he was now dead.

'Who was Malach working with?' was the question I asked Sergeant Smith, when my debriefing was finally over, three hours later. I'd met four other officers in the meantime.

We were standing near a nondescript government building not far from the Chancery Lane debriefing centre we'd been taken to.

'I can't say anything about that.' He glanced away.

'You can't tell me anything?'

He shook his head.

'I just signed the Official Secrets Act, Sergeant. And I didn't even argue. Give me a clue, at least. I'd like to know if any of the bastards got away.'

Isabel leaned forward. 'What's the official line, Sergeant?'

He glanced at her. 'We're looking into it. Be happy about that. And if there are others involved, I'm sure they'll be dealt with appropriately, sir.'

'Is there anything happening in Istanbul?' I said. 'About what we found there?'

'The Turkish authorities have arrested two people, sir. They don't take kindly to this sort of thing. That's all I can say. Goodbye to you both.'

He turned away.

We stared as the door closed behind him. The puffy clouds above our heads were tinged with purple and gold from the most spectacular late evening cloudscape I'd seen in London in years.

Isabel looked downcast.

'Are you OK?' I said.

She nodded, but she didn't look OK. 'There's a car coming to pick us up.'

She sat down on the kerb. Her clothes and hair were a mess. I'd been given blue sweat pants and a blue top. My own wet clothes were in a black plastic bag by my side. We must have looked like a couple of tramps.

She looked at me, as if she was weighing something up. Then she said, 'Why don't you come back to my place?'

I smiled. It was exactly what I wanted her to say.

She looked at me, shivered a little.

'Good idea,' I said.

She looked in my eyes. 'I don't want to be alone right now. I just found out something that's upset me.'

'What is it?'

'Not now.' She nodded toward a black Vauxhall Astra that was pulling up beside us.

She didn't tell me what was bothering her in the car either. She just gave the driver directions and sat in the back, beside me, staring out the window, looking all the while as if she was going to cry.

Was this a delayed reaction to her kidnapping? We'd been separated during the debriefing and the first person I'd seen was a medical officer who'd gone through a checklist before getting me to sign a waiver at the bottom. I knew Isabel had received the same check up, as the officer had said his colleague was talking to her, when I said he should look at her first.

All the way to her place in the car I worried about her. I tried to talk a few times, but she just kept shaking her head.

When we got to her apartment block in St John's Wood, I was exhausted and concerned. I asked her again on the way up in the elevator what she'd found out, but she just shook her head. All sorts of theories were going around in my mind. As she turned the key in the lock, she said, 'I need a shower. We'll talk about it later.'

Her hand shook as she pushed the door open. Then she stepped inside.

'You're going to tell me now,' I said. I pushed the door closed behind us. 'Please, Isabel. I'm worried about you. You can't bottle everything up. I tried that. It doesn't work.'

She stared at me as seconds ticked by. 'You're not going to believe this.'

'Try me.'

'I don't even know if I can tell you.'

'Isabel, I've signed my life away. If I tell anybody anything that's happened I'll be arrested in five minutes. What the hell is it? Come on.'

She took a deep breath.

'Peter was on our side. It was all a ruse to get the telephone numbers of Malach's accomplices.'

'But he tried to kill me. I don't believe it.'

'Neither did I, until the officer who told me asked me to explain why Malach shot Peter, if it wasn't because he was sure he'd been betrayed. Then he told me that they'd arrested two of Malach's accomplices as a direct result of a text message sent from Peter's phone to their numbers.'

'It was a ruse?' I felt angry. He'd left me to die. He'd tasered Isabel.

She nodded.

We were standing in the hall staring at each other.

'What was so important that I could be left to die?'

'Remember that threat to bring Armageddon to London? They believe it was stopped when those arrests were made.'

She looked around, as if seeing the place for the first time. 'I shouldn't have doubted him.'

'No one could blame you,' I said.

Then it came to me. That was why Peter hadn't tied my ankles. That was why I'd been able to stand in that pool. Peter had done that. He'd given me a chance. He could have made sure I'd drown. Isabel was right.

'He gave up his life.' She sounded weary. 'No one knew what he was up to, until he sent a text message saying the people his next text was going to, were all to be arrested asap. He was the most secretive person ever. He never told anybody in the consulate anything about his undercover work. We used to joke that he'd gone deep. But he died because of it.' She trembled.

It was weird thinking the man who'd pushed me into the water was a hero, but I couldn't deny it.

'I thought I was going to die back there,' she said. She stopped herself talking.

'Me too.'

I looked around. Her apartment was stark, modern, almost all white.

'Thanks for coming back,' she said.

I got the feeling she wasn't sure if she'd been right to tell me everything she'd just told me.

She was looking up at me. Her green eyes were so beautiful.

'Go on inside, you look like an idiot standing there. I'll be with you in a few minutes.'

She pointed me into her living room. Plants were thriving like a rain forest on her balcony. I sat on an enormous white sofa and looked out at a spectacular sunset as I waited while she had a shower. I listened to the sound of cars passing, the shower hissing distantly, and tried to work out what I thought about Peter now. I went through it all over in my mind again, and it felt right the more I thought about it. Doing this sort of thing, infiltrating groups, was probably what he was supposed to do.

Twenty minutes later, Isabel emerged rubbing her hair with a black towel, wearing a tight black gym suit.

'The news is coming on,' she said. 'Let's see what they're saying about that demo.'

The ten o'clock news started a few minutes later. They showed a clip of one of the princes at St Paul's earlier. He was standing on the steps leading to the cathedral wearing a navy uniform with gold braid and white buttons. I wasn't entirely sure why he was there. The voiceover said something about him paying a visit that evening. It was almost as if he was reclaiming the building.

The doors of the cathedral were closed again behind him. Apparently, after holding a small demonstration inside, the Muslims who'd surged through the doors had left peacefully without damaging anything.

The TV announcer switched to another story, about the outbreak of plague in Istanbul. A hundred people had been quarantined, he said. Six people were dead, including an Iranian scientist and an Indian national who had been discovered in a basement the day before. The mortality rate was high among those who'd been quarantined, but the authorities had been fortunate that no other sites of infection had been found.

And everything fitted together neatly.

'That was why Alek was killed,' I said softly. 'Those bastards must have found traces of plague in that chamber under Hagia Sophia. This plague outbreak in Istanbul is involved. It has to be. Plague was probably the reason why that underground cavern was sealed up for so long. It had been used to bury people who'd died of it.'

'I'm not going to argue with you,' Isabel said.

'They must have seen Alek when he went into the tunnel. Maybe he followed them. Then they kidnapped him. They had to make sure he wouldn't spill the beans. He could have stopped them if he'd gone public with what he'd found. This was why they came after me. Then they blamed fundamentalist Islamists in that video. Was that part of their plan too, to stir things up? But why the hell did all these people have to die?'

She lowered her voice.

'I'll tell you what I was told. I know I can trust you, Sean. And after what you've been through I think you deserve to know.' She was sitting near me on the white sofa.

'The two people who were arrested near St Paul's this afternoon, the ones Malach was trying to text, were about to distribute a thousand boiled sweets from two plastic carrier bags. The sweets are being tested. We believe they're laced with the plague virus, the same as from that outbreak in Istanbul. Apparently, the people giving them out didn't even know about it. They were stooges. They said they were just told to wait until they were texted, then give one to everyone they could find in the crowd until they ran out.'

'They wanted to infect people with the plague?' It was hard to imagine what kind of people would want to spread sickness and death, but when I remembered what Malach had been like I knew such people existed.

'A thousand infected people is enough to start something serious if a virus spreads quickly and is widely disbursed. Muslims would have been blamed too, for bringing the virus into communities.'

'And they killed Bulent because he helped me?'

She nodded. 'The bastards must have figured it out. Maybe someone saw you together.'

'I need some air,' I said.

She turned the TV off and opened the glass door to the balcony. We went outside and stood watching the city for a while. It was late twilight now, and four floors up, the view over slated rooftops towards the futuristic office towers of central London was as good as you could get.

I could see the dome of St Paul's glittering on the horizon. I felt a warm summer breeze on my face. The temperature was perfect, not too warm, not to cool.

'There were other people involved with that guy Malach. There had to be.'

'We're tracking them. It'll take a while. They'll go to ground when it gets out that their plan failed. But we have leads we can follow up.'

'I hope you get them all.'

She was standing beside me. I gripped the shiny steel railing.

'What did you mouth at me when I was about to be thrown into that pool?' I asked.

The tangled branches and leaves of the upper reaches of a white-skinned London plane tree, which stood at the side of the apartment block, were behind her. I could smell a mustiness from the leaves as they shimmered in the warm air.

She looked down to ground level, where a car was being parked.

'I said, *take a deep breath*.'

'You were right.'

And in that moment I knew what I wanted more than anything. The loss that had buffeted my heart, which I had lived with every single day since Irene had died, was gone. I felt normal again, as if I'd been reborn. And I felt strangely off-guard, as if my heart had left a way in.

'What are you thinking about?' she said.

'Everything's changed.' I felt a little light-headed. My life with Irene was a memory, a faded sepia picture, still valued, but from the distant past.

'You know,' she said. 'If those buggers hadn't wanted to do all this, we'd never have met.'

We looked out over the city. We were about a foot apart.

'What's your plan for the next few days?' she said.

'I'm going to rest, then see what's happening at the Institute. Get back on track.'

'Why don't you stay here tonight?' Her smile was inviting. She turned and brushed against me. My arm tingled.

'On the couch.'

Our arms touched again.

She looked up at me. 'You know, I never thought I'd trust another man after my marriage ended.'

We were inches apart.

I took her hand and pulled her to me. I could feel her skin under her cotton T-shirt.

A rush of longing rose like a cresting wave inside me. I pulled her nearer. She didn't resist. I was ready this time. It was right this time. We kissed. I felt it would never end.

I spoke softly then, 'I should warn you, I'm damaged goods. I used to roam the streets at night after Irene died. My psycho-therapist used to get calls from a nice cop in Fulham police station whenever he spotted me.'

'We're all damaged,' said Isabel softly. 'Every one of us.'

epilogue

I'd started running again, early in the mornings. The summer had turned into a perfect autumn. I always loved London when the sky was blue and the weather was warm.

I was sweating lightly. The traffic was building up on Park Road, even though it was only 6.45 AM. I took the silver key out of my pocket and held it between my fingers as if it was a lucky charm.

As soon as I put it in the lock, the door opened. Isabel was standing on the other side in a long white T-shirt. It stopped at her thighs. She looked amazing.

She kissed me on the cheek. Every time she did that, I still felt a tingle of relief. Maybe it was an echo of the relief I'd felt when I'd found her alive in that dungeon at Malach's mercy. And there was something else mixed in with it too. Happiness.

'Coffee?' she said.

'Love some.'

'It's on the balcony. I'll be out in a minute.'

I sat on one of the wicker chairs, poured my coffee and Isabel's too. I took a sip.

A lot of things had happened in the past few months. We'd attended a Greek Orthodox funeral service for Alek in Islington. His mother was Greek after all. She was traced after a week by the Polish authorities. We'd also attended a service for Peter in St James's in Piccadilly.

The manuscript we'd found under Hagia Sophia had been sent to Cambridge University for tests.

I did some research on that diagramme on the inside back page. I didn't find out anything new. It could have been a Byzantine magic symbol, an astrological chart or a puzzle, as Gülsüm had said, or it could have been something else completely.

I'd done some research on riddles from that era and I'd found out a lot about Byzantine magic. Apparently, the Emperor Heraclius had been a big collector of Jewish, Egyptian and other magic books. The manuscript we'd found could well have been from his collection, from the end of his reign. But I can't say that for sure. We were just going to have and wait and see what the researchers at Cambridge came up with.

I'd tried to get back in to Kaiser's photos on that website to have another look at them, but they'd all disappeared. I wasn't surprised.

I'd also tried to get the Institute involved in doing some chemical and spectral analysis on the manuscript, but I was told to wait until the people in Cambridge had finished their work. No applications were being considered for any further analysis until then.

I decided to be patient. I had enough to be thankful for.

Isabel had requested a swift transfer back to the UK which had been granted almost immediately. And we were trying out living together for a while.

I'd recently decided to put my house up for sale.

It was time to move on.

In Istanbul there'd been a sensational opening of the cavern under Hagia Sophia in front of TV crews. It had been on the main evening news in England. There was no mention of our involvement, or that Alek had died there.

I still thought a lot about him, and every time I did I knew how lucky we were to be alive. The world is a strange place. If Alek hadn't died I wouldn't have met Isabel.

I heard a sound, turned.

She was coming out onto the balcony, smiling at me. I held my hand out. She took it.

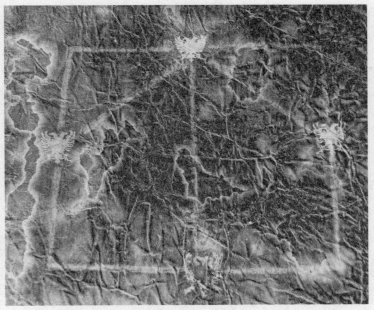

As mentioned on pp.288–289. Low spectroscopy image revealing seven connecting lines and four Byzantine double-headed eagles. The top eagle in the original is black, the bottom white, the right one green, the left red. There was a riddle beneath it.

A day in old Istanbul

Laurence O'Bryan

Hagia Sophia.

Before I first visited this city, almost twenty years ago, I imagined Istanbul as a dour colourless metropolis. What I encountered was something spectacular. Old Istanbul in particular was a revelation. Its ancient Byzantine and Ottoman sites, their beauty, power and historical significance stunned me then. They still do today. *The Istanbul Puzzle* was born from my amazement at the beauty of Istanbul.

Before deciding to spend a day in old Istanbul, and there are many modern sites and shopping experiences to occupy a more extended stay, please carefully consider the time of year you'll travel. I can now survive the 29° C average high in August, but a more enjoyable experience will be had if you go in October (20° C average high) or May (20° C average high) or during any intervening month, if you're not suited to high daytime temperatures.

If your hotel is overlooking the Golden Horn or the Bosphorus, and it has a restaurant with a view, a good way to start a day in old Istanbul is with a leisurely breakfast with an outlook that Ottoman and Byzantine Emperors would have enjoyed. I have always loved breakfasts in Istanbul. Sizzling fried salami, a selection of white cheeses, sweet jams and soft bread are enough to keep me at the table for far longer than I should. So don't rush your breakfast, relish it.

View from Zeyrekhane Restaurant, overlooking the Golden Horn, with the Galata Tower on the horizon.

The following hotels are worth considering if you want to do this. First, at the more expensive end, the Hotel Nena, Klodfarer Cad (info@istanbulhotelnena.com around £250 a night), a stunning boutique hotel within walking distance of the historical sites. The Hotel Nena features an excellent open buffet breakfast on a terrace and rooms with air conditioning and free WiFi. At the more affordable end The Star Holiday Hotel, Divanyolu Street (info@hotelstarholiday.com around £75 a night), in the same area, features breakfast on a terrace (in front of the Blue Mosque) and rooms with air conditioning too.

If your hotel is in Sultanahmet, the old part of Istanbul where the above hotels are located, the spit of land where Constantine created his new Rome, you won't be far from Hagia Sophia, our next stop. Hagia Sophia was the largest Christian cathedral in the world for a thousand years. It opens from 9-16:30, except on Mondays.

Domes of Hagia Sophia and Hagia Eirene. Taken from a rear window in Hagia Sophia looking towards the dome of Hagia Eirene.

The building was opened with a lavish ceremony by the Roman Emperor, Justinian the Great, on the 27th December 536. Hagia Sophia features an unprecedented saucer-like dome. When it was built no similar structure had ever been constructed. Its glittering mosaics and unrivalled size were considered a miracle for many centuries.

The dome of Hagia Sophia is a hundred feet in diameter. The gorgeous interior of the dome features on the cover of The Istanbul Puzzle. The dome uses forty stone ribs to support itself. Forty windows set between the lowest parts of these ribs give the dome its light, floating feeling.

This building was, in effect, the Greek Orthodox Vatican for most of the period from 536 to 1453, a Catholic Cathedral during the Latin Empire from 1204 to 1261, and a great mosque and the seat of the Sunni Islamic Caliphate from 1453 until 1935, when Atatürk and the Turkish Parliament turned

Hagia Sophia into a museum. No other building has had such an illustrious history.

If you get there early in the morning you will miss the twenty-minute queue for an entrance ticket that I encountered on my last visit in the middle of the day. The entrance fee was modest. I didn't bother with any of the offers of a

A passage inside Hagia Sophia, Istanbul. Passages such as this one on the north side of Hagia Sophia most likely date back to the 7th century, when the structure was constructed.

guided tour that I was assailed with during my wait. That was in the summer of 2011. When you finally get inside, stop in the narthex, the long outer entrance hall. It features modern wall panels describing, in multiple languages, the history of Hagia Sophia, including details about its unprecedented conversion into a museum.

View of ground floor of Hagia Sophia from upper gallery above main entrance.

After that, enjoy the stunning nave and the beautiful interior of the dome high above. Look out for the mosaics – many of the best ever made are here – and the views from the upper gallery. You can almost get lost in Hagia Sophia. Bring water and a good guide book.

A quick visit to Hagia Eirene nearby could also be fitted in before lunch. Hagia Eirene is in the outer courtyard of Topkapi Palace, which you might also want to visit. Hagia Eirene and Topkapi are both entered through a monumental gate at the

Entrance way and ramp down to main floor of Hagia Eirene July 2011.

back of Hagia Sophia. This gate leads into the park-like outer courtyard of Topkapi, the palace of the Ottoman sultans until 1853. Topkapi contains enough items of interest to fill another day. If harems, treasures, and relics of Mohammad interest you do not miss Topkapi Palace.

Another place of interest in the outer courtyard of Topkapi is the Archaeological Museum. It features a superb collection of Greek and Roman sculptures, artefacts and tombs going back to the foundation of the first settlements in the area.

Hagia Eirene, which features in *The Istanbul Puzzle*, is only open to the public during occasional evening concerts. I have no idea why. The interior would be of great interest to many. The fact that its walls have none of the grandeur of Hagia Sophia would only add to its interest, in my opinion. It was one

Hagia Sophia with ruins of Constantine I's Great Palace in foreground.

View of distant Blue Mosque from upper gallery window in Hagia Sophia July 2011.

of the very few Orthodox churches not to be converted into a mosque by Mehmed the Conqueror, when the city was finally taken by his Ottoman army in 1453.

Hagia Eirene's magnificent outer walls, the amazing open ruins on its south side, and its grandeur alone were enough to keep me entertained for twenty minutes at least the last time I was there.

Lunch will now be calling. Hot meatballs, delicious salads, natural lemon drinks all have their own distinctive voices in Istanbul. A visit to a nearby café with a roof terrace, perhaps at the Sultan Pub (sultanpub@sultanpub.com.tr) across the tram tracks beside Hagia Sophia and then to the left (at the beginning of Divanyolu Cad) might be considered if your budget allows. The views from its rooftop terrace restaurant are spectacular. Or you might just go for an afternoon coffee there, if you're on a tight budget, and enjoy your lunch at any of the other tourist restaurants nearby. The Doy-Doy restaurant not far away on Sifa Hamam Sok (doydoymusa@hotmail.com) has a roof terrace, a busy atmosphere and reasonably priced meals.

In the afternoon you could then walk a few hundred yards to the nearby site of the largest Roman hippodrome ever built. It's directly in front of Hagia Sophia. This was where dedicated city factions followed the whites or the blues (if you were an aristocrat or a landowner) or the reds or the greens (if you were an artisan or a merchant). These guys were the prototype of the football hooligan.

In early January of 532, the Nike revolt started in the Hippodrome. It was organised by rival colours. After five days half the city of Constantinople had been burnt down, including the old church of Hagia Sophia. This was at a time when Constantinople's city walls encompassed one hundred and fifteen square miles and Florence's enclosed only two.

The riots came about partly because the Hippodrome was an outlet for the frustrations of the people. Some of the factions were supported by aristocratic families who thought they had more claim to the throne than Justinian. It is said that Justinian's wife, the Empress Theodora, persuaded him to stand up to the rioters. You can read more about Theodora in *The Istanbul Puzzle*.

After a week of vacillation the gates of the Hippodrome were closed and Belisarius, Justinian's general, massacred 30,000 rioters, bringing the rebellion to a bloody close. Hagia Sophia was rebuilt after that in the form we see today.

All you will see of the Hippodrome though, is the course of the racetrack and some large items from its central spine, an obelisk from ancient Egypt, the serpent column from Delphi and the Column of Constantine. These are believed to be still in their original locations, from when the Hippodrome was in use for chariot races.

Proceed further and you will find the Mosaic Museum behind the incredible Blue Mosque with its beautiful six minarets and 20,000 blue faiences from Iznik.

The Mosaic Museum is located under a typical Ottoman-style shopping arcade. It contains original mosaics from the Imperial Roman palace, which occupied much of the area and was the seat of what we call the Byzantine Empire, until the city was sacked by the Venetians and Crusaders in the Fourth Crusade, in 1204. The Byzantines never called themselves that though. They saw themselves as citizens of the Roman Empire.

The Imperial palace had its own port, the Bucoleon, grand stairways, pavilions, gardens, towers and courtyards spread out over that first hill of Istanbul, which looks out over the entrance of the Sea of Marmara into the Bosphorus. This complex of palaces was the wonder of the medieval world. It had separate palaces for the Empress, whose walls were covered in purple marble brought from Rome, and for relatives and favourites of the Emperor.

It is a short walk from the Mosaic Museum back to Hagia Sophia from where the city's growing tram and underground network can take you to your hotel or to other parts of the city including the Grand Bazaar, Galata Tower, Taksim Square and the ultra modern shopping facilities that now dot Istanbul. If you finish your day in one of the hotels or restaurants recommended earlier you will enjoy some of the best eating in Europe in spectacular surroundings unmatched anywhere in the world.

Further ancient sights are expected to be opened near Hagia Sophia soon.

Constantine the Great created an extraordinary city here. It survived siege, plague, capture and famine until a new empire was created by the Ottomans, taking over its legacy. Now a modern republican city stands here, the largest in Europe, with a population fast approaching 14 million.

Lastly, be aware, as in all cities, of heading down dark alleys at night. And don't go along with the street scammers who try to get you to go to a bar or a shop. Just keep walking. Overpriced drinks are common at nightclubs. And in crowded places be wary of pickpockets.

I do hope you've enjoyed your day in old Istanbul. Let me know how you got on: lpobryan@googlemail.com.

Acknowledgements

I would like, first of all, to acknowledge the wonderful cities of Istanbul and London and all the warm and friendly people who live there. The many historical sites in these cities and the people who work in them are a great source of inspiration. I would like to acknowledge the fine work of all employees in the many sites mentioned in the book.

The underground and other locations I have created, under Hagia Sophia, Hagia Eirene and near St Paul's are entirely fictional however. No such sites exist, except in my imagination, and in *The Istanbul Puzzle*.

I would like to also acknowledge the assistance of Dr Antony Eastmond, Reader in the History of Byzantine Art at The Courtauld Institute, London and Dr Ken Dark, Director, Research Centre for Late Antique and Byzantine Studies, University of Reading, for their assistance, but I must point out that all historical errors and inaccuracies are mine alone and entirely.

For assistance in editing I would like to acknowledge the great help of my editor at Harper Collins, Claire Bord, who helped me shape the novel. I would also like to thank all the other writing professionals and friends who read early copies of *The Istanbul Puzzle* and helped me with their comments. Jean Jenkins in California was one. Pam Ahearn in New Orleans was another. Thank you all for your encouragement and support.

I have been lucky to attend some wonderful writing classes in the UK and Ireland and The Irish Writing Centre in particular provided a number of valuable courses. In addition, I am a member of two writing groups in Dublin, the Rathmines and Wednesday groups. Both helped me greatly. A big thank you to all the members.

My wonderful wife, Zen, my Turkish Princess, her family and mine, have all played a vital part in this book's creation. I wish also to thank my children, Isabel and Robert, for putting up with my disappearances and being told to leave the room when I was working on too many occasions to count.

Finally, I would also like to acknowledge lost friends, Noel and Jimmy, who have gone before me to a better place. They listened to my stories long ago.

Keep up to date with the Puzzle story –visit:
www.lpobryan.wordpress.com

You'll find details of many aspects of *The Istanbul Puzzle* on the site and information on the journey the book took to publication.

There will also be early details of the next instalment of Isabel and Sean's adventures, *The Jerusalem Puzzle*, due for publication in January 2013.

There are also photos, videos and links to a Twitter feed (@lpobryan) and Facebook fan page you can sign up to follow. You can find me on Goodreads and LinkedIn too.